Lindsey Barron Series
Volume 6
States Justice

Vic Broquard

Fourth Printing; ISBN: 978-1-941415-51-1

Artwork by Crooked Willow Studios.

Published by:
Broquard eBooks
http://Broquard-eBooks.com
author@Broquard-eBooks.com
103 Timberlane
East Peoria, IL 61611

For Morgan and L. Ron Hubbard

Table of Contents

Chapter 1—Sleuth Pam at Work

Pam reached a decision. If Simon Mac Fluide was indeed a student at Bradbury's and if both Professor Herbert Mac Elroy and Governor Alister were there during that time, surely Professor Herbert could tell her about Simon's years as a student. Perhaps that would help her fill in some gaps in her time line. She sent a Message to Professor Herbert.

"Lindsey, I'm meeting with Professor Herbert as soon as I help you get everyone onboard the bus for home. You can take my bags with you. I'll Teleport to the ranch later today. Maybe I'll even be there before you and the bus arrives. Cover for me please?" Pam asked.

"Sure, what's up anyway?" she asked.

"I want to see if I can get more data on my Simon time line. Professor Herbert was one of his teachers. Thanks for covering for me." A half hour later, all the teens bags were stored beneath the double decker bus, and the tally sheets verified. No students were missing the bus. Pam watched it roll out of the parking lot, before she stepped back inside the massive gates. With a quick flick of her wand, she opened a Magical Door to the Math and Science building. Stepping through the doorway, she arrived outside his office. She knocked.

"Welcome, Miss Betts. What a surprise visit. Shouldn't you be on your bus heading home?" he asked. His white hair was uncombed, and he wore everyday clothes. “Ignore the mess, Elaine and I are packing. We are about to head to our retirement home outside of Phoenix.” He moved a box so she could sit on their couch, moved a bag off his sofa, and sat down.

Elaine passed through, carrying an armload of clothes. “Oh hi, Miss Betts. Thought you were all off heading home by now.”

“I stayed a bit to visit with Professor Herbert. Thanks for seeing me on such short notice.”

“Well, Herbert, you should offer her something to drink. Soda perhaps?”

“No thanks, professor. I’ll try not to take up too much of his time.”

“Okay, then let’s chat. You said that you wanted to talk about Dominus or Simon when he was here at Bradbury’s?”

“Yes. I have been constructing a time line of his early years, hoping to gain more clues of his many enterprises. Once we capture him, we want to confiscate everything that he owns, sell it, and use the proceeds to help all those he has injured or harmed,” she explained.

“Admirable, if it can be done. How can I help,” the old man asked.

“Here’s my data thus far,” she handed Herbert her short synopsis. He read it over quickly.

Pam’s Time Line of Simon Mac Fluide (2182)

2138: Born in New Orleans

which makes him really forty-four years old 2182

looks to be at least sixty.

Parents: Ross Mac Fluide (Scottish descent) (Pervert or sadist)

Jacqueline (French)

2144: Sister Michelle born (6 years younger)

2148: Mother got diabetes (amputated arms below elbows,

legs below knees, wore corsets)

Reports of beatings by Ross

2150-2156: Attended Bradbury's

2156: (January) Jacqueline dies (found death certificate)

+ Michelle dies? (but no record)

2156: (January) Ross divides holdings

half to Simon (graduation present from his father?)

half to R. B. Folquet

Ross vanishes, no trace ever found after this

2157: Donates children's wing at hospital where Ashley was at

in memory of his loving mother and sister

2163 Captured by Rat Pack (14 years in jail)

2177 Escapes jail

"What was he like when he was here, in his early years?" Pam asked.

"Oh, he was a typical Black Hall boy," Herbert began reminiscing. "Thought he was hot stuff, as they say. Friendly to the more powerful wizard professors, but considered me not worth much, I'm afraid to say. He just had this thing against normal people, but now that I remember it, that didn't come out until later on, around his fourth year. I know that he really loved his invalid mother, and he doted on his little sister. He kept telling me to treat her right when she came here. She was supposed to arrive in 2157, but she never did. I believe he said something about her dying, as I recall. His mother, she died over the Christmas holidays, on January 1, 2156."

"You know, that must have been traumatic for him. Now that I look back on it, Pam, he seemed a changed man when he came back from the holiday vacation in January. It was as if someone had taken the restraints off him. He fought with some of the professors. I know that he was forever getting into philosophical arguments with Alister—yelling matches might be a better description. Alister chalked it up to his having just lost his mother and sister, but I think it went far deeper than that. Something happened that Christmas vacation, something that really changed him. Those last few months here—he never again spoke of his sister or his mother. He cut my math classes frequently that spring. I found him in the Library, studying spells. Typical sixth year, trying to cram every last spell they can into their brains."

"I know he shocked Alister when he mastered the Restricted Wish spell. I think that Alister still regrets that day when he pointed out to him what he was doing wrong during his attempts to learn it. Alister blames himself for Simon having learned that spell."

"Of course, you have to realize that, when he enrolled here, he went by the name Dominus Malefic and not Simon Mac Fluide. Everyone here thought that was his name. We had no idea he was really Simon Mac Fluide, the son of one of the wealthiest men on the planet. Of course, that may well be why

Ross enrolled him with that fake name, so no one would know that he was the heir to the Ross fortune. That could well have made a mess of young Simon's days here. Perhaps had we all known that he was the son of Ross Mac Fluide, things might have turned out very differently."

Pam mused a minute and then asked, "What about those arguments? What were they about?"

"You know, Pam, I don't recall the specifics, been too long. However, when he published his Manifesto a while back, those ideas were pretty much what he debated with everyone here, especially during his last term here. During his first few years here, he and I had many discussions about normals versus wizards, but that last term, he avoided me as if I carried a plague. That last term, he rarely attended my math class. Come to think of it, he skipped Jamie's class and Hardwood's as well; they were normals too. As I said—real change in personality after his mother died. Well, not so much a change, but more like all his restraints were lifted."

"What did she die of? Did he ever say? What about his sister, Michelle?" Pam asked.

"Diabetes, though why someone failed to give her an Insulin shot is beyond me. Alister got a letter from Ross explaining her death. Why didn't the man cast Cure Disease on her? I remember Alister mentioning that the letter also said that his sister had died too. Strange that you cannot find her death certificate, Pam."

"Strange indeed. And no one matching his sister's description ever came here that next year?" she asked.

"Nope, pretty sure of that. Michelle is a French name, relatively rare around these parts out west. Of course, she too could have changed her name, but if she did come to Bradbury's, no one ever knew of it. I suppose that it is possible she came here and graduated under an assumed name, but Alister would have been alerted if her parent was Ross. Dead giveaway. He's never said anything about something like that, Pam. I'd bet my money on the fact that she did die, and somehow her death certificate has been misplaced or lost. That can happen, you know."

"Okay. So he really started down his Golden Path thing after his mother and sister died?" she wanted to make doubly sure of this fact.

"Yes, that is a fair assessment of it Pam. Prior to that, he was like any normal teen, opinionated—thinks he is right and everyone else is a dummy, that sort of thing, perfectly normal, but always held in check, mind you. No, that last term, he was downright belligerent to everyone on the fact that wizards ought to be the master race. I wonder how much his mother kept his ideas balanced out. She was a normal person, not a witch, or she could have cured herself of diabetes. Yet, I don't see how a mother could have held that much hatred in check. Evidently, she must have, though."

"Say, where did Dominus and family live when he was here? I mean I was living in Sterling, but now with Lindsey near Arapahoe. Maybe if I knew that, I might be able to find out more information from that city or town," Pam asked, suddenly inspired.

"Don't know, but we can find out." He typed into his laptop and brought up school records. Ah, here it is. The bus always picked him up and left him off at 1032 Rosewood, Denver. Does that help?"

"You bet it does. Now I have something concrete to go on." After looking at her time line again, she asked, "Weird. Ross disappeared right after his wife died. Do you know anything about that?"

"Not much. When he started acting up that last term, I sent notices to his father about the conduct of Dominus. Sent five, but they all came back address unknown, no forwarding address. I thought that was strange, and told Alister about it. He promised to look into it. I never heard anything more about it. Look, there is a red flag on his last return home bus trip." Herbert showed Pam the notation. "See, Alister was going to refuse to allow the bus to drop him off at that address, and Dominus refused to give any new address. He must have Teleported home, because he sure didn't take the bus. You see, all those tally sheets that you Monitors fill out when the kids board the bus are stored in our database." Pam smiled; so those check lists she kept on the passengers were not discarded, but logged into the computer. Interesting, she thought.

Elaine came back into the room again. "You are still chatting about Dominus?" she said with a mischievous grin.

"Yes, Professor Herbert has been giving me lots to go on in my research," Pam replied.

"Say, did you ever find out about his sister? What was

her name supposed to be? Oh yes, Michelle. He bragged about her for five years, I remember that. He kept telling me she would be following in his footsteps," Professor Elaine asked, curiously.

"Nope, only that everyone believes that she also died around the same time as his mother," Pam replied.

"Dominus never said that Michelle was ill or had diabetes like her mother. Certainly, Dominus never had that illness, not when he was here," Elaine commented. "I wonder how she died."

"Well, I'm going to see if I can find out," Pam stated flatly. "Besides, I'm really getting curious to find out what happened to his father, Ross, who also disappeared. You don't suppose that Dominus killed his own mother, father, and sister, do you?" That sudden idea flashed through Pam's mind.

"Oh heavens no. Ross was a powerful wizard, as rumor has it. Dominus seemed utterly devoted to his mother and sister," Professor Elaine defended Dominus. "No way could he have killed all three, Pam, but I see why you might have such speculations. Dominus was a different person during his earlier years here."

"You know, I'm beginning to think that, if we know what really happened back there that Christmas holiday, then we might have a big clue on how to catch Simon today," Pam theorized. "Well, I've taken up enough of your time. I best be going. Thank you very much, professors. Have a good vacation down in Phoenix."

Both smiled, "We certainly will, Pam. I'm a bit

surprised that you didn't ask me about the Elementary Education elective for the fall," Herbert teased her.

Pam grinned, "That took me by surprise, sir. I do like to help others, so I ought to know all the best ways to help others. Well, thanks again. I'd best get going." The three shook hands, and Pam headed back to the main gates; once outside, she could Teleport home.

As she opened the gates, there stood Wilma and Monane, waiting for her. "Hi Pam. Sorry, but it's not safe for you to be off by yourself," her aunt explained.

Pam grinned. "Thanks, glad to see you too. Say, could we make a detour? I'd like to see the old house that Dominus supposedly lived in while he was at school here. It is 1032 Rosewood, Denver." A minute later, Pam stood beside a now vacant lot full of playground equipment. The home had been demolished years ago and turned into a small park. A minute later, they arrived at the Compton ranch, just as the school bus arrived.

"Hi everyone!" Lindsey cheerily called out, as she stepped off the Bradbury's bus, along with everyone else. A huge crowd was there to meet them, including Lena, Lloyd, and little Jonathon, who seemed to have grown these past few months. Polly hugged her daughter, Pam, while the Whitewater clan hugged as well. Amanda and Fern greeted both R. B. and Luci, who had dropped over to the Compton ranch to welcome their returning daughters. Audrey was not left out either, as both Lena and Lloyd hugged her tightly as well.

"Welcome home all of you!" Lena said, very happy that her daughters were finally home for the summer. "Come on in. Bet you are all starving. Polly, Luci, and I have whipped up a hearty lunch. Besides, we are dying to catch up on all the news."

As they walked inside, having Moved their giant piles of duffle bags inside, Lindsey commented to Lloyd, "What's with all these men?" Getting off of the bus, she saw three strangers milling around just outside the long front porch.

"Extra States Security men. We've been assigned a group of thirty men and women. Ten are always on duty now, watching over the ranch. Seven are on the perimeter. Constant vigilance is the byword this summer. After what happened to you two at Halloween, Governor Alister's request for extra security has been honored. They will stay quietly in the background, girls. Three more are watching over R. B.'s ranch as well. Come on inside," he ushered Lindsey inside, bringing up the rear. Lindsey shot a quick glance at the three bored looking men, and they smiled and nodded to her.

The quick lunch turned into a marathon afternoon session. Everyone wanted to hear all about the attack on the school in April, as well as how their studies went. Monane, Wilma, R. B., and Lloyd were keenly interested in Lindsey's incredible Dispeller skills, Wilma pumping her endlessly on details. At last, Wilma commented, "Well, Lindsey, your dad, Sam, was one fantastic Dispeller. However, it is my opinion that you have exceeded even his incredible skills as a Dispeller. I would be proud and honored to work with you as your

Eliminator. Anytime, say the word, and Bill West will go into action once again."

Lindsey realized that Wilma was treating her as her peer, not as a sixth year magic student! She grinned and replied, "Thanks, I aim to help us all capture Dominus and the lot, but this time, there are a lot of us, not just four."

Monane interrupted the two, "Wilma, for heaven's sake, let them all finish their schooling first, before we go after them all, although I admit that Amanda is now as good a Tracker as I am. How's Deiter coming along with his Eliminator training? You know as well as I that we're going to need more than one Eliminator to round up this bunch."

"Another year and he will be ready," Wilma pronounced. "He's coming along nicely. I know. You are right. Haste makes waste as they say, but I am so impressed with Lindsey's skills that I can hardly sit still. If she can keep those Disintegrate spells nullified, we stand a terrific chance of capturing them all. Remember how hard Sam had to work on those spells?" The two women began remembering their hours of training so many years ago.

"How can I forget," Monane replied. "For hours, Sam would have us shooting Disintegrate spells his way so he could work on Dispelling them. I was petrified he'd make a mistake, and I would take his head off by accident."

Wilma chuckled, "Me too, me too. Those were some times, weren't they, Monane?" Lindsey's heart ached–if only she had seen them practicing. She missed her biological father. Her only memories of him were from when she was five there on their tiny ranch.

Around three, the group broke up. Ahana, Orenda, Amanda, and their folks headed home, while the girls proceeded to unpack their many bags. Lindsey and Ashley make hasty work of this, heading off to play with Jonathon, who had entered his terrible two's and was crawling everywhere. Audrey and Fern disappeared into Audrey's workroom to figure out where they were on their backlog of wood carvings, leaving Pam alone in her room.

With quiet finally here, Pam sat down and typed up her recollections from what Professor Herbert had told her. More than ever, her curiosity was aroused about this dysfunctional family and what had happened some twenty-six years ago. Somehow, all this bore on the current situation with Simon, if only in that he had acquired billions of dollars' worth of corporations from his father. Still, the fact that Ross disappeared and the mysterious death of Michelle taunted her—mysteries to be solved. Why would his father just disappear after dividing his huge financial holdings, giving half to his son and half to this other person, this R. B. Folquet. Who was this Folquet person anyway? Was he also somehow tied into Simon and his attempt to become dictator of the world? Pam had to know, and she set to work once more with no more schoolwork to interfere.

First, she decided to see what public records were available online. After an hour, she had an electronic copy of Jacqueline's death certificate, the birth certificates of the two children, Simon and Michelle, and a bill of sale from 2156 selling the family home in Denver for two hundred fifty thousand dollars. Next, she focused on trying to find out all she could about the corporate split of Mac Fluide Enterprises back in 2156. She retrieved the electronic document that she had found months ago, the dissolution papers. She studied the documents for the tenth time, hoping to see something she may have overlooked.

She found nothing new, except there was the official witness's signature, one Herb Fry, Attorney. Pam decided to see if this man was still around; perhaps she could visit with him. After a bit of Googling, she found his law firm in Denver, Fry, Fry, and Associates. She decided to give them a phone call. While she preferred to have gone to visit them personally, Pam knew that she would have to get an adult escort and opted to use the phone instead of imposing on her aunt and the others again today.

Ten minutes later, she dialed the number. Herb Fry had retired years ago. His sons now ran the law firm, but the secretary had given her his number, a retirement home. After some delays, she finally heard the old man's voice on the phone. "Hello, this is Herb Fry."

"Hi, I am Pam Betts, a high school senior. I have been doing some historical research on large corporations of the past. A school project, you see. I chose the old Ross Mac Fluide Corporation, studying how the breakup of that billion-dollar corporation was handled. I found your name as the official witness on their dissolution papers, Mr. Fry. I was wondering if you would be willing to chat with me a bit about that time. I won't ask for any confidential information, sir, just general background information for my school report."

He chuckled, "My, my, that is ancient news. My memory is not so good these days; that was a quarter of a century ago. Yes, I remember it. It's not every day that an attorney gets to witness the dissolution of a billion dollar corporation. What would you like to know, Miss Betts?"

"How did Ross seem when he signed the papers? I mean, it must have been quite a big deal for him to divide his entire business in half. I bet Simon was very elated about it."

"Oh yes, Simon was extremely pleased, sort of a smug look, like he had achieved some major success. I guess inheriting billions would tend to do that to one. Now Ross, he seemed reserved. I believe he said this was his son's graduation present. Some present, don't you think?" Pam agreed.

"Say, one thing has me puzzled, Mr. Fry. He gave half of the corporations to Simon, but the other half went to this R. B. Folquet, not himself. I don't understand that part. Who is the Mr. Folquet?"

"Strange that you ask that. That was the funny part of the whole deal. I don't know. Ross showed up with Mr. Folquet's witnessed signatures on all the appropriate documents. I asked him about this several times. Ross alluded to the fact that he was retiring. Well, I didn't think too much of it at the time. After all, if I were a billionaire at forty, I would retire too. Yet, over these many years, that keeps troubling me. If I were in his shoes, I would have given half to my son and half to my daughter. However, I remember hearing something about her having died as well, shortly after his wife died. You know she died of diabetes some months before he divided up his corporations don't you?" Pam admitted that she did.

"So I would have left the other half to my brothers, sisters, nieces, and nephews. It's sort of bothered me all these years that he left it to this stranger." The two chatted a while longer, but Pam got no further useful information from the old man.

A while later, Pam stared at these new notes on her computer. "Why would he leave billions to this Folquet person? Who is this Folquet person, and what happened to Ross anyway? Suicide? Murdered by Simon?" Pam looked frustratedly at her computer screen. Just then, someone called out for supper, and Pam headed to the dining room, joining the others.

Nadia and Jolina arrived, joining the large group. "Well, tomorrow, girls, we have to get all your maid of honor dresses picked up and any last minute adjustments made," Nadia explained to the teens. Their weddings were going to be held in two weeks. Unfortunately, Pam had forgotten about them, so she made a mental note to find them appropriate wedding gifts—Bailey and Barnaby too.

"What with all this heightened security around you three, I have made arrangements for the dressmaker to come here to do the adjustments. I do hope that will work out," Nadia continued.

Jolina added, "We will have a dress rehearsal on Friday

before the big day on Saturday, June 15. I tell you we are getting so excited!"

"Are you going to go on a honeymoon?" asked Lindsey, remembering that Tom and Sandy Whitewater did that.

"Five days in Tahiti! Look at the brochures!" Jolina was ecstatic. Tropical beaches, sunny skies, and exotic food headlined the brochures that she passed to eager hands.

"We have to be back to run the Friday night dance," Nadia added, "so it's just for five wonderful days. It's hard to imagine that in just a few more days I will be officially Nadia Hampton. I have never been so happy!"

"What do you all think of Jolina Wessel-Hampton?" she asked. "I want to keep my last name in there. You can understand why Nadia doesn't though. She's been through that before and wants to forget the past as much as possible."

"Cool, Jolina!" Lindsey replied. "I like it, has a good ring to it." Jolina seemed pleased.

Pam exclaimed, "Eureka! What a dummy I've been!" All eyes stared at Pam and her surprising outburst. "Oh, sorry. I have been totally overlooking what the maiden name of Simon's mother was. Duh. I bet it is important. If you will excuse me, I just have to find out now." Pam hastily left.

"Sleuths!" teased Lindsey, and everyone chuckled. Everyone knew there was no stopping Pam when she was on the trail of something important.

Back in her room, she got her laptop out of hibernate mode and headed for genealogy sites, looking for clues on where to find marriage licences. A while later, she realized that in all likelihood, she would need to know the city which issued the marriage license. "Rats, could be anywhere, even Scotland; he's from there." Disgusted, she looked at the other genealogy links and came upon Genealogy-One, a site that claimed to have millions of marital records on file. Only $19.95 to join. Pam transferred the funds and created her user login and password. Finally, she was able to get into the members only section and began her search.

Three minutes later, she was staring at the marriage license from 2135! Ross Bernard Mac Fluide and Jacqueline Blanche Folquet united this 25th of May, 2135 in Marseille, France. Pam let out a loud squeal of joy! She had found yet another major clue! She now knew who R. B. Folquet was. It was Ross himself! He had not died, but adopted his wife's maiden name!

Hearing her squeal, her friends came dashing into her room, wondering what was going on with her. She pointed to the screen, and one by one, everyone began to see the connections. Lindsey scratched her head, "Pam, this still doesn't make any real sense. Now we have Ross dividing his corporation in half, giving half to his son, changing his last name, taking control of the other half, and having Ross Mac Fluide disappear from the planet. Why? Why would he do this? It is making even less sense to me."

Pam grinned, "Please, one mystery at a time." The teens chuckled. "Seriously, I don't know yet, but I will continue to work on it."

"How about starting tomorrow, Pam? We are all

starting up a family canasta game. Your mom is playing too, so come on; you have to play too," Lindsey ordered. Pam sighed. She had no choice and followed them out, though she did give her laptop a loving, longing look.

The next morning was also shot, as far as Pam was concerned. The dressmaker arrived early with the many dresses. Nadia and Jolina hovered over the proceedings, making sure that everything was just perfect. The dresses, Pam noted, were sky blue satin, and they were to wear a matching outer corset with matching five-inch pumps. Each of the girls had filled out some since Christmas, but the dressmaker had allowed for that. Still, it took time to get the dresses properly fitted for Ashley, Lindsey, Audrey, Pam, Amanda, Fern, Orenda, and Kathy.

The wedding was going to be held in the Compton's large living room, security reasons naturally. However, no matter how much the teens pleaded, neither Nadia nor Jolina would tell them who was going to walk them down the aisle, namely the long hallway from the bedroom areas to the living room. Lindsey and Ashley, as their head maids of honor, both knew, but were sworn to secrecy.

Only after lunch and the dishes done could Pam finally slip away into her room. The others had headed over to the Whitewater's pond for a swim. Pam got her laptop up and running, and then began searching. "First, we find out all we can about Folquet Enterprises," she whispered to herself.

After a half hour of browsing, she realized that, unlike the Mac Fluide Enterprises, the Folquet Enterprises seemed to be very open with corporate information. Their main headquarters was located in Marseille, France. Even their main page had links to every subsidiary company in their giant conglomerate. In the "About the Corporation" link, Pam discovered that their founder, R. B. Folquet had long ago retired from active leadership. Now a man going by the name of Simone Folquet was running the extended corporation. Furiously, Pam searched the websites for a photograph of this Simone Folquet, but found none. On the other hand, she found pictures of all the presidents of the various subsidiary companies. Simone's image was conspicuously absent. Curious, she thought. Could this be another disguise of Dominus? Could he be secretly running his father's enterprises? If so, she had to know everything about them! The ramifications were gargantuan.

Time flew by, still not a single photograph of this Simone fellow. However, he was not being secret about contacting him. She continually came across links that said:

To contact Mr. Simone Folquet, please contact his attorney, Mrs. Isabella Folquet at the law offices of Folquet et Associés at 4520 Rue Jean de Bernardy.

At last, Pam gave up on that avenue. Instead, she decided to find out the connections between the companies in the Folquet and Mac Fluide enterprises. Just what inner-corporation business transactions were occurring? She started a new database of Folquet companies and began searching for relationships, partnerships, and major business transactions—anything that might tie Simon to this new set of corporations.

At dinner, her father inquired about her research. Fred asked, “Well, do we have even more to fear, Pam? Found lots of French connections?” he teased her.

She grinned, but replied, “No, dad. They are being extraordinarily secretive about any transactions. I haven’t found one, not even one, minor sale of equipment or commodity. It’s as if he’s buried it deep underground, but I will keep on it, dad. We just have to know.”

“Let Mary Hampton lend you a hand. She’s now got access to many overseas records,” Fred suggested.

A half hour later, Pam brought Mary up to speed on what she had discovered, giving her a copy of her ever-growing database of Folquet companies. “Terrific sleuthing, Pam,” Mary complimented her. “Let me take this to my office in the morning and see what the US government has on them. Most are French or European companies, I see. Very little here in the US.”

“Yes, just that one paper mill in Oregon,” Pam replied. “I don’t see what use Dominus has for a paper mill, though.”

“Sometimes, these are merely figureheads or shell companies for money laundering and other nefarious actions. Let me see what we can find out,” Mary suggested.

The next morning, Fern and Orenda came over bright and early, while the teens were still eating their breakfasts. “Honestly, musicians!” Fern declared. “Kicked us out again.”

“Huh?” Lindsey replied. Surely Eli’s Rockers were not here; at least she hadn’t heard Ahana talking about them coming so soon.

"It's Amanda; she and Ahana are practicing. Seems Amanda is trying to get into their band!" Fern stated flatly, as if this was a total impossibility.

"Well, you two can lend me a hand in the garden," Audrey replied. "Weeds are taking over." She and the two headed outside to tend the huge organic garden. Lindsey and Ashley headed out to deal with the chores as well. Pam sighed and joined them, though she didn't like milking cows or fetching eggs. She wanted to get on with her research; still, she knew she needed to lend a hand with the daily chores and did so.

Around ten, Pam finally was able to get back to her work. Lindsey and Ashley were going to experiment more on dispersing spells. While Pam wanted to try her hand at that, this research seemed vitally more important right now. She eagerly threw herself into Sleuthing mode once more.

When they all got together for supper, Pam had still not found any connection between the two enterprises. However, the day was not lost. She had found ten more pharmaceutical companies that she had not known about, all overseas, and all needed to be checked out to see if they were now manufacturing the National Health Care pills.

After dinner, Mary dropped over to chat with her. "Sorry, dear, I was unable to find any connection between the two vast enterprises. Could it really be that there are no connections between father and son's corporations?" Mary asked.

"Normally, I couldn't believe that they would not work

together somehow. Dad and I work together all the time, but then their relationship is suspect, especially if the rumors that the dad beat the son are true. Maybe they don't want anything to do with each other," Pam suggested, though she didn't believe it.

"Well, Pam, just who is this Simone Folquet anyway? I assume that he is another son of Ross. I thought that you had said Ross had only two children and that the young daughter died around the same time as the mother," Mary inquired.

"I suppose that he could have gotten remarried and had another son," Pam suggested the most logical answer. I guess I ought to follow that down a bit too."

On Friday, the teens began to get ready for the big formal dance at B & B's Dance Hall. Nadia told them this was the fancy dress up night, and to wear their finest. Pam emailed Tom about the dance, and he replied he'd be there. Hence, Pam spent much of the afternoon adjusting her fancy Inaugural Ball gown. Indeed, with so many women staying on the two ranches, nothing got done Friday afternoon, except getting themselves ready for the dance.

Audrey's boyfriend, Bill Williams, was taking her. Fern asked her new boyfriend, Hank Tomson, to accompany her, while Orenda's new boyfriend, Bill Jones, was taking her. Now that all the teens had regular dates, Lindsey relaxed. In fact, she and Ashley made sure that both Fern and Orenda had fancy dresses to wear.

Pam set the stage by saying, "I'm going to try to look my very best for Tom tonight. I hope I don't make a fool of myself in these heels." She was planning to wear her five-inch heels from the Inaugural Ball. Of course, Lindsey, Amanda, Ashley, and Audrey had to follow suit, and naturally Lindsey found herself loaning Fern and Orenda similar heels. Even her mother was wearing the fancy dress that Nadia had gotten her. This was going to be one fine night of dancing—Lindsey was certain of that.

She was not disappointed. As she held onto Deiter's arm, they entered the revised dance hall. R. B. had doubled the inside space. Nadia had added satin draperies and Jolina added more subtle lighting so that just walking inside one felt romantic. The teens, unused to the high heels, made sure to hold on tightly to their boyfriends as they walked inside.

"Wow Nadia!" Lindsey exclaimed as the two host couples continued their tradition of personally greeting each person who came to their dances. "This place is even more fabulous than before!"

Nadia beamed, "You bet it is. We've made many changes, giving people more of what they desire. Still, I think we are going to have to expand it even further. You'll see just how packed it is tonight."

Soon the waltzes began and Deiter swept Lindsey onto the dance floor. All around them, couples danced and romanced the evening away. Before long, the DJ announced this was the last dance. The lights dimmed even further, and the hundreds of couples pulled even closer to each other. When the music ended, Lindsey found herself in a deep embrace with Deiter, loving every second of it. He whispered in her ear, “You are the greatest woman in the whole wide world.” She blushed and gave him another kiss.

They waited while the crowd of some five thousand slowly left the dance hall. Lindsey couldn’t help notice that Pam’s face was quite flushed and wondered about her. However, with everyone still packed inside, she decided against chatting with Pam about it. Tom had his arms around her, so that was a good sign, Lindsey thought.

Around one that night, they all arrived back at the Compton ranch. Because of the late hour, Lindsey was forced to say good night to Deiter quickly so that he could get home before his curfew. After seeing him off, she headed to her bedroom, passing by her mother and father who were being passionate in the dim living room, but she smiled as she passed them.

When she got to her room, Pam was sitting on Lindsey’s bed, her billowing dress folded over her legs. The clicks of Ashley’s heels announced that she had finally said good night to Jim and was joining them. Just as soon as Ashley entered, Pam finally burst out, “He asked me to marry him! Tom!” Both Lindsey and Ashley let out a loud squeal, and Audrey poked her head into their room to see what was going on. Pam repeated it.

“Wow! Super Pam! I knew he had a crush on you. What did you say?” Lindsey finally remembered to ask.

“Yes, of course! I can’t believe it! Someone pinch me!” Pam bubbled.

“Way to go, Pam! Congratulations!” Ashley added

rapidly.

"He's perfect for you," Audrey commented, not as wildly enthused as the others. She took all things in stride.

"Have you told your folks yet?" Lindsey asked.

"Er no. I suppose I ought to," Pam said. "What if they don't think he's right for me? What if they tell me I shouldn't marry him? What if?"

"Don't be silly! Just go tell them or I will!" Ashley took charge and pulled Pam up onto her feet. "Come on. I'm going with you." Not to be left out, Lindsey followed behind them, a trio of heels clicking on their hardwood floors.

"Oh Pam!" Polly exclaimed the instant Pam made her grand announcement. She hugged her daughter tightly. Fred beamed like a proud father and then hugged the two at the same time. "I'm so happy for you!"

"I hope you approve of Tom," Pam said hesitatingly, hoping they would not disapprove.

"Why of course, dear. Tom is a really nice young man," Polly replied.

"None finer," Fred put in, a little unsure just what to say. "I do hope that you two wait until you finish Bradbury's before you get married."

"Of course dad! We haven't set a date yet, but we will wait until next summer. Tom's bringing me a ring tomorrow night, a real engagement ring!"

It was closer to three am before the teens finally relaxed enough that they could go to sleep. The morning came altogether too soon for the four of them.

Pam got no useful research work done on Saturday. Everyone kept chatting with her about her engagement. Amanda and Fern came by to hear the news. Then, she had to repeat it for Ahana and Orenda. Kathy and Emilio came over to congratulate her; Lindsey had Messaged them. And so it went all day long. At least for the rock dance tonight, they didn't have to dress up. Jeans and tops were the norm.

Pam let out a squeal when the monotone voice announced, "Tom Ryker is arriving," shortly after six pm. She raced to the front door. Everyone else remained in the dining room, giving them some privacy, but Polly and Fred could barely stand the suspense.

A bit later, Pam waltzed into the room, dragging a shy Tom with her. She proudly held up the small diamond engagement ring that Tom had just given her. Polly and Fred got up at once to congratulate Tom. Polly gave him an embarrassing hug, while Fred shook his hand heartily. Then, the teens just had to see Pam's new ring, and the incessant chatter began full steam, only dying down when they finally arrived at the dance hall for rock and roll night. The live band was from Denver, Stevie's Boys.

Wilma's comment to Lloyd and Monane, who had to accompany them, providing protection from Dominus and his Death Stalkers, said mountains, "I sure will be glad when we don't have to come to these rock dances any longer. I can't hear myself think." Lloyd laughed heartily, his sentiments exactly.

After the rock dance Sunday night, things still didn't

settle down much. Preparations began for the dual weddings to be held in just five more days. Deiter and Emilio were chosen to be Barnaby and Bailey's best men. Although they had other friends, none were near, and for security reasons, they chose not to invite outside guests. The teens began decorating the living room, culminating with a large number of flowers, carefully arranged just perfectly by Audrey and Fern.

Lena and Polly worked on the reception food and the wedding cake, while the girls made the living room look like a cathedral. With a little creative spell casting, come Saturday morning, the Compton front room did look unique and gothic. The wedding was to take place at ten in the morning. At eight, the teens began dressing and helping Nadia and Jolina get ready. The two women still lived in apartment number eight, just off the teen's bedroom hallway. Barnaby and Bailey still resided with their folks, the Hamptons, in number seven, right next door.

Lindsey made last minute adjustments to Nadia's wedding gown, while Ashley did the same to Jolina's. Both wore identical white satin gowns, but both also had a matching outer corset, and six-inch white satin pumps to match. Nadia and Jolina had their maids of honor all wearing matching sky blue satin dresses, with similar outer corsets and heels to match.

"See, I told you Lindsey. It is actually easier to walk in six-inch heels than five," Nadia explained. Indeed, all the sky blue heels were six inches tall. The teens were still trying to get used to walking in them. "Remember, small steps, and oh, I'm so nervous, Lindsey! How do I look?"

"Like the most beautiful bride I've seen," Lindsey said, adding, "you too, Jolina. You both look like knockouts!" Then, they heard the start of the music and waited for the guys to pass by their door, heading into the living room. Nadia heard Barnaby ask, "You sure you have the rings?" Deiter replied that he did.

"See, he's as nervous as you are," Lindsey pointed out to Nadia, who grinned.

"Okay. That's our entrance music. Here we go! Hold onto me, Lindsey," Nadia exclaimed, as waves of nervousness came over her. Silently, Lindsey cast her Calm spell on Nadia and then on an equally nervous Jolina behind her. In these heels, they had to take small steps, but as they slowly made their way down the hallways and into the living room, Lindsey realized Nadia was right. It was easier to walk in these than in the lower ones, a fact she did not understand.

At the entrance to the room, packed with their friends, Lloyd took Nadia's arm from Lindsey, while Fred took Jolina's from Ashley. Both men wore blue tuxedos. The two women had asked their fathers to give the brides away. Lindsey felt honored; Pam, likewise.

The teens went first, taking their places up in front, opposite the groomsmen, though Deiter could not resist blowing her a kiss. Slowly, the men brought the two brides to the front, handing them over to the two grooms, and the wedding began. The foursome had written their own wedding vows, which the pastor had agreed to use. Lindsey only partially heard the words, "From this day forward, to have and to hold, to cherish. . ." She was off in a sort of dreamland.

Then, it was over; the two proud men kissed their brides. To a cheerful tune, the four walked back down the aisle, while the groomsmen came over to take the arms of the maids of honor. Everyone then met in the dining room, where the congratulations were given, photographs taken, and lunch served. Next, they opened their many wedding gifts.

Lindsey surprised the two women with a pair of matching magical earrings, which actually could store one magical spell. They only needed to say the command word to have the spells activate. Deiter had gotten them each a ring, which stored a magical spell. Hence, the two women would always have some good protections about themselves. Of course, there were many other equally fine presents.

As things wound down, Nadia wanted to make a little speech. "May I have your attention every one? I wanted to take this time once more to thank Lindsey and Lena and the all rest of you for having given me and Jolina our lives back. Without what you have done for us, we would not be here today with these incredible husbands. We can never thank you enough for what you have done for two sometimes silly, Dutch girls. From the bottom of my heart, thank you Lindsey, Lena, and all the rest of you!" Everyone clapped.

Barnaby finally said, "Well folks, please party on for us. It is time that Tahiti beckons us, if you know what I mean. We will be back on Friday in time to open the doors of the dance hall. I hope you will not be too disappointed,"

Bailey finished his sentence, "that the dance hall is closed this weekend. Thanks for everything." With that, the two men escorted their brides out of the room. After a quick change of clothes, the four Teleported away.

After they left, Deiter called out, "Say, we are all dressed up. What say we have an afternoon formal dance?" Of course, Lindsey needed no further suggestion. They partied until the late evening.

Chapter 2—Off to France

On Sunday, June 16, Pam finally got back to her research on the Folquet family and the connections between the two huge enterprises. Mary had found no information whatsoever that the US paper mill was involved in anything nefarious. She could find no trace of any connection between the Mac Fluide Enterprises and the Folquet Enterprises, none at all, which mystified her. Pam, for that matter, was equally stymied.

"Either they are geniuses at hiding their cross dealings or there aren't any," Pam explained to her aunt.

"Well, dear, perhaps they are not connected at all, though I do find that incredibly hard to believe, knowing Dominus or Simon as I do. Any luck on finding out if Ross remarried?" Wilma asked.

"No, nothing. There's hardly any information about R. B. as he calls himself over there, but I did find out that he moved to France shortly after his wife died and long before his son graduated from Bradbury's. I found an old shipping manifest. He apparently moved a whole household of goods there by boat," Pam replied.

Her father added, "You know, Pam, everything just keeps coming back to that silly link which says, 'To contact Mr. Simone Folquet, please contact his attorney, Mrs. Isabella Folquet at the law offices of Folquet et Associés at 4520 Rue Jean de Bernardy.' I have half a mind to do just that."

"Dad, I agree. It seems like we have no other viable choices," Pam replied, "but to go and see this attorney lady."

Wilma suggested, "Yes, but Fred, perhaps only women ought to go. If we go there with a bunch of men, I think that this attorney might become very hesitant. I know that I would be, if a half-dozen men suddenly showed up on my doorstep asking pointed questions. I think this may be a job best undertaken by us women."

"I see your point, Wilma. Since this is our only lead, we should take every precaution not to botch it. I believe the investigating party ought to be small, so as not to rouse suspicions. Unless there is some connection between this Folquet group and Simon Mac Fluide, you shouldn't run into trouble, I would think. Possibly we ought to see if Ashley sees anything dire in our tracking down this attorney," Fred added as a precaution.

An hour later, Ashley could find nothing threatening about their proposed visit with the French attorney. "So who gets to go?" she asked.

"Pam, Wilma, and Monane, for sure," Fred replied. "If there is trouble, having a Dispeller there would sure be optimum. However, Alister will have my head if I let Lindsey go to France without a strong backup."

"Well, I do think I should go, Mr. Betts," Lindsey spoke up. "After all, if trouble comes, I want to be there to see that nothing happens to Pam and the others."

"I would feel more comfortable with you there," Fred replied, sheepishly adding, "cause my Pam is sticking her neck out. I couldn't ask you to go, but if you volunteer, I can't say no."

Lindsey grinned, giving her a way to solve both their dilemmas. "Perhaps you, Jim, and Lloyd could tag along, but stay out of sight. You know, keep tabs on us and all that. If we are waylaid, you can always fetch Amanda, who can track us. What do you think?"

Fred grinned, "Perfect. We can stay Invisible but around nearby. I can monitor what you are seeing or hearing. If we see anything amiss, we can charge to your rescue. However, let's not bother Alister with this. We can tell him about it later." Lindsey again grinned. Fred wanted to solve this riddle as much as Pam and Mary did.

On Monday around ten, the small group left for Marseille, France. "Wow! What a large city, so strange looking," Lindsey commented as she and Pam arrived on the sidewalk of Marseille. Wilma and Monane were right behind them. While the teens stared at the buildings and people, Wilma checked the street sign.

"Yes, we have the right street, Rue Jean de Bernardy. Now to find 4520. Let's walk, shall we? My, what absolutely perfect weather!" Wilma stated.

"Smell that sea! You can smell it in the air," Monane added. Neither woman had been to Marseille before. "Ah here we are, 4520. It's the last building before the Rue ends at the Boulevard de Montrichet. Quaint old building. Three floors. Ah, the sign says Folquet et Associés. Must be the right place. Shall we?" She opened the door and the four entered, knowing the Fred, Lloyd, and Jim were milling around just outside.

They walked up to a secretary-receptionist desk. "Est-ce que je peux vous aider?" the blonde young woman asked. Pam was ready for the language barrier. She'd cast her Language spell on herself just as they entered. Lindsey silently cast hers now.

Pam answered in French, "Yes, we would like to see Isabella Folquet, please."

"Oui, chambre nombre cinq," she said, indicating a long hallway. The four headed down the hallway, admiring the woodwork, done in mahogany, carefully polished. The faint odor of the lemon polish filled the air. A lush carpet muffled their footsteps. Part way down, a door on their left had a sign that read, Isabella Folquet No. 5. Wilma opened the door and they entered, Pam taking the lead, so as not to attract too much undo attention.

A secretary with long black hair sat at a beautiful old desk. "Est-ce que je peux vous aider?" she asked pleasantly.

Pam's translation spell was working perfectly, and she replied. "Yes, we have just come from America and wish to speak briefly with attorney Isabella Folquet, please."

"Oh, oui, Americans. I speak English, little. Un moment." She pushed an intercom button and relayed rather excitedly that four Americans were here asking to see her.

She rose and motioned for them to follow her. Pam noticed that she wore a smart business suit with hose and low heels. She opened the door and motioned for the four to enter. Pam led the away. Before her was a stately attorney's office, complete with beautiful mahogany walls. A woman with long, wavy black hair rose, and with the stumps of her arms, motioned for them to have a seat. Pam's mouth fumbled as she stared at the missing lower arms of this otherwise gorgeous middle-aged woman, perhaps forty. Her makeup was subdued, but perfectly done. She had blue eyes and a kind smile. Lindsey also did a double take when she saw the woman was missing her lower arms. Wilma and Monane took it is stride, having seen far worse in their lives.

"Bonjour. I be Isabella Folquet. How may I assist you? I speak some English. You are from America?" she replied in a mellow alto voice.

"Thank you for seeing us. Yes, we are from America, Colorado, to be more precise. I am Pam Betts. This is Lindsey Barron, my Aunt Wilma Weltsi, and Monane Tumble. We would like very much to speak briefly with Simone Folquet. It is about a very personal matter and vitally important to us. Your website said that we should see you first."

The cool-headed woman suddenly lost her composure, but only for the briefest of instants. Pam suspected that she recognized one or more of their names, somehow. Were they known over here in France? That seemed such a remote possibility. "Un moment, si vous plait," she forgot to speak English, which also gave Pam and Lindsey a heads up warning that something was amiss. "A moment," she hastily corrected herself. "Dial Simone," she spoke to her phone in French. Pam noted that she had one of the fancy earphones in her right ear. She pivoted away from them in her chair as she spoke in hushed tones to someone on the phone, presumably Simone. Shortly, she pivoted back to face them, a broad smile replaced the concerned look that she had had.

"We. Simone will see you. He est mon, how you say, husban. S'il vous plait, please dine with us. Simone asks have dine with us at noon. I due in court in un moment. Please meet me here round noon. We walk, short ways. Simone says dine with us, please," she said in her budding English.

"Thank you very much! Parfait. Très bien!" Pam exclaimed, greatly relieved that the first hurdle had been surmounted. She had been armed with alternative ways to try to get her to have Simone see them.

"Parfait." She rose and walked to the large window. Now Pam could see that she too wore an immaculately cut business suit, brown hose, and black pumps with relatively high heels. She motioned for them to see. "Can visit zoo, just there. Can visit beach; take cab. Can visit history houses, short time, two hours most. Meet here noon, okay?" she grinned hoping that Pam and the others understood her.

"Great. Thanks. We have never been to Marseille before. We would love to see some sights. We will be here around noon. Thank you again, Mrs. Folquet," Pam inadvertently reached out her to shake her hand. Not surprising to Lindsey though, Isabella extended her short arm for Pam to shake. She certainly was not embarrassed by her absence of arms. One by one, the others also shook her arm and then left.

Once outside, the voice of Fred whispered, "Well?"

Wilma began leading them toward the Jardin Zoologique, located but a few blocks away. As she walked, she related what had happened. "Honestly, the woman has no lower arms, similar to the many women we've rescued from the clutches of Dominus! Yet, she seemed friendly enough and called Simone on the phone to ask him if he would see us. Amazingly, he agreed. We are to dine with Simone and Isabella shortly after noon. We are to meet her back at her office around noon. She says it is a short walk to their home. Simone is her husband, so stay alert, more woman mutilation is expected! Darn men anyway," Wilma cursed, hoping the passersby didn't hear her.

"Excellent progress. We'd better stay invisible for now. He may be sending out spies to check on you," Fred cautioned. We will cast our See True spells, just in case. Are you heading for the zoo?"

"Might as well. I don't think now is the right time to try to find the beach. We might not get back in time to meet her. Ah, there is it up ahead," Wilma announced.

"Wow, a real zoo! I've read about them, but I've never seen or been to one," Lindsey replied, becoming keenly interested. Pam gave her a strange stare, and then realized that she had grown up with no hands and lived on that remote farm with little or no money for an expensive trip into Denver to visit a zoo. For Lindsey, the two hours passed rapidly.

As they walked back, Lindsey commented, "I think I liked the lions the best. Kind of like really big cats, though not nearly as friendly." Pam smiled; she knew that if left alone,

Lindsey would have probably tried to Charm the lions so she could pet them.

It was noon exactly. Several distant church bells struck, announcing the fact, when the four re-entered the attorney's building. As they entered, Isabella's secretary was just putting the large loop of the woman's purse over Isabella's shoulders. "Bon, good, est noon. But short walk our home." Isabella spoke and then headed for the door, which Wilma held open for her and the rest of the group. She turned and headed down the Boulevard Longchamp, and a bit later crossed the street to a side street, Rue Buffon.

As she walked, she chatted. "Been long in Marseille? You like city?"

"No, we just got here today. Beautiful city. I love the smell of the sea in the air," Pam replied, having decided that she was the best qualified to carry the conversation.

"I be attorney for all Folquet business. What you do?" she asked politely.

"Lindsey and I are sixth year magic school students," Pam replied, deciding to tell her the truth, just in case she might also be a witch and could detect lies.

"Ah, magics. I no magics, but Simone do," Isabella replied.

"My aunt and her husband sell real estate in Colorado. Monane and her husband have a small cattle ranch," Pam explained, her words still came out in French for Isabella's sake. She didn't know how well the attorney understood English.

"Oh, cowboys, Indians," Isabella exclaimed, turning her head to look at Monane.

Pam couldn't help but add, "Yes, Monane is an Apache Indian." Isabella seemed very impressed.

"Only short way now," she said as she turned onto the side street, Impasse de Montbard. "That be our home there," she pointed with her short arm. The group saw a walled and fenced complex that occupied half of the block. Two stories tall, the building looked as if it were centuries old, fitting perfectly the decor of Marseille. At the main gate, she paused and pushed some numbers on their security lock, Pam noted that the buttons were overly large, making it easier for her stubs to press a single number. At least Simone had some thoughtfulness in his butchery, Pam mused.

The gate opened automatically, and Isabella headed inside. As she approached their front door, Pam noticed it was one of those automatically operated doors. Isabella merely bumped into a large button, which then opened the door for her. "This way." She led them inside the first of several buildings within this complex. Once inside, she paused a moment. Just then, a middle aged man, also immaculately dressed, came hastily into the room, French doors wagging open and shut behind him. Pam realized that made it easy for Isabella to manage the doors. He was tall and thin, but wore a full, very bushy beard. His eyes caught Lindsey and Pam by surprise, as well as Monane and Wilma, who fought hard to keep from gasping. Those were the very eyes of Dominus Malefic or Simon Mac Fluide! They were dining with their archenemy!

Simone first hugged his wife, and took her purse off her shoulders, hanging it on the hallway hook. With his arm around her, he turned to face his guests. "I am Simone Folquet, at your service. So glad that you could take this time to dine with my family."

Pam cleared her throat. What should she say? "I'm Pam Betts; this is Lindsey Barron, my Aunt Wilma Weltsi, and Monane Tumble."

"She's an Indian!" Isabella whispered to Simone, greatly impressed by Monane.

"Pleased to meet you all. Come on in. Dinner is prepared. I hope that you enjoy roast duck with almonds. We certainly do," he sounded very pleasant and did not give Pam or Lindsey any sign that he recognized his enemies. The four followed the pair into the next room, where their eyes saw a magnificent old style formal dining room, whose antique decorations alone must have cost a fortune.

He noticed the women noticing the room and said, "Isabella's work. She is not only the world's best attorney, but has a real eye for interior decoration." Isabella smiled at the compliment. If you will take a seat on that side please. I need to sit between these two seats. I hope you don't mind if my sister joins us. I know that she was very excited to hear that we were having real Americans here for lunch with us. She does not get out very much. I hope that her appearance will not startle you. I will explain in due time."

The four took their places, while Simone assisted

Isabella to sit, adjusting her chair for her, the perfect gentleman. He quickly left. Meantime, Isabella whispered, "We've only just rescued sister. He thought she dead all these years. She was, how you say, prisoner and tortured. She has mind of child still, but Simone is working with her all days. Please don't look at her funny like, please."

Just then, Simone, who probably was forty-four, reappeared, his arm around another younger woman, who appeared to be perhaps in her mid-thirties. Her appearance startled all four women! She too had no lower arms. By now they had gotten used to this aberration of Simon Mac Fluide, but she also had the thinnest waist imaginable, barely twelve inches around. She wore a beautiful pale blue gown that showed off her remarkable, tiny waist. However, her shoes, or boots rather, captivated both Lindsey and Pam. They were ballet boots very similar to those that Lindsey and Ashley had been forced to wear! This poor girl, Lindsey thought to herself, as she watched them move slowly to the table.

Much to Lindsey's surprise, she walked very steadily and really didn't need Simone's arm around her. Rather, she gave the impression that she tolerated it for his sake. Carefully, as if she were some fragile wallflower, Simone helped her sit on his right; Isabella was on his left. All were across the table from the four guests.

"I would like you to meet my dear sister, Michelle. Michelle, this is Miss Pam Betts, Miss Lindsey Barron, Pam's Aunt Wilma Weltsi, and Mon. . . I'm sorry, I didn't quite get your name, ma'am."

"Monane Tumble, it is an Apache name," she spoke up kindly.

"Wow! A real Apache! Cool!" exclaimed Michelle, much as a young child might reply. Pam took note of this. "We don't often get company. Never Americans. We are Americans, did you know?" she asked. Meanwhile, Simone rang a small bell, and a waiter entered, carrying a stainless steel tray loaded with steaming hot dishes. He proceeded to place them around the table.

Pam spoke up, "Well, I assumed that you and Simone were from America. We came to visit you and hopefully get a number of questions answered." Pam thought that might get a reaction from Simone or Dominus. The reaction that came was not what any of the four expected.

"I knew that this day would one day come, but please, let us dine first. We have all afternoon to chat, unless Isabella has another court date." She nodded that she didn't.

Simone helped the two women fill their plates, but as Lindsey expected, Michelle would eat sparingly. Freshly baked bread and the finest jams, complimented the roast duck. Indeed, this was more like a banquet than lunch, as far as the four women were concerned. Isabella explained that they ate like this every day at noon, impressing Lindsey.

Michelle dominated the table conversation, while Simone alternated feeding the two women and himself. "I've never met a *real* Indian before. Do you ride horses and shoot guns?" she asked Monane enthusiastically.

"Oh horses, yes, guns no. I'm a witch so I use spells not

guns," Monane replied.

"My mom runs our ranch," Lindsey volunteered. "We use draft horses to do all the plowing and cultivating. So I get to ride horses all the time. It is a lot of fun." She pretended to be speaking to a very young teenager, and the two of them connected splendidly.

"Wow. I always wanted to ride a horse. Maybe someday I can. My big brother here is a wizard too. He casts magic spells all the time. I wanted to be a witch too. Most say I'm now too old, but my brother thinks I still might be able to learn magic too. I'm sure trying hard," Michelle replied, but had to stop to chew another mouthful of duck.

Lindsey and Michelle really connected, and the older woman chatted merrily with Lindsey throughout the whole meal. At one point, Lindsey, unable to contain her curiosity any longer asked, "Michelle, I couldn't help but notice your unusual boots. Are they hard to walk in? I had to wear some that were sort of like those for a while."

"Oh not anymore. At first, I couldn't see for the longest time. That was hard, but I got used to them. Now that I can see again, I don't have any trouble at all. Big brother doesn't think so, but I can walk anywhere just fine. Honestly, they are just funny boots, that's all, but I can't wear any other kind. My feet aren't like yours anymore, I think." She chatted away until Simone offered her a piece of bread.

A bit later and after taking a sip of soda with her straw, she continued, "I can't run in them like I could when I was a little girl, but I can walk just fine. Please tell big brother that I can get around just fine." She was acting like a little girl, Lindsey noted, wanting her to chide Simone for her. Lindsey didn't, however.

When the lengthy meal was finished, Simone asked, "Coffee or tea or sodas?" Pam and Lindsey opted for tea after such a heavy meal. Wilma and Monane took coffee with the other two adults. While the waiter was clearing the table and bringing in yet another serving tray, Simone said, "Okay, Michelle. It's time for you to continue your studies. Isabella and I need to talk with our guests for a while. You go study and show me how much you can get done before I come back to help you again, okay honey?"

"Okay, okay. Grownup talk. I will surprise you, Simone, honest I will." She got up on her own and began walking out of the room. Naturally, all eyes followed her. Lindsey saw that Simone was very concerned for her, wondering if she really could manage this by herself. Yet, the young woman walked perfectly in the strange boots, as if she had worn them all her life. Her progress, however, was comparatively very slow.

Once she was out of the room and the coffee and tea served, Simone sighed and said, "Okay. What is it that you would like to know?" Pam took this as a signal to commence.

Pam took a deep breath and plunged in with both feet. "You are really Simon Mac Fluide, are you not? And that is your supposedly dead sister, Michelle?"

Isabella looked very surprised. Simone sighed, "I have not been called by that name for a quarter of a century or more. Long ago, I changed my name to that of my mother's last name. I am legally Simone Folquet, but yes. I was born with that name, and Michelle is my baby sister. Why does this concern you?"

"Because in the US, Dominus Malefic or Simon Mac Fluide is attempting to destroy the entire country and is pretty much succeeding at this time," Pam spared no punches. If this was Dominus, she was ready for his attack and hoped that Lindsey was ready to dispel his attack spells. None came. He sighed once more.

"I always knew that this day would come, Isabella. I guess it finally has."

Chapter 3—Simone's Tale

"It all began as one of those silly kid things. My dad, Ross, was a Black Hall graduate and, I can now say, a real bigoted idiot and sadist. As I grew up, he drilled into my head that wizards ought to control the world, that normals were somehow defective cattle, to be used and discarded as one would a cow. Stupid me, I believed it, and all through my childhood, I made grandiose plans about how I could bring about a new Golden Age for the wizarding world. I argued continually with my dad about how I ought to be supreme ruler and how I could easily take over total control of the entire world. You know how kids are. They get silly ideas in their young minds, and it rather takes them over. Well, that happened to me."

"Nearly every day, I hit my dad up with more of my ideas to conquer the world. I had it all worked out, all planned out. Dad, on the other hand, argued that to control the world, you needed to control all the major businesses, the major corporations—that was the route to total world power, not by force of arms and deception as I was espousing. Oh the late night arguments that we had. It got so bad, that he began to try to beat some sense into me. Then mom got sick. I begged dad to heal her, but he wouldn't. 'She's a pathetic normal. She doesn't deserve to get cured.' Those were his words. Right there, I decided that I had to conquer the world, so I could stop my dad and those like him. Mom, she went to the norm hospital, but to save her, they had to remove her arms and feet. Diabetes, I now know."

"Dad finally relented a little and allowed her to wear prosthetic feet so she could move around some. I always helped her into them each morning, until I went away to Bradbury's. Because dad and I were so at odds with each other and so that other kids would not pick on me because my dad was a billionaire, I changed my name to Dominus Malefic, thinking that name really described the power that I wanted. Scares people, Malefic. Anyway, Michelle took care of mom when I went away to school."

"I want you to know that until Isabella here came into my life, there are only two women whom I loved with every fiber of my being. Mom and Michelle. I doted on my little sister. I promised her that she could come to Bradbury's too, when she was twelve. I remember even telling some of the teachers there to expect her and not to give her a hard time."

Simone paused, tears formed in his eyes, and he choked up, remembering how he was getting all set for his sister to follow him to Bradbury's. He'd told her all about it hundreds of times, when he was home for vacations. Isabella put her arm on his shoulders, and he hugged her briefly. "I'm sorry. I haven't looked at those memories for so long. I failed Michelle then, but I promise you I won't fail her now."

"I was in my sixth year. It was Christmas vacation time. I came home. Yes, I was always homesick there at the school. I missed mom and Michelle so badly, but a Black Hall student must be strong and powerful or so everyone says. I kept it bottled inside and never told a soul. I came home and mom was in a diabetic coma! Dad kept refusing to help her. Finally, I cursed him and took her to the emergency room myself. Too late. She died before the Insulin could revive her. I came home and very nearly killed dad. It would have been a godsend had I been able to do that. Hindsight is always perfect, you see."

"But dad seemed remorseful, as befitting mom's death, so I couldn't do it. After we buried her, dad took me into the study and locked the door. He said, 'So do you still think that you can conquer the world by force and deception magic?' I was angry, I was foolish, I was stupid, I was morning my mother, so I said yes. I wish I could take that back now. I was thinking only of myself. I'd give anything to be able to turn back time!" His voice trailed off. Isabella again rubbed her arm on his shoulders, comforting him. Much of this was new to her as well, but she also saw how it was affecting him.

After several minutes, Simone continued. "Dad is always big on making bargains. Heck, that's how he amassed his fortunes, bargain, bargain, bargain! He said, 'Simon, I will make an ironclad bargain with you right now. I want to prove to you that your way is foolish and will never, ever wind you up as the controller of the world.' I said, oh yeh, wanna bet, stupid old man?"

"We argued some more, but then he proposed his bargain. 'Son, I will give you half of my entire fortune, no strings attached, to do with as you see fit. Yet, even with all the financial backing you could want, you and your grandiose plans will fail. However, when you fail—I do not want you to fail, son. I love you too much for that. So here's the bargain. He talked about the details for hours, but I was sick. I just wanted to mourn my mother's passing. We had just buried her an hour before all this, you see."

"What was that bargain? He refused to allow me to execute my plan and get myself killed. That he flatly refused to do. He wanted me around to gloat over once he had proven that I had failed utterly. In short, he cast a Clone spell, making a precise duplicate of me at that hour. I gave him a bit of my blood, and he cast the spell. The clone became me, Dominus Malefic, and dad divided his entire holdings into two halves, giving my clone one half. However, he told the clone me that this was where we parted company. He had Dominus, or me—it was so confusing at that time—sign legally binding papers that said if Dominus, the clone, ever had any contact with him ever again for any reason whatsoever, what remained of the fortune he had given Dominus was forfeited and would be returned to dad."

"Dad made it crystal clear to my clone that I or it, rather, should follow my plans to conquer the world, but that he was never, ever to contact dad again. My clone, er me, agreed readily, and my clone returned to Bradbury's later in January, as me. I never did finish magic school. And no, I do not know those advanced spells that Dominus or me learned during those last four months. I believe that he has learned Restricted Wish, but I certainly do not know it, though I rue the day that I didn't somehow learn it."

"As this was happening, the rest of the bargain went like

this. I had to disappear and change my name. Obviously, I could never be stateside again or ever cross paths with Dominus, my clone. God, there would be hell to pay if that ever happened. From what I have heard about him, he would kill me in an instant, if he knew that I existed. You see, the clone me thinks he is me. There is no way for him to tell the difference. He has all of my memories, skills, and knowledge that I had up to the point where dad drew my blood. So he is me, but I am not him."

"Part of the bargain was that I had to work for dad, learning how he believed one could conquer the world, by economic means. If I did that, stayed with him and out of sight, then when he died, I would get the rest of his fortune. Greedy me, I agreed to his terms, which he once more had set down on legal documents. It is truly binding. If I break that agreement, I'm disinherited, totally."

"In hindsight, I think that he had been planning this for quite some time. He had secretly purchased this estate here in Marseille, and after drawing my blood and getting my signatures on all the legal documents, I was ordered to come here and await him. One of the documents I signed was formally to change my last name to that of my mother, Folquet. So Simone Folquet I became back in 2156."

"When I got here, I found servants had much of the place ready for occupation. There are three separate buildings on this large estate. One was given to me; one held the servants; one was reserved for dad. I also signed papers stating that I would never go into dad's house unless asked, and then never leave the first floor. His study in the basement and his upstairs bedrooms were totally off limits to me. If I violated that rule, I was again disinherited. Heck, I wanted to be rid of him, so I never went into his buildings back then. God, now I wish I had had more guts and done so, but I am getting ahead of myself."

"So I arrived and I waited in my new home. I mourned for my mother for what seemed days, before dad finally came. Then, I received the worst shock of my life. I asked where was Michelle, the only other person I truly loved. Dad told me there was an accident, and she was killed. He said the Children's Hospital in Chicago had been unable to save her life. He said he then buried her beside her mother! I was crushed utterly! Everyone I loved was gone. All I had left was the distant promise of unlimited fortune."

"I didn't come out of my room for six months! When I did, I make a sneak trip to that hospital in Chicago and donated a new wing in memory of Michelle. Finally, dad got me to follow some of the news of Dominus attempting to conquer the US. I began to follow his criminal career, but I also began to see just how stupidly foolish I had been, childish notions. Slowly, dad began to get me to start taking an interest in the proper way to control things, via the business world. I worked only half-heartedly at it, back then."

"Then came the news that the world famous Dispeller Sam Rabbor and the Rat Pack had finally captured Dominus. He was sent to jail. That night I went out of the complex here for the first time since I came here and celebrated like mad.

Okay, I got good and drunk. At last, I could put an end to the stupid game that my dad had set in motion. I approached him about it the next day, but he laughed at me. 'Game isn't over until the clone is dead, proving to you once and forever that your methods are folly and that mine is the only true way to ultimate power.' Well, I was pissed as you might guess. Still I had hopes that he would die in prison. With this beard, I looked nothing like the images of my clone did on TV, so I finally was allowed to go out of the complex freely."

"By then, I was my dad's right hand man in the enterprise corporation. As such, I found that I needed some corporate legal advice, and I sought out the best lawyer in Marseille. That was the luckiest day of my entire life. I met Isabella here. She proved to be a super lawyer as well, and we fell madly in love. However, as you have probably noticed, she is a normal, not a witch."

"We dated for a couple years before I proposed."

"I thought that he would never get around to it," Isabella teased him. Lindsey and Pam grinned.

"Well, that was a fiasco. I should have never told my dad about that! When he found out that she was a normal and not a witch, he became extremely angry. I thought he was going to kill me on the spot or worse, kill Isabella! I was scared out of my wits. Yet, the next morning, he was calm as a cucumber. 'Son, you want to marry this creature. I won't stand in your way, but I will make you and Isabella a bargain to show you that she is not worthy of you, son. I will give my consent and release you from that part of the overall bargain, if she and you both agree to my bargain.'"

"You see, I had also signed away my right to marry whom I chose. Dad wanted me to marry for financial gain, not love, and certainly never under any circumstances a normal. If I went ahead and married Isabella without his consent, again I was totally disinherited forever. So he had me bring Isabella to his house, and he laid out the bargain, withholding nothing. He would give his consent only if Isabella agreed to have her arms removed at her elbows. He then gave her some options. If she agreed to do this and then marry me, he would at once transfer ten million dollars into her private account. If she later wanted out, finding the situation untenable, he would give her another ten million dollars and see to it that her arms were regrown."

"I screamed and argued and protested, but he said that we needed to give this some serious thought. He gave her the legal documents so that she could ascertain their veracity and that they were indeed ironclad, which she most certainly did verify. I think we talked about this for nearly a month. I was not about to have her do this."

Isabella broke in, "I made him agree to do it, but it took me a whole month of persuasion though. Simone is the nicest, kindest man that I have ever known. I convinced him that with some small adjustments, we would not be adversely impacted, and we would have a giant nest egg on which to build our own *independent* fortune, and so at last be able to get out from under his father's thumb. Indeed, we have multiplied that tenfold to date."

"Mostly all her doing. She is a fantastic lawyer, in high demand," Simone complimented her. So we did it. We signed the papers, and dad cast his spells on her. Then, we got married. All was going along fairly well. We both had to make many adjustments to our lives. I promised her that the day that dad died, I would get her arms regrown. I signed a legal paper so stating, by the way, and have set aside a secret account to pay for it the moment we are allowed legally to do so. Anyway, as I said, we were managing and doing well, and then we heard that Dominus had broken out of jail. Dad called me into his office and said that the game was afoot once more!"

"It was back into hiding for me. I dare not show my face around Marseille, for fear of someone thinking I was Dominus or for accidentally running into him. He was once around here, I heard. Then, we got a stroke of luck on our side. Dad contracted Alzheimer's disease, irreversible and incurable. Now he is doing so poorly that he is confined to his bed and is on oxygen all the time. The doctors give him only months to live at most. He doesn't know his own name any longer, though he still recognizes me, but not Isabella."

"That's when we got our real break. Per the legal contract, I am obligated to look after his needs until he dies. So finally, I got the run of his house. I began to notice that a servant carried dinner platters down into his basement. I thought this rather strange. One night, I followed the servant, discretely of course. Good god! There locked in a basement complex was Michelle! I found out that the servant was under similar legally binding documents to keep her presence here a secret."

"Anyway, I found Michelle. Dad had cut off her arms, blinded her, forced her to wear a binding corset. Her waist is very tiny, as you have seen. Worse than that, she had been forced to wear those ballet shoes all these years. She was locked away in the cellar room with only a servant coming to tend to her needs when she would walk over to the door and press an alarm button. The only outside contact she ever had was a small radio that was locked onto a music station. I bawled like a baby when I found her. She thought I was dead too. The first thing that I did was to Dispel the Blindness spell so at least she can see. Then, I rummaged through dad's copies of his legal papers and found that if anyone re-grew her arms or tried to get rid of those shoes and corset, again both she and I would be disinherited. Upon his death, she would receive twenty million dollars to look after her care. Okay, I admit it. I cheated and cured her blindness, giving her a good deal of life back."

"Isabella went over the documents carefully but dad goofed and forgot to mention her blindness so we were safe. I got Michelle out of that basement and brought her here to live with Isabella and me. We quickly discovered, as you probably have seen, she is mentally still a very young teenager. It was about nine months ago now that I found and rescued her. Since then, I have spent every waking hour with her, being her teacher, so to speak. I have improved her reading and math skills noticeably. I am sure that given time, I can help her reach adulthood, as she should have been. Then, I'm going to try to teach her how to use magic—what she should have been taught back in the fall of 2156. I don't know if that can be done or not. It's always taught when we are twelve, not when she is in her thirties. But by god, I sure am going to try! I owe it to her. Dad robbed her of half of her life but I'm going to try and give her the rest of her life."

"I guess that about says it all. Does that answer your questions, Miss Betts?"

Pam found her voice at last and squeaked, "Yes, I am so terribly sorry for Isabella and Michelle. Your secrets are safe with us."

"Thank you. Now am I permitted to ask some questions of you?" Simone asked.

"Sure, as long as I don't have to break any confidentialities," she replied.

"When Isabella called me this morning, I wondered about your names. Lindsey, yours is Barron. Any relation to that famous Dispeller Sam Rabnor of the Rat Pack?"

"He was my father, Dominus had his Death Stalkers murder him," Lindsey replied honestly.

He sighed. "I'm sorry. My failings have affected so many lives now." After a pause, he asked, "I've heard stories about a young woman named Betts who has been doing some marvelous things to help stop Dominus. By chance are you her?"

"Yes, I am a budding Sleuth. That is how I managed to find you," Pam answered.

"My compliments, Madam Sleuth. You are the first person in over a quarter of a century to have worked out what became of me. I knew the day of reckoning would one day come. I suppose that now you will want to arrest me or something. Please, may I have time to make arrangements for Isabella and Michelle?"

"What? Arrest you for what?" Pam asked, taken by surprise. "As far as I can tell, you've committed no crimes at all. Rather, you and Michelle are the victims of a sadist child abuser. Your dad ought to be arrested. However, you are right. You must remain a secret. If Dominus finds out that you exist, he will most certainly come after you to kill you. That is as predictable as the sun will rise tomorrow."

"Thank you. Is there anyway that I can help? Isabella and I want to help stop this clone of me somehow," he asked, a most pleading look in his eyes.

"Well," Pam began to think.

"I am in control of the entire Folquet Enterprises now. Plus Isabella and I have funds of our own that we can contribute," he added hopefully.

"Say, I notice that you have several pharmaceutical companies among your holdings," Pam began, thinking quickly. "You've heard about those darn pills that he is using to turn normals into zombies?"

"Yes, just horrible. Why? Oh, I get it. You are going to need a cure aren't you? I will make our companies' research facilities at your service. Only we have been unable to acquire any formulas or samples over here."

Just then, Lindsey heard the unusual sound of Michelle's boots on the hardwood floor. She was slowly walking towards them, grinning from ear to ear. "Hello again. It's me." Her childish voice broke in on their conversation. Pam noticed that she was carrying something under her arm. "Can I ask you Americans something?" Michelle asked as she came up to the table.

"Sure, ask away, Michelle," Lindsey replied, as Simone quickly moved to help her sit down. She dropped a magazine on the table and pushed it over to Lindsey.

"See that girl on the cover. It's called Teen Fashion magazine. See her? She's my idol. Can you find out her name for me, and how I can write to her? She's really inspiring to me, though I'm not quite as bad off as she is." Lindsey stared at the cover. The face of her sister stared back at her; it was one of her recent armless poses.

"I can do you better than that," Lindsey replied. "That's my sister, Ashley. She lives with me. If you want, I can see if Ashley will come and visit with you, maybe bring you one of those fancy dresses. Would you like that?"

The expression of pure joy and happiness on the thirty-three year old woman, going on thirteen made everyone's eyes tear up. "Your sister! Wow, oh wow! Could she? Would she? I'd love to meet her! Please ask her soon. I look at her picture every day now. She looks gorgeous, and I want to be just like her someday."

Jim, who had been listening in on the entire conversation, Messaged Lindsey.

Going to fetch Ashley. Will tell her what's needed. Bring her here in a couple of minutes. Let her know all. J.

"Michelle, we are witches. I'm letting Ashley know that you want to meet her. I'm sure that she'll want to come and meet you right away, if that is okay with your big brother here."

"You don't have to do that," Simone tried to protest.

"That would be super," Michelle continued. "Isabella, do I look okay? I mean is my hair straight and all that? If Ashley comes, I want to look good for her."

"Dear, you look just perfect," Isabella replied, brushing her arm over the woman's shoulders, as if she were still a teen and she, her mother.

A few minutes later, taking another cue from Jim, Simone and Lindsey went out to the gate. Simone gasped as he saw Ashley there. Ashley was wearing one of the dresses from the photo shoot and had temporarily Morphed into her armless form, just for Michelle. Jim had hastily briefed her on the situation, but she had been listening into Jim via a spell, and thus everyone else back home had heard it all. "My sister, Ashley. This is Simone Folquet."

"Pleased to meet you, Simone. So where is my admirer?" She carried a small backpack, which Lindsey removed as she entered the complex. Simone led them inside.

As soon as Michelle saw Ashley, she let out a squeal as only a young teen could upon seeing her idol before her, though she was really thirty-three. Michelle rose and moved as quickly as she could in her boots towards Ashley, who could not help but stare at the woman and how adept she was walking in those boots. When they were close, Ashley said, "Hug, but I have to use my feet. At least you have some arms to hug with." Michelle giggled and threw her arms around Ashley, who curled one leg around Michelle, hoping that would not cause Michelle to lose her balance, standing there on her toes. It didn't.

"I brought you a little present, Michelle. Sis, can you get it out of my backpack for me?" Ashley asked Lindsey. Lindsey brought out one of the dresses Ashley had worn at the photo shoot. "Recognize it?" Ashley asked. Michelle's squeal told all.

"Oh thank you, thank you, thank you! I look at your pictures every morning when I get up. You look so gorgeous and are even worse than I am. It gives me hope for each day. Someday maybe I can be a model too, but I think that I'm too old now. Wanna see my room?"

Ashley looked at Simone, who had large tears flowing down both cheeks. He nodded. "Sure thing, Michelle." As they started their slow walk across the room, Ashley added, "Once I tried to wear boots like yours, but they hurt my feet so, and I couldn't keep my balance well. Besides, like this, I have to use my feet for everything. At least you have some arms."

"Oh I know. I was like that at first, so very long ago. But not now. I do just fine, only my big brother doesn't think so. Perhaps you can tell him I do just fine. I can walk anywhere, just not as fast as he can walk. He's teaching me all sorts of cool things, you know. I think I forgot how to read even, but I am doing so much better. I get up in the morning and look at your pictures and think just how fortunate I really am, now that my brother has found me and is taking care of me along with Isabella. She is like a mother to me. My mother died you know, a very long time ago." Her words drifted off as they left the room.

A while later, Ashley returned. "She and I fixed her a snack, and she's eating it now. We said our farewells. I promised that I would write to her and come visit her when I can."

"What? She's fixing a snack? But how?" Simone said very worriedly.

"She can do far more than you give her credit for, Simone. My simple suggestion is allow her to tell you when she needs your help with something. She is a very independent woman, if you will allow her. Is it okay if I write her and come to visit once in a while?" Ashley asked.

An hour later, Pam finished her lengthy description to the many adults gathered in their dining room. Among them was Governor Alister, who praised Pam's detective work once again. "Pam, thanks to you, we now know the true story behind Dominus. So much now makes more sense to me. He is right; this must be kept secret, totally secret. I will merely say that you have been instrumental in acquiring overseas financial and pharmaceutical support. That will be sufficient for the many other Rodents. Let us all keep this a secret between us." Everyone agreed completely.

After Governor Alister left, Deiter, who had also

dropped by to see Lindsey and thus heard the incredible news, commented, "Pam, you have outdone yourself this time. Thank you and wow!" Pam looked pleased.

Ashley, on the other hand, said, "Well, that was an incredible breakthrough on my divination work."

"What? How so?" asked Monane.

"There are two Simon's, not one, two very different ones, identical in many ways, yet vastly different in others. Before when I was divining Simon, I often got the two confused and that messed up my divinations. Now, I know what I am doing—that there are two. My work ought to be vastly improved now," she replied. Deiter found that a very hopeful note, but wished his Eliminator training was completed so he could get to work capturing Simon.

Chapter 4—The Boston Pill Party—Bloody Monday

On Monday morning, the teens had just finished getting their morning chores around the ranch done, when Pam received an urgent Message from her father.

Turn on the TV! Boston is in trouble. F.

Pam told the others, and they all made a mad dash to the big screen TV in the family room. An announcer and cameraman were near the docks of Boston. Mass pandemonium greeted their first view. The woman was reporting, "It's chaos here. There goes another crate of the Health Care pills! Get a close up, Fred. Yes, another striker has just dumped another box of the pills into Boston Harbor. I don't know how many pills were just destroyed, but from the size of that container, it must be in the hundreds. Here comes another man with a box."

That was not quite accurate. As the cameraman swung around for a panorama view of Boston Harbor, the teens could see hundreds of men and women carrying boxes identical to the one they had just seen dumped into the waters. All were heading to the edge to throw their box or boxes into the waters off Boston. Once the person dumped their load, they raced back into the city, while more people came running down the streets to the docks. Yes, it was a chaotic scene.

Only when the station reverted to the overview from the helicopter could one see the magnitude of the Boston Pill Party, as this event was being named by the press. All throughout the city, men and women were carting boxes from the many Health Care Distribution centers. Some were miles from the waters, while others were rapidly approaching the confused docks.

"The police are powerless to stop this rampage! No, look, there is one now. He's also carrying a box! There is no law and order present at all, just rioters!" the surprised announcer exclaimed, somewhat shocked to see police officers joining the looters. "No, look, there are a number of police officers and what looks like State Militia men standing guard over the . . . well, this can't be—they seem to be protecting the looters! This is unheard of! I don't know what to say, except there seems to be a complete breakdown of law and order in Boston this morning!"

"For viewers just joining us, I'll recap. Around eight this morning, the National Health Care Program was scheduled to begin operations in three states, including Massachusetts, Connecticut, and Rhode Island. So far, there seems to be no major problems in the other two states. However, as the Health Care workers began reporting to their buildings, they uniformly found that large crowds were already there and were in the process of breaking into the facilities. Our cameras have visited one of these now deserted buildings. The looters took only the cases of pills that were scheduled to be dispensed. Uniformly, the cases of pills are being carried to the docks and dumped into the bay."

"We have learned that there are fifty-two Health Care Facilities in the greater Boston metropolitan area. All fifty-two have been looted, beginning around eight this morning. All signs point to a well-planned and well-organized raid. Authorities do not think that this is a spontaneous outbreak of looting, but has been orchestrated by one or more government officials. That the police and the State Militia are participating or providing protection for the looters suggests that the organizers are high ranking state officials, though no one would confirm or deny or even agree to be interviewed as yet."

"Yes, Bostonians are displaying their utter disgust and contempt for this National Health Care Program, much as they did during the Revolutionary War era. There are strong parallels between the Boston Tea Party and the Boston Pill Party of today! Fascinating comparison. Will Boston secede from the Union?"

"This just in! We take you live to the White House, where President Missy Snow is making an address." The screen switched to the Oval Office, the sound of press cameras snapping away could be heard, as the President walked to the podium and the wall of microphones there.

"Good morning, my fellow Americans. Today is a sad day in the history of our country. Outlaws, thugs, and common looters as I speak are looting the Health Care Facilities in Boston." Her voice was devoid of emotion; an automaton was speaking, reading a prepared speech.

"As your duly elected President, I cannot stand for such

lawlessness. We cannot allow a few criminals to block the National Health Care Program. Look at the tremendous benefits already achieved in New York and DC! No one is sick any longer. Most all hospitals have shut down, excepting two trauma centers to handle the occasional accident victim. The cost of health care in these areas is near zero, resulting in the savings of billions of taxpayer dollars. Already, state and federal tax rebate checks have been sent out to those on the plan in New York and DC, as I promised."

"Crime in New York is a thing of the past. There is no more crime. Our police have been reassigned to other duties, primarily joining the ranks of the fire fighters and other first responders. The benefits of my National Health Care Program are above dispute. Yet, disgruntled criminals in Boston have taken the law into their own hands. This cannot and will not be tolerated. Thus, I have ordered the US Army to go into Massachusetts to bring back law and order. I am declaring all the state of Massachusetts to be under martial law until further notice. General Whitney Sprague will be in charge of the task force. He assures me that his forces are already mobilizing and will enter the state by noon, bringing back law and order."

"We will make every effort to apprehend all those who have taken part in the massive looting and bring them to justice. Thank you and God Bless America." President Snow stepped back from the podium, yet was bombarded with questions from the many reporters there. Like a true automaton, she merely smiled pleasantly and ignored them all.

The station switched back to their live feed from several crews on the ground and in the air.

After a minute, the familiar face of Hugo Whitefield interrupted the local feeds. “I interrupt our live coverage from Boston to bring you this special announcement. KMAG had just learned from our sources within the White House that National Health Care Program databases for these three states has been destroyed! Yes, someone hacked into their computer systems and first deleted the backup copies and then the main database. These databases contain the names of all residents of these three states and are used to keep track of those on the program. This has temporarily halted all pill distribution in all three states! Health Care officials have no way to document who has been given their pills. Officials suggest that it will be a week before the databases can be reconstructed. KMAG has also learned who the hackers were. After performing the criminal destruction of the vital databases, the computer monitors of the Health Care systems displayed the following image, captured by a worker with a cell phone.”

The screen showed a monitor screen displaying an image of the Voodoo Underground logo along with the text: brought to you by your friendly neighborhood Underground. Pam’s face flushed as she saw the logo and text. Both she and Tom were active members of the Voodoo Underground, so was Monique Blackburn, who was now off studying to be a doctor like her father. Pam was about to Message Tom, when his Message appeared before her eyes.

Pam, I made the suggestion to others that it would be nice if their databases disappeared. Looks like someone implemented my suggestion. Cool! Ought to set them back a while. T.

Pam grinned. So Tom did have a hand in this, though not directly. She felt relieved that Tom had not violated the law on this one. Surely, the government would make every attempt to find out the identity of that hacker.

For an hour, the group watched the vivid, live pictures on the big screen. The looters did not attempt to hide their faces. Many waved to the cameras. Teens and children also got into the action, helping toss boxes of the pills into the waters off Boston. The scene almost took on a party atmosphere. No one was attempting to stop any of the hundreds of looters. In fact, large crowds gathered around the docks, cheering them on, waving, and yelling their approval.

"This is not going to end well," Ashley suddenly startled the group of teens. She'd had another premonition of the immediate future. All turned to her. She smiled and added, "I think many people are going to die in a short while." Given her dire prediction, they all stayed near the TV throughout the rest of the day.

By mid-afternoon, the Boston Pill Party was completely over, and KMAG returned to its summary of the news. Particularly interesting clips of the morning's activities were continually being replayed for those who missed the live coverage. Suddenly, Hugo interrupted, "This just in! We have heard that there was a massive explosion near West Stockbridge and I90. Our SkyCam helicopter is now on the scene. I give you Melinda Brighton reporting." The scene switched to a young woman with short black hair sitting in a helicopter, headphones on, and speaking into her microphone.

"Yes, below us you can see that there has been a massive explosion on I90, near West Stockbridge. Several tanker trucks have just exploded, destroying the bridges over the river there. All traffic in both directions on the turnpike has been halted. As you can see, there is a huge line of military vehicles backed up all the way into New York."

"It appears to be the work of some local Massachusetts militia. We can see sporadic gunfire coming from the hills. The Army is now deploying men and equipment, though I don't know how they will be able to get across the river with their heavy tanks. Now we can see the militia moving back into the rugged hills. Yes, we can see platoons of soldiers moving in pursuit. You can see for yourselves. The armored vehicles are now punching cross-country into West Stockbridge, following the retreating militia. Soon we will probably see the Army men capturing those who were responsible for the destruction of those turnpike bridges, which will likely take many months to replace. I90 is the main artery into Massachusetts from New York."

"Look, the Army is deploying several attack helicopters, which are in pursuit of the retreating militia. With that incredible firepower, I would expect that the militia will shortly be wiped out or forced to surrender. The first of the attack copters is now moving toward the line of retreating militia. Due to the likely graphic images, we will not continue showing you the live action here, but I will keep you informed of the results."

"No wait, what's that? Oh no! A wizard has just brought the attack helicopter down! It exploded in the air and subsequently crashed on the ground. I hope no one on the ground was injured. See if you can get a close up of the crash site." The cameraman zoomed in on the flames and smoke, but because of the rough terrain, there didn't appear to be any collateral damage from the crashed helicopter. "Now the other attack helicopters are backing off, but still following the retreating militia."

A while later, the reporter added, "Now I can see what may be the plan of the militia. They are pulling the Army men out into the vacant hills and hollers, where all the lakes and reservoirs are located. About the only main road through this area is Lower Tower Road, a winding narrow road. To this reporter, it seems a deliberate action on the part of the militia to pull this battle out away from populated areas."

Hugo interrupted the coverage, "We have retired General George Jones here with us in the studio to give us his assessment of this developing battle. General Jones, what can you make of the situation as it has been unfolding here live before our cameras?"

"Thank you for having me, sir. Well, this is certainly a terrible day for our country, with countryman fighting countryman. Plainly, this local militia is heavily outgunned and out-manned, probably ten to one. Their tactics are becoming very apparent—classical battlefield moves. First, they took out the bridges, effectively halting all east-west travel using the turnpike. This will give the Army trouble in deploying their heavy equipment. The lighter vehicles, as you have seen, are cutting cross-country in hot pursuit of the militia."

"The militia leader has very rightly chosen to move the battlefield into the rugged hills away from populated areas. This is a very brilliant move. Not only does it greatly reduce any chances of civilian casualties, but also it puts the militia on the high ground and levels the playing field. The many armored vehicles will not easily be able to follow the militia, forcing the field general to send in infantry platoons on foot to attack the militia."

"The militia must have at least one powerful wizard among them. I don't know what spell was cast to bring down that apache helicopter, but it certainly was effective. If I were the field general, I would keep the others back and on recon duty. Hugo, this action here today is precisely what has been plaguing us in the armed forces for quite a long time now. How do you fight a conventional battle when your opponent possesses one or more wizards? We have just seen our worst nightmare happen here today. One unseen wizard and his spells easily brought down an attack helicopter. Wizards can cast spells that can easily slay an entire platoon of soldiers! How can you fight against a force, which is fielding wizards among them? We in the Pentagon have been wrestling with this problem for over a century now, with no clear cut solution in sight, except to somehow identify the wizard and eliminate them somehow."

"I for one am glad that I am here in your studios today and not out there on the battlefield facing that wizard!"

Hugo grinned and then asked, "General Jones, if you could give some advice to the field general down there, what would it be?"

"Well, I'm not down there, but from here, why, I would get snipers into position and try to take out the militia's wizard. Of course, the only problem with that is that the wizard does not go around with a large sign reading 'Wizard.' As you know, wizards look just like the rest of us, which makes this a terribly serious problem. The field general has to be acutely aware of this. If his platoons get too close, they risk being wiped out by killer spells, long before they can even spot their attacker. No, this has got to be that commander's worst nightmare."

A loud explosion was heard in the background. Hugo hastily returned to the live image of the woman reporter. "There, that smoke—zoom in on it. Oh, welcome back. Below us, you can see the smoke rising from several destroyed personnel carriers. They were coming up Lower Tower Road, clearly attempting to get behind the militia and cut them off. However, several explosions have halted their progress completely. We can see no militia in this area. The cause of these explosions is at present unknown."

The small images of Hugo and General Jones became superimposed at the bottom of the screen. The General commented, "That looks to be road side bombs that went off, similar to what the armed forces faced centuries ago in the

Iraq War. If so, then this retreat by the militia has been very carefully planned and is not just a sudden uprising today. Our forces on the ground are now going to have to slow way down and begin careful checking for additional traps, giving the militia more time to melt into the rugged terrain. Yes, this whole operation has obviously been very carefully planned. To me, it is no coincidence that those two particular bridges were brought down."

"Oh no! Look!" exclaimed Lindsey, suddenly pointing to a greenish cloud near the bottom of the screen, barely in view. "That is a Fog Death Cloud spell. Those army men scrambling up that ridge are going straight into it! They'll be killed!" While the shocked teens watched, indeed the front line of the scrambling men reached the leading edge of the fog and began dropping like flies. The entire front wave of men fell to the ground. However, those following them frantically donned their gas masks and headed to assist their fallen comrades. Only then did the reporter realize that something awful had just happened and quickly panned the camera off that area.

Hugo, looking white and somber, spoke softly, "On behalf of KMAG, I would like to apologize for inadvertently showing those awful images of death. It is not our policy to air such gruesome events. I'm sorry for any upset those images may have caused. Would you like to comment, General?"

"Yes, that is precisely what I have been telling you today; the army's greatest fears have just been witnessed. A lone wizard and his spells has just wiped out an entire platoon of men. I admit that I did not see the murderer anywhere in those images. This is a sad, sad day for Americans everywhere. Perhaps this is even more reason to get every state aboard the National Health Care Program. It eliminates all criminal tendencies, like what we have just seen. I do hope the Department of Magical Misuse finds and apprehends the wizard who just murdered all those American soldiers, who were just doing their duty to our country, trying their very best to bring back law and order to Massachusetts."

A bit later, Hugo interrupted, "The Governor of Massachusetts is about to make a public address. We take you live to Boston, where Governor Albert Rhodes is about to speak." The image on the screen switched abruptly to the familiar wall of microphones before a podium with the seal of the state of Massachusetts clearly visible behind the podium. A tall thin man wearing a light blue suit walked defiantly to the podium.

"Good evening citizens of the great state of Massachusetts and Americans everywhere. I am Governor Albert Rhodes. Today, the citizens of our state have made it plainly obvious to anyone with eyes that we here in Massachusetts do not want to be forced into this criminal plot that goes by the name of the National Health Care Program! We have seen our friends and neighbors in New York turned into mindless zombies! While we applaud the goal of perfect health and no criminal tendencies, we deplore the criminal, horrid side-effect of turning normal people into mindless automatons, mere robots, who no longer can think for themselves and who merely go around doing what they are told. We in Massachusetts want no part of that. I have repeatedly told this to President Snow, who has completely ignored me."

"Today, against our wishes, President Snow and Aetna Pharmaceuticals have attempted to force our unwilling citizens to become drugged zombies in their misguided Health Care Program. You have seen the response of Massachusetts! The vast stores of pills destined to turn our great citizens into cattle have been destroyed in an historic Boston Pill Party. The US government then chose to respond with force of arms. You have also seen how Massachusetts deals with the invasion of its state. We are calling it Bloody Monday. We will continue to battle anyone who tries to force us to become mindless automatons. May those western state governors who support this program take heed! I warn you that your own citizens will not stand for this treason on the part of the US government and its automaton leaders!"

"I hereby urge all other states and their governors to back what we in Massachusetts have begun today. Oppose this utter tyranny by President Snow. Let's move those automatons into prison and elect a sane government. I call upon every red blooded American to stand up today. Let your elected representatives know how you truly feel about this program to turn us all into mindless zombies! Massachusetts will fight to the bitter end. We will not become zombies! We welcome all those who feel as we do to come and join our fight against this utter tyrant! That is all."

At suppertime, Fred Betts arrived, looking very haggard

indeed. "What a day! Bloody Monday is going down in history!" Over dinner, he explained some things that had not yet been reported. "The Army now had Massachusetts completely surrounded, cutoff from all other states. Good thing, because thousands have taken up Governor Rhodes' plea for help in fighting back. However, all are being prevented from entering the combat zone by the ring of troops surrounding Massachusetts. The body bags are piling up. I've heard numbers mentioned in the thousands of casualties. Probably in the next few days, the official death toll will be announced. Those things usually are, you know."

"Yes, but dad, how are those that wish to escape or leave Massachusetts going to get out? If the army has the state surrounded, won't that create even more problems? I mean in New York, those that wanted to leave were allowed to move to other places, primarily Canada," Pam asked.

He grinned, "Precisely the key point that I was working on all day, even got Governor Alister's ideas on this one. While wizards and witches can certainly Teleport their families out, it is those normals who wish to leave that present a dire problem. Many of us have sent carefully worded messages to the President suggesting that those who wish to leave the state be allowed to do so. Other states are offering to take the refugees in, promising to help convince them to voluntarily return and join the National Health Care Program. However, we will, in fact, do no such thing, rather it just sounds politically correct is all. Time will tell, if they follow our warning."

By Saturday morning, the US military was in complete and total control of all of Massachusetts. Fully forty thousand soldiers were now stationed within the state. Martial law was fully in force. The governor and other leaders had somehow escaped and were nowhere to be found. All fighting had subsided. The official dead count was one thousand five hundred sixty-three soldiers and one hundred three militia. The wounded in action was a much smaller number, some five hundred ten soldiers. The advancing soldiers, who took no prisoners, summarily executed on the spot all militia who were wounded.

Many had tried to flee the state, only to be turned back by the ring of armed forces, who allowed none to escape this first week. However, those of the wizarding world were free to come and go as they chose, since Teleport spells could not be stopped. However, as time wore on, families were allowed to leave. It was late August before new supplies of pills finally arrived for those living in Massachusetts. However, when the health care tallies were finally computed in late September, Massachusetts now had less than half of its population still residing in the state! In stark contrast, Connecticut and Rhode Island joined the National Health Care Program without a whimper. However, now the problem facing Dominus was how to find enough wizards and witches to take over control of the state governments and the major, key businesses. The automaton leaders all had to be replaced.

Chapter 5—Our Last Summer

"Hey, do you realize that this is our last summer as kids, as students?" Lindsey commented to her friends. Everyone was either splashing in the Whitewater pond or sunbathing on the shore. It was the tail end of June, the last Friday afternoon. The dry summer heat of the High Plains had arrived. She'd just realized that this time next year, they would be done with Magic School and embarking on their careers and the rest of their lives, most likely moving away from their childhood homes and their parents.

Deiter, who had strangely not been by to visit on most evenings, ever since Bloody Monday, had come to spend the afternoon with Lindsey and take her to the formal dance tonight at B & B's Dance Hall. He sighed, "I know. I've been thinking a whole lot about it, love. I am going to spend all my time capturing Dominus and the Death Stalkers. Honestly, I don't see how we can have a life of our own until I take care of them." His statement struck a chord in all the teens. Even Kathy and Emilio, who had taken the day off to spend with their friends here, felt similarly.

Kathy broke the sudden stillness, "Well, Emilio and I are going to get married right away and then put all our efforts into making Kathy's Potions a go. Those millions of people are going to need lots of healing potions if they are ever going to be able to get off those zombie pills."

He added, “Yes, and I will be kept plenty busy rounding up all the ingredients that she’s going to need. That’s my job in our business, finding all the right ingredients. Kind of a dirty job, you know, going after bat guano, frog legs, and the rest of the icky stuff that goes into them. We will be kept plenty busy for a long time, trying to help them all recover properly.”

Pam, who had completed all of her pending researches and who had identified all the subsidiary companies of the far flung Mac Fluide Enterprises, was in the dumps. “That’s assuming that Dominus *can* be stopped, you know. For all I know, we may all be moving to Singapore to escape his US domination. While Tom here and I are going to get married as soon as we graduate, we are going to have to be prepared to evacuate on a moment’s notice to who knows where, assuming that Colorado doesn’t get forced into the Health Care Program sooner than we graduate. But you are right, Lindsey, this is, for better or worse, our last few weeks as kids. Next summer, we will be adults and have all that responsibility on us,” she added gloomily.

“Cheer up, Pam,” her boyfriend Tom poked her playfully, “it isn’t all that bad. As long as we are together, I don’t care if we are in Borneo. I will be totally content! You are the greatest, Pam. Nothing ever can change or dull that!” She smiled, and they kissed passionately.

“Well, by the end of summer, I ought to be ready to join Eli’s Rockers,” Amanda changed the solemn topic. “Ahana has been working with me every day to get me ready. I’m going to sing and play the hammered dulcimer on some songs. If it works out, I'll be a member of the band, and next summer we will be going on the first world tour! That'll be something!"

Ever cheery Ahana added, "She forgot the best part, though."

"What's that?" asked a curious Lindsey.

"She's agreed to marry me! That's what! When were you going to tell them, love?" he teased her. Amanda blushed.

"What? You too? When? How?" Lindsey couldn't quite figure out which question to ask her best friend. "Been keeping it a secret?" she added, turning over on her side to stare at Amanda. All the teens did likewise.

Amanda held up her ring finger, showing off the small diamond ring Ahana had given her last night. "He only just proposed last night. See? I was keeping it a surprise for a while."

Both received a loud round of congratulations from all their friends. His sister, Orenda, and Amanda's sister, Fern, both giggled, however. Each was a year younger than their siblings.

Audrey quietly spoke up, "Well, Bill and I don't know yet exactly what we are going to do."

Bill Williams, who was also spending the day here with his fiancé, added, "She's right. We know that we are going to get married once school is done. Beyond that, we really don't know," the shy Brown Hall lad agreed. "I mean, she has a good thing going with her carvings, but she also is fabulous with plants. I'd rather like to have my own organic garden or something. Golly, it sure is hard trying to become an adult and all that, isn't it?"

Audrey smiled, "It sure is right for me to be with Bill. That's all that matters to me." Lindsey saw that Audrey and Bill were madly in love with each other and smiled. So much in the world was good just now.

"Well, I second that," Ashley added, a huge grin on her face. "As long as I am with Jim, that's all we want—you know, just to be together all day and all night long." Jim had already proposed to his Princess, and Ashley now wore a large diamond engagement ring.

"You bet, Princess. It's just going to be you and me forever. Well, we ought to take a break for meals, don't you think," he jested playfully. Jim, however, was actually on the job. His task: protect Ashley wherever she was at, the best assignment for a Security Man imaginable.

Fern's boyfriend Hank Tomson, planned to meet her just after supper to take her to the dance, likewise with Orenda's boyfriend, Bill Jones. Fern and Orenda lay beside each other, getting a tan and listening to their friends talk about such grown up things. Fern mused, "Well, Ashley, you certainly can open up a Diviner's Shop. I mean you are the world's only Class 4 Diviner now. You can make a fortune at it, I'll bet. Already Audrey is doing fabulous with her carving business. She makes three thousand a month during the summer from her part-time Internet business. So Audrey's all set too. What I don't see is what you are going to do when you graduate, Lindsey? Are you and Deiter going to get hitched too?"

Lindsey flushed. She loved Deiter, but he had not yet asked for her hand, though she was more than ready to say yes. Amanda hinted that perhaps she should just ask him instead, but Lindsey felt uncomfortable in doing that. Deiter came to her rescue. "You all know that I'm mad about Lindsey, but look all of you. It doesn't matter a tinkers darn what you are dreaming about! As long as Dominus is on the loose, everything in the world is in jeopardy. Look, by this time next year, our whole country could be a thing of the past! Automatons everywhere. Who knows, in a few years, there might not be any place in the entire world that he doesn't control. I cannot and will not try to start a family when there is no safe place anywhere to do that. Heck, we might all be dead by this time next year. Have you given that any thought at all?" He was quite upset, and he shut up, realizing his outburst had turned this brief moment of cheerfulness into the doldrums once more.

"He's right, you know," Lindsey came to his defense. "Bloody Monday is likely to be repeated over and over, as the Program moves westward. I cannot imagine trying to set up a household and family when we might have to leave everything behind on a moment's notice. I feel so sorry for the dozen families that are staying around here with us. They lost everything but their lives, getting out of New York. I aim to spend my every waking moment trying to stop Dominus. Once that is done, then I will think about the future. Honestly, I don't see how I can do otherwise."

"Right!" Deiter added vehemently, "Soon I will be done

with my Eliminator training. Then Lindsey and I are off to capture Dominus and his thugs and put an end to all this once and for all. Then, we can plan for the future. You want to know why I haven't asked Lindsey to marry me? Well, I'll tell you. I want more than anything to be with her, but I might be killed trying to apprehend Dominus. No way do I want to have her become a widow at eighteen! Besides, if we were married, I'd be petrified that Dominus was going to hurt or kill her."

"Yes, but Deiter, have you considered what Dominus has said that he will do to Lindsey and me just as soon as we turn eighteen?" Ashley spoke up, her defiant attitude rising within her. "You know as well as we do that Dominus intends to capture Lindsey and me and turn us into his private play toys, torture us, and then kill us. However, if Jim and I are already married, maybe he will rethink his plans about me. I'd rather be dead and buried than become another one of his play toys. God, the torture that those women had to endure. Honestly, Deiter, you ought to give that some serious thought. Marrying Lindsey might keep her from being brutalized by Dominus, you know," she added tartly. Deiter's face flushed. She knew that he knew that she was quite right in her observation.

"Well, sis, I think that we can now stop Dominus from capturing us again," Lindsey defended Deiter. "Without his Restricted Wish, he is unlikely to get us again."

"He's just following in his father's footsteps with women, that's all," Pam put in her opinion. "Look what Ross did to his own daughter, Michelle. God, the torture that woman has endured—thirty some years of it, to say nothing of his own wife. I wonder how Michelle and Isabella are making out?"

"I don't see how that poor woman manages to even walk," Deiter replied. "I mean those boots that you two were forced to wear were something else." Images of Lindsey and Ashley trying to walk to classes wearing those steel ballet boots last November flooded his mind.

"Well, we did sort of get used to them near the end," Ashley admitted, "but I'll kill him before I let him do that to me again!"

"You had better move faster than me," Jim interrupted her, "because I'll kill him before you get the chance, if he ever tries to harm my Princess ever again, ever!" He was emphatic in his determination, though in his mind he recalled his utter helplessness when he suddenly found himself holding onto the severed lower arm of Ashley last Halloween there in Telluride. Realizing this, he added, "I swear that I will never rest until I kill him, Ashley, if he ever hurts you again. I will devote my whole life to tracking him down and killing him," he promised, thought he still felt more than a little inferior to the task. Dominus was vastly more powerful than he was, and he knew it.

"My point exactly," Deiter felt that they all were finally seeing his entire viewpoint. "How can you plan for the future when the threat of Dominus is close at hand? It is just ignoring what we are all facing in the here and now. We need to make plans to capture him, bring him down, and all that. That's what I think."

"True, but don't you think we ought to finish our sixth year first," Pam astutely pointed out. "After all, we will be learning to cast the most powerful of spells—spells we will need to bring Dominus to justice. I think we need to be patient; let the adults deal with all this until we are fully prepared to meet the challenge." Deiter was completely silent. He knew that Pam was one hundred percent right. She always was right, he noted. Still, he wanted to contribute in some way and grinned as he recalled what he had been doing in secret to stop Dominus. One day when the time was right, he would tell his friends about it.

Levelheaded Audrey had the last words. "Pam's right. We need to study and learn all that we can and then go after him. In the meantime, we do not know if we have mere months to live or another sixty years. So I intend to spend my days enjoying each and every one to its fullest. I will not succumb to the threat of Dominus. I will continue to make my carvings, snuggle with Bill, and plan our future. We are going to the fancy dance tonight, and I aim to enjoy myself fully. If I'm dead next year, so be it, but I will not succumb, sit, and mope around until then. I say, we get on with our lives, and the heck with Dominus. We'll just have to deal with him when the right time comes our way."

Lindsey sighed, "She's right, you know. We must not succumb to the threat of Dominus. Okay, how about a swim, Deiter? Race you to the diving platform."

"Okay, you are on, but no cheating this time. No magic

use," he teased her.

"You are just grumpy because I can cast them silently while I am swimming," Lindsey playfully teased him.

"Yes, that's why I won't play basketball with you," Ahana joined the teasing of Lindsey. Everyone laughed, recalling the games where Lindsey tossed the ball remotely in the direction of the hoop, cast Move Object on the ball, and had it somehow go through the hoop.

After they all cooled off with a swim—Pam merely getting her feet wet as she hated anything athletic—the girls began to chat about what to wear to the formal dance this evening. Deiter spoke up, "Say Lindsey, wait until you see my new suit that I'm wearing for the first time tonight. I bet you won't be able to keep your hands off of me and it," he teased. However, no matter how much Lindsey begged and tickled him, he refused to say more, keeping it a surprise.

"Well, I'm going to wear my Inaugural Ball gown," Pam decided.

"I certainly hope so," Tom playfully teased her. "Pam looks so incredibly sexy when she wears it. I just want to hold her tightly all night long." Pam blushed, but knew that she felt utterly different when she was wearing it and loved that Tom thought so too.

"Nadia keeps telling us that we ought to wear more fetish looking gowns instead of the fancy ball gowns," Lindsey mused.

Ashley laughed, "Of course, she and Jolina are crazy about them, but they are so tight and confining."

"Yes, but the ball gowns are so big and billowy that I can never see where I'm putting my feet," Lindsey playfully countered. "Say, Deiter, which do you like seeing me wear the most: those slinky, tight fetish dresses or the billowing hoop ball gown?"

Deiter's face reddened slightly. "Er, I like to see you in both of them, Lindsey. Either way, you are the most beautiful woman on the dance floor." At that, an argument broke out, with Tom, Jim, and all the other boys claiming that their girlfriends were the most beautiful women ever. Everyone was soon rolling with laughter.

"Seriously, which look do you like better, Deiter?" Lindsey finally insisted on asking.

Before he could answer, Ashley also asked, "How about you, Jim, which look do you like best?"

Jim admitted, "Ashley, I fell in love with you the moment I saw you as an armless waif in rags first coming to Bradbury's. I knew right there and then you were the one for me, a feisty girl after my own heart. You were then and now the sexiest woman I've ever seen. Armless in rags to Inaugural Ball gown to slinky fetish look with short arms, it doesn't matter. You are the greatest period."

"Isn't that just like a guy!" Ashley teased him. Lindsey giggled. "You ask them a serious question, and they just simply cannot answer it." All the girls giggled even louder.

"But he was telling the truth," Deiter came to Jim's defense, unable to see the mirth in the situation.

"Of course he was, Deiter," Lindsey tried to explain.

"We women like to dress up to please not only ourselves but also our boyfriends, silly. So we ask you what you like to see too. He didn't answer Ashley's question, now did he? Ashley maybe can read his mind, but I can't do that with you. Sometimes you boys need to really answer us, you know."

"Okay, okay, I get it," Deiter chuckled. "Wear that green slinky fetish dress for me. There, I've said it." His face flushed, and Lindsey realized that Deiter really did like her looking similar to Nadia and Jolina. She grinned and gave him a kiss for being honest with her.

"Well?" Ashley demanded Jim give her his honest opinion as well.

"Darn. What a tough decision!" Jim finally admitted to his Princess. "How do I choose between stellar looks, Princess? You could wear rags, and I'd love you no less. I like the photo shoot dresses, but that huge ball gown looks fabulous on you, but then so too does that fetish outfit that you wore last November. Okay, okay, I will make up my mind, Princess, but it is so hard."

Ashley pointed out, "Well, now you see what we have to go through all the time, just trying to figure out what to wear!" The girls giggled again. Ashley had stated it precisely.

"All right, wear that slinky fetish outfit for me will you?" Jim finally made a decision and then whispered something in her ear. She blushed and smiled back.

"Are you sure, Jim?" she asked, and he blushed, but nodded.

"Okay then, armless it is," she replied.

"What? You are going armless?" asked a rather surprised Audrey, beating Pam to the query.

"Look, I don't give a rat's ass about what others may think of me," Ashley retorted. "I have spent most of my life armless. I do what I want to do. I look the way I want to look. If someone doesn't like it or thinks it weird, then that's their problem, certainly not mine. Occasionally, Jim loves to wait on me hand and foot, and I like him doing it, so that's that. I've never cared what others may think of me, and I'm not about to care now, well," she added hastily, "excepting for mom and all of you, that is. The rest of the world can do what they want and think what they want. Meantime I will be me, period. Besides, look at the inspiration I've been to poor Michelle. I've given her hope each day. You should have seen her and her room. She had pictures of me taped on her wall, you know, from that last photo shoot I did. While I was chatting with her, I realized just how much impact I had made on her life—how much true hope I was giving her. Besides, Jim is going to take a picture of me tonight, and I'll send it to her. I promised to write to her, and I aim to do so."

"Thanks, Ashley, I could sense it too, with Michelle, that is," Pam replied, supporting Ashley now that she saw the larger picture.

"Well, gang. I say let's enjoy ourselves this last summer together, shall we?" Lindsey suggested. Everyone agreed, though many sensed that this might be their last summer together as a large group.

Around two, the girls adjourned to their rooms to begin

getting ready, while the guys continued to swim and relax. Unlike their girlfriends, they didn't need that long to get ready. "Gosh, we are going to need to wear a corset just to fit into these dresses," Lindsey commented as she and Ashley began to lay out their proposed wardrobe for the formal dance.

"Either that or make a mad dash to some clothing store," Ashley commented with a big grin. Both teens knew that was not an option. They were under strict orders to stay here or at the dance hall, under the watchful eyes of the many Security men and women. "I'll help you into yours and you help me into mine," she proposed. A bit later, both teens agreed that these corsets were manageable, unlike the incredibly tight ones that Dominus had melted into their bodies last Halloween.

By suppertime, they were ready, as were the many adults. As they all sat down for supper, Lindsey finally saw Deiter's new suit. His fancy tuxedo was custom-made of camel hair, soft and warm to the touch. Although traditional in black, his look was vastly different from the other tuxedos worn by the other teens and adults. He was right. Lindsey could not keep her hands off him that night.

As the large group assembled to Teleport to Denver and to the B & B Dance Hall, along with Nadia, Jolina, Barnaby, and Bailey, Ashley cast her Morph Self spell, appearing as her familiar old self, armless. Jim put his arm around her and Teleported them to the dance. True to his word, he took a number of photos of her with his cell phone and had Lindsey take some of the two of them.

After the large group arrived, Nadia took Lindsey and Ashley aside for some brief words of validation. "Gosh, I am so glad that you two chose to dress similar to Jolina and me. You both look positively stunning, Ashley especially so. I take it Jim is going to wait on you all night?"

Ashley grinned, and Nadia added, "Let me know what you think about the heels. I see you are wearing the six inchers. Jolina and I find that they are easier to manage than lower heels. You both look like a million!" She gave them each a hug, and the trio joined the others. Soon the dance hall began filling and the music began. Midnight arrived in seconds, according to both Ashley and Lindsey.

As they waited for the crowd to leave, Pam commented, "How did it ever get to be midnight, Tom? It seems that we only got here, excepting my feet are saying otherwise."

"Hey, next time try these higher ones," Lindsey noted that her feet were not as uncomfortable as they had been when she wore the five-inch oxfords that she wore to the Inaugural Ball. Among the women, a lengthy discussion about heel heights ensued, leaving the fellows rather bored, and they chose to grab a bit of the remains of the catered food.

The days passed slowly for Pam, who continually lamented that she now had no Sleuthing projects to concentrate upon; her mind was idle as she put it. Thus, she jumped at the opportunity, the moment Ashley mentioned it. "Pam, I just got an email from Michelle, though I don't know if she actually typed it herself or if Simone did. However, she needs my help and support right now." Ashley had printed off the email message and handed it to Pam.

Dear Miss Ashley,

Help. I am scared. My father has just passed away. Simone insists that it is time for us to get our arms regrown, but I am scared of it. I don't know what to expect or anything. I'm doing mostly fine as I am, but both my brother and Isabella are so insistent. Can you please come to visit me? Please. Simone says that it is okay for you to come, if you want to, that is.

Your friend,

Michelle

"Wow, that was unexpected. Ross is history. I'll be honest, Ashley, I really didn't think that Simone really meant what he said about getting their arms regrown. You know—Dominus and all that. Well, I didn't think he'd actually do it. Are you going to go?" Pam asked.

"She is counting on me. I owe it to her to go, Pam. After all, not too long ago I was in a similar situation. Michelle can use all the moral support she can get," Ashley replied.

"Good for you. I'm coming with you," Pam insisted. "Who else is going?"

"Well, Monane and Wilma have agreed to go. Jim, too, naturally. Lloyd believes that they will be enough protection for me—well us now. After all, no one but us knows about them, so we should be safe enough in Marseille," Ashley explained. "Go pack some clothes. I want to go in an hour, if possible. We'll probably be there at least a week or so—

however long it takes to regrow their arms."

Pam hastily packed some clothes and her laptop, but sent Tom a quick email before she shrunk the computer into a tiny form. Then, she shrunk her entire duffle bag and put it in her purse. "Should we take our Staves of Power?" she called out to Ashley, who was in her bedroom next door packing her things. Both teens decided that was a good idea and shrunk them as well, stowing them into their purses.

A bit later, the five said their farewells, and Wilma cast her Teleport spell, landing them perfectly before the entrance gates of the Folquet estate in Marseille, France. To their utter surprise, Michelle was just inside the gates waiting on them. Her face looked downcast and troubled, but the instant she saw Ashley, her eyes brightened up, as if a huge weight had been lifted from her shoulders.

"I'm *so* glad you could come, Miss Ashley. One second while I open the gate," Michelle said. The five watched her unusual gait as she walked the short distance, bent down, and using her arm, pressed the button that automatically opened the gate. Ashley still could not help but notice her tiny waistline, accentuated by the red, flaring party dress, which ended above her knees. Her long black, curly hair draped over her shoulders; her smile, infectious. That she walked on her toes was acutely obvious; the red ballet boots came part way up her calves.

Michelle chatted away, though both Ashley and Pam noted that her simple childish manner of speaking had noticeably changed since their last visit. They all followed her towards the main building, in which they had first met this family. Michelle had no trouble walking in her boots, Ashley noted, though she walked slower than a normal person might. "I don't know what you said to Simone last time, but whatever it was, he stopped treating me as if I was a baby or something. I get to walk around the estate here on my own now. He even lets me fix my own snacks. He should; after all, I just had my thirty-third birthday. I've been studying hard too. He works with me all day long and into the nights too. But two days ago, our dad died, and now I'm really scared. Simone wants me to get my arms regrown just as soon as possible. I am a bit scared. I don't know what to expect, you see. Thank you ever so much for coming, Miss Ashley," she chatted away.

"Ashley, just Ashley," she replied. Michelle grinned and nodded. As they approached the main front doors, Michelle moved over, pushed the large button of the automatic door, and led them inside. Simone was waiting patiently by the large dining room table. Pam saw at once that he was secretly holding his breath, hoping that Michelle could manage all this on her own without his help and was exceedingly proud of his sister at the same time.

"Simone, they are here!" Michelle announced, unable to contain her relief and excitement.

"Thank you all for coming on such short notice. My sister is grateful that you could come. I warned her that you might have other business and might not be able or even want to come," Simone addressed the five, and then shook their hands.

"Oh, you have arms!" he said rather surprised when he shook Ashley's offered hand.

"Yes, I had mine regrown just a couple years ago, when I was about to be a fourth year student. I have been through what Michelle and Isabella are facing. I just had to come," Ashley explained. "However, I still sometimes Morph back into the way I grew up. Here, Michelle, I brought you some photos of Jim and me at our Formal Dance a couple of Friday's ago." She laid out ten photos of herself, one with the two of them.

"Wow! You look incredibly beautiful, Ashley," Michelle replied as she stared at each one. "Can you help me put them up on my walls? See, Simone, I really don't need to get arms. I've not had them since I was twelve, that's twenty-one years. Doesn't Ashley look just fabulous, Simone, and she has no arms, whereas I have these." Ashley realized that Michelle was trying again to convince him that she was just fine as she was.

Ashley agreed to help her put them up, and Michelle used her arms to attempt to slide the dozen large photos back into a single pile. Ashley had to restrain herself from instantly jumping in and taking over. Simone had already moved halfway around the table with the very same idea. However, Ashley realized that she had to wait and allow Michelle to do what she could. Memories of her own fierce independence came into her mind and she smiled. Yes, Michelle was very awkward in her attempts to pick up the pile of photos, but given time, she managed to slide the pile slightly off the table and then squatted low and picked them up holding them securely between her arm and side. “This way,” she said, though Ashley already knew the way into her bedroom. Ashley walked slowly alongside the older woman and chatted with her.

“Amazing, Ashley is right, you know. Michelle is not some helpless cripple after all. I mean, when I first saw her, I thought oh my god; she is utterly helpless. Yet, I tried to follow Ashley’s advice. You remember: let Michelle tell me when she needs help. I’ve never had a harder thing to do in my whole life! My heart nearly burst there just watching her do that simple thing of picking up the photographs. Yet, I have been practicing restraint, and Ashley is so correct! Michelle has really adapted well to her unique situation. I’ve found that she can walk all around the estate on her own quite well in fact, though I constantly keep an eye on her from a distance.”

“Michelle and Ashley are a lot alike,” Pam explained, memories of Ashley’s first year at Bradbury’s came vividly into her mind. “When I first met Ashley at school, I felt so sorry for her, figuring we would all be having to do everything for her. Well, was I ever wrong? Though she had no arms at all, as you have seen from the photographs, she did everything that we did, only often in unusual ways.”

Jim could not help but butt in, “You should see her play pool! She had no arms then, but she was a real pool shark, a real master of the table. She could run the table on me and just about everyone else—darn near a professional pool player and with no arms at all, just incredible. Used her feet as arms, you see.” Jim was incredibly proud of his Princess.

"Amazing, almost unbelievable," Simone replied. "But didn't she just jump at the chance to get her arms back, regrown?"

Pam realized that he was now asking the key question that had been bothering him the most. "Oh, Ashley was terribly worried about getting it done. We spent months taking about it, and we even had a plan formed where if she didn't like them, they could be removed again. It was a hard decision for her to make. You see, she is a witch and was casting her spells with her feet. Now she would have arms and hands, but what would that do to her spell casting skills? Michelle is fortunate in that she does not have that additional heavy consideration with which to deal, Simone. She is just heading into nearly unknown territory, that's all. She just needs time to get more used to the idea, most likely," Pam theorized.

"Well, although I promised her and Isabella that I would have their arms regrown the moment that dad died, I can wait a little longer. I've talked with Isabella about this," Simone replied.

"How is Isabella doing?" asked Pam.

"Oh, she says that she is not in any urgent rush, claiming that she has adapted well to life without her lower arms. She's said that she can wait until Michelle is ready. My wife is a treasure; honestly, she's just fabulous," he replied. "Yet, I know that it has really been traumatic for her. She's not like Michelle and can't do many of the things that I have now seen Michelle do. Isabella likes to decorate our rooms, and she's been able to do none of that herself, relying on me to carry out her ideas. She likes to cook but can no longer. The list goes on, so I know that she really wants to get this done, but still she is patiently waiting for Michelle. She told me that it may well be traumatic for my sister."

"Is Isabella at work?" Wilma asked, wondering where the woman was.

"Yes, she works weekdays at her law firm. Even there, she is now so dependent upon others to be her hands. I know that has to bother her deeply. Maybe I should just go ahead and get hers regrown and not wait on Michelle," Simone threw out the key idea that he was considering.

"A day or two won't matter much," Wilma suggested, "but a month might. I'll talk to her tonight and see how she really feels about it. Women are more likely to confide in other women, you see." Simone grinned and thanked her profusely.

Monane commented, "Well, Simone, I must compliment you on your teaching of Michelle. There is a marked improvement in her manner of speaking and her vocabulary and understanding since we were last here. Remarkable change."

Simone smiled, "I spend twelve hours a day with her education. I'm glad that she is making such good progress. I only hope and pray that there is some way that she can learn to use magic. It is her birthright." Monane didn't know about birthrights. She did not consider that magical skill was an inherited thing.

Just then, Ashley and Michelle returned to the dining room. "Mission accomplished, big brother!" Michelle proudly announced. “Can I show them around the estate?”

“Oh forgive me,” Simone gushed. “As you may recall, we have three separate buildings on this estate. Now that dad has gone, I have been slowly cleaning up his building. There are plenty of bedrooms in there for all of you. We should show you to your rooms right away, and let you get settled in, unpacked, and all that.”

“I can take them, Simone,” Michelle insisted.

“Okay sis, but remember, that building has no automatic doors in it. You are going to have to rely on them to open the doors for you,” he hinted to his sister, who grinned.

“Of course, silly. I haven’t found a way to turn doorknobs yet,” Michelle wiggled her arms around. Ashley understood. Without the use of her feet and toes, for Michelle, many things were vastly more difficult to accomplish than they had been for her.

“I’ve been going through piles of dad’s old papers and stuff, tossing most of it out. I have a huge pile of it in my study in that room over there. If you need anything, just Message me,” Simone suggested, though he kept a close eye on Michelle, as she slowly led the five-some out of the front door. Only when she disappeared from view did he reluctantly go into his study.

“Aren’t these flowering bushes just perfect here? They smell so nice,” Michelle commented as she led them along the cobblestone walkway. Indeed, much of the estate grounds was devoted to formal gardens. This was definitely the estate of a wealthy family. Proudly, Michelle led them on a tour of the entire estate, quite a long walk in ballet boots, Ashley thought. Michelle gave no sign of any discomfort, however. At last, she stopped, and allowed Ashley to open the main door into what had been the private domain of Ross Mac Fluide or Folquet after he had adopted his deceased wife's maiden name.

Pam half expected the place to smell awful, since Ross had died in here, but Simone had been very thorough with his Clean and Fresh spells. Her nose could catch no scent of anything except the many flowers growing outside. "These are the bedrooms," Michelle pointed out. "There are three of them, but if you want more, big brother can quickly get some more beds ready. This stairs leads to the upstairs, but mostly the rooms are still filled with dad's old junk. I have a harder time with stairs, so I have only been up there a few times. It really is a mess. I wish that I could help him clean it all up; Simone works so hard you know." While the group picked their rooms, un-shrunk their clothing, and unpacked, Michelle chatted away.

By the time that they went back to the main house, dinnertime was approaching, and Isabella arrived home. As before, she entered wearing her professional black suit, white silk blouse, and matching skirt. She wore nylons and black heels that Ashley guessed were probably four inches high—a perfect looking young attorney, who, except for her missing lower arms, would fit in perfectly. "Welcome to our home. I'm so glad you come," Isabella greeted them in her broken English. "I've been practicing my English. Hope I sound better."

"You were good the last time we were here," Wilma complimented her. "Michelle has given us the grand tour, and we are settled into our rooms."

"Good, good. Michelle does really well," Isabella complimented her sister-in-law, "far better than I do. That is just incredible, amazing."

"Well, she's had many more years of practice than you have," Wilma pointed out, making sure that Isabella knew that she would not be held to the same standards as Michelle. Isabella nodded to Wilma, acknowledging Wilma's intent.

A bell sounded, signaling that dinner was about to be served. The group headed for the table as a waiter entered carrying a large silver tray. As before, Simone sat between the two and assisted each with their meal. Michelle whispered to Ashley, "I still can't figure out any way to feed myself, but I can hold a glass and drink, if it is tall enough, just not cups. For those, I think I would need to use my feet, which I can't." Ashley understood perfectly.

With a wonderful dinner finished, Simone suggested that Michelle work on some of her homework while he chatted with the guests. She sighed, but agreed and left for her study room. Simone chatted a bit more about the marvelous progress that his sister was making and that he had discovered just how independent she actually was. Then, he excused himself to continue sorting out his father's papers, asking Jim to lend him a hand. Jim realized at once, that he was attempting to leave the women alone, so that they could talk privately with Isabella.

"I've made Simone hold off on his promise to me," Isabella opened up to the women, as soon as they were alone. "He'd always promised me that the very day that his dad died and the contract thus ended, he'd get my arms regrown. However, there is Michelle to consider. She's scared about it, though I don't know why. I've told him that I can wait a while longer, but gosh, life like this is so hard."

"We understand," Ashley spoke up before the others could. "It is so embarrassing to have to have Simone feed you and dress you, isn't it?"

She flushed, "Very much so. Humiliating, I found it so humiliating at first, but I have made adjustments, yet it is still so very hard for me. I worry about Michelle. Simone and I talked about possibly my going ahead and getting it done, and let Michelle do it when she is ready. I rather vetoed that notion. After all, she is scared, and what better way to alloy those fears than for her and I to have it done at the same time?"

"Yes, doing it together would likely be the best way," Wilma agreed with her.

"I'm glad you see it that way too," Isabella replied, relieved that she had found more support for her opinion. "Simone did surprise me, though. Apparently, he has fully researched this and found the very best médecin, how you say, doctor, in all Marseille. Ross was dead less than an hour before Doctor Rochelle arrived here to examine Michelle and me and make his recommendations."

Pam thought to herself. So Simone did intend to really

follow through on his pledge. Maybe he isn't the monster that his clone is! Wonder why?

"What were the results, Isabella, if you don't mind my asking?" Wilma asked.

"He said that in my case, the process would take about a week, and that in a month's time, why, I'd never know I had lost them," she replied. "However, it is how you say problem-filled, no, problematical with Michelle. He said that her arms were not the problem; they could be as easily regrown as mine, a week or so. No, it is the rest of her body that is causing problem. Her back muscles are very weak cause of wearing corset so long. She may still need to wear corset, but there is some chance her back muscles will regenerate too, but he is not hopeful of that."

"No, it is her feet that are the real problem. They are now different than mine. She cannot put her feet flat onto the floor. They remain, how you say, up, no vertical, not bend flat." She tried to indicate this with her missing hands, but flushed as she realized she had no hands anymore.

Wilma came to her rescue rapidly. "Ah, you mean the bottoms of our feet are flat on the floor, and Michelle's toes meet the floor, and she cannot bend them to get the bottoms of her feet flat on the floor."

"Yes, yes, oui, parfait. The médecin does not think that this can be corrected. Simone asks if we removes her feet and then regrow them, if that will work. Alas, no, he believes that Michelle's feet will come back just as they now are. Something about having been this way for so long, that this is the way the body thinks it is supposed to be. I do not understand dis magic things, though."

Ashley thought to herself. Wow, so there are limitations to magical healing after all. I wonder what Doctor Caterwall would say?

Pam, however, took action, sending Doctor Caterwall a long explanation of the situation and asked for his medical opinion. "You do magics?" Isabella asked, as Pam's wand activated.

"Yes, I'm asking for a second opinion about Michelle's waist and feet, Isabella. I'm asking our school's doctor. I'll let you know what he says."

"Oui, merci, merci!" she replied, relief in her face. She then went on, "Michelle, she is afraid. I try to get her to tell me, but she no tell me fears. I not sure of fears, but she is afraid. Maybe you can find out?" she asked Ashley.

"That is one of the reasons that I came at once. I've been in her shoes. I know what I went through, and it may be similar to what Michelle fears. I'll talk to her."

Just then, Pam received a lengthy Message from Doctor Caterwall. She sighed. "Well, he said that to be absolutely certain, he would need to give her a comprehensive medical exam and all that. However, he says that due to the twenty-one years that she has been this way, it is highly unlikely that anything short of a magical Wish spell could fix up her feet, probably the same with her waist, though he said that in time her waist would again slowly fill out. Not very good news, I'm afraid."

Isabella's face fell, though she had expected to hear it. "What is dis Wish spell thing?" she inquired. Pam then gave her a lengthy description and how incredibly expensive they were, if one could even find someone willing to cast it.

"Well, I think I'm going to go have a chat with Michelle," Ashley announced. Isabella looked very relieved, and Wilma poured them all another round of coffee. She had been assisting Isabella drink her after-dinner cup.

Ashley found Michelle in her study room. Books lay everywhere, stacked neatly in piles. The woman was studying an American History text when Ashley entered. "See, I'm reading about the Revolutionary War now," Michelle explained. "Simone says that I now know as much as a first year student knows, excepting of course for the magic."

"You are doing remarkably well, Michelle; keep up the good work."

"Oui, Simone says that I will be able to get my GED saying that I have made it through high school."

"Cool! Say, can we talk about getting your arms regrown now? The others are off chatting or sorting out your father's old papers and stuff. We are alone now."

"Oui, I bit scared, Ashley. Were you scared too?" Michelle readily accepted this chance to speak with her idol.

"Plenty scared, plenty worried, Michelle." For some minutes, Ashley confided in Michelle many of her worries, fears, and concerns that she had when she was facing getting her arms back.

"Like you, I spent all my life without them, learned to

do everything with my feet, my way. Now, all that was about to change. I didn't know if I could even use my arms to do anything once I got them."

"Exactement! What if I get arms and hands and then cannot do anything with them because I forgot how? That was twenty-one years ago! Perhaps they won't work. I'd look stupid with arms and hands that just dangle there! What if they don't work? I mean I am fine now. I've been like this so long that, like you, I've figured out other ways to do things, had to, because I couldn't see anything for so very long. So I'm fine now, really."

"I'll level with you, totally honest, Michelle. You will have to relearn how to do many things. I was a hot pool player when I had no arms. Once I got arms and use them to shoot pool, I'm terrible at it. When I need to beat someone, I still have to resort to using my feet only. However, Michelle, and this is a really big and important however too. So many other things in life are now so easy to do that it totally makes up for the few things I still haven't learned how to do properly yet."

She thought about this a bit. "So many things are now very easy for you?"

"Very much so. I expect it will be the same with you. You probably will have to spend hours learning how to write again, for example. Yet, think how great it will be to be able to feed yourself at meal times?" Michelle grinned; that struck a chord within her.

Ashley figured she'd won that battle and moved on to the rest of the situation. "Isabella has told us that the doctor isn't so sure about the rest of your healing, that you may still need to wear these tight corsets, that your feet will not heal right, and you will still have to wear these kinds of shoes or boots."

Ashley expected the worst and was very surprise with Michelle's response. "Oh, I'm not worried about those at all. Don't tell Simone, but I've been surfing the Internet when he isn't looking. Women sometimes like small waists. I read that and saw pictures, so I don't mind that. Besides, without it, I can't sit up properly. I think the doctor said I am too weak. I can walk just fine, but not run, and I don't want to run anyway. I'm just slower than Isabella and Simone. Is there some reason I must learn to walk faster?" she asked.

"None that I can think of," Ashley replied.

"Good. I'm slow, but that's all. I don't mind my feet anymore. Don't get me wrong. At first, it was horribly painful, but that passed years and years ago. I couldn't crawl, so I had to walk, but I couldn't see anything. I learned to count my steps to find things. Really, Ashley, I don't mind my boots at all anymore, unless someone thinks I need to go fast or to run."

"That's really encouraging, Michelle. Just as soon as you get your arms regrown, you will be able to feed yourself, bathe yourself, put on your own clothes, and even brush your own hair. While I could do these with my feet, it was hard, and everyone always looked at me like I was some freak or something."

"Well I don't look at you that way, Ashley!" Michelle

replied, slightly aghast that anyone would think less of her idol, Ashley. "You think I will be able to do all those things?"

"Sure, those are simpler things. Now writing, well you might have to relearn how to make your letters again. I certainly did, but then I always wrote with my feet before."

"Will you be with me while I get them regrown?" she asked timidly.

"You bet I will! Pam and I will be right there with you and Isabella all the way. Of course, you may want us around here when you come back to your house too. It's our summer vacation, so I can stay as long as you and Isabella need me."

Michelle threw her arms around Ashley, "Oh thank you! Thank you!"

"Come on; we ought to let the others know that you are ready to get it done," Ashley said encouragingly. The older woman smiled, and led Ashley back into the dining room. "Everyone, Michelle has something to tell us."

She walked slowly closer to the table and then said meekly, "I'm ready to get it done. Ashley is going to be with me the whole time; Pam too, and with you too, Isabella."

"Oh that is wonderful, Michelle. I'll go tell your brother," Isabella replied. Wilma noted the tremendous relief on the woman's face. A minute later, Simone came rushing into the room. Michelle had just sat down.

"Are you sure?" he asked. "I don't want you to rush into this, sis," he asked, hoping that she really was ready, but Pam saw that he did want to make very sure that his sister was ready to accept the regrowth of her arms. She replied that she was and that Ashley and Pam were going to be with her throughout the whole process.

"Terrific, sis. I will let the doctor know and see how soon he can schedule it." Simone rushed off to send a message to the physician. Meantime, Isabella chatted gaily with Michelle, outlining all the many things that the two of them would soon be able to do for themselves.

About a half hour later, Simone returned with the news. Because of the intensive care that the two women would need for at least a week and because of the money that Simone had at hand, the doctor would perform the operation here in his home. However, a nurse would also be staying with them as well. He would check on their progress each day, suiting everyone perfectly.

When they were in their own building getting ready for bed that evening, Wilma pointed out to her group that this would keep their presence here even more of a secret. Having the five of them constantly around some hospital rooms for a week would certainly raise many questions, especially since they were Americans.

At nine, the doctor and his nurse, Arianne, arrived. Of course, both spoke only French, so the five cast their Language spells so that they could follow along. However, the process was nearly identical to that used by Doctor Caterwall back at Bradbury's. Both were given the regrow potion and confined to their beds. Both of their arms were fastened down so that they couldn't move them for the first two days. "Drink lots of this specially fortified milk," the doctor explained, but both were shocked by the amount that they were supposed to be consuming. Ashley grinned, for she'd been through this before.

Once everything medically was setup and operational, the doctor left, promising to return to check on them later. "Don't worry, Michelle, the first two days are the roughest cause you are not supposed to move the new arms and hands. Probably after that, you will be allowed up and about. Until then, Pam and I will be your constant companions. Wilma and Monane will be with Isabella, so we are all set. In a week, you will be better than ever," Ashley sounded a hopeful note. Both women now wore only a thin nightgown. This also meant that Michelle was not wearing her tight corset or shoes. The doctor wanted to give the potions a chance at remedying those areas, though he still told Simone that the odds of anything beneficial occurring with her waist or feet were slim. We'll wait and see was his attitude.

To help the women pass the time, Ashley and Pam read some of her textbooks to them. They found that Michelle was a very quick learner. Her mind was sharp, perhaps making up for her physical difficulties. At the end of the first day, both women could see the ghostly outlines of new lower arms and hands reforming. By the end of the second day, they were becoming rather solid, and the doctor released their arms so that they could move in bed a little.

"Oh, they itch something fierce!" Michelle commented on the third day. The nurse made sure that neither woman attempted to itch their arms and hands. By the fourth day, the intense itching subsided, and the two women found that they could now move their hands and fingers, though they were under strict orders not to use them for anything yet. On the fifth day, the doctor allowed them to start using their hands to feed themselves, though not to lift their milk glasses, which were still too heavy for the regenerating arms.

During this time, Jim kept himself busy helping Simone sort out and discard tons of his father's junk, old suits, shoes, and other brick-a-brac.

When the eighth day came, their final checkup at the end of the process, Ashley was astounded at how much of American History Michelle had learned during the past week. She'd absorbed and could repeat back well over half of the entire thick text. The doctor examined both women and stated, "Perfect, just perfect. You are now back to normal in the hands department. However, I don't want you lifting anything too heavy for another week and do not lift anything over ten pounds for a month. After that, you can do what you wish." Both women were very pleased with his prognosis. At no time had Michelle felt any pain, which was her primary concern.

Next, he examined Michelle's spine and back muscles. While she had grown slightly stronger from the healing process, she still was still not going to be free from the corset. "I'm afraid that you will still probably find that you will want to wear your corset for back support, Michelle. Yes, we can see that it is stronger, but I will leave that up to you. Try dressing without it, but if you have any difficulties at all, please put it back on, dear."

Next, he carefully examined her feet. Unfortunately, he

still was unable to bend her ankles much at all. Her foot bones had more or less fused into their current position to support her constant walking on her toes. Simone sighed when he saw the doctor was unable to bend them, but he realized that there was only a slim chance this process would repair her feet. The doctor then Summoned his portable x-ray machine and took a set of after images. He and Simone then compared the results, but no visible changes could be seen. After those twenty-one years, her bones had fused and reformed to fit her boots. The doctor could do little else, though Simone vowed to dig further into other alternative medical solutions.

Isabella readapted to having lower arms and hands rather rapidly, commenting mostly on how weak her arms felt, compared to what she remembered from several years ago. However, she was able to take care of all her own personal needs easily, and her spirits soared. Simone's too. Ashley and Pam assisted Michelle in relearning how to do various personal chores, such as brushing out her hair, feeding herself, and dressing. However, Michelle needed assistance in getting into her corset, which she found almost at once that she still needed to wear.

A week later, Michelle was making full use of her arms and hands, requiring no assistance for anything but her corset. Her attitude toward life changed to one of bubbling enthusiasm. "Now I'm a whole person again! I can do everything for myself again!" Simone merely wiped his watering eyes all that day. To see his sister back to her old self was almost more than he could emotionally handle.

During this time, Pam fixed up Michelle's laptop so that she could easily email them via Bradbury's anytime that she wanted to chat. Of course, this really pleased Michelle—that she could email Ashley at will. Simone then said, "Honestly, I don't know how to thank you all for everything you have done to help up out these past two weeks."

"I know," Ashley piped up. "How about taking Michelle and us on a guided tour of Marseille, then let's take her to a movie, and then stop by a pizza hut! I'm craving a pizza."

"Please, Simone, please! I've never been out of our estate. I would love to see the rest of the city. I can walk fine. Honestly, I can. And I've not seen a real movie since you took me to see one when I was eleven. Please, please, can we go out now? I'm a whole person now, really I am." Michelle pleaded with her brother, who could not help but honor her request and Ashley's.

"Okay, but you must promise me that if your feet begin to hurt or you get too tired or exhausted, you will let me know at once. Let's not overdo it on your first time out. We have all the time in the world to go places and do things," Simone insisted. Isabella merely grinned in a motherly way.

"Oh thank you! I promise," she paused and then added somberly, "I hope that I won't slow everyone down too much. If I do, tell me, and I can come back here and let Simone show you around. I don't want to be a burden for you." Ashley so promised. Meanwhile, Simone and Isabella spent an hour working out the best sights to visit and a reasonable order. They would take their car, just in case Michelle couldn't handle so much walking at one time.

Ashley realized quickly that this was the first time that Michelle was out of her residence since she was twelve years old. Thus, the day held monumental significance for the young woman. Ashley also suggested that Michelle wear long pants instead of her usual party style dresses. She magically elongated the legs. "There, now your boots are mostly hidden from view Michelle. You won't constantly attract undo attention from those around us. It's a little trick that Lindsey and I learned when we were forced to wear boots similar to yours." Simone also took keen note of what Ashley had done. She now realized that he would follow her lead, suggesting that she wear clothing that did not at once reveal her unusual footwear, not until she wished it to be seen.

Walking through art galleries, through the zoo, and the many other places that they visited, Michelle quickly discovered that she did better when she was holding on to another for support. Hence, she quickly accepted Ashley and Pam's arms around her on either side. Later, the teens fell in love with the many public beaches. Ashley declared that one day she would return here and go swimming in the warm waters of the Mediterranean Sea. The only major trouble that Michelle ran into during the long afternoon was in the movie theater. There she had to negotiate steps and a very sloping ramp up to their seats. While going up was easy, going down was another story entirely. By suppertime, Michelle finally admitted that she was tiring, but she radiated intense happiness and joy.

The next day, the five said their farewells, but Ashley and Pam promised to return for a visit whenever they could. This, of course, pleased Michelle. "I promise that I'll study really hard. I want to get my high school GED as soon as possible. Then, Simone says I can try to learn to do real magic." Both Ashley and Pam were very careful to say nothing about this. Whether she could ever learn magic at her age was in question. They did not want to get her hopes up with this, not even remotely. The five arrived back home around the third week in July, spending nearly a day telling their friends about their adventures and learning what had been going on in their absence, which was not much.

"Mostly boring," Lindsey said dolefully. "Even Deiter has not been around as much as I would like." He still was not saying what he was actually doing this summer, a big secret. In private with Ashley, Lindsey asked many questions about how Michelle actually did wearing the ballet boots. She soon realized that if force to wear them constantly for many years, the body adapted by fusing foot bones to support them. That even the healing potions had no effect on Michelle made her even more thankful that Deiter had managed to find a way to get them out of their steel versions.

From their visit, Pam brought back one curious piece of information that Jim had discovered while helping Simone for so many days. Jim had asked him about his grandfather, Ross' father. Jim told Pam that he had learned that his name had been Argus and his wife had been in an automobile accident shortly after they were married and had lost her arms in the crash. Pam now had a new, albeit minor, project to research: Argus Mac Fluide and Anne.

Two days later, Pam had found many newspaper reports from a library in Aberdeen, where they had lived. She discovered that Argus was a wizard, but Anne was not. After careful scrutiny of the accident reports as reported in the newspaper, she dug a bit deeper. Using her special access code as an official member of the new Department of Magical Misuse, she obtained the actual police reports of that event. As expected, said reports were online. “I thought so!” she declared aloud.

The circumstances surrounding the accident were suspicious. The accident recreation report could not explain how Anne could have had the accident, which she had apparently had. However, no other explanation was put forward, since Argus was the Police Commissioner at the time. What Pam found most curious indeed was that Argus never had her arms regrown! This detestable aberration was being handed down through at least three generations of the Mac Fluide line! She couldn’t trace it back any further because those far older records were not online. She would have to visit Scotland and personally search archives if she wanted to know about the parents of Argus. Thus, her new Sleuthing project was short lived.

Chapter 6—Rodents Meet

On the last Friday of July, Governor Alister called a special meeting of the entire Rodents Pack, the many governors of the coalition of western states, and the heads of the States Justice departments. For security reasons, the meeting was again held in his large conference room at Bradbury's School of Magic. The place was packed with men, women, and the teens. Santa Claus, Lindsey observed, was noticeably absent.

"I apologize for the lack of refreshments. The kitchen staff is also on vacation," Governor Alister opened the meeting. To Pam, he seemed much older than she recalled. Perhaps the stress was taking a heavy toll on him. "I wanted us all to have a midsummer update on how things are going. You are all keenly aware of Bloody Monday and the Boston Pill Party. You have seen precisely how Dominus responds to direct confrontation."

Governor Al Waters of California called out, "You were right, Governor. He used the US Army to back his plans, just as you suggested last year. I admit that had you not spoken out, I would have done the same thing as the governor there did."

Alister took the compliment gracefully and the huge round of applause from the governors. He continued, "What you may not know is that we have been getting support from some unlikely places. The computer underworld of hackers did us a favor by totally wiping out the government's population database in those three states. This has caused them a six week delay in getting their databases back online." Again, these unknown hackers received a round of appreciative applause.

"Their pill production took us a bit by surprise. All spring, we attempted to thwart their plans for new production facilities within the States. However, Dominus cleverly brought a number of foreign drug companies online. Those are the ones responsible for the sufficient buildup of pills that allowed them to attempt to subdue the three states. While the unexpected Pill Party put a huge dent in their pill supplies, they were able to replace those losses rapidly. However, two factors have now shifted to our favor. First, due to the tireless efforts of Miss Betts, we now know just what foreign drug companies are producing the pills. Every effort is being made to have sympathizers in those countries deal with the problem. A certain individual and his comrades are assisting in that area and cannot attend this meeting." This was an obvious reference to Santa Claus, alias Erin Sacs. He too received a round of applause in absentia. Many eyes found Pam and nodded her way.

"Yet another unexpected individual has appeared upon the scene. We now know that they have imported a huge supply of the pills, far more than enough to bring the three states into the Health Care Program, which as you know began this past week. They are storing their massive supply in a heavily fortified bunker, well-guarded and protected. Yet, this unknown individual has been systematically stealing pills from their storage facilities and has accumulated several million of their pills, more than was dumped into Boston Harbor. Unfortunately, the individual was not sufficiently swift enough to steal enough to prevent them from bringing the three states into the hideous program. As yet, this individual remains anonymous." As he spoke, Alister's eyes met each of those of the teens sitting off to one side of the room. Lindsey wondered if this thief was one of them, but who? She had no idea who it could be. Alister caught a subtle flinch, as his eyes met those of Deiter. Alister now knew, though he probably suspected Deiter for some time. He did not reveal anything, however. He added, "I hope this thief in the night stays very alert for traps, for Dominus will surely now be laying traps in hopes of catching the thief." Deiter flinched once more, but only Alister detected it.

"In fact, this outright theft of over half of their current pill supply has likely seriously crippled their plans for further state expansion. We know that New Jersey and Delaware were scheduled to join the program on August 1. This date has been postponed indefinitely. I am hopeful that with continued vigilance, we will be able to continue to keep their production to a minimum, delaying the program for a long time, but not forever, I'm afraid."

"That is about all that I have to report. I know that Mrs. Mary Hampton, High Plains Department of Law and Justice wishes to say a few words before I turn it over to you," Alister wrapped up his brief summary.

"What about that attack on Bradbury's?" some governor

called out. “What’s the scoop on that? Were you really attacked? We’ve heard all sorts of impossible rumors about a Dispeller. Can you clarify? Is Sam Barron not really dead?” Lindsey’s face reddened. She squirmed in her chair. People still remembered her father, whom she’d give anything to see once more.

“Alas, I am afraid that the rumors are true. Bradbury’s School of Magic now has the dubious distinction of having been the first magic school in the world to have been attacked outright.” He explained that fifty Death Stalkers had blown a hole in the perimeter wall and came charging onto the campus, where by chance Professor Janice Smith was holding her spell casting class. Battle was joined, but soon, all the upper class students appeared to help defend the school. Alister knew that he could not keep Lindsey’s amazing skills and abilities secret any longer.

“Yes, we have a new budding Dispeller, the daughter of Sam Rabnor, Miss Lindsey Barron. She Dispelled many, many Disintegrate spells being cast by the invaders. Her actions saved the lives of the students and faculty that day. We were fortunate that no student was seriously hurt, though Professor Janice Smith took a brutal burning, but she has fully recovered. So yes, when Miss Barron has completed her studies, you may expect that she will take up the mantle dropped by her father. She may well become the world’s greatest Dispeller, but enough bragging about Miss Barron. We don’t want all this to go to her head,” he winked playfully at Lindsey, who grinned. Lindsey had no such notion, rather wishing she could once more become invisible. Like Pam, she hated being the center of attention.

"Now then, I believe that Mrs. Mary Hampton wishes to say a few words of encouragement." Alister motioned for her to rise and face the assemblage.

Dressed in her formal business suit and looking every bit the lawyer that she was, Mary began, "Thanks to the tireless efforts of Sleuth Miss Betts here, we now have a full and complete list of every holding, every company, and every subsidiary of Mac Fluide Enterprises. In keeping with the States Justice guidelines, I have prepared takeover plans. The instant that Simon Mac Fluide, alias Dominus Malefic, is apprehended, members of the Security Department will appear at each of these businesses, taking over total control of them, preventing any illegal transfer of funds and the like. Our men have their assignments now and will drop everything the instant the signal is given by me. Once we have confiscated all those assets, we will begin the tedious process of providing compensation for all the victims of Dominus, though that will be a very lengthy process. Said compensation will be based upon the new guidelines of the States Justice Department, with death ranking the highest, followed by mutilation and raping a close second. At this time, my staff are attempting to come up with a total net worth estimate, though that will of course be subject to revision once we take over those companies. So, fellow Rodents, it only remains for us to capture Dominus." She received a loud round of applause, for she provided real hope for the future, at least in terms of reconstruction and recompense.

"Now, I believe that Professor Delius Dogs wishes to explain another ally that has recently joined with our movement," Alister nodded to Delius.

With his hair more well-oiled than normal and wearing his best suit, Delius rose and faced the group. "I am very pleased to announce that we have gained the support of another very large overseas group who wishes to remain anonymous at this time. They have made some of their pharmaceutical research scientists and facilities available to analyze the pills that have been turning people into zombies. Specifically, they are working on finding a cure for those who have become victims of this diabolical plot. Their secondary charge is to see if there is any way to reconstitute these pills such that these horrific side effects are gone, yet the ability to heal and remove criminal tendencies remain. I have shared our preliminary findings about the chemical nature of these pills with their scientists, namely that they are laced with heroin to make them highly addictive. At this time, they are making some progress on the chemical analysis. When I get their initial report of their findings, I will email each of you a copy for your study. Again, I repeat, their top priority is to find a cure for those who are now addicted. Perhaps in time, we may reap further benefits along the health lines, but that is secondary right now. Thank you."

Slowly, clap by clap, the applause broke out. Soon several called out, asking the name of this mysterious benefactor. Delius refused to say any more. Lindsey smiled;

the real Simon was keeping his word.

"Next, Governor Al Waters wishes to address the group," Alister motioned for the outspoken governor to rise. Indeed, he was the spokesman for all the assembled governors.

"Governor Alister's plan to pretend to go along with this debacle has been fruitful up to this point in time. True, we have all seen the response of Dominus to outright resistance to his program. Bloody Monday will go down in infamy." To Lindsey, this sounded more like a political speech.

"However, and as a direct result of Bloody Monday, we governors are now facing an entirely new situation: rebellion amongst our own populations! As we all know, our average citizens are outraged over this Health Care Program and have been protesting wildly and savagely against the position we western governors have taken. Many of us have narrowly averted a recall election. So yes, it is that bad. We have virtually no support for our position among our citizens! True, a few trusted others know that our public position is the complete opposite of what our true stand is, but the average person fully believes the lies that we have been espousing."

"I'm afraid that Bloody Monday has irreparably changed all that. We are now facing a huge buildup of local militias. In LA alone, over fifty different para-military organizations have formed. Some are gangs thirsting for more control and action, while others are more legitimate. All are arming their members and threatening to head into the next open battle in whatever state comes next."

"Yes, in secret, many of us have been funding and supplying the more reputable militias with arms and munitions. However, at this point, our public position has been compromised!" This brought a stir among the other governors.

"Yes, it could not be helped in California. A band of one of the more powerful militias out of LA infiltrated the Governor's mansion complex, their leader demanding to meet with me. I had no choice but to meet with him. Yes, he was extremely angry about my public position on the Health Care Program and demanded that I see reason. I had no choice but to fill him in completely on the situation. I explained to him that while I openly show unfailing support for the program, behind the scenes I am doing everything I can to thwart it. I explained what would have happened if we had all rebelled, citing Bloody Monday as that result. He was mollified after I gave his militia access to significant weapons and ammunition. However, that was just the tip of the iceberg. I've had to repeat that message to several dozen other militia leaders since Bloody Monday. I am afraid our cover story is not likely to hold up much longer. Surely, Dominus now knows that armed militias are forming up in all the western states and that his original battle still looms on the horizon." He sat down. Several other governors had similar stories.

"Governor Arne Bellweather, Colorado. I need to bring up another issue before us. Several more state governors have been in contact with me asking if they might join our coalition. From what they have told me, they are aware of our two-faced approach, saying publically that we support the program, while behind the scenes doing what we can to stop it. To date, Michigan, Wisconsin, Minnesota, Missouri, Mississippi, Alabama, Arkansas, Indiana, and Ohio wish to join up. I told their governors what they must do to be considered, namely remove all Dominus ring wearers and supporters from their state governments, take over control of the state owned facilities that are rented by the federal agencies, and so on. I guess the ball is now in our court. Are we going to allow late joiners? If so, how will this be done?"

A lengthy discussion followed in which they decided upon a procedure to follow to allow more states to join their coalition. Then, Alister recognized Governor J. J. Jones of Arizona. She rose and spoke softly. "Seceding plans are coming along at a reasonable pace. Of prime concern will be the financial arena." She talked for over a half hour outlining the proposed actions to be taken when the states seceded from the US, forming their own country. The barriers were monumental; yet these desperate leaders were doing their best to formulate a plan to do just that, should all else fail. "Bottom line, governors, we need at least two more years of planning if we wish the process to avoid total and complete chaos across the entire financial arena." It was a grim assessment. Obviously stalling the slow moving Health Care Program was unlikely to provide them that much time, especially now that the proposed Health Care Program implementation in other states that were closer to New York had already published.

Amos Slaughter, the head of the new States Justice

Department, which oversaw all the new departments, spoke last. "While I know this is relatively minor, I would like to make a report on how our new Justice procedures are working. We have been enforcing Justice for crime victims now for just short of a year. The results are, in my humble opinion, stellar. First, just as Governor Alister suggested, the average man and woman in the street have whole heartedly accepted this reform, with open arms, I might add. Some say it's about time. We have now gotten our procedures in place at all prisons within our jurisdiction, save only the maximum-security ones. The few die hard criminals who flatly refuse to cooperate and begin making amends for their crimes have been transferred to these maximum security prisons."

"Presented simply: work and begin to make amends or starve. Our program is beginning to have an impact on society. While crime victims are now starting to see some compensation, I am very pleased to report that this is having a very noticeable impact on our overall crime rates. Yes, they are down twenty-five percent already in just these past few months. We have seen a steady month-by-month drop in the crime rates in all states participating in our program. The only area that seems unaffected thus far is drug addiction related crimes, wherein the perpetrators are hooked on illegal street drugs and in many cases are no longer rational beings. In the armed robbery, hold-ups, and rape categories, we are seeing a most pronounced drop in the overall rates. That the perpetrators will be forced to make amends, to compensate their victims until the victims are satisfied with the amends, is definitely causing would be perpetrators to withhold committing such crimes. At this time, there is a clear pattern of cause and effect of our Justice program developing."

"Our next step is to tackle the hardened criminals in the maximum security prisons. This will be a tougher nut to crack, so to speak. With all the planning going into seceding from the Union, I would like to propose another avenue of exploration. Why not do a thorough review of all laws on the book? Let's eliminate the greater percentage of these and spell out in simple language that the average person can understand what the laws of our land will be. I totally agree with Mrs. Hampton, namely that lawyers spend weeks trying to figure out one simple legal question. Let's revise the hundreds of years of congressionally passed laws and get this down to a manageable, key set, written in an understandable fashion. I believe our citizens will back us all the way on this one."

After a short discussion in which Amos was praised for his contributions, everyone agreed that the Justice Department should begin this overwhelming task. Amos and Mary looked very pleased with this go-ahead order, Lindsey noted.

Governor Al Waters rose again, "Excuse me, before we adjourn, there is one matter which I would like clarified. It has to do with the deployment of our clandestinely supported militias. If one of our member states is invaded, I would like everyone's agreement that all states will send in or give the go ahead to their many militias. Yes, I know this is likely leading to another Civil War, but I don't think I can possibly withhold the militias in California. However, if a non-member state is invaded, such as we've seen with Bloody Monday, let us do all that we can to prevent our militias from intervening."

J. J. immediately pointed out that they were obligated to do just that, send in their militias if one of their member states was invaded. "However, the moment we do, we had better be prepared to secede, because it will be as Al says, the start of a huge Civil War." Although some discussion followed, they all agreed to Al's proposal; they could not do otherwise. A set of grim faces finally left the room, heading back to their states. The teens stuck around, however.

"Sir, do you really think it will come down to that, a new Civil War?" Lindsey asked Governor Alister.

"Dear child, I certainly hope not. The carnage and losses would be staggering. However, I will say this, the wizarding world and the normals are fully aligned together on this one, something perhaps Dominus has overlooked. Only shady wizards and witches are backing him. I find that to be encouraging. Don't you?" Lindsey smiled, but was still very worried. She didn't see how a horrible Civil War could be avoided, not unless somehow Dominus could be captured.

Chapter 7—Summer Doldrums

August arrived hot and dry on the High Plains. During the week, the teens helped around the ranch, doing various chores and helped with the farming as well. There was little else for them actually to do this summer. Pam had no Sleuthing projects and was incredibly bored. Because of the ever-present threat of Dominus, the girls couldn't travel anywhere, not unless they could get the many adults to accompany them. None felt much like inconveniencing them just to go shopping in Denver. Besides, they made the adults accompany them Friday, Saturday, and Sunday nights to the B & B Dance Hall. Indeed the dances became the only bright spot in their weekly routine.

"I'm bored," Lindsey sighed.

"Me too," Ashley added, equally listless.

"Same here," Pam stated flatly.

"Perhaps you should take up carving, like Fern and me. Maybe you three need a hobby," Audrey replied. "Fern should be here directly. Please tell her to come to the workshop when she gets here." Audrey left the three teens, who were watching little Jonathon this afternoon.

"Well Amanda isn't bored," Ashley began to strike up a conversation.

"Yes, she's working really hard to get her musical skills up to speed. She's really excited about joining Eli's Rockers,"

Lindsey replied. “I do hope she makes it. She seems to have her heart set on a career in music and entertainment.”

Just then, Fern arrived on the Teleport Pad in their front room, carrying all her carving tools and wood. “Hi all!” she said cheerily.

“Hi Fern. Audrey is in the workshop,” Lindsey replied, still bored. Fern headed off to join Audrey.

“What do you want to do?” Lindsey asked.

“Dunno,” Ashley replied. “Maybe I will go shoot some pool. I wonder where Jim is at? Maybe he and I can do something after a while.”

“I can’t wait to get back to school,” Pam volunteered.

“You and me both!” Lindsey felt a sudden surge of excitement. “I kind of feel like we are locked up here with nothing to do but chores.”

“You know this is our sixth year,” Ashley commented. “That’s when we are supposed to get the chance to learn how to cast spells sans wands, sans words, if we can. I know that I can cast quite a few that way already. Why don’t we all go outside and work together on doing spells this way? After all, technically we are sixth years now, and school starts in just a couple weeks. I know that we will be lacking whatever instructions the professors will be giving us on how best to cast this way, but still, Lindsey is an expert at it already. What have we to lose by trying?”

“Good idea!” Lindsey exclaimed, enthusiasm suddenly flowing again.

“I don’t know, perhaps we are missing some key data

that will make it easier to do," Pam hesitated. "Well, what the heck! We haven't anything else to do. Jonathon, how about going outside with us a while, eh, little fellow?" He was all for that!

Lindsey assumed the role of teacher for the moment at least. "I think that perhaps casting sans wand, sans words has more to do with your personal conviction that it will work that way, Pam, Ashley. Let's give that a try. Ashley, you review and practice the spells you can already do this way, and I will work with Pam to see if she can get some cast without her wand and maybe silently."

Sitting on their long porch with Jonathon playing with his toy pile, the teens began casting their simple spells. Lindsey coached Pam on her useful spells of Grade 0 first. After all, those were the very first spells that Lindsey learned to cast in her special way. That they were also very easy helped.

Pam tried and tried to cast a Clean spell to remove a bit of dirt from the porch. The more she tried, the more frustrated she became. "I just can't get it to work!" she exclaimed. Lindsey did her best to coach her, but slowly became more and more frustrated with Pam. Then, Lindsey realized that something just must be interfering with Pam's conviction. Pam was very familiar with the Beyond, so her conviction was enormously stronger than the average student's was. Already everyone had seen how Deiter had easily Disarmed the entire class, so strong was his personal conviction. Pam ought to be similar to Deiter, having been there nearly as often as Deiter, as far as she knew anyway. Yet it was not working.

"Pam, are you really and truly convinced that the spell will work this way," Lindsey said accusingly.

"Heck no. I *know* the rules. I know how we are supposed to cast the spells. This is violating those rules, you know," Pam said huffily, certain that she was precisely correct in her statement. "Rules are the rules and can't be broken," she uttered. Suddenly, a silly expression came over her face. "Now that is a stupid thing to say!"

"Well it does sound like something that you would say," Ashley offered, having just finished casting all the Grade 0 spells that she knew she could cast silently and without her wand.

Pam flushed, "That obvious?" Ashley nodded. Pam looked sheepishly at the ground, before saying, "Well, I've always tried to follow the rules, you know, and not get into trouble or fail or make a mess of things."

"We know," Lindsey giggled and Pam managed a smile. Lindsey suggested, "Say, why don't you just relax and let go of that consideration. Let go of the rules. After all, there is no one around but us, and we won't say a thing about you. Give it a shot, relax and let go of all that."

Pam sighed. Did they know just how hard this was for her to do? She doubted it. Ashley was highly independent and did what she wanted to do, though far more when she was armless than now, she observed. And Lindsey, well she broke the rules by even entering Bradbury's without hands back in their first year. No, it is very hard to let go, she thought to herself. Nevertheless, she tried to relax and slowly her mind became blank. At last, she thought Clean! Before her eyes, the pile of dirt vanished, as a bit of magical energies flashed over the dirt.

"Holy cow! I did it! I actually cast Clean without my wand and without saying the words!" Pam exclaimed, shocked by the spell's activation. Lindsey and Ashley both cheered her and encouraged her further. "Wow, it did work. Incredible! I wonder if I can ever do it again?"

Pam put a little more dirt on the porch and tried it again, and then again, and then again. Only after she vanished a dozen piles of dirt, one after the other, was she herself convinced that she could actually cast this one spell sans wand, sans words. Finally certain that she did it, Pam began working diligently with all the other Grade 0 spells. Lindsey felt herself Chilled, grinned, and asked for another chill from Pam. It felt refreshing in the heat of the day.

By suppertime, Pam was elated; she was able to cast a dozen of her simple, useful spells. "We must keep on doing this every day!" she declared. The teens chatted about how long it might take to learn to cast all their spells this way. However, Lindsey pointed out that even she could not cast all the spells that they knew this way, just a large percentage.

"Perhaps no one person can cast them all this way," Lindsey suggested. That did not stop them from trying. Each day, once their many chores were finished, the trio went to the front porch and continued to practice their spell casting. "If nothing else, we have a leg up on spell casting when we get back to school." Pam wholeheartedly agreed.

By the time that they headed back to school, Lindsey had added another five spells to her lengthy list of spells she could cast in this manner. Ashley added another twenty, while Pam was ecstatic at her progress. Pam was able to cast all Grade 0 spells this way and nearly all of her Grade 1 and 2 spells. As they sat around on the porch after their last session before leaving for magic school, Lindsey realized something. "Hey, gang, for we three, magic is everything in our lives. Yet this is not so for everyone else. Audrey is into carving and growing things, Fern too. Amanda is into making music. Tom is into computer programming. We all have different interests, but we three are really into magic itself. Isn't that interesting?"

Pam said, "Well, what else is there that is really important, other than our fellows," she added, her face crimsoning.

"Dancing," Lindsey teased.

"Dressing up," Ashley teased back. Then, she added seriously, "Honestly, I'd be lost without magic. It's everything to me."

"Same here," echoed Pam and Lindsey a fraction of a second apart.

"Say I wonder if that also plays a part in one's ability to cast the way we are casting?" Pam mused, thinking this through, drawing as many parallels to others as she could. "I'm going to see if I can tabulate the results of this when our class begins to learn to do it this way at school. I can make a column that is my estimate of just how dedicated the person is to magic and then another column to reflect how successful they are at casting this way. I'll let you both know the results." Pam had another research project started. She built a database and entered all the names of the students who she remembered were in their class. She decided to rank them on a scale of one to ten, putting herself, Lindsey, and Ashley down as ten's in the dedication column. She was a bit frustrated, because this was all that she could do at this time and barely ten minutes had passed.

Each Monday morning when Lindsey rose, she began yearning for Friday night and the next formal dance at B & B's Dance Hall. True, the teens often took a refreshing dip in the Whitewater's pond, and they all had nice tans going, but they found it all boring, excepting their daily spell casting attempts. As the end of August drew nearer, Lindsey found herself marking off the days until her departure on her bedroom calendar.

The last Saturday night live rock band dance came. Eli's Rockers were presenting their last concert before the band members headed off to their respective magic schools, Ahana and Amanda to Bradbury's, and the other three, to Toronto School of Magic. Tonight would be Amanda's debut with the band, and she was both excited and very nervous. True, she had practiced every day, sometimes for hours at a time. Still, stage fright loomed heavily upon her. "I hope I don't screw it all up tonight!" she wailed to Lindsey, who was helping her get her things together.

Silently, Lindsey cast Calm on Amanda, who suddenly felt more relaxed. Then, she realized that Lindsey had cast a spell on her and said, “Thanks. I needed that. I guess I am as ready as I ever will be. Wish me luck. See you all there.” Amanda and Lindsey hugged each other tightly, and then Amanda headed off to join Ahana and his fellow band members. They had to arrive at least an hour before the doors opened. Setting up their equipment took some time, even with plenty of magical assists. Lindsey watched the five Teleport off to Denver and then rejoined her friends at her house—time for her to get ready.

While the young women spent hours getting ready for the Formal Dances, only minutes were really needed for the rock dances. Jeans and tennis shoes were the norm, and their only major decision was what top to wear. Finally all set, they waited patiently for their boyfriends to arrive. One by one, the young men’s arrivals were announced by the monotone voice of R. B.’s alert spell. At last, the voice announced, “Deiter Cross is arriving.” Lindsey rushed to the door.

“Oh my god, what happened to you?” she asked as Deiter entered the large living room. His hair was singed and now very short. A faint odor of a fire still lingered about him. Even his eyebrows showed damage.

He squirmed a bit before answering, “Er, I got a bit careless with a spell and had a Ball of Fire go off in my face. No real damage, nothing broken or badly burned. Only don’t put your hands around my neck tonight, because it’s kind of sore there.” Naturally, Lindsey just had to peek under his tee shirt.

It was still fiery red, as if he had gotten a very bad sunburn.

"I guess I'll have to tell my story over and over tonight," he said sheepishly.

At first, Lindsey thought about saying, "Of course, you ought to be more careful." However, she began to suspect Deiter was not being entirely accurate in his statements. True, he certainly was not outright telling her a falsehood, just probably not all the truth behind it.

Ashley and Jim walked into the room, ready to head off to the dance. Without thinking much about it, Ashley commented to Deiter, "Forgot to check for traps, did we?" She gave him a friendly smile. Lindsey watched Deiter's face turn a slightly stronger shade of red and knew that Ashley had spoken more of the truth. It was hard to put something over on Ashley, a Class 4 Diviner.

As Deiter and Lindsey prepared to Teleport, she whispered, "So when are you going to tell me all about it?"

He squirmed a bit, but whispered, "Later, after the dance. Okay?" Lindsey smiled and agreed, making a mental note to make sure that he did.

The usual smoke cloud appeared on the stage, and Eli's Rockers slipped into their positions. Amanda stood behind her hammered dulcimer; a flute was in her hands and a microphone in front of her. Ahana counted out the beat, and they began to play an Antique Rock song by Jethro Tull, Amanda was playing the flute part. The crowd yelled and danced wildly, though many nearer the band stood and listened, enthralled.

When they finished, Ahana spoke, "Welcome one and all. Tonight, as you can see, we've added a new band member, and now we have an expanded set of songs. Please give a hand to our new flutist, dulcimer player, and singer, Amanda." The appreciative roar and clapping was deafening. When it died down, he continued. "One of the Antique Rock groups who pioneered the voice as an instrument was Dead Can Dance. With the addition of Amanda, we are privileged to be able to reproduce some of their vast body of works. I'm pleased to announce that this next song goes out to P and N and J. Enjoy!" The amplified sound of the rapid repeated notes of Amanda's dulcimer echoed in the vast hall, and then her voice, sounding more like an instrument came in, followed by the rest of the band.

Pam, Jolina, and Nadia squealed as they recognized this famous old tune, and the three yelled and cheered as loudly as they could, such was their enthusiasm at hearing one of their old favorites. These three women dearly loved Antique Rock. The hours passed by rapidly. After the concert was over, the band signed autographs as usual. Lindsey saw that many more fans were asking for Amanda's than the fellows, and she grinned.

After the last fan left, Amanda slumped exhausted into a chair. "What a rush!" she exclaimed. "That was incredible, fantastic, no real words to describe it, but what a rush!" Ahana sat beside her. He knew precisely what she meant. One had to perform before an enthusiastic crowd to know just what they both felt or so he tried to explain.

"Well, you have been totally accepted by the fans, so looks like you have your spot," Ahana teased her.

"After we graduate, in July, he's booked our first major tour of the US," Amanda explained.

He added, "Yes, booked in thirty cities. If all goes as planned, we ought to gross at least fifty thousand each, maybe more."

"Wow! I had no idea! Perhaps, we should let you support us, eh," R. B. teased his daughter. Both he and Luci had come tonight to hear their eldest daughter perform. "Amanda, you were amazing tonight. Well done." She beamed, thankful that her father approved of her venture into the music industry. Luci gave her a warm hug.

"Er, sorry mom. I'm completely soaked. Occupational hazard," Amanda apologized. Everyone roared; all five were soaking wet from their musical exertions under the hot lights. Just then, Barnaby came by with their payment for their performance. Amanda could not help but flash her pile of bills in front of her parents.

"Look, almost a grand for one night's work!" Amanda was truly happy. Even R. B. looked pleased. That was a lot of money, from his point of view, just for singing and playing music. He was impressed with his daughter even more so than before.

A while later, the teens and their dates returned to their ranch. The couples silently split off into different rooms for a brief private moment. Lindsey and Deiter found themselves in her living room. "Okay, now spill the beans, Mr. Cross. How did you get burned?" Lindsey asked insinuatingly, though a bit playfully.

He grinned sheepishly. "Well, you remember Alister saying that someone has been stealing the pills right out of their main warehouse? Well, that's me. I've been going to the Beyond at night, becoming Invisible and all that, then sticking my head and arms down into their warehouse, pulling boxes of the pills up and into the Beyond. Lindsey, I've got nearly one million of those pills stacked in the Beyond now."

"Wow! Clever, Deiter. But isn't this terribly dangerous? What if Dominus get wise to you and lays some traps and all that?" she asked, worry in her voice.

"I got careless last night. I forgot to check for traps and set off a big Ball of Fire. Duh, I forgot to cast proper protection spells on myself and just barely got back into the Beyond. Only got a little singed is all. Nothing major. Honestly, love, I'm making a dent in their supplies of pills. We all got to do our part, you know," he attempted to justify his actions. "Say it is late, and I have to go, curfew and all that. See you tomorrow night as usual?" Lindsey gave him a loving kiss and he departed. She laid in bed worrying about his safety until sleep finally took her.

Lindsey awoke and scratched another 'X' on her calendar. With renewed enthusiasm, she got dressed. Tomorrow the bus would take her back to Bradbury's and school again. Tomorrow couldn't come too soon for her and the other teens. This had been the most boring summer yet, due mainly to the fact that they were house bound because of the serious threat of Dominus—house bound except for the weekly dances. Had those been denied her, Lindsey would have found the summer unbearable. She was up early and breakfasted with her mother and then set to work on her chores just as the others rose. "Last day," she reminded everyone, though none needed her notification, as they, too, had been counting the days until they could return to school.

Both Lindsey and Ashley spent most of the day doing every chore that they could think of doing to help their mother. This included all the things that they had been putting off until later, such as cleaning the toilet, and mopping the floors. "My, you are industrious today," Polly commented, as she began cooking everyone's lunch. Even Pam got into the cleaning act.

Jonathon wanted to help as well. Hence, Lindsey was kept continually busy trying to find or invent little chores that he could manage. He particularly enjoyed scrubbing the floors, since he could play with the soap and water and make a big mess. In the late afternoon when none of the teens could think of anything else that should be done or that they had been putting off, they finally dove into the chore of packing everything that they would need to take with them to Bradbury's.

At supper, everyone chatted furiously, as if they had forgotten to tell everyone this and that. "I do hope you girls don't get attacked by Dominus this year," Lena said quite seriously. "I'm getting sick and tired of hearing my girls are hacked up again. I worry about you every day."

"I know mom, we do too, but we are stronger now, and I think that Ashley and I can totally resist and repel any more of his fancy Restricted Wish spells. So we should be pretty safe this year," Lindsey explained, hoping to lessen her mother's worry.

"I certainly hope so," Lena replied. "Say, Jonathon is really going to miss you. How about sending him some postcards or something often? I know that you will be really busy with your studies, but he will really enjoy getting a card every so often."

Turning to her little brother, Lindsey said, "Jonathon, I promise I'll send you a card at least once each week. How's that?" He clapped his hands and hugged her, getting applesauce from his mouth onto her blouse.

"Me too, little buddy," Ashley seconded the idea, but was careful to avoid the applesauce mess.

Shortly after supper, the passenger lists for the floor monitors arrived. Pam, Lindsey, and Fern compared lists. Pam stated, "Look, the bus will be completely full this trip! We must be adding even more students than last year."

"Probably some come from those three states," Fern suggested. "We will be really busy this time."

Chapter 8—Back to School at Long Last

The next morning at ten, the large group sat on the porch, waiting for the yellow bus. "Oh I get it. All of us are going back early this year," Lindsey realized. "Normally, it is just we monitors and the first years who go back early."

"Must have made a big change this year," Pam concluded.

"Nah, it's just that Governor Alister thought it best if all of you from here go back together, better security," Jim explained what he'd been told. "He's afraid that Dominus will try something, so he is asking all of you to go back together. I guess Amanda can figure out something to do there for a couple of days."

"Well, I wondered why Audrey, Fern, Orenda, and I were going back so early," Amanda retorted. "You should've told us this, Jim." She glared at her brother, who smiled back at her, teasingly. Ignoring him, she began stuffing her bags into the cargo hold, as did everyone else.

"Wow! Six Security men," Ashley commented, as she counted the men in black, who alertly stood around the bus, watching in all directions.

"No, seven, don't forget me, Princess," Jim teased. He was in good humor this morning. School was about to begin;

his Princess was now in her last year—the power year, as far as he was concerned. In nine more months, she would be finished, and finally, they could marry. Jim, who was not known for patience, had the days until her graduation all counted out. Besides, he, too, was bored, unable to take his Princess anywhere—his hopes for a fun summer dashed by Security concerns. No way would he risk having her harmed as she had been last Halloween; that had been a nightmare for him. Indeed, during that frantic month, he had searched high and low for a cure for her. Unable to find a single hint, he had felt utter humiliation for the first time in his life, sobering him considerably.

Ashley was a rare breed of woman, as far as Jim was concerned, and not because of her unique skills as a Class 4 Diviner. That had nothing to do with it, except making things more difficult for him. No, she was a fighter. She took nothing from no one ever—feisty, yet loving and beautiful. His mind recalled when they had first met. At the time, he had fallen for Lindsey, who at that time had no hands, but she rapidly became a distant second to Ashley. He remembered how the armless girl had rapidly run the pool table on him, giving him the biggest shock of his life. Until then, inwardly, he felt a streak of pity for the young girl, but after that, she had his undivided attention. No matter the adversity, Ashley kept her independence and never gave up. He smiled.

"What are you smiling about?" Ashley asked Jim. The two were sitting in the back of the top deck of the double-decker bus and holding hands.

"Just remembering when you ran the table on me, Princess. I'll ever forget that day! That's when I knew you were the one for me," he whispered.

She hugged him and whispered back, "We are quite a pair. I love you too."

Meanwhile, Pam, Lindsey, and Fern, the floor monitors, compared lists and chatted. "I've never seen seven Security men on the bus before," Lindsey commented. "Do you suppose that Governor Alister suspects Dominus or his men will attack our bus again?"

"Dunno," Pam replied. "He's tried it several times and failed. He must know that security has been beefed up, so perhaps he won't try anything. Besides, this bus is going to be packed. Just look at all the names."

"I know, we are going to be really busy with all these first years," Fern replied. "Maybe they all won't be first years, though," she added, recalling that there were a large number of transfer students last year and they had to attend orientation week too.

"Shall we divide them up like we did last year?" Lindsey asked. "You two take the first years and I take all the others?" She liked that best, dealing with the older students. Besides, she saw that Pam and Fern both really enjoyed working with the first year students. The three agreed. Soon, they began to work as the bus began making the first of many stops, often at smaller towns out here on the High Plains, towns that they had never used to visit before.

Secretly, Lindsey anxiously awaited their arrival in

Colorado Springs, where Deiter Cross would board. Though he was the Black Hall floor monitor, she hoped they could sit together during the long hall through the mountains to Bradbury's. By the time Deiter boarded, the bus was three quarters full, keeping all them very busy. At least Deiter got the chance to blow Lindsey a brief kiss, as he began introducing himself to the twenty Black Hall first years now onboard.

When they finally embarked on the long run to the school, every seat on the bus was taken, and two Security men had to stand the whole way there. The five hall's monitors were kept quite occupied, answering questions, not only from the new first years, but also from everyone else. The big topic: why was everyone going back a week early with the first years? This was their orientation week; the older students always came back at the end of orientation week. Unfortunately, the Floor Monitors had no answer. Jim did, but no one asked him about it.

Lindsey was exhausted, when she finally headed down to supper, accompanied by her many friends. It had been a hectic day indeed, unlike any other start of term for these floor monitors, who had to deal with not only the new first years, but also all the many transfer students as well as all the other older students and all in the same day! Pam was so tired, that she could barely walk down to the dining room. Fern teased her, "See Pam, this is why you need to do more exercises in PE class. I'm not tired at all."

"Yes, but you are an Apache runner. I'm not," Pam

retorted, thankful that it was downhill to the dining room.

Their dining room was packed, far more densely than last year, Lindsey noted, as Deiter finally dragged his tired body over to sit beside her, ignoring the many stares from the Black Hall first years. Lindsey was in Yellow Hall. "Everyone's here," he commented.

"Tell me something I don't know! I am so pooped. I think my feet are going to fall off," Lindsey replied. "Look, here come all the professors."

The faculty filed in and took their usual seats. Governor Alister rose to address the throng; silence quickly fell. He didn't even have to ask for silence this year.

"Welcome one and all to the start of a new year of school. For you new students, I am Governor Alister Broadwell, that's head man, if you didn't know." A few chuckles echoed around the room. "Many of you are probably wondering why I have asked all students to return during this year's Orientation Week—why I have cut your summer vacation short one week. I did so for several reasons. One is for your safety, for Security reasons. As most of you know, Bradbury's School of Magic was savagely attacked last spring. As a result, twenty Security men are now posted here at the school to ensure your safety. They will be on guard at all times, day and night."

"These men and women of the States Security Department have doubled as your bus guards. Since they cannot be in two places at the same time, I thought it prudent to have all students return at the same time. Second, we have added quite a number of transfer students this term. You see, the Boston School of Magic has temporarily closed its doors. As a result, some of their students have transferred here to Bradbury's. This term, instead of our usual maximum of six hundred students, we will have one thousand. Yes, this means things will be a bit more crowded than normal. As you have already discovered, each dorm room now houses five students, not the usual four. If you are dissatisfied with your accommodations, please notify one of your Floor Monitors."

"Since all this is placing an extra burden on our volunteer Floor Monitors, for this week, we are adopting a new policy. Hence, for this week, we will use the buddy system. Shortly, each of you will receive word of the new student for whom you will be assisting. The Floor Monitors will still handle taking the new students to get their books, supplies, computers, cell phones, and so on. Your task will be to show your buddy around the campus, walk them through their daily schedules above ground and then through our tunnel system. Make very sure that each new student is very familiar with our campus. If any new student gets lost on their first day, I will send their buddy to detention for failure to properly orient their new student. Am I clear?" Alister was very stern, Pam thought, but then this whole Dominus mess was taking a very heavy toll on him. She thought that he looked positively awful tonight.

"Now then, a few announcements," Alister continued. "This year, as last, there will be no National Track Meet, for very obvious reasons." Lindsey was glad of this, knowing that this year they would have more homework than ever, leaving her little time for track meets and soccer games. "For you older students, there will be no Telluride Days. As you may know, Dominus struck our students while they were in Telluride last Halloween. I don't want to endanger any student needlessly." Massive groans thundered through the dining room.

Alister raised his hand, "In place of these outings, I am bringing in live rock and roll bands. We will have four rock concerts this year." The grumbling vanished, instantly replaced with wild yelling, cheering, and whistling. Lindsey smiled, suspecting Eli's Rockers would be one of the bands playing. Besides, she didn't want to go through what she and Ashley had experienced last Halloween in Telluride.

Then, Alister dropped into his now familiar speech for the new students. This being the sixth time she had heard it, Lindsey's mind drifted to other matters. As captain of Yellow Hall's Track and Soccer teams, she needed to get tryouts scheduled. Since none of her team had graduated last year, there would be no holes to have to fill. Indeed, they had actually had several extra players than the bare bones minimum of nine. She smiled as she recalled that she had not even played in their last game last year.

She ate quickly as did Deiter, who also had Floor Monitor duties to handle. Lindsey made her way around the Yellow Hall tables, chatting with all of last year's team members. At last, she relaxed, because everyone wanted to continue being on the team. Still, she posted a sign for tryouts on Friday at ten, getting a head start on the season and the big rush of the first week of classes. If she could get this responsibility handled in short order, then she would have more time for her studies. Lindsey remembered how busy all of her now graduated friends had been in their sixth year. Almost as if reading her thoughts, Hank Walls, the boy's PE teacher who was in charge of the track and soccer teams, approached her.

"Since we have time this week, I want to hold a meeting of the team captains to set the schedules for the meets earlier than normal. Let's meet tomorrow after dinner, Lindsey," he explained. She readily agreed, as did the other four captains.

A while later, Lindsey used a Magical Door to get up the stairs to her room. She had walked miles and miles this day, helping all the students, particularly some of the new ones. Even Deiter was so tired that he suggested they hit the sack early tonight, which she greatly appreciated. In her room, her companions were sorting out their bags. Amanda, Pam, Ashley, and Kathy again shared a room. This year it was number thirty, slightly larger than the ones from the previous years.

"I say Lindsey, have you noticed that we have a larger room this year?" Amanda chatted away, stowing clothes into a chest of drawers beside her bed.

"I sure am glad that we do," Ashley added cheerily. "Honestly, how did we ever get all this stuff? How many dresses do we really need anyway?" Everyone giggled, but knew that they needed many more than those they brought. Well in their minds, they did anyway.

Pam alone was using her wand to unpack, move, and stow all her things. It looked a bit strange. She saw Lindsey watching her. "My legs don't work anymore! Honestly, we should have more Floor Monitors. I may have to crawl my way around campus tomorrow."

"Hey, I had to use a Door to get up here," Lindsey consoled Pam. "What a work out."

Changing the topic, Kathy broke in, "Hey, my buddy is Anna; she's from Boston. She has been telling me about the Pill Party. She herself dumped six boxes of pills into the harbor. It was exciting at first, before the battles came. She says things got nasty there quite quickly. She and her family got out of there just in time. Can you believe it? Her house was blown up during the battle for Boston. Now they are living in Greeley."

Lindsey figured that in the next few days, she would be hearing many more horror stories from the new arrivals. However, she had Kathy tell her all the details that she'd heard from Anna. Inwardly, she was thankful that she had had a safe summer, even if it was completely boring, or nearly so.

The next day, Lindsey and Pam spent helping the many new students acquire their schedules, books, supplies, cell phones, and new laptops. That took the better part of the day, and both were very glad that now the buddies took over. Pairs of students began walking the campus, learning where their classrooms, buildings, and paths were located, including the underground tunnel system used primarily in bad weather months.

At the short evening meeting of the five track and soccer team captains, Lindsey once more got first choice of matches. Always the team who won the school cup the previous year got first choice of schedules. This year, Lindsey made all the four other captains happy. Her schedule went as follows.

2nd Saturday September—Yellow Hall versus Black Hall, track

3rd Saturday September—Yellow Hall versus Red Hall, soccer

1st Saturday May—Yellow Hall versus Brown Hall, track

2nd Saturday May—Yellow Hall versus Blue Hall, soccer

No playing or running in the mud, rain, or snow for her this year. Indeed, when Lindsey told her teammates their schedule, she was cheered and patted on her back, all except Emilio, who longed for diversions from his studies. Little did he know or suspect that his opinion of schoolwork would be drastically altered within a few more days.

Evenings, the teen couples spent wandering or sitting in the Formal Gardens, amid the flagrance of the late summer flowers. On August 28, Deiter was more nervous than Lindsey could ever remember him being. Arm in arm they had wandered the gardens for a time, until they found a secluded spot. “Deiter, you are actually trembling. Is something wrong?” Lindsey asked, making no attempt to hide the concern in her voice.

“Er, well, yes, no, I mean sort of, well no,” he fumbled, but was unable to speak clearly or decisive. “Lindsey, I am madly in love with you. I can’t imagine living life without you by my side.” Having said this much, his nerves calmed a little.

He had made a start, now perhaps the rest of the words would come.

"But I know that you and I are different than all the others. We both know that in the end it is going to have to be us that somehow stop Dominus. The adults don't have any real chance; he's just too powerful for them. After all, you are now the world's greatest Dispeller, and I aim to be every bit as good as Bill West, and everyone knows that he, well Wilma really, is the world's best Eliminator. I just know that it's going to come down to you and me, of course, with lots of help from the other Rodents, naturally, but it's going to be you and me that have to face Dominus. We might not, well, we might not survive it. That's why I have been hesitant. I know that all of our friends have already gotten engaged, and you must be feeling just awful about my reluctance."

"However, I've decided that even if I get killed, I still want to have done this one thing." He got down on one knee and asked, "Lindsey, will you marry me? I mean once this Dominus thing is over. Please, will you?"

"Of course, silly. I've been waiting for you to ask me, though Amanda suggested that I should ask you instead. I know what you mean about Dominus, Deiter. We both know how badly Dominus wants to capture and torture me, just as soon as I turn eighteen. Honestly, I was quite scared last Halloween, when he mutilated us so badly, and it took you and everyone else a month to free us from that torture. Next time, I might not be so lucky. Just look at what's happened to poor Michelle. Are you really going to want me if I end up becoming a hopeless cripple or something utterly dependent upon you for everything?"

"No matter what, Lindsey, you will never be a burden, not ever! No matter what happens or how badly that pig mutilates your body, you will never, ever be a burden on me. But Lindsey, there is something that I must have your solemn promise about, you must swear something to me." Deiter's face muscles all tightened. Lindsey had never seen him look so serious.

"Lindsey, if, if something happens to me, if I get killed, I must have your solemn, unbreakable promise that you will forget me, move on, and find some other man to love and marry. I don't want you becoming an old maid, moaning over my loss the rest of your life. Lindsey, you have to promise me, that if I get killed, you will try to find someone else to love, to marry, and to raise a family. Please, this is very important to me, you must promise me this, please."

Lindsey sighed, "Deiter, I'm in love with you, but if something awful happens to you, I promise you that I will honor your memory, but I won't become an old maid. If I can find someone else to love, I will. Honestly, mom had to do that too, and she eventually found Lloyd. If she can do it, I can too, Deiter, but will you do the same? I mean if I get killed, can you move on and find someone else too?"

"I don't know if I can, Lindsey. I've only loved you, but," he sighed, "I promise you that I will try, though I don't know how just now. Is that good enough for you?"

"Yes, I will do the best I can. You do the best you can.

Okay?"

"Good." Deiter's muscles relaxed completely. He slumped for a second from the suddenness of it. "Okay, then, Lindsey, I have this for you." He handed her a small box. Lindsey held her breath as she opened it, knowing that it most likely contained an engagement ring.

As she opened it, she gasped involuntarily as she saw the golden ring. Two small diamonds were set in a gold band, but the band was unique. It was as if two separate bands of gold had been twisted around each other, then binding to the diamonds.

"I had it specially made for you, Lindsey. The twisted gold represents our lives, joined together for all time. The diamonds are one for each of us, reflecting the love and life of each of us. I hope you like it. I wanted to spend more, but that's all I could afford just now."

"Deiter, it is the most beautiful ring I have ever seen! More importantly, what it symbolizes is incredibly romantic! I love it! Thank you!" She gave him a strong, loving hug, and passionate kiss, and then allowed him to slip it on her finger, followed by a Shrink spell to make it fit perfectly.

After a bit of time, Deiter said, "As far as getting married goes and all that, I've given it some thought, but I have not gotten very far with it. At first, I thought that we should get married as soon as possible, that way, Dominus might be dissuaded from trying to turn you into one of his play toys when you turn eighteen. You know that they have all been single women; he's never messed around with those who are married. That way, I would sort of be protecting you. But then, I thought about how badly he wants you and all that, and I figured that would probably make little difference with him. Then, being more realistic, we probably shouldn't make any serious plans until we've got Dominus captured. After all, one or both of us might not survive that, so plans would only make the loss even worse to bear. I don't want to make you grieve even more that way. So I don't know what to do."

Lindsey suggested, "Well, getting married is a time to share with all those we love, so we shouldn't do it in haste just to try to keep Dominus off me. If he wants to torture me, he's going to do it anyway, I think. After all, I really have caused him a whole lot of trouble. I think that we should just take our time and plan a perfect wedding once we graduate. Who knows what the situation with Dominus will be by next summer. I for one will not have that vile man dictating to me how I run my life. The very worst that could happen is that on our wedding day, we need to postpone it so we can go after Dominus. I think that Ashley can divine us a good day to get married where that won't happen. After all, Deiter, we shouldn't let a madman control and influence our lives."

"Cool. You are right, as always, my love. Have the others made their plans yet? All of our friends are getting married after we graduate, so I hope the dates don't conflict," Deiter commented.

"None have really set a date yet. Perhaps we can all get together and work it out. If Dominus is still on the loose, maybe we all should get married together at one time and place, better for security. We'll have to chat with everyone, don't you think?"

"You bet. I agree. I have only one consideration, Lindsey. Let's not delay it too long after we graduate!" Lindsey flushed, knowing precisely what he was suggesting.

Later that evening, Lindsey proudly showed her ring to her four dear friends. "Gosh, it is really beautiful. Deiter certainly has great taste and style," Kathy pointed out.

"Well, it's about time that he proposed! Honestly," Pam stated flatly, as if he ought to have done this months ago. The five girls compared each other's rings, commenting on their beauty and sentiments. None had really made any solid plans for their ceremony yet, much to Lindsey's relief.

Lindsey then took a photo of her ring and emailed it along with the news to her parents and other friends back at her ranch. A bit later, her mother called up, excited about the news. The two chatted far into the night.

On Friday, Lindsey and last year's team members gathered at the stadium to hold tryouts in case any new students wanted to join their Yellow Hall team. Venus and Ali, the third year twins, originally from New York, were the first onto the field, taking warm up exercises. "Hi ya, Lindsey. We've been practicing all summer," Venus happily explained.

"Yah, we are going to be better and faster this year, you'll see," Ali added. "Think we'll have any new additions? We only lost Dirk who graduated."

Lindsey didn't get a chance to speculate, as the other sixth years arrived in mass. Lil Ames, Amanda, Ashley, Emilio, and Andy jogged onto the track, all saying hello to the twins. Shortly, Glen and Alan, second and third years respectively came running up, trying not to be late. Only Fern had not yet arrived. Lindsey stalled a bit for her, while wondering if any one new would try out this morning.

A bit later, Fern arrived, bringing three others were with her. "Sorry we are a bit late, track shoes mess. Got three who want to try out, Lindsey. This is Bob Franks, fifth year transfer from Boston. He's run in the Boston Marathon, if you can believe that! These are the Mc Birdey twins, first years, Sally and Pete. They've played soccer since they could walk."

Of course, everyone wanted to know all about what it was like to run in the Boston Marathon. Bob wasted no time in telling his many stories. "Hey, we can talk about that later. Let's get down to business. We lost our right fullback and mile relay racer; Dirk graduated. So that position is open. However, if you have the stuff to make the team," Lindsey explained, "you are on it. I promise you that everyone will get to play."

"Hey, she's right!" Amanda broke in, pointing out, "Last soccer game last year, Lindsey didn't put herself into the game at all. We still won. Cool. So she's right. On this team, everyone gets play time." This was good news to the two first years, who doubted that they would be able actually to make the team, this year anyway."

Lil retained her hold on the sprinter position; none could catch her on such a short run. Smiling, she knew that she was hot. Next, the mile relay racers took the field, twice around was a mile, though in the relay race, each runner only had to go a quarter of a mile. Although only twelve, both Pete and Sally managed to keep up with the pack, and Lindsey decided that they would get their chance in the mile relay races.

Of course, everyone wanted to see how Bob did in the twenty-mile relay race, in which each runner had to race five miles before handing off to the next teammate. Venus, Ali, Amanda, and Lindsey would be his competition. Soon the five were off, the Apache Amanda setting the pace as usual. Lindsey was amazed that Bob could keep up with this fast pace, for few could match the speed of the Whitewater clan.

As the five finally approached the last half mile, Amanda began to pour on the speed for the sprint down to the finish line. She easily pulled out in front of Lindsey, who had never yet beaten her dearest friend. However, right behind Lindsey were the other three, pouring it on as well! Lindsey came in second, a hundred feet behind the fleet footed Apache, while Ali, Venus, and Bob were in a virtual tie just a few feet behind Lindsey.

After cooling down and catching their breaths, Lindsey exclaimed, “Wow, you two have really improved, you almost took me!” The twins grinned; their long summer workouts had paid off. “Bob, absolutely great going.”

“Yes, but darn it, I came in nearly last. I thought I might actually beat you all, but man, you four are hot runners!” Bob stated, rather disappointed in his performance.

“Hey, you did great. This means that we have a spare twenty-miler. Okay, here’s the plan. We race against Black

Hall first," Lindsey began to work out playing times and orders.

"Hey, I heard that Black Hall has also just added two more Boston Marathon Runners," Amanda broke in with her warning.

"Yes, I know them," Bob added. "She's right, they are good."

"Okay, then it will be Amanda, Ali, Venus, and me against the Black Hall bunch. In May, we race against Brown Hall. Bob, you are going to take my place there. Now against Black Hall in the mile relay, it will be Fern, Ashley, Glen, and Alan. Against Brown Hall, it will be Fern, Ashley, Pete, and Sally. Now on to soccer." Here, Bob took over as right fullback. However, with five replacements, everyone could get a chance to play and rest up. For the first time in six years, there were plenty of backup players. Lindsey vowed to make sure that everyone got plenty of actual soccer playing time.

As they were heading to the showers, Lindsey took Fern aside. "As you know, as captain, I get to appoint my successor. I am letting you know ahead of time, Fern, my pick is you."

"Wow! Way super cool! Thank you! Thank you!" exclaimed a very excited Fern.

"Yes, but you are going to inherit a mess, Fern. Five of us are going to be gone next year. That's going to be hard to replace, so it's my intention that this year, I'm going to give younger players every possible opportunity to play, as long as we can continue to win the school cup, that is. I want you to have the chance to pick first next year. It's no fun playing in the snow and mud."

"Hey, that would be great! That way they will have more experience. If they all stick around next year, I'll have enough for a team, but the twenty miler is going to be a challenge. Maybe I ought to practice up to fill that hole. I'll see if I can do it. Thanks again Lindsey. Is this supposed to be a secret until the end of the year or not?"

"No secret. I'll tell everyone next time we are all together, okay?" Fern walked back to the dorms with her head held high. She would be Yellow Hall captain, just like her older brother Tom had been. Not even Jim or Amanda had been captain, just Tom and herself!

Chapter 9—The Lessons Begin

Monday classes began. The group looked over their schedules as they ate their breakfast, Emilio chowing down on the pancakes and bacon.

```
 8:00 PE
 9:00 English Literature and Composition
10:00 Calculus
11:00 Elective
 1:00 Spell Research II
 2:00 Spell Casting Grade 7
 3:00 Spell Casting Grade 7
 4:00 Spell Casting Grade 7
```

Pam groaned, “Nothing worse than eight o’clock PE! Ugh.”

“Maybe you’ll get finger lifting,” Emilio teased her, making lifting motions with his finger, while stuffing another whole pancake into his mouth. Kathy giggle, and Pam glared at him.

“Well, looks like we all split up at eleven; we can exchange notes at lunchtime,” Lindsey suggested. Indeed, Kathy was really looking forward to Potion Making III. Of all the sixth years, Kathy was the best potion maker. She already had made lots of plans on going into business with Emilio’s help, just as soon as they graduated and got married, of course. To be of the best possible assistance to Kathy, Emilio was taking Business Math as his elective, so that he could help run the business, since Kathy had always been poor or slow in math.

Audrey was taking Plant Biology, while Deiter took Eliminator Theory II. Tom couldn't wait to go to his new Advanced Programming elective class. Music Performance was now perfect for Amanda. Ashley would continue her specialty with Practical Divination. Only Pam and Lindsey were a bit worried about their electives, as suggested by Governor Alister personally. Lindsey was to take Administration Management, while Pam took Elementary Education.

At PE class, Lindsey realized that their class sizes were going to be larger than ever. Over forty girls took the field, as Betsy called roll. "Okay, that's that. Now then, young ladies, this is your sixth and last year for PE. This fall we will take up tennis lessons. When the weather gets too cold for that, we will play badminton. From January to May, you will be allowed to do whatever activity you desire, within reason naturally. You chose. Okay, then let's get started. First, the rules of the game."

An hour later, refreshed with a magical shower, they assembled in the English Hall, awaiting the start of their English Literature and Composition class. Professor Elaine Mac Elroy quietly called role and then began. Lindsey counted forty-one students; nearly ten new faces were present, though not all had transferred from Boston.

"This year is devoted to two activities that run parallel to each other. First, we are going to examine the famous poets throughout history. Second, we are going to get your composition, that is, your writing skills, up to passing standards. It is a state requirement that you must pass in order to graduate. So no sloughing off in this class. Now let's begin with Chaucer."

At least Lindsey found this interesting, though she worried about the writing aspect. Many papers meant lots of night study time. Calculus class went as expected. Professor Herbert continued with his grandiose project of getting the kinks out of every student's math skills. Nevertheless, Lindsey expected to have to do a batch of problems every evening.

Professor Cho Lin welcomed her, "Good morning, Lindsey. Ready for your Administration Management class?"

"Yes, I guess so, but I really don't understand why he thinks I should take this class," she replied honestly.

"Lindsey, neither do I, neither do I. That's why I'm only Number Two around here. However, he thinks that you need to know how to run an organization, so let's tackle that, shall we?" Lindsey nodded.

"Now the text will give us the basic principles, but I have to admit that I have never been in charge of a company. I have only helped run this school. So I'm afraid that I will have to draw on Bradbury's operations for all of my practical applications of the theory. I guess you are going to get a good understanding of how this school is run, administratively. Let's get started, shall we?"

Lindsey mused on what she'd just said. Surely, this would be more interesting now, given that she was about to hear all manner of things about how the school was run. This interested her, and the hour passed rapidly.

At lunch, Ashley commented, “Well, people sure want to know the answer to the craziest things!” She’d just had her introduction to Practical Divination with Professor Mary Ann. “What should I wear to the dance? What is the best stock to buy? What is the best day for me to do my laundry? Will I get wrinkles when I am fifty? Geesh, people sure ask silly questions, but they pay well.” Lindsey chuckled. Ashley was not going to have a hard time making a living, she reasoned.

A bit later, Professor Arthur Thornby welcomed everyone to Spell Research II. After calling roll, during which Lindsey tried to learn the names of the new students, he began, “Welcome to Spell Research II. Yes, this year, you will be seeing quite a lot of me, as I am also in charge of your three period Spell Casting Grade 7 class. I have a lot of explaining to do for you sixth years. You see, this is the year that you attempt to achieve the highest of spell casting skills. Once you graduate, it is rare that a wizard or witch later on learns any of the more powerful spells that we will be studying.”

“Thus, this year, we go for broke, as the normals say. I and your other professors will push you to your limits, in hopes that some of you will be able to master one or more of the most powerful spells that we have. It doesn’t stop there. As most of you have heard, we will be giving you an opportunity to see if you can learn to cast one or more spells without speaking and perhaps without ‘proper wand activation,’ as you have so often heard in the past.” Half of the class giggled, for this was a clear reference to Professor Janice and Lindsey, back in her first year here.

"Of course, several of you can already cast sans words, sans wand. It is my fondest hope that many more of you will be able to do some spells this way. Yet, I caution you, most often spells cast in this manner tend to be the little, useful spells, like Clean. So don't set your sights into the sky on this aspect of casting."

"Now some of you may be joining various trades when you graduate, such a becoming a baker, an electrician, perhaps a carpenter. Many such areas, as you know from last year, have very specialized spells. Hence, this year, you will be given an opportunity to attempt to learn those spells within the areas you believe that you may desire employment." Many oh's and ah's echoed around the room. This promised to be an exciting year indeed.

"Now as far as this class goes, Research II, normally it is offered as an elective. However, considering the times we face, Governor Alister has moved it into the mainstream. In this class, you will continue the research project that you began last year, adding whatever spells you can to your database. Further, you will be allowed to research and develop new spells, spells that have never been created as yet."

The thunderous echoing cheering and applause was what Professor Arthur always received when he made that statement at the start of this class. It had never dawned on these students that new magical spells could be invented. They all thought that spells were fixed and finite, never changing. "Indeed, class, new spells are frequently created, though I will say that they are usually equivalent to lower Grade spells and are usually found in specialty areas, such as car maintenance, the baking industry, the shipping industry and so on. However, please note, that to pass this course, you are not required to invent a new spell! Actually, I will be quite surprised if anyone in this class actually does create a new spell. Such is relatively rare, but nevertheless it does happen."

"Finally, once you feel your database is complete, you may then attempt to learn some of those spells that you have uncovered." More cheers.

Pam whispered to Lindsey, "This is going to be the greatest class ever!" Lindsey nodded. She never knew that new spells could be invented! It was news to her and everyone else for that matter.

"Now as we get to spells other than those based upon alteration, I will have the appropriate professor come here to assist you in learning those. When you are inventing new spells, I will again have the appropriate professor assist you. We have all seen just how important a wide knowledge of specialty spells actually is. Miss Barron and Miss Stokes-Compton are proof of this. Now then, does everyone still have a copy of your spell database from last year? If not, I can provide you with a copy of what you submitted." Nearly everyone had theirs on their laptop, however.

"Oh yes, one final detail. The Restricted Section in the library is now no longer restricted to sixth year students. Just contact Lillian Angel if you want access to that section." Pam let out a squeal of excitement. Even Deiter was extremely pleased to hear this. He had heard that there were some incredibly powerful spells locked away in that section.

"Now then, shall we head for the Library?" Everyone made a mad dash out of the room, many casting Magical Doors to get to the Library more quickly. Absolutely every student headed for the Restricted section!

Lillian Angel laughed as Pam strolled up, for she was the last in line to seek permission to enter this very special section. Her classmates had made such a show of it that she purposely took her time. "Hi Pam. You are cleared too," Lillian smiled.

Before Pam could enter, Deiter came out carrying a large, very old volume entitled Dark Arts Spells. These books could only be studied in this special section of the library. Pam watched as Lillian made a computer entry that indicated that Deiter had checked this one out. Curious Pam asked, "Does all accesses to the books here in the Restricted section get logged into the computer?"

"Absolutely! In fact, if a student attempts to leave without turning the book back in, an alarm sounds. Honestly, Pam, these books must never fall into the hands of the younger students. They may be severely harmed by some spells and data."

"Say, how long are the checkout records kept?" she asked, not fully certain where her mind was leading her.

"Forever, Pam. They are archived on the main computer. Ask Professor Herbert about it, if you are concerned," she replied. Pam thanked her and headed into this special section. True, while Governor Alister had her researching the Restricted Wish spell, she had been given access to the Restricted Section, but only limited access to books that might relate to her research. Now she had complete access. She observed her classmates running frantically among the shelves, looking at random titles. She decided to approach this whole thing in a more educated, professional manner. Today, she concluded, she ought to make a listing of major areas and the number of volumes in that area. Then, she could decide upon the optimum line of research. After all, she cared nothing for the volume Deiter had just taken a fancy for—Pam hated the Dark Arts. By the end of the period, she'd accomplished her mission, fifteen categories, and over five hundred books to scrutinize.

Finally, the period over, they all headed back to the Hall of Alteration for their three-hour Spell Casting Grade 7 class. "Isn't this just fabulously incredible?" Ashley chatted with Lindsey and Pam as they walked across the sunny campus.

"Unbelievable. No wonder the sixth year is so hard. Just look at what we have to accomplish," Lindsey replied.

"More importantly, this is really our one and only chance to learn the most powerful of spells!" Pam cautioned. "No wonder all sixth years work so hard. It's now or never for us!"

Lindsey had a sinking feeling in her stomach, that this would be her last year studying magic—the only thing that she was truly interested in, and this bothered her greatly. She resolved to ask Governor Alister about this.

"Okay everyone, for the next two hours, we will be working on a pair of related spells. Suspend Gravity nullifies the force of gravity on the caster, an object, or another person. When successfully cast, the object or person now weighs nothing. If Miss Barron should cast this on an automobile, she would be able to pick it up with her finger, since it is then weightless. The companion of this spell is the Reversal of Gravity spell. This spell takes the cancellation one step further and causes gravity to exactly reverse its force direction. Hence, the object or person goes flying upwards, unless they can find a means to hold themselves down. Okay, let's get to business. Page twelve please. Each partner come up and grab one of these steel plates. Your objective is to make the plates weightless. Your partner will verify that you have done so."

"Ah, Professor?" Deiter interrupted the class. "Can this spell be used on Dominus? You know—to shoot him up into the sky and so on?"

"Yes, but if the other person is a wizard, then just like the Dispel Magic spell, he or she has some chance to negate its effect on themselves. Considering the power of Dominus, I would give you about a thirty percent chance of having this spell actually affect Dominus."

Deiter's hopeful look was dashed, not good odds at all. Nevertheless, he could find uses for the spell. He and Lindsey began reading the spell details. "Gosh, this is one of the longest descriptions yet," Deiter commented.

Lindsey flipped through a few pages and replied, "Hey, they all seem to be at least this long or longer. These are certainly more complex aren't they?"

A half hour passed before Deiter was ready to try it. Lindsey noted that they had never taken this long just reading about the spell and how to cast it. "Better take this one slowly. Practice the wand motions first, Deiter. Then, let's try to get all the words down properly."

The wand motion was simple enough, rather a waving motion, up and down over a very small distance. The wording of the spell, however, was rather intricate. Lindsey heard Pam and Tom also working on getting the words down. Finally, Deiter thought that he had it.

"Okay here goes nothing," he said. Making the proper motions with his wand, he spoke the words. However, he forgot to be specific on which object the spell applied. His wand activated in a brilliant flash of magical energies. Suddenly everyone in the entire classroom was crying out. Everyone and everything in the classroom was now floating weightless, just above the ground or surface on which it had been resting, people and things, including Professor Arthur, who had the strangest look on his face as he pivoted to look at Deiter.

"Mr. Cross, once again you forgot a detail of the spell. What was it that you neglected to specify?" he commented patiently. Red faced, Deiter hastily cancelled his spell, and Lindsey felt solid floor beneath her again.

"Er, which object?"

Grinning, Professor Arthur replied, "That's right son. However, I must say that in my long teaching career, I have never seen a student Suspend Gravity for the entire class. Very interesting use of the spell. However, Mr. Cross, I suggest that you be a bit more specific about the object. Please continue to practice." Deiter nodded and began again, making very sure that he indicated the steel disk in front of Lindsey.

Soon, all their classmates moved their attention off Deiter and back onto their own books and wands. Lindsey noted that Professor Arthur fired off a Message spell. She guessed that it had gone to Governor Alister. By the end of the day, the class as a group had made up a new expression, not wholly derogatory, mind you. It was "doing a Deiter," meaning causing a vastly larger effect than intended.

Careful not to do a Deiter, Lindsey was very specific in indicating the disk. Gravity was cancelled on her first attempt as well. She looked over at Pam and then Ashley and finally Amanda. All three were being quite successful with this new spell. However, at the end of the two hour period, these were the only students who had mastered this spell. None of the five knew that they had set a new school record. The average time to master this pair of spells was one week, not an hour.

Incidentally, the next day, Lindsey saw that Professor Arthur was now keeping a log of each student's progress, noting just how long it took for them to learn to cast the spell.

"Now then, this last hour of the day we will spend on learning how, if possible, to cast without saying the words." This naturally got everyone's interest way up, because most were downcast because they had not been successful with the Suspend Gravity spell.

“Conviction and intention are the requisites for casting silently. You must firmly think the words in your mind as if you were casting the spell. You must intend for the spell to work, but it is your conviction that it can indeed be cast without your uttering one syllable that is the key to all sans words casting. Now I’m going to divide the partners up a bit for this hour. As many of you know, and for those new students, Miss Barron here can cast an incredible number of spells sans words, sans wand. Just how many she can do this way no one has tallied yet, but I will be doing so shortly.” Most of the new faces stared in disbelief at Lindsey, who again wanted to become invisible, though she dare not cast that spell, though she could do so silently and without her wand.

“I also know that Miss Stokes-Compton can also cast a number of spells sans words, sans wand. Thus, I presume that some of the rest of you can also do this to a limited extent. Show of hands, how many of you are able to cast at least one of your spells sans words. Keep them high please. Mind you, this is no reflection upon you. It is just random probability; some of you will have encountered this phenomenon before now, all on your own.”

Of course, all eyes darted around the room, looking to see just who could do this incredible action, besides Lindsey and Ashley. Only Pam’s hand rose; her face turned noticeably pinker.

“Excellent, Miss Betts. Okay, then with the exception of these three young ladies, the rest of you divide up into small groups and begin experimenting. You should attempt only the useful spells of Grade 0." He motioned for the three of them to come to his desk.

"Congratulations, Miss Betts, I was unaware that you could cast this way. Any sans wand?" Pam nodded. "Very good indeed. Now first, I need to find out just what you already can and cannot do, both sans words and sans wand. With Dominus on the loose, this is very sensitive data, and I promise you that I will protect the information you are giving me and then destroy it at the end of the school year. However, if I'm to guide you three effectively, I must know what you already can do. Let's start with you, Pam. What spells can you do this way? Even better, just tell me the spell and which way."

Pam rattled off the spells that she had worked on with Lindsey and Ashley during August. She now had all the useful spells down, all the Grade 1 spells, and nearly half of the Grade 2 spells. Ashley went next; hers were a hodgepodge of spells from Grade 0 through Grade 4, a little here and there. In contrast, Lindsey's listing was extensive. Only the necromancy spells, the spells she never did master or choose to master, and a few other scattered spells were off her list, all the way through Grade 4. Unfortunately, she only had a few of the higher Grade spells down this way; she'd not had the opportunity to work on them yet.

Professor Arthur looked over the three lists and scratched his head. "My, oh my, do you three realize that this has never happened before? That is, I have three of you who can do this with many spells, though I'm not surprised with Miss Barron here, since she's been doing this since the first year here. I'm not sure how best to proceed with you three."

"Well, I don't want to cast the necromancy spells at all, Professor Arthur," Lindsey volunteered, "and the spells that I don't know, I don't want to know. I just haven't had a chance to work on many of the higher spells this way. Deiter helped me get a few of these down during the casting classes. I suppose I should pick up where I've left off."

"Yes, I do believe that you have a valid point. You three are going to be twinned up starting now during this portion of the class. Begin with the lowest level spell that you want to learn to cast this way and slowly work your way on up to the top. When you get to the more dangerous spells, let me know, and I will make special arrangements during this period. How does this sound to you three?" All totally agreed with his suggestion, and he sent them off to work on their casting.

However, by that very Friday, Professor Arthur had to make a fundamental change. Both Deiter and Amanda were making such rapid progress casting this way that he had them join Lindsey, Ashley, and Pam. Otherwise, they would leave their fellow classmates in the dust, so to speak. He didn't want anyone who was succeeding at this to be slowed down in any way. Casting silently and without a wand was a powerful skill that most wizards and witches could not do. Normally, he would expect about half of the class eventually to be able to cast some of the useful spells of Grade 0 this way, but not much more. Clearly, this class was somehow fundamentally vastly different. He had three already far advanced along this line of casting with two more rapidly progressing at a great pace. Something was different about these five students. That they represented the Dispeller, Eliminator, Diviner, Tracker, and Sleuth professions may be the root cause, he theorized in his messages to Alister, who, as always, was carefully monitoring the progress of the students.

Monday night after supper was finished, Pam approached Professor Herbert. “Excuse me Professor, but I have a question for you.”

“I’m all ears, so to speak, Pam,” the kindly old man replied. It was not often that students sought out his opinions. He was not a wizard.

“Today, I discovered that Lillian Angel always logs the books in the Restricted section out to the students and then back in again before they leave. She said that these records are archived on the school’s computer. Sir, how far back do these records extend?”

“Oh my, such a question. Well, I set that system up myself when I first came here so many years ago. Before that, the Librarian had to do it manually and mistakes were made. Since my system went into operation, we’ve had no errors. Let’s see the first year of logging was back in 2145. Why?”

“Fantastic! Sir, can I possibly have access to those records? You see, I want to compose a detailed listing of every book in the Restricted section that Dominus ever checked out. Then, I will examine those books to get a better idea of just what Dominus might know or be able to cast.”

“Splendid idea. I don’t know why no one has thought of doing this before. Certainly,” he replied, writing a short note on a post-it pad, which he always carried with him. "Here, take this to the computer center. You know where it's at. Show this to Sam, our operator, and he'll let you in. Let me know if this proves useful. Perhaps you will find a way to help stop this criminal."

Pam thanked him, opened a Door to the computer installation in the basement of the Admin Building, and stepped through. A few minutes later, she was setting up a database search, with Sam looking over her shoulder, just as curious about the research as she. It was eight that night before she joined the others in the Yellow Hall study hall.

"Where have you been?" Lindsey asked. "We're all swamped with math and poems that don't make any sense. Help."

"Been doing a little research of my own, sorry. I now know every book that Dominus ever checked out of the Restricted section. I aim to see if I can find anything useful in what he examined. Oh my!" she declared as she opened her Calculus book to see the number of problems that had been assigned. During the excitement of the afternoon, she had completely forgotten about them, to say nothing of the poems.

"Well, at least we don't have a science class to worry about," Pam commented flatly.

"No, I just got *two* math classes not one! Help, anybody!" Emilio wailed like a wounded puppy. The girls giggled.

"What's worse is that none of you can help me on my management homework," Lindsey added.

"Nor my education class homework," Pam added dryly. "I think that I will work on the poems just before bed." Everyone agreed with her idea, very glad to put those books away.

"You know, this is going to be one incredible year," Deiter pronounced. "After all, we are going to become as powerful as we possibly can before we graduate."

"Yes, but think of the work that you are going to have to do to achieve that, Mr. Cross," Pam said didactically. He groaned. They swapped calc papers and began checking each other's work, while Pam frantically began to work hers.

Later that night in their bedroom, Pam said disgustedly, "I don't get these poems at all. Gibberish." She'd only read half of today's assignment.

Lindsey yawned, "I don't either, so don't feel bad."

"Hey, I thought they were kind of interesting and all," Kathy replied, turning out her bed's reading light.

By Friday night of this first week, everyone discovered that Kathy was the poem hot shot, taking to them very easily, while most struggled to make any sense of them at all. She found herself being the poem tutor this year, which gave her an immense sense of pride. After all, until now and with the sole exception of Potion Making, she had been heavily dependent upon everyone else's help getting her math, science, and English homework done. Now she was able to help the others.

The following week, Professor Arthur had them working on the Destroy Object spell. "When successfully cast, the object arrives above the sun and is disintegrated by the sun's intense heat. Thus, the object is gone. This is one method of destroying very dangerous items, including evil relics of past magical ages."

Next, they learned to Create Shelter. Pam excelled at this spell, which created a large home-like construction, which was invisible to all, once entered and the door shut. This spell provided a safe haven when a wizard or witch was doing extensive traveling. Several other less useful spells were also covered. As before, the five excelled in these alteration based spells; they were again the first in the class to be able to cast them successfully. As the end of September came, nearly everyone in the class had these spells mastered.

What of sports? The track meet against Black Hall was a close one, primarily because of the addition of two Boston Marathon runners to their team. However, Amanda crossed the finish line a few steps ahead of their best runner, clinching a Yellow Hall victory. At the soccer match against Red Hall, Lindsey herself did not even play. No need. Red Hall was never known for being a tough team to beat. Instead, they were playing for the pure fun of playing soccer. Lindsey made sure that all the newcomers got to play at least half of the game, whose outcome was never in question.

Chapter 10—A Challenging Fall

Professor Blake Smith joined Professor Arthur the first week of October to assist the teaching of the complex conjuration based spells. In sharp contrast to the alteration based spell, these spells, Lindsey and her friends found incredibly challenging to learn how to cast.

They began with the Summon spell which, when properly cast, would summon any object to them instantly. It was a Teleport Object spell, as Pam described it, when she finally got it right, the first student to succeed with this spell. One could also Summon a person, but if they did not wish to be summoned into the caster's presence, they could resist it. Again, the more powerful the person was, the less chance the caster had of a successful casting. Once more, Deiter was frustrated, because he so hoped that he could somehow utilize this spell to capture Dominus. Indeed, capturing Dominus was constantly in the back of his mind, constantly dwelling on just how he could do it. His and Lindsey's future utterly depended upon finally getting rid of Dominus.

After a very rough week of Summon, they then embarked on the Summon Beasts spell, which went a whole lot easier for those who had successfully gotten the base spell down the previous week.

"Okay, this week we are taking up perhaps one of your most powerful combat spells, one which is very difficult, if not impossible, to defend against—yes, Mr. Cross, this is one that you could use on Dominus, assuming you could get sufficiently close to him for the spell to work. The maximum range is fifty feet; any further away and it fails. The spell is Stun. I believe that several of you have been the victim of this spell in the past. It is one of Dominus' favorite spells, that's for sure. When successfully cast, the recipient is truly stunned, completely helpless, frozen to the spot. It lasts for at least an hour before it begins to wear off slowly. Because of the current situation with Dominus, Governor Alister has asked me to take as many days as is needed for each of you to become very competent with this spell. Please note, that once you have mastered this spell, it is one that can be cast very rapidly, but you must hold rigidly in your mind the desired effect. The usual way that you fail with this spell is that your mind wanders during its casting, which completely nullifies the spell. Now let's get cracking."

"This is one spell I absolutely must get down perfectly and be able to do it rapidly!" exclaimed Deiter to Lindsey as they began to read the extensive instructions for its casting.

"You and me both! He's stunned me several times now. Gosh, I wish there was some defense against this spell," she replied.

"Only distance," Deiter said encouragingly, "stay way back from him."

"Yes, but then our stuns won't reach him either," Lindsey pointed out. Deiter grimaced.

Several days later Deiter and Lindsey, as well as most of

the class, were routinely Stunning their partners. However, ten in the class never did manage to master this spell, even after Professor Blake extended the time for another couple of days.

As the end of October approached, Professor Blake began the class with a very serious mien. "This week, you have a choice to make. The next spell, as some of you have rightly guessed, is the Restricted Wish spell, the spell that Dominus has used repeatedly against some of our students and many others as well."

"It is restricted in that you are limited in the amount that the reality of the world can be changed. If you wish for a million dollars, you will likely fail in its casting. If you wish for ten thousand dollars, it will likely appear, though do not be surprised if the pile of money vanishes a day or so later. You cannot wish someone dead, Mr. Cross." Deiter already knew that.

"Now Dominus has become a master of this spell, choosing to couple his spell with other spells. I am picking on Miss Barron here to illustrate some optimum ways of spell coupling. Please note that his choice of spells was particularly vile and evil. She has given me permission to use her as a learning example. Please note that what I'm about to say was not the totality of his casting nor were these his precise words. Those are very personal to her."

"His Restricted Wish last Halloween went something like this: I wish that Miss Lindsey Barron would appear before me with her arms removed at her elbows by my Slice spell and that my Paralyze spell and Idiot Mind spell would be in effect on her. See how he couples his Slice, Idiot Mind, and Paralyze spells into the wish? This way, when the Restricted Wish spell detonates, he has total and complete control over Miss Barron. However, if he does not then follow it up, the spells will wear off, she will regain control over her body, for example. Yet the Slice results and the Idiot Mind spells would be permanent, thus giving him total control over her. In addition, by virtue of the Idiot Mind spell, she would be unable to cast any spell whatsoever."

"You see, with this spell, the caster must put in a very great deal of forethought to get the wish precisely stated. I bet Dominus stayed up many nights trying to get that wording worked out precisely correct. He is one of the greatest masters of this spell, unfortunately for the rest of the world."

"However, as many of you already know, there is an Achilles Heel to this spell. Each successful casting causes premature aging of the caster's body! Yes, real aging. Ten casts and your body is ten years older! This is a terrible price to pay for the casting of a spell, in my humble opinion. Further, if any of you become successful with its casting, I will have to register you with the Universal Registry as one who can cast this spell. At this point in time, there are ten known wizards and witches in the entire world who can cast this spell. Dominus is one of them."

"Thus, consider very carefully whether you wish to embark on learning to cast this spell. When you are successful at casting it for the first time, your body will age one whole year. While I know you are all heading towards eighteen, this is a very serious side effect, one not to be taken lightly. Do I make myself perfectly clear?"

The room was so silent that you could hear the breathing of the students. Pam raised her hand. He nodded to her. "Professor, could we study it and learn how to cast it, but just not actually cast it? Then if we ever needed to cast it, say against Dominus, why, then we could go ahead and actually cast it for the first time."

"Yes, Miss Betts, you could make such an attempt. However, and this is a big however, when you finally get around to trying to cast it, you might not be able to do it or you might find yourself having to try to do it hundreds of times before you got every tiny mistake out of your casting. It is a tough one to cast and takes weeks of practice to get down perfectly. So yes, in theory you could study up on it, but I would not put much faith in your ability actually to cast it when you decide you need to cast it." Pam looked crestfallen, her bright idea shot down in flames.

Deiter was in a quandary. This would be a super cool spell to have in his arsenal; however, the cost was steep. Plus there was Lindsey to consider. His mind held images of him being old and grey, while Lindsey still had her youth! Yet, he also saw images from last November, where Lindsey was in desperate need of his help, going through a living torture every day. He thought that this spell could have saved her. "Do I or don't I?" he wondered.

Then, he remembered when he was twelve and his father was lecturing him about magic school. "Son, you will get the chance of a lifetime, when you get to be able to learn the Restricted Wish spell! Only powerful wizards can cast this spell. You learn this one, son, and you will be among the dozen most powerful wizards on the planet! Nothing can stop you; power will be yours!"

"Yeh, power, but dad neglected to mention the cost," Deiter mumbled.

"What's that?" Lindsey asked, hearing this bit of news.

"Nothing, well something. I don't know what to do about this spell, Lindsey. I mean I always looked forward to learning this one, ever since I first entered magic school. You know, the ultimate power is yours if you have this one mastered. Just look at Dominus. If I had known this one, Lindsey, last November I could have saved you and Ashley a month of pure torture! But. . ." His voice trailed off.

"But," Lindsey prodded him.

"I mean if we get married, I could end up an old man while you are still a gorgeous young woman! How can you love an old man when you are only say twenty-one? It's not fair. I mean if I use it to help you, then I grow old and that hurts nearly as much, though I wouldn't regret doing it for a second, mind you. I'd do anything for you. You are the most importing thing in my life, but don't you see, it would end us up with me being really old while you were really young."

"Look Deiter. You didn't need that spell to rescue Ashley and me, now did you? Of course not. That spell would only have been a quick shortcut. Besides, we got along fairly well until you worked out how to do it. I think that what you figured out was far more intelligent, far more powerful than just using a Restricted Wish spell. You are selling yourself short, Mr. Cross."

"I know, but what if Dominus does something to you that I can't fix without it?"

"I think the real question is, Deiter, do you and I really *need* this spell in our arsenal?" Lindsey stated, thinking about her own question. Something Pam had said bounced around in her mind. "Say, there is the even more powerful version of the spell, the full Wish spell. I have an idea. Instead of messing around with this lesser version, especially since we want it so that we can undo something awful that's happened, why don't we delay a while and see about the full Wish spell? If you are going to grow older, why not have it as the price of the top spell?"

He smiled, "I like your thinking. You bet, why mess around with this one, when the best one is out there. If we can't learn it, then we can always come back and try this lesser one. Brilliant, love, brilliant."

"I hope that your dad will not be too disappointed in you, though," she tested him.

"Ah, heck, that's his problem, not mine. He's too much into force and power for my tastes. Yes, we should be strong and powerful if we are taking out Dominus, but we have a purpose for it. He doesn't; none that I can see," he replied, satisfied that he had finally reached a mutual decision.

After allowing his students plenty of time to consider this spell, Professor Blake asked for a show of hands, "Okay, who wishes to make an attempt to learn the Restricted Wish spell?"

Peaches hand shot up without the slightest hesitation. To Lindsey's surprise, Andy's hand rose, along with two boys who had transferred from Boston. Professor Blake had the four come up to his desk; he would be working closely with the four. Meanwhile, Professor Arthur had the rest of the class working on the Protection Barrier spell, which created powerful enclosing walls around whatever the caster chose. Anyone who attempted to pass through that wall was met with the equivalent of a powerful Ball of Fire, a massive electrical discharge, a cloud of poison gas, and several other horrible death-causing effects. Lindsey and her friend now realized that this was one of the spells that Governor Alister had used to protect the Rod of the Apocalypse during their first year here. That spell had nearly killed Dominus, who was trying to steal the rod.

During the ten-minute break between sessions, Lindsey asked Andy why he wanted to learn this spell. At the same time, Deiter asked his friend Peaches why she wanted to learn it. A bit later, they compared findings and chuckled. The two had put their heads together and were going to make their initial casting of Restricted Wish to wish to be that, when they got to a certain spell, they would have no trouble learning it perfectly. Peaches desperately wanted to learn how to Make Permanent a magical enchantment, because she had always wanted to make and sell magical items. Andy, on the other hand, wanted to be able to learn the Grade 9 spell that would give him the most powerful divination spell, the ability to have Foresight in his archaeological digs. Thus, he would always seem to be incredibly lucky and become a foremost expert in his field.

As the Halloween Dance approached, these sixth year students finally realized that they were deep into magic, totally immersed, so much so that they paid little attention to anything else but these studies. That this was the case came when they received their first comprehensive poem test in English class. “Oh no! I’m flunking poems!” declared Pam, wailing that all was lost.

Lindsey had never known Pam to fail anything. She looked over Pam’s shoulder at her test. “Pam, that’s not a failing grade! You got a C on it!”

“Well that’s tantamount to failing for me!” She began crying. “I wish they would just write simple English so we could understand them.”

Kathy decided right then and there that Pam needed help. Kathy had aced her test, one of the few A’s that Professor Elaine had given on the big poem test. “Pam, let’s plan to spend an hour each night working on them. I’m sure I can help you. Besides, you have been getting A’s on all the writing assignments, probably that will average out to be a B.” She tried to lessen the impact on Pam.

“I’m spending too much time on magic, I guess, but that’s what I’m supposed to be doing,” Pam countered. “After all, what use is a poem’s meaning going to be to me if Dominus ends up controlling the world? None at all.” Pam thought better than to say that this one class would ruin her straight A's throughout all of Magic School. That was wise of her.

Lindsey decided to change the subject. "Say Pam, I've been meaning to ask you. How's your research into the books that Dominus checked out of the Restricted section coming along?"

Pam wiped her tears and began explaining. "I've learned a lot. He gave up totally on most of the highest Grade spells, checking them out only once. It appears that he concentrated heavily on learning the Blind spell and the Charm the Masses spell. He dabbled in all the Dark Arts spells—you know, those having to do with dead bodies and all that. I get the distinct hunch that he was not very successful with these key power spells, except Blind and Charm the Masses, which he seems to favor quite a lot."

She went on, "Compared to us, he checked out far fewer books than most of us already have looked at. I think that he spent his time researching the Specialty area spells, like Slice, Wrap, Leather to Plastic, and Plastic to Steel. I'm sure that those Specialty spells are far more useful to him than the superpower spells. I think that we got our first real break here. If only some of us can learn some of these top spells, maybe we will have a chance to stop him." Pam had now forgotten all about her C in poems, she was back into magic once more.

During this time, New Jersey and Delaware were brought online in the National Health Care Program. They went down without a protest or fight. The scare and death toll of Boston and Massachusetts loomed large in the minds of many people there. Besides, both states were small and would easily be overrun by the army. Pam did note that three months had gone by since Bloody Monday, which meant that Erin Sacs and his men were being effective at slowing the production of the pills. More than likely Virginia would be next or else the Carolinas, and given the pitiful slow progress that Dominus was experiencing, that would not happen until probably next February or maybe late January. Pam was sure that they all had time to learn superpower spells with which to stop Dominus.

On Halloween, the dining room was decorated in the spirit of the holiday. Bats hung from the ceiling; black cats adorned the walls; spiders and webs filled corners and decorated the tables. Eli's Rockers performed live for the students and were a smash hit. When the final slow dance came, Lindsey whispered into Deiter's ear, "Well, this was a fun Halloween. I sure am glad that nothing bad happened this year."

"Me too," he replied. "I really needed this study break, even if it is only for one night. We have so much to learn if we are going to capture Dominus. Wilma says that I need to find a way to get him to use his Restricted Wish spell, and then immediately after that he is vulnerable to capture. If I wait two minutes after that, he is back to battery, as she says. Honestly, Lindsey, I have no idea how I'm going to get him to do that."

"Let's worry about that later," she said and began kissing him as the light dimmed even further.

That night a heavy snow fell on Bradbury's, forcing everyone to use the tunnels to get about the campus. However, Lindsey was not particularly pleased with Spell Casting. Professor Delius Dogs was now their teacher for the necromancy based power spells. He entered with a swirl of his black cloak, his black hair shining from the oil. "Power, power, power spells. Yes, today we embark on learning true power spells. With one pointing of your finger, you can cause a person to die instantly! That is true power, the power of life and death, the Death Finger spell. Turn to page eighty-eight, and we will begin. However, I caution you, I expect only a few of my Black Hall students actually to master this spell."

Deiter raised his hand, "Professor, could we use this spell against Dominus?"

"You could, Mr. Cross. However, you would probably find it useless. He can likely throw off the spell's effect, rather like Dispelling Magic. If you were several times more powerful and experienced than Dominus, then yes you could slay him and end this tyranny of his. On the other hand, if you could somehow take him by total and complete surprise, you stand some slight chance of slaying him." Deiter's face fell; this was not going to be the answer either.

By the end of the week, many Black Hall students were pointing their fingers at lab rats and watching them instantly die before their eyes. Lindsey and most of her friends found this repulsive and disgusting and only went through the motions, pretending to be learning the spell. She wanted no part of this spell!

Next, Delius created or brought, no one knew for sure, three zombies into the classroom. Dead bodies somehow animated, these stinking creatures attempted to claw and attack the students, who were supposed to be practicing their skills at Controlling the Undead Creatures. While again most Black Hall students excelled with this spell, Lindsey ignored it as well, whispering to Deiter, "I'd just as soon Disintegrate it as control it!"

Next, Professor Janice came to teach them one charm based spell, Control Plants. Lindsey noted that she looked as fresh and pretty as ever. By looking at her, you could not tell that last year she had been terribly burned by the Death Stalkers who had attacked the school. Lindsey found this spell very boring. Deiter was sure that he could not make a plant strangle Dominus, so the spell was mostly useless, he thought.

By mid-November, Deiter finally cast some useful spells of Grade 0 sans words and sans wand. In fact, nearly half of the class was able to cast a few of these little spells without saying the words. Only six had thus far been able to cast them sans wand, however. Their conviction that the wand provided the power was too strong.

However, now Professor Jerry Thalmus came to work with them on two spells of abjuration. Lindsey hoped that he would not be too boring, recalling how many times she had fallen asleep in his first year history of magic class. He was not an inspirational lecturer. "Greetings. I am Professor Thalmus, abjuration, for the new students. I am here to help you learn, if possible, two powerful abjuration based spells. The first spell is called Hide, a simple enough name, which encapsulates precisely what it does," he drolled on in his usual monotone.

"A successful casting causes objects and persons of your choice within the area of effect to become invisible to all observers, save those using See True of course. Erin Sacs is a master of this spell." Suddenly, he had the full and complete attention of nearly everyone in the class!

"So this is why no one can ever seem to find him," Lindsey whispered to Deiter. He vigorously nodded his agreement and began taking notes.

"The army could Hide several of its battle tanks on a field, and no one would be the wiser, unless, of course, they walked into the invisible machines. Again, you must truly be convinced that no one will be able to see the objects or people that you are trying to hide," he lumbered onward, his voice tending to put them to sleep once more. Soon they woke up again, as they began to read about the commands and wand motions required. The needed wand motion was a rather peculiar one, a sort of rolling motion, as if one was repeatedly making small hills.

This time, Lindsey fetched their box of blocks, which they were to hide, while Deiter eagerly began reading how to do it. After a bit of practice motions with his wand, he excitedly called out "Hide!" His wand flashed rather brilliantly this time, and the entire class, professors, their desks, the chairs, the ceiling, the floors, and the four walls all vanished from sight. Startled screams filled the room. Someone called out, "Deiter's done a Deiter again!" Loud invisible laughter now filled the room, as Deiter cancelled his spell and all returned to normal once more, though over forty were laughing hysterically.

Un-phased and as if he'd seen this a thousand times before, Professor Jerry advised, "Mr. Cross, I believe that you need to be a bit more specific on just what it is that you wish to Hide. I believe that we are to make the blocks hidden." This was too much for Pam, who now laughed so hard that she fell out of her chair. Even Deiter began grinning; he'd done it again. Poor Lindsey, she fought valiantly to keep from laughing, but it was so funny hearing that monotone voice, that she too burst out laughing. Even Professor Arthur sported a smile, as he made due note of this in his logbook, Lindsey noted.

Later Deiter explained, "We can use this spell to sneak up on Dominus and his gang. I get us all hidden; we creep up, and then attack, taking them by surprise, and capturing him."

"Yes, but that assumes that none of them is using the See True spell while on guard duty," Pam pointed out didactically. Deiter was unmoved, however; he had a useful spell here, and he wasn't about to discard it.

However, the next spell everyone thought was terrific, Reverse Spell Back at Caster. The whole class sat on the edges of their chairs while Professor Jerry drolled on about this spell. "In essence, you cast this spell upon yourself. It lasts about an hour before it dissipates. While it is in effect, when a spell is directed at you, you simply say Reverse, and the spell reverses direction and detonates on the caster, not on you.

Please note the fine print. It only works on a spell that is directed at you, not the area around you. So if Miss Betts launches a Ball of Fire into the classroom here, nothing would happen by virtue of this spell, assuming that one or more of you had it in effect at the time. However, if Mr. Cross had the spell in effect and Miss Betts had centered her Ball of Fire directly on Mr. Cross, then she would find that the Ball of Fire when it detonates is in fact centered on her."

"I know for a fact that Dominus knows and uses this spell. Thus, an Eliminator must be prepared for this spell, if Dominus enters the battle fully prepared. Remember, the spell is in effect for only an hour. Worse, would be Eliminators take note: it cannot be dispelled by the Grade 3 Dispel Magic spell. However, it is not an endless spell. Rather it can Reverse only one Grade 6 or higher spell before it is exhausted or two Grade 3 spells or six Grade 1 spells. That is its limitations. A suggestion for would be Eliminators against a so protected Dominus: hit him with a Disintegrate spell, which he will surely Reverse Back to you. However, be prepared to dodge or you are eliminated instead."

They soon began to practice this one. Unfortunately, the wording that must be said with utter conviction was intricate and involved. Pam was the first student finally to get it cast, some three days later. Deiter got it to work on the fifth day of trials.

The first week of December came, and Professor Huan Su joined them to help them master, if they could, some evocation magical spells. "Our first spell is of great historical importance, Vice Hand. Yes, this is the spell that the famous Eliminator Bill West used to capture Dominus Malefic back in 2163. You will note that there is a reference to this in this current edition of your Grade 7 spell text. Essentially, when successfully cast, a giant hand grips the target person as if it was steel vice grips, pinning the person's arms at their sides. The duration lasts for ten minutes, ample time to subdue the party further. Whether Dominus will be using a Reverse Spell Back at Caster on this one remains to be seen. It is my opinion that he will very likely do so, since this was the spell that entrapped him last time."

Lindsey had never seen Deiter so enthusiastically throwing himself into the learning of any spell before now! She knew why; he intended to use this one to capture Dominus, emulating Bill West, or rather Pam's Aunt Wilma. If he did so, she wondered if in future editions of their spell text if Deiter's name would be mentioned. If it did, Deiter would have some measure of future fame and notoriety.

The spell was not an easy one to learn quickly. By the fourth day, both she and Deiter had mastered this spell, and Lindsey set to work on seeing if she could cast it sans words, sans wand. However, she found this to be a trifle difficult and put such casting off until later when they had more time.

The next spell was a Timed Ball of Fire. Still a Ball of Fire, however, now the wizard or witch could chose the moment of its detonation. While the class easily picked up this new spell, Lindsey didn't think she would have much use for it. Neither did Deiter.

His last spell just before Christmas break was Imprison. When cast, the person found himself or herself surrounded by a steel prison cell, just big enough to hold them. Yes, the person imprisoned could still cast spells out through the openings in the bars, but they could not Teleport out of the cell nor could they use any other magical means to leave the prison cell. Deiter thought that this might be useful in capturing Dominus, but the real problem was that to active the prison, the caster had physically to touch the person to be imprisoned. This would be quite a challenge in the middle of a big battle.

Worse, the spell was very complicated to cast, requiring several minutes to get all the requisite words out. Again, one stumble, one slightly incorrect word, and the spell would fail. Only half the class was eventually able to cast this one, and Deiter was not among them, much to his chagrin. Lindsey and Pam, however, were successful with this one.

At their last class before the long holiday break, Professor Arthur told them, "Class, when you come back in January, there are only two more Grade 7 spells to tackle, both are divination oriented. Hence, right after that, we will be spending our time on learning whatever Specialty spells you desire and making attempts at the even high Grade spells. For just about all of you, this will be your only opportunity to attempt to learn these incredibly powerful spells, so be prepared to spend vast amounts of time working on them."

As the term grades came out, Pam wailed, "I only got a B in English! My first failure!"

"Maybe you can still bring it up to an A this spring.

After all, it is only the final grade that counts," Lindsey tried hard to cheer Pam up.

Kathy added, "Look Pam; we worked real hard and got it up from a C, so we'll just have to work harder on it together this spring. Say, maybe you could do some extra credit assignments, Pam. I mean we have been given our choice of two or three topics for each composition paper. Maybe you could write one on each of them, and Professor Cho Lin will give you enough extra credit to pull it up to an A."

"But I want to work hard on the power spells this spring! This is my only chance to learn them! You head what Professor Arthur said. I'm doomed," Pam wailed.

"Boy, she sure doesn't take getting a B at all well, does she?" Emilio whispered to Kathy. "Heck, I only got a C in English, and I'm happy I did that well." Kathy glared at him and offered a hankie to Pam so she could wipe her eyes.

"Come on, Pam. We need to get dressed up for the Formal Dance tonight," Amanda took a different approach. "You have to look great for Tom, and we only have three hours left before dinner." Reluctantly and with reddish eyes, Pam followed Amanda back to their room, all the while wondering how she could face Tom, when he now knew that she had failed so miserably and gotten her first-ever B.

After those two left, Lindsey sent Tom Ryker a Message, alerting him to Pam's "failure." She hoped that he would be extra considerate of her feelings tonight at the dance. Then she asked Deiter, "Okay, what should I wear tonight? It's going to be formal, so I have to dress up."

Deiter didn't directly answer her question. Instead, he replied, "Did you know that Governor Alister is allowing some visitors to come to the dance tonight? I heard that Nadia and Jolina are coming, along with Barnaby and Bailey. Of course, Jim will be here for Ashley. I wonder who else is going to come?"

"Cool, I'm sure that they will dress in their slinky, fetish outfits. Maybe I ought to dress that way too," she thought aloud.

"You do look incredibly sexy when you dress like that. It's okay with me if you want to," he replied, finding a clever way to suggest that she dress like this.

"Okay. You have to wear your new fancy suit. I just love how it feels when I have my arms on your shoulders," she teased him. He leaned forward and gave her a kiss, ending their banter. They, too, headed for their rooms.

Lindsey had no more gotten to her room, where her roommates were starting to undress and head for the showers, when both she and Ashley received a Message.

Please come immediately to the Infirmary. A.

"Wow! I wonder what Governor Alister wants," Ashley said, very surprised. She began hastily redressing.

"Dunno, but you all didn't get the Message, so it must just be us he wants. Why the Infirmary? Is someone hurt?" Lindsey asked.

"I think it is very strange, perhaps something bad happened at your ranch, Lindsey," Pam speculated. Two very worried teens stepped through Lindsey's Magical Door right into the main emergency exam room of the Infirmary.

Doctor Caterwall and Governor Alister were standing there waiting for them. “Is everything all right back home at the ranch?” Lindsey blurted out her fears the very instant she stepped into the room. Ashley was right on her heels, still buttoning her blouse.

“Oh, I’m sorry. Yes, everything is perfectly fine at your ranch. Forgive me. I didn’t intend to startle you so, but I couldn’t risk saying more in a Message that could possibly get intercepted. No, this concerns the Folquets.”

“Has Dominus found them and killed them?” Lindsey jumped to conclusions.

“No, no, no disasters,” Alister grinned. “Let me explain a little. We have received the preliminary findings from Simone’s French pharmaceutical labs on the composition of the pills. Isabella sent their findings to Delius yesterday. I must say that we are all very encouraged with the initial report. In all likelihood, they will have a cure pill within a few more months. Even better, they believe that they may be able to re-design the pill to continue to make people healthy, though perhaps not curing the criminality aspect.”

“No, I have asked you here on another matter related to your summer excursions. Simone and I have had a number of lengthy phone calls, over a totally secure line, mind you. I have taken every precaution. The calls cannot be traced or intercepted, 128-bit encryption I am told, though Miss Betts would be better at trying to tell you what that means. Because of his invaluable assistance to our cause, I have agreed to have our doctor examine Michelle, especially her feet, to see if there is really nothing that can be done about them. Also, you will remember that she was supposed to come to Bradbury's that following term, before her father disfigured her. I thought it might be a nice gesture on our part to have her come and attend the Formal Dance tonight."

Lindsey read between the lines and said, "Ah, you want to observe her and see if she still has the potential to use magic, don't you?"

Alister's face flushed; he gave a silly laugh. "I'm found out at long last! Yes, yes, that too, though her seeing the good doctor here is really the primary mission. Now Simone and I both agree that it is far too dangerous for him to bring her, so I have sent several whom I trust to bring them to Bradbury's. Isabella and Michelle will be coming. That is the primary reason I have invited several other adults to the Formal Dance this evening. Obviously, Michelle will have to look, how do you say, fetish? Is that the right word for your long, slinky dresses with the enticing corsets on the outside? With her waist as small as it is and with her feet, we need to disguise it as much as possible. Could you and Ashley possibly wear those outfits that are similar to those of Nadia and Jolina? That way, there will be five of you looking similarly attired, drawing less attention to Michelle."

"Sure, we planned to anyway," Ashley answered before Lindsey got the chance.

Alister looked relieved. "Thank you both. The cover story we are going to use is that they are a pair of distant

French aunts of yours, who have just come stateside to visit you both. Due to holiday travel arrangements, they have to return tomorrow, a short visit. Tomorrow morning, Doctor Caterwall will do his examination of Michelle, and they will be returning to Marseille right after that."

"What about an outfit for Michelle?" asked Lindsey. "Where are we going to get the right dress and stuff for her?"

"Nadia and Jolina will be arriving shortly and are handling that aspect. Perhaps, you two would be kind enough to drop by here say around 5:30 just before dinner and escort them all to the dinner and dance?"

"Perfect, but does Jim know?" Ashley asked.

Alister grinned; his eyes twinkled, "Who do you think I trust enough to fetch them here?"

A smile appeared on her face, as she realized that he was talking about Jim. "Way cool!"

"Good. Then I think that you both need time to get ready, so off with you," Alister shooed them out of the Infirmary.

Once back in their room, Pam, Kathy, and Amanda just had to know that this was all about. The two explained while they began getting ready for the dance.

Kathy, who was wearing one of the Teen Fashion gowns, was ready long before the others. She excused herself and went to visit Professor Delius to find out about this pill analysis report. A half hour she returned very pleased indeed, though she waited until later to explain the findings to her friends.

At 5:30, Ashley and Lindsey were finally all set; getting into their outfits in such short a time took some doing. While Amanda, Kathy, and Pam headed down to the dining room, Lindsey and Ashley headed to the Infirmary to meet their guests. Lindsey wore her blue full-length satin hip hugging gown, which had the tiniest of walking slits, a matching blue and white striped outer corset, and matching heels, very similar to those that Nadia was usually wearing. Ashley's was nearly identical, save it was green. Holding hands to keep each other balanced, the two stepped through Lindsey's Magical Door into the Infirmary.

"Hi Lindsey, Ashley," Jolina called out. "My, but you look fetish tonight." She grinned. The two sister's gowns looked strikingly similar to those worn by Nadia and Jolina, having been picked out some time ago by the two friends. Barnaby and Bailey wearing their camel's hair suits stood near the back of the room. From their vantage point, they could casually watch all the women, a fact that they didn't attempt to hide.

More importantly, Nadia was just putting the final additions to Michelle's new outfit, while Isabella watched them carefully, memorizing each action the women took to dress Michelle properly. Isabella wore a navy blue satin gown with matching four-inch heels, her typical style of dress apparel. However, Michelle's new gown was much the same as Nadia's, sky blue satin, extra-long, very form fitting, with matching blue and white outer corset. Lindsey noted that Nadia had purposely lengthened the dress very nearly to touch the floor, completely hiding the fact that Michelle had to wear ballet boots. At least, Nadia had been able to find a blue pair that nearly matched the color of Michelle's dress. Jolina had done up Michelle's long, thick black hair, loaning her some jewelry to accentuate her look. Indeed, Michelle now looked like a stunning middle-aged woman, much as Isabella did.

"Hi Ashley! Hi Lindsey! I'm so incredibly happy to be here and to come to your dance and see your school and all," Michelle called out, becoming very excited and animated. Although forced to take small steps, the two sisters rushed as quickly as possible to Michelle's side and took turns giving her a warm hug. Then, they shook hands with Isabella and gave her hugs as well.

Isabella said sternly, "Ve have lots to say, but maybe ve talks after dance, eh?

"Sure thing, we've got lots to ask you two as well. Right after the dance, we can return here and talk as much as you want," Ashley answered.

"Remember, watch what you say to others, Michelle," Isabella warned.

"I have to be careful when I am around others. We are supposed to be your aunts from Marseille. Simone explained it all to me very well. I can't wait for the day when we don't have to come in secret," Michelle added. She was still extremely happy. "We all look so similar now, and these dresses are really just fabulous. I've never owned clothes as fine as these!"

Lindsey asked, "Say, Michelle, do you know how to formal dance, waltzes in particular?"

"Yes, a little, Isabella has been teaching me, but Lindsey, I have learned a lot since your last visit. I'm having a hard time with some things. I thought I was doing okay with these boots when all I had to do was walk around my room or even the estate. Now as my world has suddenly grown so much larger, I'm finding that is not the case. Going downhill is hard, and I'm afraid dancing is very difficult for me. I go so slow in public that others get impatient with me." She was about to say a lot more, but Isabella pointed to her watch, and Michelle stopped short.

"I understand. Lindsey and I were force to wear boots much like yours for a month here. We managed to find a way to sort of waltz, so I'll dance with you tonight and show you how we did it, if that's okay with you," Ashley volunteered, hoping that Jim wouldn't mind too much. Michelle eagerly agreed. She was about to dance with her idol!

Taking this as their signal, Barnaby and Bailey moved silently to their wives, slipped their arms around their waists, and prepared to escort them to the dining room. Lindsey opened a Magical Door to the dining room for everyone, explaining, "This is a fast way to get there, Michelle, a bit of magic."

"That is good. You have so much snow outside, and I was very worried I would have to walk in that snow, which is so very hard for me to do."

Barnaby added, "Yes, nearly six inches of snow already, Michelle. By the middle of the winter, it gets well over a foot deep, sometimes three feet, but not often." Michelle was impressed, not having seen snow since she was a little girl. With Lindsey on one side of Michelle and Ashley on the other and holding on to Isabella, they stepped slowly through the door into the dimmed room, now becoming packed with other students, dressed in their finest gowns and suits.

Professors Janice and Elaine had decorated the dining room for a romantic evening's ball. Overhead, hundreds of candles provided a soft, warm glow over the room. The smell of fresh lilacs was in the air. All the tables were also covered with elegant tablecloths. Every few feet, a candle flickered in an ornate holder. Michelle and Isabella began looking around; neither had ever seen such elegance before, though Michelle was awestruck with the room.

Jim and Deiter came quickly up to the group. They had been waiting patiently for their arrival. Ashley did the introductions, "Michelle, Isabella, this is my fiancé, Jim Whitewater, and this is Lindsey's fiancé, Deiter Cross. Guys, these are our *aunts* from Marseille, Michelle and Isabella Folquet." At once, Deiter understood.

Jim spoke first, giving Michelle a warm shake and a hug. "You look smashing, Michelle." She grinned and hugged him back. Deiter merely shook her hand, figuring that a hug might not be appropriate, since he had never met her before. Jim also shook Isabella's hand, and she insisted on exchanging hugs as well.

"This way ladies, I have our seats reserved," Jim took charge, leading them to a group of seats at the front of the Yellow Hall tables, where they could see the professors clearly, as well as many of the other students. Ashley was careful to assist Michelle in being seated, and Jim quickly caught on, doing the same for Isabella.

However, before Barnaby and Bailey could seat Nadia and Jolina, they were recognized, and several teens came rushing over to them. One sixth year young woman said, “Oh your dance hall is just the greatest! Sometime can you hire the Acid Black band to play live? I know lots of us would just give anything to see them live, you know.” Soon, all four were actively involved in numerous conversations, surrounded by teens that had been to their dance hall.

For the women’s sake, Ashley explained just what the B & B Dance Hall in Denver was all about. “Honestly, someday I would love to take you all there. I just know that you would love it.” Governor Alister entered, leading the faculty to their seats, the dinner was about to begin.

After everyone took their seats, he rose and spoke clearly, “Tonight, is our Christmas Formal Dinner and Dance. However, I am very pleased to announce that we have some guests with us. Many of you recognize Nadia, Jolina, Barnaby, and Bailey Hampton. They are here to see just how fancy we can be. I believe they wish to borrow some of our ideas for their Dance Hall.” Several chuckles echoed around the room. “Finally, the two women sitting with Miss Barron and Miss Stokes-Compton are aunts of the sisters and live in France. They are here for a very short visit, and I thought this would be wonderful Christmas present for them to attend this Formal Dinner and Dance with their nieces. Mind you, they are not witches. Now let the festivities begin." He waved his wand and trays of food magically appeared above the tables, slowly lowering to the top. Eager hands began taking scoops and passing them on around the tables.

"Ah, roast duck with almonds," Isabella commented, helping herself. Lindsey suspected this dish would be a hit with her and was not disappointed. Christmas was one of the few times during the year when they were served this delicacy.

Dinner passed by rapidly, and then with a wave of his wand, Governor Alister whisked all the dirty plates and dishes away. Lindsey knew that they were appearing in the hidden basement washroom. "Let the dance begin," he called out, and the first slow waltz of the evening began. To Lindsey's surprise, Governor Alister came quickly over to them. Taking Isabella's hand, he said graciously, "May I have the honor of this first dance?" She grinned and accepted.

Ashley helped Michelle up and the two moved slowly onto the dance floor. Ashley whispered to Michelle what she should do, namely the pattern to step. Standing on your toes made actual waltzing vastly more difficult and awkward, but merely by moving in the right pattern, no one would notice. In her tall boots, Michelle was a good four inches taller than Ashley was, so it worked well for them.

Before long, Michelle's self-confidence rose, and she forgot about not being able to dance properly and began just having the time of her life. A bit later, Jim cut in on them. "May I?" he asked, sliding his arm around her waist, steading her as he had watched Ashley do. He whispered in Michelle's ear, "Just keep on doing what you were doing; it works great, Michelle." Indeed, as Ashley stepped back, she could now actually observe them. As long as Michelle took the tiniest of steps, she gave the appearance of waltzing just fine, especially with Jim holding her tightly.

By the middle of the second waltz, Governor Alister interrupted Jim, taking a turn with Michelle. He said something that caused her to blush, Ashley noted, while taking a spin with Jim. Meanwhile, Lindsey began noticing some of the other young women's gowns. About one in ten now wore a fetish gown somewhat similar to hers! This was the first time that Lindsey realized that between the four of them, they were actually setting a fashion statement, and others were adopting their look, complete with tall heels and tight gowns with outer corsets to match. Never in a million years did Lindsey ever consider that other teens would choose to dress like her.

Some waltzes later, when Nadia drew close, she whispered, "We are starting a fashion trend! Seriously, isn't it great that other young ladies are choosing to dress as we do?" Lindsey smiled, not quite sure what to make of all this. Yet there was Peaches in a long, slinky, red satin gown, with matching red and white striped corset and tall, matching heels. She also noticed that Andy held her close to his body, really close.

By the fourth dance, Lindsey forgot all about Michelle being a problem, and midnight came again in just a few minutes—well as far as she was concerned. Someone had obviously moved the clock hour hand again, and she vowed to learn that spell so that she could dispel it! As the young couples slowly left the dining room, Lindsey gathered her "aunts," while Ashley opened a Magical Door back to the Infirmary. A few minutes later, the four arrived at the make shift room in which the two French women would be spending the night.

"I've got to sit down. My feet are aching!" Michelle declared and hobbled to the nearest bed. "That was so much fun! I kept wishing the night would never end! Isabella, do we have anything like this in Marseille?"

"No, I am afraid that we don't, dear. Not quite like this, but I will see what I can find," she replied. "Lindsey, your Governor Alister—why, he is de perfect gentleman! He dances divinely!"

"I wish I could dance, too," Michelle broke in, "I was just pretending."

Ashley came to her defense, "You did just fine, Michelle. Did you notice that many couples were dancing very close together and moving their feet much as you were—in very tiny steps? You did great." Michelle accepted the compliment, but knew she still wasn't doing it properly.

They chatted a bit longer before Michelle told them, "I'm now up to what my brother calls fifth year studies. He thinks that I will get my GED in about three more months." Both teens congratulated her on her stellar accomplishment.

Isabella added, "She is an incredibly fast learner. I'm very impressed with her progress. Simone, he is still working with her for nearly twelve hours every day." She then asked them if they had seen the pharmaceutical reports that she had sent to Professor Delius. Since neither had, Isabella outlined the overall results.

Meanwhile, Michelle wanted to talk with Ashley, and she confided a number of her many observations and worries to the teen, her idol. “Honestly, I’m really having a hard time with my feet like this. I have to be so careful you know when I am out in public. It is so hard. So many people give me all sorts of strange looks and comments, but I can’t help it. My feet are this way, and I have to wear these kinds of boots.” She went on for some time, bearing her soul and inner feelings to Ashley, who listened to her every word and tried to encourage her where she could.

Finally, the hour was getting very late, and the teens said goodnight, promising to return in the morning. Back at their room, Kathy was telling Pam all about the chemical makeup of the pills. “You see, it contains the healing enzyme but it is highly concentrated—like one thousand times stronger than in any healing potion. They think that this is how it can cure diseases so rapidly and keep everyone healthy. However, the heroin seems to be needed to get the body to absorb this much of the enzyme. If so, that is a bummer. They have suggested that they might be able to concoct a derivative pill that will ease those addicted off heroin gently, while still maintaining a high level of health. Yet, they are not sure just how the pill eliminates criminality or how it is turning the takers into automatons. More research is needed, but the bottom line is that there is some hope for the future. They really do expect to have an antidote pill by summer, though not in the quantity that we will need to get so many off of Dominus' pills."

Lindsey heard no more. She had fallen asleep. Still dressed in her fancy outfit, she had lain down for a moment and had fallen sound asleep. Ashley, too, was very tired, and said, "I'll undress in the morning." A minute later, she was asleep as well, though she managed to pull a sheet over her.

Kathy asked, "Sleeping in their dresses?" Pam nodded, sleepy-eyed. Kathy covered Lindsey as best she could and headed for her bed. Amanda had been asleep for an hour already.

The next morning, after changing, the girls began packing for their trip home for the holidays. Although the bus would leave at ten the next day, they had a good deal of packing to do, far more than they had as first years. Promptly at ten, Lindsey and Ashley excused themselves and headed for the Infirmary to check on Michelle and Isabella—well Michelle really.

Both Doctor Caterwall and Governor Alister were now studying x-rays of her feet. "Ah, just in time," Frank called out. "Come have a look." He pointed out the key features. Lindsey, who had never seen an x-ray of feet before, had no idea what she was seeing. Doctor Caterwall quickly realized that neither teen understood what he was saying. "Here. We need a comparison sample." He took an x-ray of Lindsey's feet. Soon, he had the two up side by side.

Now Lindsey could see the difference. It was not the

fact that her feet were flat on the floor while Michelle's were pointed toes downward. All the foot bones in Michelle's feet had somehow grown together, fused was the doctor's term. No visible cracks between the bones were visible. "You see, her feet are one solid bone mass. Thus, she is unable to bend them at all." Now both Lindsey and Ashley fully understood Michelle's problem.

"The question that we are now raising is just how can this be put to rights?" the doctor explained. Alister suggested a healing potion. Unfortunately, that will not work in this case, as there is nothing to heal. The bones have become one solid, single bone. This is a particularly tough case to heal. Most normal methods are going to be useless because of the fused bones, which has come about from wearing these boots non-stop for a quarter of a century. Well, that's my guess anyway. Perhaps her father cast some spell of which I am unfamiliar, but from her story, I don't believe that was the case. More research is needed in that area."

"Now, I don't know if you have yet studied the Regenerate spell or not, which potions can also emulate. If you haven't, then allow me to explain. I believe that Regenerate is probably the only real hope she has, but even that spell has its limitations. So much time has passed, you see. As near as I can tell, she had normal feet for twelve years and then had them this way for the next twenty-seven or nearly so. Regenerate puts things back to the 'normal state'—normal being defined as that state which has been most prevalent. In this case, fused feet."

"Her case is most disconcerting. She can't even walk or stand without the assistance of these boots. Her feet do not bend at all. We were discussing the possibility of amputating her feet and then regrowing them. I seriously doubt this will produce anything but what she has now, since the predominate condition has been fused feet. The only hope I see for her is Regeneration. But will it work? I don't know yet. I'm afraid that I will need to research this one."

"What about her tiny waist and having to wear that corset all the time?" Ashley asked, since her feet seemed doomed.

"Same story with that, I'm afraid. She's been this way so long, that her body has adapted. Even her lower ribs have grown wildly inward." He showed them Michelle's chest x-ray. Indeed even their untrained eyes saw the lower ribs shaped vastly different from the upper ribs. He teased the girls, "I know that you ladies pride yourselves on having a small waist, but hers goes too far." They giggled.

"No, the cure for the feet will be the cure for her waist," Doctor Caterwall pronounced.

"We'd better let these teens say goodbye. I know Jim is anxious to get them safely home," Alister interrupted them. "We can talk more in a bit." He led them to the room in which the two women were staying. Jim was there chatting with Michelle and Isabella, who were pleased to be talking to a full-blooded Apache Indian. Jim didn't seem to mind though.

"Ah, morning my Princess," he said as Ashley entered. The two hugged. The teens spent five minutes saying their farewells. Repeatedly, Michelle kept saying she now realized how much she had been denied by her father imprisoning her instead of sending her to Bradbury's as he had promised. Ashley felt awful for the woman, but could do nothing about it.

Finally, Jim held their hands and Teleported them home. The four returned to the x-rays and the diagnosis. Alister asked, "When you return from vacation, will you and Miss Betts please research the Regenerate spell? Let's see if we can get a handle on some form of cure for Michelle, shall we?" He didn't have to ask twice. Both promised to do so. Then, they returned to finish their last minute packing.

Finally, they spent time on their laptops, ordering Christmas presents. Both girls had been so busy with Spell Casting that they had completely forgotten the holidays were upon them. Much had to be purchased in short order.

The next morning and hundreds of Move Object spells later, the packed yellow double decker bus rolled out of the parking lot and onto the freshly snow-plowed, state highway, heading for their homes, far out on the High Plains.

Chapter 11—A Fretting Dominus

"Now we are getting someplace!" Dominus confided in his assembled Death Stalkers. "Bloody Monday will teach them all a valuable lesson—that I am serious. We have total control over five states now. How soon can we add more?"

"Boss, I just don't see how they found out about the five overseas places," Ames Selig avoided the question. He didn't dare answer it. "All five new plants you brought online have been attacked and production crippled. How did they find out about them anyway?"

Elated over his Bloody Monday achievement, Dominus was in rare good humor. He had been miserable ever since he discovered that Sam Barron's kid, Lindsey, was perhaps the world's most powerful Dispeller, totally thwarting the Death Stalker attack on Bradbury's last spring. Yet, the total force subjugation of Massachusetts had turned this all around, putting him back on his path to US and then world domination.

"Ames, we will just have to figure that out, now won't we?" he replied covertly. Ames breathed a sigh of relief. Dominus had not taken his head off with screams or worse. Dominus swivelled in his chair to face the man at the other desk, his business associate, Melvin Hoggs. "Production figures, Melvin?"

"Right. Counting the warehouse stocks and the limited

production from six facilities, we can maintain the current five states for now. Initial estimates on repairs are still coming in, but I guess all five overseas plants will be back to capacity by late fall. Based on populations, I would recommend that New Jersey and Delaware be taken together as the next targets. Sir, do you anticipate heavy resistance there? If so and if there is also a significant population evacuation, then I can add North Carolina to that takeover."

"I seriously doubt that they will resist. Both are so small and so industrialized that they will not likely offer resistance. Darn, this whole thing is going slower than expected," Dominus lost his good humor.

"Boss, what are we going to do about the western states and Broadwell?" Len Striker decided to pose the question that had been lingering in his mind for days now, ever since Dominus had finally worked out what was going on with the alliance of western states.

Dominus smiled, his good humor returning. He was pleased, very pleased, that his information ring had finally uncovered the exact approach that Broadwell was taking. Further, he didn't need Diviners to work it out, only his spies, his men controlled by his rings. Admittedly, he had taken far too long to resort to out-right spying, but in the end, he had found out. "Yes, we know that Broadwell was the instigator of that conspiracy. They are putting on a public front that appears to be totally behind the National Health Care Program. However, in fact, behind the scenes they are in effect seceding from the Union, forming up armed militias and the like. They do not intend ever to join the Program peacefully. You'll have to admit that was a pretty smart countermove on Broadwell's part."

Dominus sneered, "Yet the cat is still about to pounce on the mouse. Haven't you seen the news? By publically backing the Program, these stupid western governors have turned their own citizens against themselves. Not one of them stands the slightest chance of getting re-elected. Broadwell's grand plan is about to come back and eat him up." Dominus laughed heartily and his men joined in.

"No, let's allow the states to implode before we take any real action against them. When the time is right, I'll send out the Assassination Squads to level the field some more. Let's let them stew in their own pots a while longer."

"However, I am beginning to come around to your viewpoint, Len. Broadwell is becoming a real pain in the ass. I may have to compromise my ultimate plans for him, but I won't with those darn teens. Go ahead, Len; let's see what you come up with this time."

Len's chest puffed out. He'd been given the chance of a lifetime, to prove his ultimate worth to Dominus. Yes, he had failed to take out Broadwell at Bradbury's last spring, but time had shown that it had not been his fault. No one knew that Barron's kid would be so good or that she would accidentally be outside on the day of the attack, let alone right in their path. Stroke of incredibly bad luck. This time, he would not fail; he would become the top Death Stalker, knocking Ben Johnston out of that place.

"Gentlemen, I will be at my London house if you need me. I have to work out just how they are finding our new overseas plants and how to deal with that." Dominus waved his wand and Teleported from the Georgia office.

He arrived in a plush home in the heart of London's wealthier district. "Hello Sam, all okay here?" he asked the older man who guarded this secret hideaway for him.

"Yes, I've let Millicent know of your arrival. I do need to make a grocery run now. Is there anything in particular you wish? Will you be staying long this trip?"

"Yes, the finest chocolate and bring me a latté from Starbuck's Century 2200 please. Probably a couple weeks, though I may run some errands from time to time. Message me on your return, Sam." The older man nodded and Teleported from the plush front room. Dominus took off his coat and hung it in the closet. Thick carpeting covered the floors; mahogany trim contrasted with the velvet wallpaper he had used to refinish this room. He headed upstairs to the toy room.

"Ah, good afternoon, Millicent. I see you are looking well, and your charges are as beautiful as ever," he said covertly to the middle-aged woman, sitting on a red pillow, the stumps of her legs covered in the same walking pads, which he had invented for that stupid Venezuelan woman he'd trapped in that abandoned gold mine. The woman was matronly, but wore a tight fitting corset, as did the other four women he kept here. He'd improved upon his toys, however, and inwardly thanked the teens for continually giving him more opportunities to improve them. They kept discovering his secret houses and stealing his toys from him. However, no more. This house was very heavily protected from any kind of divination and scrying. Instead of just putting his Idiot Mind spell on the matron, the caregiver of his toys, he also put it on the toys themselves and found this far more satisfying.

“Oh yes, sir. I have them all ready. Don’t they look like beauty queens? I’ve done my best to make them all look just gorgeous for you. Aren’t they just perfect this afternoon? Who do you wish to take with you?” she asked enthusiastically, quite proud of her work.

Dominus eyed his four new beauties who were sitting patiently on the edges of the velvet davenport. Each one’s arms ended at their elbows, but this time he had their upper arms gently narrowing to only an inch in diameter at their ends, far more elegant looking he thought. All wore very tight fitting, wasp waist corsets with the finest black nylons. Their feet wore shining black patent ballet boots. He had carefully chosen each of their glass eyes’ color to match their hair. Their enlarged breasts were both huge but very well shaped. Dominus admired his latest handiwork with a grin. He was improving his talent with age. However, each of the young women was also under his Idiot Mind spell, a touch that he found delightful, having removed all traces of resistance on their part, so much more enjoyable.

“Hello ladies, you all look absolutely beautiful this afternoon. How are you doing? Have you been practicing your walking like I asked?”

"Oh thank you. We have been trying very hard, Dominus," the blonde woman replied. "It is so hard to do, but we try, don't we, Millicent?" she turned her head roughly to where she thought their matron was sitting.

"Oh yes, I have them walking as much as possible," Millicent confirmed the woman's story.

"Well, this afternoon, I will spend with the lovely Czech Milankova." The gorgeous brunette grinned, though the other women could not see it. "Come with me, Milankova. You have all been so good that I have sent Sam out to fetch you all some of the finest chocolate in all of London. My treat." All five squealed with happiness. Then, Milankova attempted to get to her feet. It was quite a wobbling struggle, however. Very awkwardly, she managed to stand, her arms wiggling to help her gain her balance.

"Which way are you, Dominus?" she asked.

"Over here. Let's see how your waking has improved, Milankova," he smiled and gazed upon her, watching her every struggling, miniscule-sized step. When she drew close to him, he put his arm around her and began to lead her to his bedroom next door.

A bit later, he helped her to sit on the edge of his bed. She asked innocently, "I'm so happy that you chose me. How is my waist? Is it small enough for you yet? I think I may still be too fat."

"Well, let's see shall we?" He measured her waist. "Well, it is fifteen inches, Milankova; fourteen would be better."

Her face fell. "Oh darn. It is so tight now that I can

barely breathe, but it must be tighter still. Can you make it smaller, please, please Dominus? I want to have the perfect waist for you." An evil grin creased his lips; he waved his wand and cast a shrink spell, tightening her waist another inch. She gasped for breath, nearly fainting. It was now so tight.

"How is it now?" she gasped. "Is it perfect?" She gasped again. "I do so want to be perfect for you, Dominus," she asked, while struggling to keep from fainting.

"Ah yes, my beautiful Milankova, it is now just perfect indeed. Lie back and let's enjoy the afternoon."

An hour later, Sam had returned, and Dominus handed out five chocolate bars to Millicent, who then helped each woman eat hers. "Ladies, when you can walk really well in your boots all by yourselves, I will take you to hear a play and to the hottest night dance club in London." The women cooed and promised to work very hard; they all greatly desired to go to the dance hall. Invigorated, Dominus went downstairs to his study to think.

He had two issues to work out. How were they finding out about these overseas plants? How could he get around this continual loss of product from the warehouses and plants? He began to map out on paper just what all had been happening during the last year, hoping to see a pattern that he had missed before.

His mind digressed, and he recalled watching the lovely Milankova, as she walked back to her bedroom and the others. "Ah, the perfect women," he mused. From out of nowhere, the image of a stern looking Lindsey Barron appeared, haunting him. She stared mercilessly at him, and then proceeded to Slice his body into small pieces. “Darn it! Daytime nightmares!” he cursed and took a large gulp of his latté. He tried to morph that image of Lindsey into his play toy, but somehow the image refused to be so altered. “Women are just play toys!” he screamed in protest.

The image of Lindsey now spoke, “I’m coming to get you, Dominus. Women will be your downfall.” Way back in some discarded section of his mind, Dominus knew that this was the truth, that women were as powerful as men. Quickly, he squashed all such notions, and the image of Lindsey vanished as rapidly as it had come. Dominus relaxed and took another sip of his latté and set to work.

After some time, a pattern began to emerge. “Eureka, that is it. Now I know how they have been able to find these overseas plants! Darn, I should have seen this from the beginning! No overseas plant will ever work out. I need a new approach entirely!”

Next, he set his mind reviewing the thefts of millions of type A pills, the ones for norms, stolen from his main warehouse. He’d installed video cameras, but they had only shown boxes mysteriously vanishing. He’d laid numerous traps, and one Ball of Fire had actually detonated, but that had caused more damage than the thefts. However, of late, the thefts had pretty much ended, ever since the middle of September. In the back of his mind, he knew that figuring out how these pills were being stolen was vitally important to him, but as always, he came up short. He had no answer to this one.

Resigned to this enigma, he turned his attention onto possible ways around the thefts. Clearly, if they could produce more pills than could be stolen, the thefts would become irrelevant. Also, he considered creating several more secret warehouses and placing US soldiers on guard duty there. At last, he picked up his throwaway cell phone and dialed President Missy Snow.

Overjoyed with the smashing success of the conversion of both Delaware and New Jersey, Dominus began to draw up plans for Virginia next. However, the field reports from his numerous spies raised some concern. The number and sizes of the western militias were growing rapidly. He knew about the mutual defense packs these sneaky governors had signed, and it worried him, primarily because of his overall pill production levels. If only he had been able to manufacture these pills in a much larger quantity, then he could have proceeded drastically more rapidly, giving these renegades far less time to prepare.

Finally, Dominus was convinced. He would just have to let go of his long time desires to torture Alister Broadwell until he begged for death. He would have to take more drastic measures. Alister—the mastermind behind the resistance movement and the sole blocker of his Golden Path—yes, Alister had to go. He Teleported back to his Georgia office to meet with Len Striker. He sighed because this was not what he had been looking forward to for so long, and yet it simply had to be done. Nobody, but nobody, was going to interfere with his plans for those annoying teens this June.

"Boss, hold on a minute. President Snow has been

calling for you," one of his Death Stalkers interrupted his travel to his meeting with Len. Reluctantly, he grabbed the disposable cell phone and dialed her number.

"Oh yes, Simon, so good that I was able to reach you. I wanted to tell you the good news. I'm told that six US facilities are now about to begin your Saude Dourada pill production. Isn't this just wonderful news, Simon? Why, in just a few more months, my program can be extended to many more states as I have been promising. Do you suppose we will encounter more renegades fighting us? Are they infiltrators or terrorists do you suppose?" Her poor automaton mind was struggling to comprehend how anyone could possibly be against her wonderful program. Everyone on it was so perfectly healthy now, and there were just no criminals to be found among the pill takers.

"Ah, well done Madam President, well done indeed," Dominus poured it on heavy, knowing that her automaton mind would relish the praise. "Did you do as I asked and station a large US army force at each of your government plants?"

"Oh why yes, yes I believe I signed that order. Now where could it possibly have gone? Dear me. I will ask Martha just to make sure," she valiantly tried to think where those papers had gone, but could not recall that, only that she had signed them at Martha's insistence. It was what Simon wanted—to ensure the safety of the plants from the outside terrorists. Yes, now she remembered that Simon had called them terrorists. She was finally about to ask him something else when he spoke again.

"I'm sorry, Madam President; it seems I have an urgent conference call that I must take. I will be in touch with you later. Goodbye." The phone went dead, and Missy Snow promptly forgot what it was that she was going to ask Simon, but then, that seemed to be happening a lot these days. No matter, must not be important, she concluded.

Dominus met with Len Striker to go over Len's plans in late November. "Hey Boss," Len looked up, as Dominus entered the office that Len had confiscated for his use. "Hey, I came across those girl's birthdays. Do you realize that you don't need to wait til June to grab them? You can strike them both as early as April, if you want." Dominus grinned; in fact, he might just do that. Oh the pleasure that would give him.

"Thanks, good idea. Now let's go over the plans one more time. Absolutely nothing must go wrong this time. Is the warehouse in Montrose all setup and ready to go?" Dominus inquired.

"Yes, the ring making machinery has been scrapped, and the place cleaned up, ready for our use. Honestly, it makes a really good meeting place for a hundred of us at a time," Len relished being able to give Dominus good news for a change. "Now about the plan. I've tested it out on a mockup of the place. Two minutes is all that it will take. Let me show you." Len re-conjured his demonstration buildings, here inside the mammoth warehouse. Dominus followed Len through the steps. Indeed, two minutes tops would be needed. He gave his okay to Len to proceed as planned.

Chapter 12—The Worst Christmas Ever

At last, the school bus materialized at the Compton ranch, parking before the long front porch with three main entrances. Snow was several inches deep, and footprints tracked in all directions, but more so to and from the barn. Under the watchful eyes of the seven Security men, Jim included, the teens cast their Move Object spells to unload their many duffle bags directly into their rooms or by the teleport pad, in the case of the Whitewater group. Then, they all headed inside where many had gathered to welcome them home for the holidays.

Jonathon was now a walking, talking, mischievous boy, and he dashed to his two sisters, hanging on to their jeans, demanding attention. After numerous hugs and kisses, Lindsey picked him up, much to his pleasure. "So you want to play, eh. How about I tickle you?" He giggled and protested, but wanted her to do it anyway. She was home, and it felt good just to relax. Lindsey hadn't realized just how much her attention had been locked onto the advanced magical studies until she dropped everything to just tickle her little brother.

"If I hurry up, I might be able to get the school newspaper edited and out before Christmas," Ashley explained to her mother and father. "Really, this sixth year is something else! We've never been so busy before."

Pam told her mom, "I'm a failure. I am getting a B in English. It's those darn poem things. I very nearly flunked the test. Only the essays kept me from a dismal failure. I'm sorry mom. Do you think dad will forgive me?" she asked mournfully.

Polly chuckled, "Dear, a B is hardly failing. Besides, honey, it's magic that is important, not poems. I never got on well with them either."

"You didn't?" Pam asked, as if she had just had a startling, major revelation about her mother. The two moved into the kitchen, and Lindsey couldn't catch the rest of their conversation.

Lloyd asked her, "So, are you picking up the good spells now dear?"

"Wow! You bet, great ones, though none of us is going after the Restricted Wish spell, except Peaches and Andy. They wished they would be able to learn another spell that they really wanted. I think that is silly of them. I would have waited and seen if I could have learned it in the first place. If not, then is the time to waste a Wish spell," Lindsey chatted away, while not ignoring Jonathon.

"I put your postcards on my wall. Wanna see, Lindsey?" She found herself being pulled to his bedroom. Indeed, he had taped all the cards that she and Ashley had been sending him onto his wall. There were quite a few of them now.

"Are you going to get me a Christmas present? I want a Fisher red wagon so I can help mommy in the gardens, bringing her things and bringing tomatoes back to the house," he explained.

"We'll have to see. That sounds like a good present to get. Say, are you getting me anything?" she asked.

His eyes lit up, "Yes, I got you —." His hands slapped his mouth shut. He pealed his little hands back and said, "I'm not supposed to tell you. It a secret!" Lindsey giggled and chased him around his room. "Wanna play ball? Wanna play in the snow? Pull me on my sled, please?" he begged. Lindsey realized it would be a full time job keeping up with him now!

"Let me unpack my stuff and then we can play, okay?" He agreed, but followed her into her room to watch, ready to play the second that she finished. A short while later, Lindsey found herself outside pulling Jonathon around the barnyard on his small sleigh. Only by promising him a cup of hot cocoa could she finally coax him back inside.

At supper, Lindsey showed her mom her engagement ring, and they chatted for quite some time. Meanwhile, Ashley was on Jonathon duty. Only when Lena took him for his bath and then to tuck him into bed did the others get a chance to chat seriously. Wilma, Monane, Lloyd, Fred, Jim, and Polly quizzed the four teens on what they had learned this fall term. Jim had a good idea of what they had done, but not the details. Besides, Governor Alister had altered the program with the addition of Spell Research II from when Jim did his sixth year. All the adults gave them some advice for the spring, since this would be the primary opportunity in their lives to learn the top spells, if they could do so.

As Lindsey and Ashley prepared for bed, Ashley commented, “Well, this spring is going to be vitally important to us all. I never knew why the sixth years were so darn busy, but now I know. I guess we should enjoy our vacation before we go back and work harder than we have ever worked before.”

“No kidding. I never knew it would be this intense. Say, we’d better get our Christmas presents ordered soon. It sure will be nice to be able to go shopping again. We don’t dare ask the adults to take us shopping. They have too much work to do,” Lindsey replied.

The Monday before Christmas, Audrey was carving a duck, while Fern was working on her fawn. “Ouch, darn it. I cut myself. This is not a good day. I have a very bad feeling about today. Something is not right,” Audrey commented.

“Let’s see,” Fern asked, very concerned. “Come on. I’ll help you get it fixed up. It’s only a little one.” The two headed for the bathroom, but met Ashley and Jonathon running around playing tag.

“Audrey cut her finger,” Fern pronounced. “She says it is a bad day.”

“Not exactly. Ashley, I have a bad feeling about today. It wasn’t there when I got up, but it sure is now. Can you sense anything? Maybe we should turn on the TV. Fred usually notifies us if something is happening that we ought to know about, though,” Audrey stated in a most worrisome manner, almost begging Ashley.

Pam came out of her room where she was surfing the

Net, wondering what she should be doing. "Are you okay, Audrey? I feel kind of funny too."

"Okay, so do I," Ashley admitted. "Here, you play tag with Jonathon, and I'll see if I can pick up anything. Fern, you and Audrey go check out MAG News when you get it bandaged up." She headed for her bedroom and laid down on her bed.

Ashley quickly let go of all her thoughts and expanded her consciousness. This was she used to pick up general things, general emotions—ones that were so strong they pervaded the world. If she had a specific person in mind, she would use a more direct approach to her divination. Time passed, though she was not conscious of it. There was a very strong, powerful emotion out there. She homed in on the source and then let out a yell as she recognized who it was! Ashley wanted to jump up and yell her warning to everyone, but steeled herself to divine instead, picking up all the key information that she could, before she sounded the alarm.

All the teens heard her scream, however. Lindsey knew well what that meant, and she came running to their bedroom, the others right behind her. Ashley was white, grief swamped all other facial characteristics, but she was still concentrating, divining. Lindsey motioned for quiet, and they waited, growing more and more worried with each passing second, which seemed like hours. At last, Ashley opened her eyes, but she was balling.

"It's Alister! He's been captured and killed. Alister—he's dead! Dominus has just killed Alister!"

Polly heard the commotion and had run to the room.

Standing in the doorway, she heard Ashley's cries. "Okay, Ashley, what can you tell us? Where is he right now? At the school? Pam, start Messaging everyone."

"No, they took him from the school a short while ago. His body is in some big warehouse somewhere. I can't tell where. No one is saying its name. He's lying there on the floor, dead. Now no one else is around. He's dead! They killed Alister!" Ashley succumbed and began crying again. Lindsey found her own eyes watering so badly that she couldn't see, and then realized she was crying as well. In fact, all the teens stood there stunned by the news. As the shock wore off, intense grief took its place, so much so that Pam could not even cast a single Message spell!

Polly did. Rapid fire, she shot off Message after Message. Before she even finished, Lloyd came racing inside. R. B. and Monane came darting off the teleport pad, followed closely by the teens from the Whitewater ranch. Wilma came out of the shower, a towel wrapped around her head. Jim dashed inside; he was chatting with the Security men standing guard outside the ranch home. Ashley was in no condition to tell them; Polly hastily repeated what Ashley had divined, after Audrey's warning.

"Oh dear god!" exclaimed Wilma.

"Not Alister! This is bad!" exclaimed Monane.

"We must get to him pronto," R. B. added. "There might be some chance that we can revive him. Monane, Amanda, to the Tracking. We know it is a warehouse and that they began their trip at Bradbury's. See if you can pick up the trail."

"We're on it," Monane replied, taking Amanda aside, who was about to break down from the shock of the horrid news. By making Amanda begin to trace the magical energies left by the many Death Stalker spells, Monane hoped to keep the surging grief in Amanda at bay, so that she could function. Ashley was now a basket case. While they were concentrating on picking up the trail, many others began arriving, so many so fast that the monotone voice, which announced the arrivals, could not keep up. Deiter, Kathy, Emilio raced in almost simultaneously with Tom Ryker. Not long after that, half of the faculty of Bradbury's came.

Professor Cho Lin's face was taut and her whole body tense. "He's gone, left his tea partially drunk, his roll half eaten. Is he really dead? How did Dominus break our school's security? Where is he at? Why?" Huan Su put his arm around her; her hand reflexively grasped his. Polly repeated what Ashley had discovered after Audrey's warning.

Meanwhile, Deiter got the girls propped up a little, "Okay, get some warm clothes on and grab your Staves of Power. We are going after him just as soon as the Trackers have located him. Get cracking, Lindsey. We need you if the Death Stalkers are still around. Come on, get moving." Mechanically, the girls obeyed, throwing on some heavier coats and fetching their staves. Meanwhile, the adults also began preparations.

"We have his location. It is west of Denver. Come on! Let's Teleport to Denver and take another reading," Monane called out, as she and Amanda joined the others. "It is a trail that a blind man can follow! Must be close to fifty Death Stalkers came to the school and took him away. Everyone ready? Teleport to Denver Airport." Almost at once, dozens of wands flashed, and the large group vanished from the Compton ranch.

At the airport, Monane and Amanda picked up the trial once more. It led still westward. Amanda guessed Montrose might be a likely next hop, and a minute later, the group began appearing in the snow-covered city park. "We are really close now! It's in this town. Fly!" her wand activated, and quickly the others followed her. Monane carefully allowed Amanda to take the lead, though she verified every twist and turn that Amanda took. Amanda simply followed the intertwined mass of Teleport spell energy trails left by at least fifty Death Stalkers.

She soared down to the abandoned warehouse where the Dominus for President gold rings had been manufactured. The Rodents had long ago searched this building, but found it abandoned and empty. Wilma took charge now, carefully opening the door. The other adults, led by Delius Dogs followed right behind her, the teens brought up the rear.

"Wow, this place has been stripped!" Lindsey whispered to Deiter, as her eyes looked around and found that all the equipment she had seen in here before was now gone, leaving a huge empty shell of a building, several hundred feet across.

"He's over here!" Wilma's voice called out. Everyone ran after her. Nothing could have prepared the teens for what they saw next. There lying on the floor was their beloved

Governor Alister. A large bullet hole lay in the middle of his forehead. He had been shot with a gun, a normal's gun, not wizard spells! The back of his head was gone, splattered across the floor of the huge room behind his body. He lay on his back in his pajamas; his loafers were still on his feet, as if they had taken him while he was just getting up in the morning.

The adults attempted to shield the teens from the ghastly sight, but were too late. They all saw him lying there. R. B. examined him and rose, tears streaming down the old Indian's face. "He's gone. Nothing we can do for him now but take his body back home." Lindsey began crying, her grief flooding over her. Many of the teens were likewise overcome with grief, unable to function at the moment. Lindsey felt like a zombie, as Delius cast his Teleport spell, taking her and Pam with him back to Bradbury's Infirmary. Likewise, other adults brought the other teens with them, unwilling to trust their casting skills just now. R. B. brought his lifetime friend's body back and laid him on Doctor Caterwall's emergency table, as the good doctor, teary-eyed, examined the body. He shook his head, but they all knew what he meant. There was nothing that he could do. Alister was gone.

Delius spoke very softly, "Cho Lin, you should do a thorough search of his office. See if anything is missing. It is likely that Dominus stole one or more things when he took Alister. Janice, take the kids to the dining hall and somehow get them calmed down, please. Arthur, Jerry, Blake, Huan Su, you are with me. We must go over every inch of the school and check every security measure. We must make sure all the protections are back in place, if they are gone. Doctor," he nodded to Frank.

"I'll go with Janice and help her with the students," the doctor said softly. "Nothing I can do here." Lindsey had no idea how she ended up in the dining room. Someone pushed a mug in front of her and said to drink. She didn't feel like drinking, but her body mechanically obeyed. Soon, she began to relax. Her muscles eased their taught tension; her mind calmed, as the potion worked its calming magic.

How much time had passed, she had no idea. Lindsey looked around. There were all the familiar faces, all but one. No Alister. Her mind tried to grasp that there never would be Alister again to sooth her, to help her, to guide her, and to aid her. She realized how much she loved the old man—how much she really had depended upon him, but she was now at least calm.

Other professors now joined them, pink from the cold. They had traversed the entire perimeter of the school, wading through the deep snow. "All protections are in place. Nothing has been disturbed," Delius explained. "I don't understand how the Death Stalkers and Dominus could have possibly gotten through all these protections!"

Cho Lin's Magical Door opened, and she stepped into the dining room, her complexion white as snow. "Nothing has been stolen as far as I can tell. I found this, a note from Alister."

Professor Herbert came running into the room. "You have to see the surveillance video!" Huan Su Summoned a player and TV. Herbert inserted the disk, and everyone stared at the screen. Pam never realized before that there were security cameras around the main gates. Everyone entering or leaving was captured on camera!

Professor Herbert had positioned the feed to the right spot. As they all watched, they were shocked to see Ashley and Lindsey walking up to the gates! "But that's not us! We were at home! Honestly, we were!" Lindsey fairly screamed in protest.

"We know, Lindsey, we know," Cho Lin spoke softly, but not taking her eyes off the screen. Shortly, the gates opened, but the two girls seemed to pause overly long, holding the massive gates open. "They must be allowing others to enter," Cho Lin spoke what many were thinking. "There, a foot print in the snow just appeared! They are letting a whole bunch in!" Then they passed beyond the camera.

"Keep watching," the old man spoke. Herbert now seemed very old to Lindsey. "There's more." Less than two minutes later, Dominus appeared on the screen, leading Alister beside him, followed by dozens of Death Stalkers. Lindsey recognized Len Striker, but Pam recognized at least thirteen immediately. They figured prominently in her database of Death Stalkers and their crimes. Then, the screen image returned to merely that of the gate area. Professor Herbert turned it off. "Apparently, he didn't offer a fight. By all appearance, he went quietly to his death. I do not understand what I have just seen."

"I—I found this letter on his desk," Cho Lin spoke, her voice trembling. She read it aloud.

If you find this, know then that I was right in predicting my own death at the hands of Dominus. For some time now, I have known that it cannot end in any other way. I have been the instigator behind all resistance to his Golden Path. Inevitably, he will discover this truth and have no choice but to kill me. My affairs are in order. Professor Cho Lin will be assuming the daily duties of running the school. She is more than able to do an excellent job. Please back her fully. More importantly, do not seek revenge. Please my dear young friends, do not rush to stop Dominus. You must finish your education first. That is my last, dying wish, for you all to finish your education. Cho Lin, you will find my papers in file forty-two.

Goodbye my dear, dear friends.

Alister Broadwell.

"He knew about this all along and didn't tell us or try to stop it?" Lindsey wailed, her grief once more flooding over her.

An unexpected voice broke the sobbing of many gathered in the dining room. Doctor Caterwall spoke softly. "I'm now free to tell you all what Alister swore me to secrecy. Alister was dying anyway. He had at most another three months to live."

"What? You couldn't cure him?" shrieked Professor Cho Lin, suddenly very angry with the doctor.

"No, there are limits on magical healing and even more limits on normal healing methods, I am truly sad to say. Some months ago, I discovered an inoperable tumor growing inside of his head. To operate using normal's methods would have resulted in his death. Yes, he and I tried all manner of magical healing methods over these past months, but none had the slightest effect on his tumor, which just kept growing. We kept this information from all of you. He didn't want his illness to interfere with the students and their education or with you faculty. However, had he not been murdered today, you would have begun to suspect something by the time you came back from vacation, slurring of speech, misfiring spells, perhaps even involuntary muscle reactions. I had his agreement to notify you when he reached that point. So it looks like Dominus really did him a favor. The next three months or so would have been unbearable for us all—to watch him slowly succumb to the tumor. It is perhaps a real blessing in disguise. Oh, Cho Lin, he wishes his body to be cremated and his ashes spread over our grounds. I believe you will find those instructions among his papers that he mentioned."

This news startled everyone. "I didn't know," muttered Delius. "I just didn't see."

"None of us did, Delius; you can't blame yourself," Cho Lin consoled him.

He sighed. "Okay, I will take it upon myself to notify the governors and those in the States Justice departments. I will also let Erin know as well, Cho Lin."

"Thank you. I'll have my hands full with the school's affairs. We can be thankful that all the protections are still in place. We're going to need to conduct a funeral very soon. Huan Su and I will make the arrangements, but I believe that only his closest friends should attend that. I propose we hold a wake in his honor afterwards, in which as many who would like to show their last respects can do so. I suspect the turn out for that will be rather large indeed, straining our security to its limits."

Delius spoke up, "Cho Lin, I know among the rest of us, you are the only one who can cast Make Permanent, which is the keystone to all of our protections here at the school. I'm very concerned that all this now lies only in your hands. Before, Alister did cast that spell as often as needed, and you were his back up. You must not take any undo chances whatsoever or our school may be unsafe for the thousand students."

Lindsey decided to speak up, "Professors, Cho Lin isn't the only one who can cast Make Permanent." Suddenly, all eyes looked at her bloodshot eyes. Utter silence filled the room. "Some of us also can and have cast it. We learned how from R. B. when we were building our extra houses last summer. I can cast it, as can Deiter, Pam, Ashley, and Amanda. If you need it cast, ask one of us, we all want to help anyway we can."

"What? That is a Grade 8 spell! We haven't yet covered any of those spells," Professor Arthur exclaimed, completely shocked.

"I will vouch for them. I taught them that spell last summer to thank them for all their help in building the many new homes on both our ranches," R. B. spoke up. "I know that it is surprising. It shocked me. I talked at length to Alister about this most unusual situation."

"Why doesn't this surprise me?" Cho Lin attempted a little humor, wiping her eyes. "Lindsey, Pam, Deiter, Ashley, Amanda, I will be sure to call upon you if I need assistance with this spell. I will also make sure that all the other faculty here knows about this, and if needed, they will call upon you as well. Thank you all for volunteering. The safety of our students here is our prime concern."

Lindsey saw Delius staring wide-eyed at the five of them. She sensed envy coming from him, tantamount almost to jealousy. He couldn't cast this spell, though not for having tried on numerous occasions. Quickly that emotion vanished, however.

Professor Janice finally spoke up, surprising Lindsey. "Cho Lin, all the students should be notified personally by us before they hear about it on the news. We owe them that courtesy, don't you think?"

"Yes, Janice, you are ahead of me again. Would you please see to it? I'm going to need a lot of help and support. Running this school is a full time job, and I already have a full time job teaching. All help is most welcome. Somehow, we will get through this spring term, somehow," Cho Lin said, though she was not very convincing just now—her grief and shock all too real.

Jim then offered, "I'll gather the data necessary to document this crime and present it to the legal department. We should hold his cremation as soon as possible, right doctor?"

"Yes, son. I know that he only has one living relative, a

brother Ashton. Lives in Maine, I think. They're not close. I haven't seen him in several years, though I believe Alister goes to visit him sometimes during the summer for a week or so," Doctor Caterwall replied.

"Okay, will this evening be acceptable to everyone, assuming that I can get a hold of his brother?" Cho Lin asked. Both Jim and Frank agreed. "Now then, I believe that we should take these students back to their home and set to work on making all the arrangements. Kids, we will keep you informed of any developments. Unless you hear otherwise, we will all gather here tonight at say seven to conduct his funeral and spread his ashes."

Two minutes later, the teens arrived on Lindsey's front porch. Jim led the party inside. Wilma and Monane stayed behind to help Cho Lin and the faculty with the many arrangements. R. B. returned with them and was the last to enter Lindsey's home. Of course, everyone else had congregated there; the living room was full. The smell of coffee, tea, and cocoa filled the air. Lindsey nodded to the others and sank onto the sofa. Pam and Ashley followed suit; all were devastated.

Quietly, R. B. filled Luci, the Hamiltons, and all the others in on what had happened—all that they had learned, though he did not describe the awful scene there on the warehouse floor, merely that he had been shot in the head. Many sobbed as they heard the news, though.

"Why didn't he tell us? Why didn't he say something about it to us?" Lindsey wailed. "We could have been there for him."

Her answer came from her father, "Lindsey, think about his situation for a moment. He knew his days were numbered. There wouldn't have been anything you or anyone else could have done for him. What would have happened if he had told you or all the others? Wouldn't you have spent lots of your time trying to comfort him, looking valiantly everywhere for a cure?"

"Well, yes, of course," she bawled. Red-eyed Ashley nodded that she would. Pam was too grief stricken even to cry anymore. She sat there like a dead statue.

"Precisely his point," Lloyd said softly. "That would have taken away much of the time that you needed to learn and research all the powerful spells that you all can now do, now wouldn't it? He knows as well as all of us here just how vitally important it is for you teens to get through your last year. The spells you will be learning may well be the spells that finally bring Dominus down and put an end to this reign of terror. I know that was uppermost in Alister's mind."

He continued, "He, like many of us adults here, know that it will be you teens, the Rodents, that have any chance of bring Dominus to justice. You have skills, Lindsey, as do your friends, which in all likelihood a wizard or witch has never had before, skills, which when perfected, stand a good chance of stopping Dominus. To Alister, this is what is and was important. He served a cause far greater than himself. He was serving all mankind—all of you, Lindsey. He is living proof that there is more to life than just oneself: your family, your groups, mankind, plants, animals, the physical universe. Dominus is working only for his own self. Alister worked for all the rest of them, and I know that he went with no regrets, no self-recriminations—no 'I wish I had done this instead.' He knew that his friends would have wanted to and given anything to care for his needs, but that would have likely sacrificed all these other areas to serve only himself. That he could never do and be true to himself. Do you understand what I am trying to say?"

Lindsey nodded, but couldn't bring herself to speak. It was logical—deep down she knew this was what Alister intended, but her raw emotions, her intense sense of loss was still too great.

"But I want to go after Dominus now more than ever!" Deiter nearly screamed. "I swear that I'll make Dominus and his Death Stalkers pay, pay dearly, pay horribly for this. I do! I swear it!"

"We all share those feelings, Deiter. You are not alone," Wilma, who had just returned from the school, decided to intervene with her student, her budding Eliminator. "I know I certainly do. Now is not the time. That is where we have the advantage, Deiter. We have Audrey and Ashley on our side. One day, Deiter, they will finally tell us that 'now is the time.' Then, you and I and all the rest of the Rodents will act. We will get him, and he will be made to *pay* for his numerous crimes—he and all his followers. Just now, we owe it to Alister to morn his passing, for he was a dear, dear friend and companion to us all. Honor his memory now; work and study hard in the coming months; perfect your crafts, so when our Diviners tell us that 'now is the time,' we will be ready. I know that this is what Alister wanted the most—to have us all be ready when the time is right."

She went on, though she also stared at Pam, who was still frozen in shock. "Right now, we are all in shock and grief. This is a measure of just how much we all loved Alister Broadwell—how important a role he played in our lives and those of so many others these many years. Tonight we mourn, as in the days to come. In time, the grief will give way to anger, hostility, and antagonism towards Dominus and his vile men. Yet, we must resist those urges too, because in time those too will pass. Our minds and heads will clear. We will be able to think freely and act freely once more. Then, Deiter, then, we will be ready to strike back and obtain justice—justice for Alister and justice for the millions that he and his men have harmed."

The statue that was Pam slumped hard into a nearby chair, and she started crying harder than she had ever cried before. Tom put his arms around her, and she buried her head in his chest. Together they cried.

"I still swear," Deiter said quietly, but found his arms holding Lindsey tightly, though he didn't remember doing it.

Just then, Tom and Sandy Whitewater arrived from college in Denver, their eyes red from crying. "We heard; came at once," Tom said. "How's everyone holding up?" He fought back his grief valiantly. Luci hugged her daughter-in-law; Sandy laid her head on her shoulders.

"Mostly," Jim managed to answer his brother. "Glad you're here, Tom." Amanda and Fern, both still crying, mobbed their older brother, hanging on to him for dear life.

Jim, while comforting Ashley, explained to Tom and Sandy all the news, particularly about the tumor. No sooner had he finished than the monotone voice announced, "The Blackburns are arriving."

Sure enough, the entire Blackburn family stepped through the doorway, Doctor Henry Blackburn, his wife Lottie, and daughters Monique and Ellie. Both of his daughters were hysterically crying, totally out of control. They were from Red Hall, where emotions rule.

Lloyd welcomed them and found some chairs for the four. Jim once more explained everything to them, and Henry was most appreciative of this kindness. Pam saw her former dearest friend and one time love, and finally pulled herself out of her fit of crying. She had not seen Monique for nearly two years now. Memories came flooding back to her. Pam got up and pulled Tom with her, as she walked over to Monique who was bawling out of control. She still looked positively gorgeous, though her makeup was now a complete mess.

"Monique!" Pam said, sniffing her nose, wishing she had a handkerchief. To her surprise, Monique rose and grabbed a hold of her, hugging her tightly, almost like vice gripping arms.

"Pam! Pam! How I've missed you! Horrible! So horrible! I can't stand it. Alister!" she wailed on and on, totally out of control. Pam sympathized with her, but soon realized that indeed Monique had gone off the deep end, so to speak; she was being carried away by her emotions.

"Red Hall," she whispered to Tom and then cast her Calm spell. At once, Monique's wild crying began to die down. Tom grinned at Pam, knowing what she had done and why. "There, there, Monique. That's better."

"I feel so awful. I really loved Governor Alister. He was the greatest, you know. Who's this?" Monique finally noticed that Tom was standing there too, one arm around Pam and one around her, helping steady her.

Pam grinned, slightly embarrassed. "Her fiancé," Tom replied. "I don't know if she has had the time to tell you about us or not. We are going to get married once we graduate. Pam has told me a little about you. Studying to be a doctor?"

"Pam! Pam! Oh, I wish you had told me sooner! This is incredibly good news. You don't know how worried I was about you! Say, what a coincidence, Pam. Ace has just proposed to me. Ace Brill and I are going to wed as soon as I graduate later this summer! He's with the States Justice Department of Defense for all Colorado. Say, your Tom's cute, Pam," Monique finally got her attention back onto her present surroundings.

Tom flushed. He now knew precisely what Pam had meant when she said that Monique was gorgeous. She was that and more. Pam said, "Congratulations on both—becoming a doctor and getting married. I kind of thought that Ace had fallen for you at the Inaugural Ball. I was right, wasn't I?"

Monique blushed and replied, "Pam, when have you

ever not been right?" Both girls managed a little giggle.

"Come on. Let's get you to the bathroom. Your mascara is a total wipe out," Pam suggested. Reluctantly, Tom let go of both girls, and Pam led Monique down the long hall to one of the many restrooms, though the older girl still knew the way. Memories, fond memories, came sweeping back over Monique's mind, memories of when she lived here with Pam before she graduated and went off to magical medical school.

In the bathroom, Monique began to clean herself up. "I know now that I must have hurt you terribly, Pam. Can you ever forgive me?"

"Of course, Monique. I'm so glad that you found the right fellow too. Have you set your day yet? We haven't. This Dominus business is messing everything up, you know."

"Thank you, thank you Pam. Say, how did you meet Tom? He is rather cute isn't he?"

"At the Inaugural Ball. You were so into Ace that you didn't see me dancing with Tom all night. We hit it off well. He's deep into computers, you know, deeper than we are. You've chatted with him before in the Voodoo Underground."

"What? Really? Does he know who I am there?" Monique asked, suddenly becoming very curious indeed. Pam explained in detail, while Monique kept saying "Oh wow!" over and over, very much impressed with Pam's fiancé. The huge upset between Pam and Monique evaporated into the past.

When the two girls rejoined Tom and the crowd a bit later, Monique once more looked like the stunning Red Hall graduate beauty that Pam had known. Tom was quite impressed, even more so when he found out that he had often chatted with her in the Underground chat room. The two friends had a lot of catching up to do and took this opportunity to chat like mad.

Chapter 13—The Death of Alister Broadwell

"Ah, come in Dominus. I have been expecting you," Governor Alister said calmly, putting down his morning newspaper and partially eaten roll. "Have a seat."

Lindsey and Ashley had just walked into his office. Minutes before, they had buzzed him from the main gates of Arthur Bradbury's School of Magic, and he had let them in.

Dominus was startled. How had he seen through this Morph disguise? Had the Stokes teen divined this attack? Lindsey's eyes darted around the room, half expecting that he'd walked into a trap. Seeing nothing unusual, he canceled his spell. The form of Lindsey morphed back into that of Dominus Malefic. Beside him, Ashley turned back into the Death Stalker, Len Striker. Both had their wands pointing at Alister.

"Ah, much better, Dominus. Have you come to your senses and wish to surrender to me now?" Alister said calmly, trying to hide the slight involuntary twitch in his left arm. The tumor must be acting up this morning, he thought.

"What? Are you completely mad? No, I've come to stop your infernal meddling in my Golden Path. Take him boys!" Dozens of Invisibility spells cancelled, and many Death Stalkers were now in the room, all pointing their wands at

Alister. "You will come with us. We don't want to kill you here—think of the students," Dominus sneered, already regretting that he had agreed to the outright killing of his archenemy. Yet it had to be done. There was no time to play around with torture. Any second now, the pesky teens might divine what was happening and bring a large force to rescue him.

"As you wish, Dominus." Alister rose and decided to hold his left arm with his right, disguising it further. He didn't attempt to reach for his wand lying on his desk. Dominus watched for that, as did dozens of other eyes. Calmly, he walked out of his office for the last time, through a Magical Door to the main gates and then out into the parking lot. At once, over fifty Teleport spells activated, and he found himself inside a huge, but empty, warehouse, which he thought he recognized, though it had been altered significantly since he had visited here last year.

Dominus pulled out a 45 caliber gun. "Any last words? I'm afraid this must be done quickly."

"Dominus, do not do this. You have made many, many errors in your career, but shooting me here will be your greatest mistake ever. I wish you would take my advice and not make a blunder of this magnitude," Alister spoke calmly, though he had no way to know that those would be the last words that his body would speak.

Bang! The gun discharged, the bullet pierced his forehead. His body died instantly. Dominus watched as his long-time enemy slumped to the ground. What had he meant about his greatest mistake ever? Suddenly, Dominus felt that surge of fear, which he hated more than anything.

"Boss, we have to get out of here immediately. Who knows how long it will be before they discover what we've done and send in an army of wizards," Len urged Dominus, who stood motionless, staring at the lifeless body on the concrete floor. "Come on," Len pulled at the sleeves of his jacket. Reluctantly, Dominus obeyed. Over fifty Teleport spells activated. The next second, the warehouse was empty of all life. The dead body of Governor Alister Broadwell lay in the center of the huge, empty space.

Chapter 14—The Funeral

At seven, the large group gathered at the Compton ranch Teleported to the gates of Bradbury's. The main gates were open, and they all filed through and followed the simple signposts that had been conjured up to point the way. Out on the snow-covered lawn between the swimming pool and the pentagram dorm many, many close friends were now gathering.

Lindsey noticed that the staff had cleared a large area, piling the foot-deep snow in giant mounds around the open area, revealing brown tufts of grass. A newly constructed pyre stood in the center of this large square. Professor Blake had conjured a ten-foot tall golden pyre. The body of Alister Broadwell lay on top. Lindsey saw that they had dressed him in his finest suit, the one he always wore for the opening of each school fall term.

Over a hundred people gathered within this open, cleared area, all somber or crying softly to themselves. Yes, it was cold, and a light snow had begun falling, but no one really noticed either. When no more arrived for several minutes, Professor Cho Lin Sung Levitated to the top of the golden pyre. Using the Magnify spell that Professor Blake used to announce the track and soccer meets, she began speaking to the assembled, grieving friends.

"It is with the saddest of hearts that I must make this

my first official act as acting Governor. Thank you all for coming. I know your presence is a comfort to Alister. Be it officially known that we are following his last request to the letter. That said, I would like to offer a few words of my own. Yes, I know we will be holding a large public wake in his honor on Christmas Eve here at the school. Yet, I want to say these things before all of you—we who were his family. Alister never married; he devoted his life to the many young wizards and witches who came through this school."

"Alister was one of those rare people who touched so many, many lives. Many of us here tonight owe him a debt that we can never repay. It is said that wisdom comes with age. Alister, though not that old, has proven that adage false. His long reign as Governor here at Bradbury's is packed with untold wisdom. Time and time again, he has proven to all that he was not only wise, but perhaps the most able wizard this world has seen in decades."

"Alister had the uncanny knack to see the true potential within people and students. He never failed to nurture his students to achieve their full potential. This, we faculty have seen repeatedly through the many years of his service. Alister was one to stand behind you all the way. Yet he had that rare ability to stand back and allow students to do it for themselves, lending a hand only when actually needed. So many of us cannot resist jumping right in and helping because we know what must be done. But Alister resisted those urges and allowed us to work our way through it and get the task accomplished ourselves, though he was not above giving us a hint along the way."

"Alister had a keen ability to see and recognize the true source of problems, of situations, and thus make them vanish, almost as if by magic. Yet, Alister was generous, generous beyond all measure. Often he assisted many of us with financial donations from his own pocket. In short, Alister Broadwell was a perfect gentleman and a dear, dear friend of mine and of yours."

"Now as we give him this final send off, Ahana is going to join me in song, while the men light the fire." Cho Lin cast her Gentle Fall and landed before the group. She joined Ahana off to one side and picked up her bagpipes. Until now, few knew that Cho Lin could play them. The nasal sounds from the pipes playing Amazing Grace filled the area, and then Ahana's young voice began to sing the words. Lindsey's eyes swelled with tears, dripping down her cheeks; most all were teary eyed before the music ended.

Shortly after the music began, standing in the shape of a pentagram, Professors Huan Su, Delius, Jerry, Arthur, and Blake cast their Ball of Fire spells onto the golden pyre, where Alister's body lay. Evidently, they had also soaked his clothes with a flammable liquid, because it burst into flames. For the next several minutes, while the music and words floated over the group, the men continued to periodically and in synch with each other cast more Balls of Fire, their final salute to this great leader of their school.

When the music ended, everyone quietly headed for their homes, while the five men remained at their pentagram positions. They would see it through to the end and see that his ashes were scattered over this area. Come tomorrow, the field staff would put the thick layer of snow back over the ashes and ground. The pyre would be gone, just as Alister Broadwell was now gone.

The next day the teens sat around Lindsey's front room. The shock had worn off, and now they all felt so listless—the vigor gone. No holiday spirits were left. They were a somber bunch, though occasionally one would play with the ever-insistent Jonathon. Around ten Deiter arrived and things began to change.

"How are you holding up, Lindsey?" he asked, though he could well see that she was subdued and very quiet.

"He's gone, really, really gone," she lamented. "I never, ever thought anything would happen to him, not Alister." The others agreed with her.

"Me either. That got me to thinking, gang. I've been up all night thinking about the situation with Dominus."

That sparked Pam, who said caustically, "So you are planning to go after him soon and ignore what Alister wanted."

"Not soon. Not until we learn all that we can, and Audrey and Ashley tell us that it is time. No, I was thinking about just how we are going to capture him. Look, I've pumped Wilma about the details on how she and the Rat Pack caught him the last time. The situation now is very, very different. Look, when she got him, he always had his dozen Death Stalkers with him. Now, he has at least fifty that go with him wherever he goes. Plus, if he is out in public, President

Snow has Secret Service men also guarding him, to say nothing of other Federal Security forces."

"So?" Pam added caustically. Deiter ignored her attitude.

"So we cannot use the same methods that the Rat Pack used. That's what I am saying. It won't work a second time, not unless Lindsey here can cancel or absorb fifty plus spells at the same time."

"Not really, Deiter. I was hard pressed to just keep the many Disintegrate spells from activating. I had no time to do much else during that attack last spring," she replied.

"My point entirely. With fifty of them, we have to figure out a new way to get them. That's what I was up all night pondering."

"So pontificate us," Pam said sarcastically. She was really in the dumps. It was as if someone had ripped off a part of her.

"Look, we have a few weeks free time now. I think that we should at least read up on all the remaining spells that we are going to study this spring. Let's see if any one of these fits our needs. If so, I'm willing to learn the Restricted Wish spell and wish that we all could learn it."

Amanda cheered up, "Say, he's right. We should start planning. We must come up with something. Who knows when the right opportunity may come? We have to be ready, Rodents."

Pam smiled at last, "For once, you are right. We need a plan. Okay, count me in. Let's grab our stuff, meet back in here, and go over what's left for us to try to learn." The teens scrambled to fetch their additional spell books.

Soon Lindsey, Ashley, Pam, Audrey, Amanda, Ahana, Jim, and Deiter were scouring their books of top Grade spells. After some time, Deiter said, "Hey how about this one, Kill? That ought to do the trick. I wanted to capture him alive, but now I'll settle for Kill."

The spell looked promising. Pam flipped its description and began studying its details. She insisted on reading all the "fine print." A bit later, Pam shot his plan down. "Deiter, it says here that wizards who have mastered at least one Grade 7 spell are immune to the spell's effect. We probably could get some of the lesser henchmen, but probably not even one Death Stalker."

"Rats, it looked so hopeful," Deiter replied. "Thanks Pam." They all continued to read, suggesting all manner of wild scenarios in which they might be able to make use of one of these top level spells.

"Well, we could Blind him. There's no defense against that one," Deiter suggested.

"Yes, but then he is very likely to just Teleport away, Dispel it, and then Teleport back. It's not really going to stop him long enough for us to get our hands on him," Amanda countered. "Somehow, we have to be able to grab his body, hold on to it, and well, handcuff him or whatever."

"You're right," Deiter agreed and went back to looking at the spells, envisioning how he might get Dominus.

Sometime later, Lindsey asked about two more

possibilities. "Look there is the Prison spell and the Suspended Animation spells. The last one puts him into a state of suspended animation somehow and the other does the same, only he is in a prison somewhere under the ground. I don't quite see how that would be, though."

A bit later, as all read up on these two, Pam said, "Well, with both, you are going to have to touch Dominus. Undoubtedly, he has an In Case I Am Touched, then cast, well I don't know, Teleport somewhere. Besides, in a fight with fifty of them, how can you possibly get close enough to touch him? Remember their attack on us last spring? We held our ground, and they never got past Professor Janice even. While the results would be fine, I'm very dubious on just how you're going to touch him and what counter-spells he will have for that." Deiter sighed, another pair down the drain.

Close to suppertime, Deiter made another suggestion. "Hey, how about this scenario? I cast Stop Time. I know it is only for a brief few seconds, but then I get closer to Dominus and open fire with a normal's gun. See, he might have Skin of Stone on himself, so the first few bullets might bounce off him. But if I keep on shooting as fast as I can pull the trigger, sooner or later I will finally hit him, hopefully before time starts up again."

While no one could find any reason this would fail, no one really liked it either. What if he had other In Case I Get Hurt, then Teleport on him? The teens closed their books and moved them back into their rooms, as Polly called supper. Only one spell seemed at all workable, the full Wish spell. With that, the caster could capture him; this seemed the only real way to do it.

Plus they had in their possession the gift to Ashley from Erin Sacs, the Wish scroll. He had intended it to be used to save Ashley, but perhaps they could use it to get Dominus, which would be nearly the same thing, protecting Ashley from the clutches of Dominus. The whole bunch sat down to eat, convinced that the real answer did not lie in these more advanced spells. What had Alister in mind when he was so insistent that they continue their education? Did he think that one of them would be able to learn the full Wish spell? Lindsey began to think that must be what he had in mind when he wrote out his last notes to Cho Lin. What else could there be?

After dinner, Pam suggested, "I think that maybe what Alister had in mind was our searching for some Specialty area spells that might be useful in capturing Dominus. When we get back to school, I'll see what I can dig up." They all agreed with her; this must have been what he wanted them to pursue.

Jonathon kept the teens busy and off their sorrows. Actually, if it had not been for his continual cheerfulness and insistence that someone play with him "right now" and all day long, the teens would have spent their holiday moping about, constantly thinking about the loss of Governor Alister.

On Christmas Eve, the teens really wanted to go to the formal wake, but were not allowed. Professor Cho Lin carefully explained that much of the school's security measures would have to be lowered to accommodate the rather large number of people coming to pay their last respects to Alister. "I just cannot guarantee your security, Lindsey," she had said reluctantly. "However, for security reasons, we will be video record the entire affair. When you have some free time, you can watch a replay of it. That's the best I can offer."

Feeling perfectly miserable, the teens sat around the living room doing mostly nothing. "Say, who is going to be coordinating everything?" Pam suddenly realized the far-reaching impact of Alister's death. "I mean, he was working with all the western governors, probably with Erin Sacs, and who knows who else. Someone has to take over for him, don't they?"

"Yes, but who? Delius maybe," Deiter suggested.

"Yes, but they have a full time job teaching we students. Governor Alister had lots of free time, since he wasn't teaching," Pam pointed out.

"Mary Ann says I'm to relay any divinations to her. I suspect she will relay them to Erin," Ashley added, dolefully.

"It more like everything is going to fall apart," Audrey commented disheartened by it all. "I think I will go carve some more."

Lena could not help but see the state the teens were in as she passed by the room. "Say, why don't you all put your heads together and see if you can come up with some kind of permanent memorial to Governor Alister, a statue or a bust or something really nice."

"Thanks mom. That *is* a good idea. We *must* make some kind of memorial to him, if only to let future students know how important he was," Lindsey stated, becoming more alive once more. This was Lena's intention in making the suggestion from the sidelines. She left the teens chatting about what form the memorial would take.

Lloyd hoped that going to the Formal Dance and the live rock dance on the weekend after Christmas Day would bring the teens back to life. It didn't. While they were dancing, they at least forgot about their grief, but as soon as they returned home, uniformly they all just sat around and did pretty much nothing. Days before, they'd decided upon a life-sized bronze statue of Alister mounted on a marble base out in the middle of the grassy area, near where the funeral pyre had been.

On Sunday, Lloyd decided to take a more drastic action. "Okay, I have an announcement to make. Teens, I need your undivided attention, all of you—yes you too, Deiter, Tom, and Jim." Everyone looked at Lloyd; they were sitting around in the living room doing nothing in particular.

"Pack your bags. Tomorrow, we're all going to take a week's vacation. We're going to Tahiti! Deiter, Tom, your folks have given me permission to take you along, as well as Kathy and Emilio. Audrey, Fern, Orenda, yes, your boyfriends can come along too, only I'll need to contact their parents, if you want them to come."

"What? Tahiti?" Lindsey asked, suddenly becoming interested. She had never been there, though she knew that Tom and Sandy had honeymooned there.

Jonathon exclaimed, "I'm going to get to play on the sand at the beach! I bring my new diggers!"

"Don't forget to pack your swimsuits," Lloyd teased them. It worked. The teens got out of the doldrums. The tanned group returned in time to get ready to go back to school.

Chapter 15—Back to School Once Again

The Floor Monitors again got a workout as they unloaded the fully loaded buses. A blinding snowstorm only made matters more difficult. A very tired Pam, Fern, Lindsey, and Deiter finally got to sit down at suppertime. Pam's legs felt like they might fall off.

The Floor Monitors had also received orders from Cho Lin to watch the students carefully for any signs of depression over the death of Governor Alister. If they saw any signs, they were to report it directly to her. Lindsey figured that part of her new duties was to watch out for lingering aftereffects of his death on the many students. So far, they had not reported anyone because if she reported one, she'd have to report everyone in the school!

This first evening's meal was strained. It was Saturday night, Cho Lin wanted the students back a day early so that they could chat about his death and get comfortable at school once more and not waste an actual class day doing this. This was the first time that everyone in the school noticed Governor Alister's absence. He was not at his usual place at the faculty table and he was not there to give the opening welcoming remarks. This now fell to Professor Cho Lin.

"It is with a very sad heart that I welcome you all back

to Bradbury's for the spring term. All of us have experienced a great loss. We will all miss Governor Alister. However, his last wishes were that you students continue your studies of magic, and that's precisely what we are doing. Take a day to chat among yourselves, express your grief. On Monday, classes will resume as usual. I'm told by the other professors to expect the usual workload. No loafing this spring. Now let the banquet begin." She waved her wand, and the trays loaded with food began appearing over the many tables, slowly descending, while many hands began helping themselves.

On Monday, Lindsey began to realize just how valuable their schedule, their familiar routine, actually was. Almost at once, she was "back in the groove" of studying once more, much to her great relief. Maybe this was what Alister had in mind, not their learning of more spells, she theorized.

Professor Arthur Thornby granted the teens their request. At this point in Spell Research II, they were supposed to begin learning those Specialty spells that they wished. Pam pointed out that she and the others had not fully finished their search for spells. "Perhaps we have overlooked one that can be used to help capture Dominus," she argued successfully. Professor Arthur agreed to allow them another three weeks to research spells, before beginning to learn those that they wished. They scoured the library like never before, in search of new and unusual spells. During this time, Pam added another dozen spells to her database, spells that she had somehow overlooked.

However, when the three weeks were up, all were

dejected. They'd found no super spell that would be the answer for which they were looking. Now each began to make a list of which spells they wanted to attempt to master. Professor Arthur insisted on Okaying each list before they began, plus he needed to oversee and assist them. With all the strange and unusual spells, Pam realized that Professor Arthur was going to be run ragged trying to keep up with forty students all attempting vastly different spells!

When Lindsey reported to Professor Cho Lin on Monday for her elective Administration Management course, she received a bit of a surprise. "Lindsey, there's nothing like good practical experience. This term, as we study various principles, I'm going to have you help me with the related Bradbury tasks. The first one will be to set up all the students' next year's schedules. We put them into the computer database with several basic assumptions. First, we assume they will pass the courses they are now taking. Second, we assume they will be returning to Bradbury's next year. However, at the end of the term, we then go back and make a few corrections and additions, primarily those of electives. Let's get to work; there are a thousand students to handle."

Lindsey was excited about this. To her, the appearance of their next year's course schedule had always been a mystery. Now she was seeing how it was done by actually doing it. She launched herself eagerly into the project.

On that first Monday, Professor Mary Ann joined Professor Arthur to work with them on their last Grade 7 spell, See the Past. "This spell has put many private eyes out of work.

With it, you can get a vision of what has recently happened. For example, you come upon an unconscious woman. You cast the spell, and you may see what has happened to her. This spell is vital to those who wish to join the Department of Magical Misuse, as it is one of their key spells to determine if a misuse of magic has happened."

"Don't misunderstand me. It is not just visions of bad things that have happened. The spell shows you anything that has happened in the area of the casting. Now let's get to work on this one. No one is to cast this spell on the lawn where the funeral pyre was held. Detention for anyone who does." Lindsey wondered why anyone would want to revisit all that grief; she certainly didn't.

Ashley got this spell down perfectly within a matter of minutes. Everyone teased her, saying that as a Class 4 Diviner, she had an unfair advantage in learning this one. However, by the end of the week, well over half the class had it down perfect. Lindsey's entire group mastered it. Indeed, Pam was the second person to master it, claiming it would prove invaluable for a Sleuth.

The next week, Professor Arthur began having them work on the power spells of Grades 8 and 9. "Most of these spells will be beyond many of your reaches. Do not fret, worry, or think less of yourself because you fail to learn even one of these very advanced spells. These are most difficult spells. Even Dominus only knows a very few of these. The first pair that we will take up are the Dimensional Shift, used to enlarge a space beyond its real physical dimensions, and the Make

Permanent spell, which is used to make magical items by making permanent their magical enchantments." Many in the class responded with cheers, these were interesting spells indeed.

"Now there are several of you who already know these spells. I would ask that you practice your sans words, sans wand casting during this period when I am working with the others."

The next week, Professor Arthur explained, "I chose those two spells last week because nearly all students want to try to learn them. From now on, I will cover a spell and then ask for a show of hands of who desires to try to learn that spell. If no one does, we will move on to the next one. This will take about an hour to survey the Grade 8 spells. Once I know who wants to learn what, I will be working out a schedule so that I can assist you. This means that some of you will begin this three-hour period working on sans words, sans wand spell casting, and later on, working on one or more of these power spells. Now then, let's get going."

An hour later, most of Lindsey's group had decided to attempt to master the Crushing Fist, a variation on the Vice Hand spell, only this one crushed the recipient, causing great harm and pain. They chose to work on the Exploding Cloud, which was vastly more powerful, damage-wise, than their usual Ball of Fire. These, most thought, might be useful in combating a swarm of Death Stalkers. Finally, they chose to learn the Blind spell, primarily because Deiter thought that this might somehow be useful in capturing Dominus.

No one in the class chose to learn the Make Clone spell, which Lindsey now knew had been cast by Ross Mac Fluide to create the clone known as Dominus. Very few other students wanted to learn the Order spell, in which one could issue an order to someone else, and they would be compelled to carry it out. The same few, mostly from Black Hall, desired to know Charm the Masses, which did precisely that. Pam knew that some variant of this spell had been cast into all those rings, which Dominus handed out during his "run for President." Again, no one wanted to learn how to wipe out all of a person's memories; this was too terrible ever to use.

A couple weeks later, Lindsey's group had finally finished mastering the spells that they desired from this batch. Simultaneously, Peaches and Andy finally mastered the Restricted Wish spell. Of course, they got their wishes, to learn the spell that they most wanted to know. However, for the next couple of days after they successfully had cast it, everyone in the class covertly or overtly stared at them, looking for signs of aging. Peaches got very annoyed with classmates suggesting that an age line had appeared on her forehead. She insisted it had always been there.

In the middle of February, Professor Arthur did the same thing with the handful of Grade 9 spells. "Remember that these are not necessarily a grade above those in 8. There are no higher classifications, so they are all lumped together. Again, with many of these spells, if you are successful, you must register your skill in the National Database. If you learn the full Wish spell, for example, you must register or be instantly expelled, and your Professor will have to register you anyway. Now then, who wants to try to learn the Prison spell and the Suspended Animation spell?" He described both related spells. Naturally, Deiter wanted at least to try them. Likewise, they all decided to attempt to learn the Kill spell, though they all swore that they would only use it on the Death Stalkers and then only as a last resort. If successful, you had to register in the National Database.

Nearly all the class wanted to learn the Change Your Shape spell, which could be used to physically alter your own body into nearly any living creature. This was one of the two alteration based spells, and Lindsey's group easily mastered this one. Ashley suddenly appeared as a lion, startling the entire class. Deiter turned into a grizzly bear, causing even more of a disturbance. Lindsey changed into a farm cat, however, while Pam, a hawk. Amanda chose a wolf form for her first successful attempt.

The last three spells, everyone in the class wanted to try, although two already were doing the result of this spell innately: Have Foresight. Audrey and Ashley giggled; they had been doing this as long as they could remember. All wanted to be able to Stop Time, and of course, everyone was very curious about the full Wish spell.

This segment of their education ended with the close of March. Peaches actually mastered Have Foresight. None mastered the full Wish spell. Lindsey, Pam, Amanda, Ashley, and Deiter could all Stop Time, though they really were not sure if Deiter's idea of trying to gun down Dominus would actually work. Deiter and many Black Hall students mastered the Kill spell. None was girls, however. No one mastered the Prison or Suspended Animation spells.

"There is one final spell to try," Professor Arthur explained during their last session in March. "Governor Alister specifically requested that I put this Specialty spell from the Magical Healing area on our agenda. It is the Regenerate spell. With it properly cast upon someone, you can regenerate or regrow missing arms, legs, fingers, eyeballs and the like."

Lindsey smiled; it was almost as if Alister had put this spell here for her. She had inherited a Regeneration Ring from her father and had used it to regenerate Ashley's arms and those of a foreign exchange student. Now she would have the chance at least to study the spell, even if she could not master it. After the days of study were done, only Lindsey was able to cast this spell. She had to register her skill in the National Database. Inwardly, she thanked Governor Alister. She knew that he would have been most proud of her accomplishment.

Already, most of the class had given up on the sans wand, sans words type of casting, finding it next to impossible. The few that were being successful had pretty much attempted everything they already knew. It was now time to move into the desired Specialty spells arena. Because this whole class had taken a beating from the attacking group of Death Stalkers and their meat packing Slice spell last spring, the whole class wanted to learn this one!

Indeed, the days passed rapidly. These spells, for the most part, were easy to learn. Actually, the students were now fully competent wizards and witches, so these lesser, ungraded spells came easily to them, raising their morale considerably. All except Deiter, who continually complained that he was not learning anything useful to capture Dominus.

This, he continually confided in Lindsey and Pam, who also gradually became as worried as he. How were they ever going to capture him? Where was this all-powerful spell? At last, Deiter realized that he would actually have to invent something!

In their traditional courses, Pam finally gave up completely on deciphering poems. Rather, she did all three of the composition assignments instead of choosing one to do. She hoped that Professor Cho Lin would consider them, but finally resolved to take her first F grade gracefully.

In mid-March, both Emilio and Kathy shared the best news that they had ever had with respect to math. Both had finally gotten a perfect score on Beginning Calculus. All their confusions and difficulties with math up to now had been uncovered and cleared up. Both actually understood what they were doing. Further, Emilio was now getting an A his Business Math class. The two were elated over their victory. Pam vowed to find out Professor Herbert's secret formula before he retired.

Chapter 16—The Preparations

While the teens were spending every waking hour trying to master the most difficult spells, they were in effect insulated from the expanding chaos that was accompanying the expansion of the National Health Care Program. With their coordinator gone, that is, Alister Broadwell, the resistance members began to pilot their own courses. Inevitably, some worked at crossed purposes, sent mixed signals to each other, and no longer formed an effective team.

Under election pressures, many of the western governors began to explain why they had done what they had done. It was common knowledge now that Dominus had already figured out that their political move of seeming to back the President's program was merely a ploy, which in fact they were dead set against it in every possible way. One by one, all the governors at last publically revealed their true positions and stopped pretending to support the program.

Most continued openly to supply either funds or arms and munitions to any militia group who asked. Consensus was that these states would not go down without a fight to the death. The real question that arose in the early spring was whether to secede from the United States. On this, they could not agree. So many financial hurdles simply could not be crossed. Major companies owned and operated facilities in many states, including those already in the President's

Program. More than half of the governors viewed seceding to be the worst possible thing they could do, an action that would destroy their economies utterly.

Instead, they did agree on fighting to prevent the introduction of the President's Program in their states. Hence, they did everything possible to recruit more men and women into their State Guard forces, while backing and supplying every militia group they could find. The idea was to create a large enough force to prevent the US army from forcing entry into their state.

Meanwhile, the States Justice Department continued to attempt to bring order. The actual crime rates in these states continued its steady decline. That they would have to work and pay restitution to their victims or else starve to death in a cell continued to have an impact on some types of criminals. It had no affect whatsoever on the crimes associated with drugs, particularly those committed by drug users seeking to fund their addiction.

One small action did cause quite a stir in the legal system, however. The prisoners in the maximum security prisons refused to participate. Clever wardens secretly acquired some of the stolen Saude Dourada type A pills and fed them to these hardened criminals. After all, in New York all the prisons were now closed, and their inmates were now automatons dutifully working menial jobs. The wardens were amazed at the results, and the pill use at these prisons, right or wrong, escalated. Brazen criminals became polite automatons, eager to please and to work any kind of job for the lowest of pay and were happy to do so. This pleased those in charge of the penal system, and they backed it all the way. By April, the crime rates had plummeted to incredible lows; would be criminals thought long and hard before committing a crime, for who wanted to become an automaton? Only the drug addicted ignored all this, but they were ignoring life anyway.

Erin Sacs did not need Ashley to tell him where the pills were being produced after January. President Snow herself highly publicized this complete change in plans. The various governmental drug centers were being converted into facilities to mass-produce Saude Dourada. Complicating matters was the fact that many of these facilities resided in states not currently on the Program. Hence, President Snow issued orders to have the US military forces take over total control of these facilities, providing a very large garrison force at each facility. There would be no more destruction of pill processing plants, at least that was the idea behind this move.

New sets of problems developed immediately. Locals protested these companies. Any trucking firm making deliveries to these plants was attacked, and trucks were burned or heavily damaged. Snipers attempted to pick off workers going to work there or leaving. The violence only escalated until at last, President Snow ordered a total sealing of these vital pill production facilities. The workers were force to live in the plants! Either that or be shot for treason. Hearing rumors of this happening at other facilities where people simply vanished from sight, some abandoned everything, including houses and families and fled. Others who were force to work began doing little sabotages, such as an accidental spilling of the acid, which ruined an entire batch of a million pills.

Dominus cared little about all this. In fact, he paid almost no attention to it at all. He was back on his original Golden Path, his path to total rulership. He knew he didn't have to make the entire country into automatons. The states would finally resist, just as Massachusetts had done, playing right into his hands. The US military might would actually conquer the entire country for him, state by state. These local militias couldn't possibly stand against the highly trained and very well equipped soldiers. Plus, he now had the Air Force with its many drones to assist in the battles. They had not been available during the brief Massachusetts battles, but now he had their full support. Any militia would be wiped out in short order.

The elimination of Alister Broadwell had made this all possible. By spring, Dominus could easily see just how much that man had been coordinating the resistance to his Golden Path. Without him, all was crumbling and rapidly at that. Via President Snow, he had the military Generals draw up plans for the takeover of each state. The takeover order he left to their determination. Accordingly, in March, President Snow reported that they had decided that Virginia would be the next state brought into the National Health Care Program. The military forces were ready; troops moved into position; drones armed with deadly bombs—all waiting zero hour.

On the other hand, Erin Sacs and his band of wizards

and witches had not been idle. Once they were no longer needed to sabotage overseas plants, they returned in secret to the States. He knew well that his small band of two hundred could do little to stop these new federal facilities from producing the pills, thus he chose to intercept their deliveries. By raiding intermediate warehouses, he continued to confiscate large quantities of the pills. Indeed, he found all manner of people were very willing to share delivery information or warehouse locations or even suspicions of such to his forces.

However, as the date for the conversion of Virginia drew nearer, Erin decided to intervene. Along with many others, he was totally convinced that a major battle would be fought within the hills and mountains of this state. He sent out scouts into the Arlington and Alexandria areas just outside Washington DC. Scouts watched all major bridges across the Potomac River, including the greater Virginia Beach area.

Dozens of fired up militias from many of the western states also wanted action. Unwilling to sit and wait until the US military came to invade their states, these hotheads decided to make Virginia their battlefield. That the governor there put out daily pleas for military support from all who would help protect Virginia only flamed the fires of these militia men and women. They came by car, by trucks, and by chartered buses, entering Virginia via the safe routes through the Appalachian Mountains to the west of the state. All the motels of Richmond, Lynchburg, Petersburg, Charlottesville, and Roanoke were filled beyond capacity by those who had come to fight for Virginia.

Erin knew well that a massive slaughter was imminent. These militia men and women couldn't possibly stand against Big Red One, with the Air Force backing them. Erin Sacs faced the biggest decision of his life in mid-March. He longed to discuss this with Governor Alister. The ramifications of the decision he had to make were massive and might change forever the relationship between the wizarding world and the normals. Erin knew he couldn't make this decision on his own, but Alister was gone. To whom should he turn?

On March 31, the students of the Rodents Pack received a summons from Professor Delius: Report to the giant lecture hall in the Hall of Necromancy immediately. Delius, unlike Alister, preferred more direct orders. Lindsey and her friends dropped everything and via several Magic Door spells arrived in the hall. "Oh!" Lindsey involuntarily exclaimed as she stepped into the room. It was half-filled with adults, none wearing any disguises. She recognized Erin Sacs standing beside Delius Dogs at the front of the assemblage. Deluis stood tall; he was taking immense pride in his current role, she noted.

Pam recognized everyone the instant she arrived. "Oh my," she whispered. Amos Slaughter, the head of the States Justice Department sat in the front row, along with the three major department heads below him. There was Misty Wells, Security, Fred Angel, Law and Justice, and Casper Williams, Magical Misuse. She spotted some subordinates, those from individual state's departments. Ace Brill, Monique's fiancé and head of the Colorado Security Department, sat in the second row. Bill and Elaine Ryker, Tom's parents, and Kathy Jacks of the Arizona and Colorado Department of Law and Justice sat on either side of him. Her father, Fred Betts, Colorado Department of Magical Misuse sat beside Mary Hampton, the High Plains boss of Law and Justice. All told, forty men and women from these departments of the western states were present, but no governors.

Delius motioned for the teens to sit behind these powerful leaders, which they rapidly did. Pam waved to her father, however, and Tom did likewise to his folks, who smiled. Last to arrive were Jim, Wilma, and Monane. Only then did Delius finally speak.

"Thank you all for coming on such short notice. I have asked you all here because Erin Sacs must make a decision, perhaps the most critical decision any of us in the wizarding world has ever faced, since the decision to become public over a century ago." Delius relished the spotlight.

"I have some additional good news to present, once this monumental decision has been made. Erin, the floor is yours." He sat down beside the other professors. Lindsey noted that the normals were also present, professors Herbert and Jasper!

Erin stepped forward and conjured a map of Virginia. "As you are well aware, President Snow and Dominus are about to launch the takeover of Virginia, adding it to the states now under the National Health Care Program. The Governor of Virginia, Abe Smith, has made it very clear that his state does not want to participate. He has been making daily pleas via all major media outlets for militia assistance, and I quote, ‘I beg all red-blooded Americans to come and help us defend Virginia from our treasonous President Snow and the viciously evil wizard Dominus Malefic.’”

“I have many spies now located around Quantico and the DC area, where the US military is staging its army divisions. Others are watching the Appalachians, where truckloads of ill-equipped militia are arriving every hour. Heck, you can’t get a motel room anywhere in Virginia today—there are that many volunteer fighters there already.”

“I have uncovered some details of the military’s current plans. Once they have secured an area, then military trucks will bring in loads of the pills for those people. They will be unloaded at the different Health Care Centers and distribution will shortly thereafter begin. Well, that won’t happen. I am seeing to that one. I have a Destruction Squad ready to go. Once the pills are unloaded, these men and women will be Invisible, sneak into the building, cast the Time Delay Ball of Fire spell, activate an Illusion that will notify all those inside that building to evacuate in two minutes or be blown up, and then they are to Teleport to safety. Boom. There go the pills. We will be able to take down a dozen centers at one time.”

“But this is not why I have asked my good friend Delius to call this meeting. I face a decision that could only be answered by Alister himself. I sorely miss his council. I’ve decided that I cannot make this decision on my own. Far, far too much is at stake, far beyond this Dominus mess. Let me explain.”

"We are looking at the total slaughter of tens of thousands of Virginians and the group of 'want to help' militia men and women. Look, these rag tag volunteers are poorly armed, have no training, and poor, if any, leadership. Some are no more than street gangs, really. Facing off against the highly trained, superbly armed US Army, supported this time in full by the Air Force, they will be slaughtered to the last man! We are looking at the worst loss of life this country has seen since the Civil War centuries ago! Can you imagine the reaction of the rest of the country when they see and hear about the slaughter of hundreds of thousands in Virginia? I can foresee nothing but a brand new Civil War resulting. I know that the western Governors are this close to seceding as I speak. A slaughter of this magnitude will push them irrevocably over the line. Come May, the whole country will be at war with itself. You don't need to be a Class 4 Diviner to predict this. It is as plain as the nose on my face."

"Now, can it be stopped, prevented, halted? No, I don't see how, but it can be slowed down tremendously."

"Just how? What are you suggesting?" Amos asked, he being the senior person here.

"Glad you asked. I have two hundred forty wizards and witches under my command. Invisible, with Skin of Stone spells on them, they can position themselves at the proper locations from which to take out airplanes and wreak massive death upon the US military forces. You know well the many, many spells that we of the wizarding world have at our disposal—Balls of Fire being the least. It would be a simple matter for my forces to obliterate completely an entire regiment or brigade and then move on to face the next group. Yes, that would be the ultimate slaughter of our own men and women in uniform, the helpless pawns of the treasonous President Snow and Dominus Malefic. Yes, the Idaho Red Brigade could prevent the loss of the Virginians and those who have come to aid them in their hour of need, but only by murdering those in the US military, who are also innocent pawns."

"The ramifications of such an action are horrific to the relationship between us of the wizarding world and the normals. We would be violating our sacred pledge that was made centuries ago, when we came openly into society. Think of the reaction of the parents, wives, and children of those soldiers that we would be murdering! I guarantee you that they would be screaming for our arrests and hangings. Yet, their slaughter of the Virginians and volunteer militia would be prevented."

"Good god! It is this bad!" Amos exclaimed, wiping his forehead in his hands. "We are facing a catch-22 situation. We are damned if we do nothing and damned if we take action."

Everyone started talking at once. Ideas flew in all directions. Lindsey heard many times someone lamenting the fact that Alister was greatly missed at a time like this. Deiter listened to all this and knew that he just had to figure out a foolproof way to capture Dominus and soon. But how?

After a half hour of mass discussion, old Casper Williams rose, "Please, please, this decision really falls under our area, Magical Misuse, the mass killing of normals via magic." The group chatter died down. He continued, "Fred has come up with an idea. I for one like it, as I can see no other way out of the mess. We certainly can't sit back and do nothing, for that would surely lead to the destruction of the United States, as we know it. There is no effective way to 'capture' the marines. After all, have you ever heard of a marine giving up? No way. Fred's idea may well minimize the awful consequences. Fred, since this is your idea, why don't you explain it?"

Pam nearly squealed! Her father was becoming one of the most important men leading the resistance. Fred rose with a solemn countenance. "The use of magical spells to kill thousands of normals is by its very nature a total breech of the laws of which the wizarding world agreed to follow so long ago. On that, there can be no disagreement. However, that breech can be minimized. We go before the western governors, perhaps Virginia's too, and fully explain what is very likely going to happen, the total slaughter of those attempting to defend Virginia. Allow them to give us their likely response, which we all know will be to secede from the Union and that leads inevitably to a massive Civil War, the likes of which has never before been seen on this planet. We then present them Erin's alternative, to allow wizards and witches to join the battle, doing all that is possible to stop the US military in its tracks. We *ask for* and seek their *permission* to use magic to aid Virginia. If they give it, then we have the *backing* of a large percentage of the country, minimizing the damage to our relationship with the normals of the country. It still doesn't make it right, but it minimizes it."

Once more, the group began chatting. The consensus was that Fred's idea was a good, solid one, perhaps the best that they could do. After the group agreed to adopt it, Misty Wells rose to ask what had been bothering her throughout the whole discussion.

"I have been thinking about all of this. Look, suppose that the governors give Erin permission to begin attacking the US military with deadly spells. What happens after that? We are really dealing with Dominus here, not the US military, who are mere pawns in his plans. What will be his reaction to seeing his pawns being obliterated by Erin's magic spells? I know what I would do, throw all my Death Stalkers and other wizards into the fray, counter-attacking Erin's forces. Now we are talking a major wizard battle. Are you prepared to take on Dominus and all of his Death Stalkers, Erin?"

"You have a point, Misty. I think that initially we will be completely effective. However, Dominus is indeed likely to take countermeasures after that. My forces, while able and dedicated to maintaining the basic freedoms of our country, are no match for his force of Death Stalkers. If they show up on the battlefield, I will be forced to order a retreat. However, will he actually do that? I mean he depends upon them for his own security. Will he throw them into a wizard battle?"

She replied, "If the stakes are high enough, I bet he does. If your forces take as devastating toll on the US forces as we all expect, he may have no choice but to counter. Still, he may enlist the assistance of other dark wizards from all over the world. That's a real possibility, as he is already doing that in the occupied states. Who else can run their businesses and the government? Not the automatons."

"Okay, then we should expect either the Death Stalkers and Dominus on the scene or a bunch of unsavory wizards. I hate to ask this, but what about back up from anyone from your departments?"

Misty sighed, "If and when Dominus falls, it is imperative that my Security forces immediately take over all the businesses and corporations owned and controlled by Dominus. As soon as those presidents and CEOs hear of the capture or slaying of Dominus, they are going to transfer all their funds into overseas secret accounts and then vanish themselves. We will have no way to recoup any funds, and billions in restitution are going to be needed to rebuild what has been destroyed thus far. I have just enough personnel to take over his vast enterprise. If I lose some in a battle with Death Stalkers, we take a terrible risk in losing the funds that will be needed to set things right. Further, if I pull them off their security assignments, I expose key men, women, and children to Dominus and his men."

"Thanks for being honest about it, Misty. I already assumed that would be the situation. Any chance that we could recruit a volunteer wizard force?" Erin asked.

"Not many would be willing to go up against Death Stalkers, let alone Dominus," Casper answered him truthfully. "They are nothing more than a bunch of trained killers, whereas the rest of our world is not. Our hesitation on killing gives the Death Stalkers a clear advantage. Honestly, I wish the old Rat Pack were still around and in operation. Now those were a fearless bunch, and they wouldn't hesitate for an instant going after Dominus."

Wilma squirmed a little in her seat. She and Monane were still around and still very active, only they needed a Dispeller and a Diviner to make it work. However, she also realized that her body was aging; she no longer had the lightning fast reflexes that she used to have. The many lessons with Deiter had acutely pointed that out to her. This she confided to Monane, who agreed with her. No, much depended upon Lindsey, Deiter, Ashley, and Pam, perhaps also on Amanda, but they needed to finish their education first. Sixth year was the key to everything magical.

Indeed, it was in their sixth year, so many years ago now, that the four of them began training together, the formation of the Rat Pack. Wilma hoped that Lindsey was also working that angle. Just give the teens a few more months, and then the world would see some decisive actions once more.

The group discussed the situation further, but nothing of consequence resulted. Casper agreed to implement the proposal of Fred Betts. He would meet with all the governors in the alliance and get Erin some measure of protection against retaliation from the breaking of the Magical Misuse Laws.

A while later, the teens were once more back in their

usual spot in Yellow Hall's study hall. Pam frantically tried to write three different compositions, ignoring completely the poem assignment. The others worked on their math problems. All but Ashley and Deiter, that is.

Deiter's mind began thinking about the Dominus problem: how to capture him. "How do you capture a wizard that is more powerful than you?" he asked himself. No answer was forthcoming, so he asked, "Well then, do I or we know anything that Dominus does not?" His mind went over their spells and the complete listing Pam had made of the likely spells that Dominus knew. This did not seem at all fruitful, since they completely overlapped, save the Restricted Wish spell. For a minute, he toyed with the idea of getting Dominus to use that spell a whole lot of times and thus die of old age. He chuckled at his final image of a withered Dominus kicking the bucket after casting one last wish.

Then, he thought of something! "Hey we know about the Beyond," he inadvertently blurted out. Others around him said "Huh?" and he brushed that off by saying he was just doodling and needed to get going on his math problems. He picked up his pencil, but drifted back into thought almost at once. The Beyond. Could this be the key he was looking for, the key to everything? His vivid imagination suddenly ran wild with all manner of scenes. Just as he was about to blurt out that he was on to something, Ashley startled everyone.

"That's it! Our time for action!" Ashley exclaimed, rather startled by her divination. She had found it hard to concentrate on the poems, having pushed her math aside. She was not into being very logical, not after that meeting. Her mind had begun to drift onto Dominus once more. Vivid images of what might be happening in the presumed battle that Erin had discussed flashed in her mind, imagined images based on what he suggested might happen.

Then she had an actual premonition. She saw Dominus addressing a large force of Death Stalkers there in that same abandoned warehouse where he'd killed Alister. She realized that at this point in time, they would know where he was and could go after Dominus and his men without any collateral damage. No innocent civilians would be anywhere around that place. She exclaimed, "That's it! Our time for action!"

Suddenly, everyone dropped what they were doing and stared at her. "Premonition, gang. Dominus is going to retaliate in kind. He's going to send in his Death Stalkers to take out Erin and his group! He's going to meet with them in the same warehouse where we found Alister. That will be our time to strike and get him! I just know it!"

"Well done, Ashley!" Lindsey replied. "Now we can really plan out how to do this! I feel better already."

"Yes, but just how are we going to do it?" Pam said quietly putting the dampers on Ashley's premonition. "We don't have a plan. We have yet to find the spell that we know for sure will work to either capture or kill him, now do we?"

At this point, Deiter spoke up, "I have a plan that will work, only it isn't tested yet, but I know it will work."

"Out with it, man!" Amanda insisted, hating the way that he dragged things out.

Deiter looked around. There were many other students nearby. "Not here. Privately. Amanda, Ashley, Lindsey, Pam, come with me." The others gave him a strange look. Kathy was very annoyed that he left her out of this. Emilio brushed it off saying he was just being melodramatic Deiter. Several chuckled at his jest.

"Where are we going, Deiter?" Lindsey asked as they walked through the tunnels below the snow-covered grounds.

"Someplace safe from prying eyes, where we cannot be overheard," he replied.

"Okay, then I have just the place," Lindsey replied. They were close to one of the secret side rooms that she and Amanda had discovered a few years back. "Hide!" she called out. To Deiter's utter surprise, a secret door suddenly opened. Pam grinned. It was the old storage room where she and Alister had captured the supposed mad bomber.

Now Lindsey had to explain about all the secret rooms, while Deiter, casting Light spells began to look at all the old, cool junk, as he called it. "Come on, Deiter, out with it!" Amanda brought him back to the present. She was growing more annoyed with him by the minute.

"Okay, okay. We have something that Dominus knows nothing about, the Beyond. Now here's my plan so far." He began to outline to the four girls what he had dreamed up.

"But will it work with someone as intelligent as Dominus?" Pam wondered.

"Look, everyone knows that just seeing the Beyond causes convulsions or whatever. If you can do your part the very instant I get him, it has to work. I'd like to test it, but I don't think we can get any volunteers, besides, Doctor Caterwall will ask too many questions when we bring the guinea pig in to be cured of the Idiot Mind spell."

"This is going to take a whole lot of coordination," Pam said thoughtfully. She didn't admit it to Deiter, but she loved his plan. No sense in further adding to his overly large ego, she rationalized. "We will need plenty of prison guards and members of the Law Department on hand to receive them. They will have to be notified and ready to go on a moment's notice. We will need to take every precaution we can imagine, but I think we ought to try it. After all, the worst that can happen is that we all are killed. I for one would prefer that to trying to live in a Dominus-ruled one."

"Some are inevitably going to escape via Teleport spells. Monane and I can go after two of them at a time, but we will need a goodly force coming with us," Amanda added. "Perhaps, we can organize two strike teams to go with us after escapees."

"I like it," Ashley giggled, "when the time is right, we can strike. That's my poem for tonight." Pam gave a fake moan of disgust.

"Yes, but we must keep precisely what Deiter, Pam, and Ashley are really doing and just how they are captured a total secret," Lindsey pointed out. "Even from Wilma and Monane and from everyone but ourselves." They all concurred totally on that point, though Pam hated to withhold information from her aunt.

"Then, there are seventeen of us. I don't want to ask Fred or Lloyd to come. If anything happens to us, I want my family and your family well taken care of, Pam," Lindsey added. "The adults all have their jobs to do. Honestly, Dominus goes first, and then immediately after that, all the Security force will go after his companies, so we can't count on them. I guess it all comes down to whether or not I can deal with so many at one time."

"We should practice it Lindsey," Deiter suggested. "Let's get Delius to arrange more mock combats, only for real this time. Let you work on seeing how many you can handle at one time."

"Yes, but what if she cannot handle as many Death Stalkers as are present? We can get creamed," Amanda pointed out.

"Yes, but we three can strike from the Beyond, if needed, taking them by total surprise," Ashley pointed out. "It's a very workable plan, I think. I suppose if you think we need more Rodents, we can ask around. Probably other sixth years might consider joining us."

"Well, if Fern and Orenda are going to be with us, they ought to have a Staff of Power too," Lindsey thought aloud. "That way, they can absorb spells that get by the rest of us. Pam, see if you can find where I can buy a couple, please." Pam grinned, that would cost her a good deal of money, but Pam also knew that Lindsey wanted to do her best to insure the safety of these two fifth years. There was no way that they could keep these two from coming. Fern would just follow them anyway.

"The key will be to watch the news carefully. We need to be prepared for immediate action, which will come sometime after Erin's intervention," Pam pointed out. "We need to make that very clear to all the Rodents. We'll not have a minute to spare when our time to strike comes."

Kathy added, "We should bring along all the healing potions we can, in case we get hurt. Quick fix might save lives. I'll see what I can do to brew some more before our time comes," she volunteered.

"I think we should hold a Rodent meeting and go over the plan with everyone," Pam suggested. "Let's get everyone organized so that they can have everything at the ready and know what defensive spells should be cast before we go into action. I'll make a list of the spells that we ought to have on us."

"Good thinking, Pam. I'll arrange a meeting for the whole bunch, including Wilma and Monane. How about on Saturday afternoon? I'll see if Cho Lin will let us have a room in the Hall of Illusions," Lindsey volunteered.

That settled, they rejoined the others and promised them that they would learn all, come Saturday. Professor Cho Lin was curious about Lindsey's request, but didn't object. She knew that these teens needed to organize, to work out defenses, and so on. That they really could take out Dominus, now that she doubted very much.

Saturday afternoon, the seventeen Rodents entered Number 5 in the Hall of Illusion. Lindsey silently cast a number of protection spells that would prevent anyone from overhearing their conversations.

"I called everyone together today because we Rodents now have a plan to capture Dominus and many of his Death Stalkers at the same time. Part of this plan must remain secret. Only five of us know the specifics. Perhaps one day, I can tell you all about it. We'll see. We know the location of our attack, roughly the number who will be there besides Dominus, only just not the when. Our time will come sometime after Erin Sacs counterattacks the US military in Virginia, causing massive casualties to the troops. Sometime after that will be our time. In all likelihood, we will have but a few minutes' notice to go into action. Thus, it is critical that we all be prepared and ready to go at any time after we hear about Erin's actions on the news."

"Our attack will take place at that abandoned warehouse where Governor Alister was killed. Dominus will be there giving final orders to his Death Stalkers. We believe that he will be sending them in to take out Erin's forces. We will have two Eliminators with us. When we enter, my first priority and what absolutely must be done first is for me to dispel all protections that Dominus may have on himself. The instant that is done, Deiter, Pam, and Ashley will do their secret thing, capturing Dominus and depositing him at the state prison in Denver."

"While I am thus engaged, your task is to keep all really harmful spells from harming either mef or yourselves. The instant that I'm free from Dominus duty, I will dispel as many of their protections and spells as I can, and that is quite a lot. Following Bill West's orders, you can then begin to capture or kill as many of the Death Stalkers as you can. Pam, Deiter, and Ashley will continue to capture some, one at a time, just as soon as they get rid of Dominus. Yes, Pam will also notify Misty Wells the second that they place Dominus in prison. At that time, she will then send out all the Security forces to take over his many companies."

"Inevitably, some are going to manage to escape us. Once the battle is done, we will divide into two groups. Able and Amanda will be the two Trackers. We will track down every one who was at that warehouse, two at a time. Once we have captured the lot, then we will have Pam prepare a list of the others that need to be captured. I suspect that we will be plenty busy for quite some time after that."

"Kathy will be in charge of the healing potions. If you are injured, see Kathy and have a dose of emergency healing. We are only going to get one chance at this, so we must make sure it works. You are all my dear friends, and I want nothing bad to happen to any of you. Hence, Pam has written out a list of protection spells to cast upon yourselves just before we join together to do it."

"When you get the word that 'now is the time,' cast these spells upon yourself, and immediately meet with the rest of us by the main gates," she explained. "That will be our rendezvous point. Questions?"

"Lindsey, how are we going to get out of Bradbury's? The gate is locked and protected." Fern wanted to know.

"Leave that to me. I will get it opened when we need it," Lindsey replied confidently. As many times as she had been through that gate, she certainly knew all the protective spells Governor Alister had placed upon it. It would be a simple thing for her to lower them temporarily so they could leave.

"We are going to be outnumbered at least three to one," Wilma pointed out.

"I will even that out just as soon as I remove any spells Dominus has on himself. How long that will be I can't say, because it depends upon how many protections he has up at the time. I know I can keep at least twenty to thirty Disintegrates from hitting you at one time. I am going to practice doing more. Just in case, we will be giving several of you our Staves of Power and your job will be to absorb all dangerous spells that get by me."

"Okay, but what about this secret plan of yours? Will it really capture Dominus? Have you tested it?" Wilma wanted to know. Besides, she was terribly curious from a professional standpoint. Another Eliminator had out-thought her!

"If he has no protection spells on him, then Deiter's strike will be a success, when combined with Pam and Ashley's spells. No, we haven't actually tested it yet, partly because it involves the Idiot Mind spell." Wilma grinned! That would serve him right—to become an idiot as he had done to so many other women over the years. "More than that, I simply must not say at this time, Wilma, though I know just how badly you want to know. We can't risk anything coming out about this until we are done using it. Dominus is too intelligent, and we don't want him finding out about this in any way before we use it on him." She hoped that would satisfy her.

Pam handed each a list of protective spells that they were to cast upon themselves before they headed to the main gates. Monane read over the list: Skin of Stone, both Major and Minor Spell Protection spells, In Case of Becoming Badly Wounded Teleport to Bradbury's Parking Lot, See True, Anti-Scrying, Reverse Spell, and Multiple Images of Self. What surprised her was the next item on the list: just before we enter the warehouse, everyone is to Morph Self into Lindsey to confuse the enemy further. The last line read: finally, if anyone gets badly injured and can't escape, the person next to him or her is to cast the Magical Barrier spell on them. That way no further magic can harm them. Monane chuckled to herself. Pam had done an exceptional job with this list; nearly every possible defensive spell would be used before combat was engaged. This shifted the odds significantly, she thought.

Chapter 17—Prelude

Aneta Deniska wiped the fog off her night vision goggles. "Cursed fog. Hate London. Why did it have to be here?" the thirty year old Czech witch whispered to herself. Her long brunette hair was braided and piled beneath her stocking hat. Dressed entirely in black, she continued her watch. Eventually, she would show up, at least Aneta hoped and prayed. A year ago she finished her tour of duty in the army where she had been an expert marksman, assigned to the Special Ops corp. Yes, she had been a sniper. Since then, she worked as a night watchman for a factory. That, she believed was what caused the whole mess with her sister.

Aneta had a sister, a stunningly beautiful brunette, who was twenty-one, her little sister. Their parents had died some years ago, and Aneta looked after Milankova. Unlike her sibling, Aneta hated partying, possibly because she lacked all those facial features that made Milankova so striking. Not homely, she never considered herself pretty. Nevertheless, she was a witch. Her sister was not, never having shown any signs of such ability. In fact, the two sisters were as different as could be. Partying, dancing, movies, dating, flirting, wearing fancy dresses—all were up Milankova's alley. She had become a teen model and now had a good modeling career going. Aneta, on the other hand, hated these things. Instead, she loved magic and guns—no, make that powerful rifles.

Always Aneta had looked out for Milankova, being nine years older. It had been her responsibility for ten years now. Only five months ago, Aneta had failed, failed in the only responsibility that mattered to her, Milankova. While she was at work guarding the factory, Milankova, dressed in one of her provocative gowns, had gone out partying and dancing at some of the fancier dance clubs in Prague, in defiance of Aneta's stern warnings. When Aneta came home, Milankova was gone. She waited up for her, but at sun up, Aneta knew something was very wrong and went in search of her sister.

After some investigation, she picked up her nightclub trail. At Milner's, she was seen dancing in the company of a foreigner, and they had left together. Frantic with worry, Aneta checked the hospitals and even the morgues, but her sister was nowhere to be found. She submitted a missing person report, but was told not to get her hopes up. She'd probably run off with this man. Aneta had gotten a good description of him from the bartender at Milner's and began prowling the city at night, after quitting her job of course. The stranger and her sister had just vanished. Aneta began to suspect the man was a wizard and had perhaps kidnaped Milankova.

A month passed and still no word, no clues, but not for her lack of trying. Every night, Aneta went on the prowl of Prague's nightclubs, which yielded nothing at all. Then she got a call from the police station. It was the strangest call she'd ever received. It seems that her sister's arms were found in the Thames River in London! DNA had been used to make the identification. Aneta cried for days, but finally concluded that since her body had not been found, perhaps she was still alive, having met with some tragic accident. Certainly, she was now convinced that the man had to have been a wizard. Milankova did not have enough funds on her person to afford to travel to England, and her bank account remained untouched. Two months ago, Aneta arrived in London to continue the search for her sister's body or her sister.

After spending several weeks long the Thames, she decided that her sister must be alive, probably somewhere in London. Next, she checked all the hospitals, looking for any woman admitted who had somehow lost both of her lower arms. That yielded many strange looks but nothing more. At last, she could only think of one more thing to try. Milankova loved partying and dancing. If she were alive, then eventually she would show up at one or more of the fancier nightclubs of London, only which one? After checking out several, she decided on Danny's Spot, which catered to a very exclusive clientele, namely those with much money. Women entering wore elegant gowns; men, tuxedos. Aneta began to stake out this place. Yes, she had patience.

Towards the end of March, the weather suddenly turned spring-like, unseasonably warm; the temperatures rose into the middle seventies. Dominus had been spending many nights here of late and had taken a fancy to Milankova. True, she was breathtakingly beautiful, particularly after his modifications to her body. Under the Idiot Mind spell, she was most willing to do anything for him. He had encouraged

Milankova and the three other women he held prisoner here in his plush home that if they learned to walk well in their ballet boots, he would take them to one of the finest nightclubs in London. Little did he know that this was precisely the encouragement that would motivate Milankova. The other three women complained about not being able to see anymore, that their feet hurt, that they couldn't breathe, and that they could barely walk in these boots. Not Milankova. The thought of going to the finest nightclub in London drove her mad with desire—her normal cautions gone because of the Idiot Mind spell.

Now Dominus watched as Milankova maneuvered around the house, using her short arms to feel for the walls. True, she moved slowly, but well, and continually asked him if she was walking well enough to earn her that special trip to the nightclub. At last, Dominus yielded to her persistent pleadings. Besides, it was unseasonably warm, and he had not been to a nightclub in weeks. He visited a dress shop and purchased an elegant, satin, full-length gown—one which would nearly touch the floor, hiding her boots for the most part.

"Milankova, tonight we are going partying at Danny's Spot," he announced in the presence of all five women.

She let out a squeal of glee. "Oh thank you, thank you." She gasped. "Oh, what will I wear?" Again, she had to gasp for air. "I think that I am mostly naked." She gasped again. "I can't go like this."

"Not to worry, my beautiful Milankova. I have just

bought you an elegant, green satin, long dress. Here, have a feel," he held it close to her short arms.

"Oh, that feels wonderful." She gasped from lack of air because of the extreme corset he had on her. "Can you help me dress?" Again, she had to gasp, before adding, "I don't think I can manage it anymore."

Dominus had to cast several spells to make the dress fit. The enormous size of her bust caused him the most grief in getting the dress altered. At last, she was properly attired. Dominus then had the legless toy keeper, Millicent, do her makeup and hair. At last, gazing at this rare beauty, Dominus was satisfied. He quickly donned his tuxedo and Teleported the two of them to the garage. He talked her into position to get into the Rolls Royce and then drove to Danny's. Holding on to her arms, he helped her out of the car, while an attendant took the keys to park it for him. With his arm securely around her thin waist, they walked into Danny's.

"Oh, you must tell me," she began and gasped, "what is around us." After another gasp for air, she added, "I seem to be unable to see anything for myself." Gasp. "I hear the band." Gasp. "There are many smells." Gasp. "Please tell me all about it," she gaily chatted away, as she took her small steps moving wherever Dominus gently guided her. At last, he began to describe things around them. The lights were dim, and the fall of her dress over her shoulders hid the fact that she had nothing below her tiny elbows. He didn't want to chance tiring her out, so he escorted her to a table and helped her sit down. A few drinks later, he was chatting away with her, describing the ambiance that was uniquely Denny's.

"Oh, let's dance, shall we?" she begged. Reluctantly, Dominus gave in; Milankova was melting his heart. In her boots, dancing proved most difficult, but she gave it her all anyway. When she began wobbling a bit too much and gasping for breath, they returned to their table to listen to the music. He really liked this woman and her attitude; he began to consider marriage with her. Nadia had been a complete disaster, but Milankova was not a witch, and she was many times better looking.

After another hour of constant chatting, Dominus wanted to return home. Milankova whined and begged to stay longer, but lost the battle. Again, they walked very slowly, but reasonably gracefully to the car pick up area. They had to stand there for several minutes until his Rolls appeared. Once more, he talked her into position and helped her get inside. As he got into his side, he sensed that someone was watching him. Covertly glancing around, he saw no one, but the sensation was still present. As he drove the car down the lane to the street, he Teleported the car to his home and put in into the garage, shutting the door behind them.

Aneta, dressed in black, stared through her night vision goggles. Another Rolls drove up to Denny's. She cursed, "Darn Londoners. They all have Rolls." Her car was a rusted junk pile constantly breaking down. Suddenly she gasped. That woman getting out of the car. Could that be Milankova? No, this woman had a huge bust line, not at all like Milankova. Her hair—that was right, at least as near as she could tell in this light. As the woman stood up and began walking slowly into Denny's, Aneta could clearly see that she was missing her lower arms! Aneta's pulse began racing. What had happened to Milankova? Dressed as she was all in black, she could not possibly get into this club. Further, she had seen no single women entering all night. Men, yes; women no, not unless upon the arm of a man, so she suspected that, even if she conjured up a fancy outfit, she would not be allowed inside.

They had come in a car. They must leave in that car. Aneta formed a plan. She watched where the guests went to pick up their cars. Once she worked out that detail, she cast Invisibility and opened a Magic Door to that area. She found a hiding place just to the left of the exit door, from where she could get a very close look at the woman when she came out. Now she waited, though for some reason her patience seemed to evaporate this evening.

Just when she though that she could stand it no longer, the man and the woman came walking out to pick up the car. "Why is she walking so slowly?" Aneta wondered. Then, she spied the boots that the woman was wearing and stifled a gasp. It was her sister! She was positive of that. Yet, Milankova was chatting away, seemingly very happy indeed. As she got into the car, Aneta saw her sister's eyes, or rather the absence of them. She was now blind wearing a pair of sky blue glass eyeballs, totally unlike her real brown eyes. Aneta knew this man had very likely tortured her sister, mutilating her body. Hearing Milankova chat, she recognized the Idiot Mind spell at work. Her stifled gasps drew the attention of this wizard.

Aneta held her breath, but he calmly got inside the driver's side. That he knew she was there became evident a moment later when the Rolls disappeared at the end of the lane, dashing any hopes that Aneta could follow them and rescue her sister from the clutches of this butcher.

So close and yet so far. Aneta stood there for several minutes wondering what to do next. At last, she waved her wand, conjured herself a fancy gown, and canceled her Invisibility spell, stepping out as if she had just come from inside. "Excuse me sir. That man who was just here, do you know his name by chance? He dropped a diamond cufflink, and I want to return it to him."

"Ah, so kind of you. I believe he is called Simon Genteel, but I'm not sure of his last name. He comes here on occasion, if you would be so kind as to give the cufflink to the lost and found department and tell them it is Simon's, they will see that it is returned to him on his next visit here." She thanked him and followed his directions to locate that man. However, she walked on past his lost and found desk and out the main entrance. There, she Teleported back to her cheap motel room. She drew a hot bath and lay in the tub for an hour, crying to herself. She had gotten to within three feet of her sister, but was unable to rescue her.

The next day, she set out to track this Simon fellow down. Obviously, he must live somewhere in London. A week later, she sat in her room dejected. There was no such person listed anywhere in the city. There was no one with that last name. The attendant had not gotten Simon's last name correct, of that she was certain. She turned on the tele and began idly watching the news.

On April 5, General Bragge was ready. All his men, some forty-five thousand of them, were in position. Some were ready to explode out of the Marine base; some would come across the Chesapeake Bay Bridge, but the vast majority would move out of their DC staging area across the many bridges into Arlington and Alexandria. Once those cities were secure, some forces would swing west into the hills all the way to the border with West Virginia, while the main deployment would travel on down I95 to Richmond. His other group, having subdued the greater Norfolk area and Virginia Beach, would sweep west along I64, meeting the main strike force at Richmond. From there, they would sweep west by south, subduing the remainder of Virginia. He expected this would take three weeks, mostly because they had to arrange for the pill deployments at each distribution center that they secured along the way. Pity the MPs could not be used for this purpose.

Worse, a dozen news helicopters would be flying over the battlefield, bringing live news and footage to the watching millions. While this would not likely be a problem, except possibly for the Air Force, he found it a bit unnerving. The reporting of modern warfare had been totally altered for all time back in the Gulf War with Iraq back at the start of the Twenty-first Century. At least, he didn't have to deal with embedded reporters. At ten, he gave the launch signal, and his men began moving out.

Just as soon as the point men and vehicles crossed the state line, snipers began opening fire upon them. The battle for Virginia began. The Big Red One initially faced the Virginia National Guardsmen. APCs and the main battle tanks poured into the cities, blasting every building from which enemy fire came.

By sunset, the army division had secured a fifteen-mile circle around the bridges. All day long, the TV coverage showed house after house, business after business being blown up by the HE (high explosives) from the tanks. Collateral damage was horrific; bodies were simply piled up in a dozen large piles in the parks around the greater metropolitan area. At least the news crews didn't show those, merely the numbers. Nearly five thousand guardsmen and women were in those piles, but also several thousand innocent men, women, and children whose homes had been turned into rubble. Many thousands more filled the hospitals far beyond their capacities. Wounded were being treated in hallways, before supplies ran out.

The nation watched in utter shock, glued to their TV sets. Across the nation, all businesses closed; their employees refused to do anything but watch the event unfold. Anger rose to the level of outright madness. Some proposed that everyone head to DC and slaughter the President and all the automatons in Congress. As soon as that hit the airwaves, angry men began heading there to do just that. All roads into the New York-DC area became jammed with violent, angry madmen bent upon extracting revenge against their governmental leaders. Mass pandemonium had been finally unleashed.

General Bragge had anticipated this upheaval and had his Second Division in position. Those heading into the area found themselves facing a barricade of army men. Some chose to attempt to drive through the soldiers, who naturally opened fire. Casualty counts grew by the hour.

On April 6, General Bragge's forces moved out into the more distant suburbs of the two metropolitan areas. Erin Sacs and his forces were waiting for them. Now with some space to fight, fight they did, only using spells not bullets and explosives. The news reporters had a field day this day. "There goes another battle tank up in flames! Can anyone see where that attack came from?" the startled reporter called out to the other members in the copter.

A platoon of foot soldiers moved out down a deserted street. A green cloud of vapors drifted over them. When visibility returned, the TV crews saw nothing but their dead bodies lying in the street down which they had been walking. Overhead, the Air Force sent a dozen unmanned drones, armed with HE bombs, ready to strike back against the resistance. One by one, these drones mysteriously blew up, harming no one.

When evening came, the body count had risen dramatically, over seven thousands US troops lay in piles awaiting removal. No militia, guardsmen, or civilians were in the tally. The talk of the news reporters was just how incredibly effective Erin Sacs and his small force of wizards and witches had been. To many, they seemed the saviors, but to others, deep fear flooded their minds; the wizarding world could easily wipe out normals without taking a single casualty. Some began calling for a crusade against all those who used magic, but they were at least in the minority here on day two.

Chapter 18—Now Is the Time

All that day, the students at Bradbury's crowded the commons. Classes were cancelled. Everyone watched history in the making, albeit a horrific history. That evening as the massive losses by the military were announced, Lindsey and the Rodents knew that the time for their action was fast approaching. During that day, some students were crying, others, outright angry. None was unmoved by the graphic scenes of the battle unfolding. However, uniformly many cheered when they saw the US soldiers taking a terrible beating, making up for what they had delivered the day before. Most of the kids believed that they were seeing the start of the next Civil War.

On the morning of April 7, the students swarmed the dining room early, eager to get in front of the TVs to see what would happen today. Would the army try different tactics? Would they retreat? Some speculated that the President would simply Nuke the whole state.

Around nine that morning, Ashley sighed, waved her wand, and cast her Mass Message to sixteen others. Lindsey saw the simple message flash before her eyes.

Now is the time. A.

Hastily, she went down Pam's list of spells, casting them on herself one at a time. She grabbed her Staff of Power and opened a Magical Door to the front gates. Deiter was already there waiting for her. Within a minute, all fourteen had arrived. Silently, Lindsey temporarily lowered the protection spells on the gates, though no one saw her actually cast any spell. Silently, they filed outside; Wilma, Monane, and Jim were waiting for them. Lindsey stepped through the gates and turned to face them. Silently, she raised the protections back into full force. “Now,” she said soberly. Seventeen Teleport spells activated, and the group vanished, just as Professor Cho Lin responded to the alarms going off, that the gates had been breached. She saw the group just as they Teleported away. She said a silent prayer and Messaged the other faculty.

The next instant fourteen arrived just outside the abandoned warehouse in Montrose. The streets were nearly empty. Everyone was home, glued to their TV sets, waiting for the next episode to unfold. “Where’s Deiter, Pam, and Ashley?” Wilma called out, alarmed and worried something happened to them.

“They are in their secret positions. We are ready. Cast your Morph spells, and here we go,” Lindsey commanded. She was a bit unnerved suddenly to see thirteen duplicates of herself standing behind her. She grinned. “Okay, Magical Doors, spread out, cover me, and give me time. Now.” She silently opened her Magical door inside. All were Invisible as they entered, giving them a brief space of time to get themselves oriented. Dominus was standing on a large box, addressing his men.

“Men, I want the head of Erin Sacs today. Kill every

wizard or witch that you can find. Let's show them *real* fighting. Ten thousand dollars for whoever gets Erin." The group of sixty-five Death Stalkers and a few hired wizards cheered him.

"What the hell?" Dominus now noticed the many Magical Doors opening up in the back of the room. He flicked his wand and cast a Dispel Magic spell, revealing a Lindsey Barron. Hastily, several other Dispels flew, revealing more Lindsey Barrons, unnerving only Dominus, however.

Lindsey appeared in the room and spotted Dominus. She concentrated and began seeing the magical energy lines of his protective spells. She was in luck; he only had two, the Major Protection from spells and an In Case Of spell on his person. While she was disrupting both of these, Deiter stuck his Invisible head down from the Beyond and cast his Mass Disarm spell upon the sixty-five men. After this "doing a Deiter," wands flew in all directions. A mad scramble for wands ensued, though three In Case Of spells activated, and those wizards vanished from the warehouse. Several other In Case Of spells activated, and their wands returned to the owners via a Summon spell.

Now. L.

The Message that Deiter had been waiting for appeared before his eyes. He leaned over, pretending to reach under his bed. His arms seemed to stretch out as if he were some kind of rubber man, though he was completely Invisible, but not to the Rodents, who had See True in force. He grabbed Dominus by both shoulders and returned to the Beyond. It took only a split instant for this to occur, however.

Dominus arrived in the Beyond quite confused, totally at a loss to explain what was happening to him. “Idiot Mind!” Ashley cast her spell. “Idiot Mind!” Pam cast hers a split second after Ashley’s, but from behind Dominus. Confused, disoriented, totally lost, Dominus was unable to grasp what was happening to him during those two seconds. Both spells activated and his body turned into a rigid statue. He was still living and breathing, but he was utterly stupefied. Intelligence was king in the Beyond. Right then, he had none and thus could not move a muscle.

Pam sent another Message and nodded to Deiter. He grabbed Dominus and bent over. Suddenly, Fred Betts and Casper Williams, who were at the Denver Maximum Security Prison, saw Dominus standing before them, taking them by total surprise. However, alerted by Pam, they had their wands at the ready. “Duh, what is this stick? Silly, I don’t need a stick.” Dominus dropped his wand onto the ground. “Where am I? Who are you? Should I know you?”

“Come with us; we will help you to a nice bed. You would like a nice bed wouldn’t you?” Fred took command. Casper was too flabbergasted to say anything.

“Oh how nice. Yes, yes I would. I feel rather sick. I might vomit. I wonder why. Maybe I have the flu. Do you have the flu? Oh I am sick.” He threw up his breakfast onto the ground. Several prison guards rushed up and took him off to a secure cell.

“How the bloody hell did they do that to Dominus?”

Casper asked.

"Heads up, here come more," Fred called out. He sent a Mass Message spell. Misty Wells, one of the receivers acted at once, sending out another Mass Message to all of her Security forces.

None of the Death Stalkers saw Dominus vanish. They were madly grabbing whatever wand they could find. "Disintegrate!" many voices began calling out. Their spells completely fizzled. Balls of Fire detonated harmlessly all around the Lindsey's. A volley of Dispel Magic spells began to undo some of their protective spells or the Morph spells. Now the Death Stalkers spied their archenemies, none other than the famous Bill West and Able Monument. Fear began to creep into their minds, especially when their killing spells continually fizzled.

Soon, they changed tactics and began casting Slice spells, hoping to gain some hits. Already, Bill West had three Death Stalkers entrapped and out of the battle. Deiter stuck his head down once more and cast his Disarm spell, okay his "doing a Deiter," Mass Disarm spell. Wands went flying in all directions once more. He then grabbed Len Striker and lifted him into the Beyond, where Ashley and Pam cast their Idiot Mind spells. A second later, Deiter gently lowered Len beside Fred and Casper. He went back for more.

After the mad scramble and diving out of the way of spells, thirty managed to regain their wands. The rest were encased in piles and piles of sticky webs, totally out of the battle. Three more were encased by Vice Fists, unable to move or do anything. The remainder attempted to cast Slice spells and Dead Fog spells all over their attackers. Once more Deiter did a Deiter, casting his Mass Disarm spell, wands leaped out of the Death Stalkers hands. This time he pulled Ames Selig to the Beyond and a bit later deposited him beside Fred.

Jim and the others now figured out a new tactic, based on Deiter's spells. When he reappeared the next time and cast his Mass Disarm spell, they were prepared. The instant the wands went flying, fourteen Sticky Web spells fired, entrapping the confused men. Three more In Case Of spells activated, and those men vanished.

Lindsey Messaged Deiter and shortly Deiter, Pam, and Ashley materialized in the warehouse. "Where the heck did you come from? Were you up on the roof?" Emilio asked, as that was the only explanation that made any sense of what he had seen.

"Yes, that's pretty much it," Deiter lied, well it was sort of right, he justified to himself.

"Okay, Deiter, we have them all but a few who escaped. Now comes the hard part. If we attempt to take them into custody, they may have In Case Of spells on their person," Bill West explained.

"Anyone hurt?" Kathy called out, worried that someone would urgently need her healing potions.

"I stubbed my toe," Emilio replied, "but I don't think that counts." Everyone looked around making sure all seventeen Rodents were accounted for, and then they broke out laughing.

"Let me go from man to man," Lindsey requested. One by one, she carefully examined the struggling men entrapped in the mountains of sticky webs. They had all manner of spells still in force, particularly In Case I Get Arrested. One by one, Lindsey silently disrupted every spell still in effect. As soon as she was finished with one, Wilma or Deiter took him into custody, casting a Tie spell. Once secure, one of the Rodents then Teleported the man to the Denver Prison, handing him over to Fred and Casper, who became more and more amazed at the incredible captures.

Less than an hour after they entered the warehouse, the last man was taken by Ashley to Fred. When she returned, Bill West was deciding upon the next course of action to take. "Okay, five escaped us. Plus there is the President and the host of others that Pam has identified. We should probably go after the government officials and their wizards next. What do you think, Ashley?"

"Give me a bit of time, please," she requested and sat down on the floor and began to relax, focusing her mind on President Snow.

"This was almost too easy," Monane commented to Wilma.

"She's a hundred times better than Sam, just unbelievable. Yet, what I still don't understand is how Deiter, Pam, and Ashley could take out Dominus so quickly. He never got the chance to do much of anything at all. They must have been up on the roof, because we did see him coming down from up there. Yet, how could they have subdued him? Even without his wand, he is dangerous."

"If I hadn't seen it with my own eyes, I wouldn't have believed it possible," Monane replied.

"Hey, she and all her cabinet members are sitting watching the TV in her office. Now is a good time to fetch them," Ashley replied, rubbing her face and then standing back up.

"Okay, everyone get your list of spells back on yourselves. Amanda, this time you are with Deiter, that way we can get four of them at once. The second that any of us appear in that room, you had better believe all the Secret Service alarms will go off. Armed men and wizards will come dashing in, so here's the plan." She outlined what the four should do, explained what she would do, and then what the Invisible Rodents were to do. "Remember, we want the wizards captured, but the Secret Service personnel left unharmed, as much as possible."

Two minutes later, thirteen stood Invisible on the street outside of the White House. When Deiter's group was ready, Lindsey whispered, "Now." Thirteen Magical Doors opened, and they stepped through the door and into the office of President Snow. Just as they entered, they saw all the automatons sitting quietly watching the news unfold on the TV. President Snow, and three others of her administration suddenly vanished, and a loud alarm began clanging. The Rodents had just enough time to fan out across the back of the room before Secret Service men and women raced through the doors, along with four of Dominus's wizards who were on guard duty here at the White House. Four more of her cabinet members suddenly vanished.

Lindsey focused on the wizards, but they had many defensive spells on them. One by one, she discharged these, while the Secret Service men yelled, “Where’s Snow?” The remaining cabinet members looked completely confused, utterly baffled. One answered, “She is right here,” pointing to the empty seat. “Oh!” he said, blinking twice. Then, he too vanished, along with three more, leaving only three members left.

“Get them to the secure location,” one Secret Service man screamed. A volley of Stun spells struck all them and they froze mid-stride. Now the wizards began to cast Disintegrate spells, but Lindsey was on to those. She saw the first one forming, stopped what she was doing, and caused that one to fizzle. Then another and another. Half of the Rodents shot Dispel Magic spells, while the other half shot various entrapment spells. Two minutes later, the four wizards either were held by Grabbing Hands or were entangled in a mass of webs. One by one, these men vanished from the room.

“Retreat, and I’ll free the Secret Service men,” Lindsey ordered. Once the Rodents had left, returning to the warehouse in Montrose, Lindsey concentrated on the magical energies surrounding them and dispersed them. They were free, but tremendously startled. The room was empty except for themselves. Lindsey was the last to Teleport to the warehouse.

“Nicely done, Lindsey,” Deiter called out, as she

materialized among the Rodents. "Now what?"

"Wilma?" Lindsey asked. She'd just run out of plans. Wilma laughed hysterically. It was contagious. Soon all seventeen Rodents were roaring with laughter. About an hour had now passed, and they had taken care of the top two key sets of personnel.

"If I'd known it was going to be this easy. . ." Wilma roared with laughter. Easy it had been, but only because of Lindsey's skills and her friends' clever use of the Beyond.

Finally, Wilma calmed down. "Okay, let's go back to Bradbury's now. We will have to go after everyone on Pam's list, one by one, but we'll leave that for another day. Right now, the country needs a bit of time to come to grips with what has happened. We have just pulled off the coup of the century. Honestly, the adults are going to need some time to handle such a drastic change in power. Trust me, Rodents. I have been in communication with those in power. Let's give them time to adjust."

"Okay, Rodents, back to school," Lindsey teased.

"Ah, but I was just starting to have some fun," Ashley teased her back.

"Ah, do we *have* to?" Deiter whined in a pleading, childish tone. Everyone laughed wildly again. A few minutes later, the warehouse was empty once more. At the gates, Lindsey waited for Professor Cho Lin to lower the protections so that they could enter. While she could have simply let everyone in herself, Professor Cho Lin was the one in charge of the school now, and Lindsey allowed her to have that responsibility.

Once inside the gates and the gates closed, all received a Message.

MY OFFICE! NOW! PRONTO! C. L.

"Do you think she is mad?" Deiter asked, a bit mystified by the shouting message.

"I've never gotten a shouted Message before," Pam noted. "Maybe we are all being expelled. After all, we did leave the school without permission."

"I think that we should walk to her office," Audrey calmly suggested. "That feels right." Lindsey smiled and stopped casting her Magical Door. The seventeen walked along the path heading north to the Hall of Illusion. When they finally entered the door, all the faculty were assembled, stern faces staring at the three adults and fourteen teens.

"Well it's about time. I don't know whether to expel all of you or to hug you. What did you think going off like that without notifying me?" Cho Lin was very angry and very elated at the same time. "It's all over the news! What have you done?"

Lindsey stepped a foot closer to her. "It's my fault. I asked them all to come. Ashley divined when the time was right for us to strike. It was this morning. Honestly, we had only a couple of minutes to prepare and get there or we would have missed Dominus. I, I didn't want to be delayed, so I didn't tell you. Besides, if anything had gone wrong, no one could fault you, since you knew nothing about it."

"We got him! Dominus! He's at the Denver Maximum Security Prison. Fred and Casper locked him up and over fifty

Death Stalkers too, along with President Snow and her whole cabinet!" Deiter blurted out, since Lindsey was not answering Professor Cho Lin's direct question. "We stopped because we sort of ran out of people to arrest just now."

"Don't you *ever* go off again without telling me first! Do I make myself perfectly clear?" Professor Cho Lin nearly yelled, her anger coming to the fore. The teens nodded.

Her anger evaporated. "Now sit down and watch the TV. The whole country has gone topsy turvy! It's utter madness out there. You are on the news, obviously. Casper Williams and Fred Betts were just on. Amos Slaughter is supposed to be on shortly. Misty Wells has sent dozens of Messages here for Pam. With the exception of Pam's parents, I have been deluged with calls from your parents demanding to know if you were safe. Please, before you do another thing, Message them, and let them know that you are okay. Oh, are any of you wounded? Do you need Doctor Caterwall?" She suddenly realized that one or more of the students might be badly wounded

"No, Emilio stubbed his toe. That was our only injury," Lindsey, as their leader, reported. Cho Lin visibly relaxed, and the teens fired off their Messages and received some back from their worried parents.

"The TV," Professor Delius pointed out. Everyone gathered around her TV. Elsewhere on the campus, the five hall commons were packed with the other students who had been watching since early this morning.

A harried Hugo Whitefield was speaking, "Honestly, the

news is breaking so fast that we here at KMAG simply cannot keep up with it. We are going live to the office of the States Justice Department where Amos Slaughter is about to speak. He is the head of their entire magical departments, most of whose members used to be in the federal departments. Amos." The scene switched to a small room. Amos sat behind his desk and a wall of microphones, hastily installed.

He spoke slowly and calmly. "Good morning, Americans everywhere. Liberation Day, that is what we are calling today, for America has been once more liberated from tyrants. First, I want to confirm what has happened this morning thus far. No, the Rat Pack is not back in operation. Rather a new group has been formed, the Rodents. Yes, the two surviving members of the old Rat Pack are now part of the Rodents. Bill West and Able Monument have indeed reappeared and are now officially on the job."

"This new group, who call themselves the Rodents, is led by none other than the Rat Pack's Sam Barron's daughter, Miss Lindsey Barron, who after today, may be seen as the world's best Dispeller ever. She has in her group not only the famous Bill West Eliminator, but also an even more powerful Eliminator, one Mr. Deiter Cross. Also a part of the Rodents are Diviner Class 4 Miss Ashley Stokes-Compton and Sleuth Miss Pamela Betts. Yes, they have indeed captured the tyrant Dominus Malefic."

"This morning, one by one, Miss Betts and Mr. Cross dropped off the captured Dominus and fifty-nine of his top Death Stalkers at the Denver Maximum Security Prison, delivering them personally into the hands of Mr. Casper Williams, the States Magical Misuse head, and Mr. Fred Betts, head of the State of Colorado Department of Magical Misuse."

"Not long after that, they also delivered into their hands President Missy Snow, her vice-president, and all the members of her cabinet. They are being treated for their pill addiction as I speak. Later, they will have to face a trial for their deeds. I have been in contact with General Bragge, and he is at this minute withdrawing all the US military forces, returning them to their home bases. The conflict in Virginia has ended. I would urge all the volunteer militia to return to their homes at once."

"We in the States Justice Department have compiled a very lengthy list of all those wizards and witches who have participated in these many criminal actions over the last many months, as well as those normals who have been involved. To all these men and women, I have only this to say to you. Report within the next few days to the Denver Maximum Security Prison and surrender yourself to our new Justice Department. If you do not voluntarily surrender, after that time, the Rodents will come after you. Just between you and me, I would not want this new Rodents pack after me. Dominus lasted less than two minutes against them, when he had over sixty Death Stalkers with him. Please give that serious thought before you attempt to flee and hide. The Rodents have two very able Trackers in Able Monument and Miss Amanda Whitewater, so there is no place in this world where they cannot find you. Please do the right thing and surrender and that will be taken into consideration at your trial."

"As you know, the US Government is in a total shambles and has been for some time now, ever since the introduction of those vile pills, masquerading as a benefit to mankind. The normal chain of command has been severed because all of those who would inherit the running of our country, should the President be unable, are themselves automatons. The entire Congress must be replaced as well. I have been asked by the governors of forty states to assume the role of Acting President, which I have reluctantly accepted on *one* condition."

"That condition being we must hold national elections four months from now. On August 7, all states will go to the polls to elect a new President and all members of Congress. However, there are five states that are currently unable to participate, as their entire populations have been turned into automatons. Their seats in Congress will remain vacant until they are able freely to elect their new Representatives and Senators. Those of you out there with political ambitions, now is the time to move swiftly. I know I am giving you very little time, but I do not want our country to be without a duly elected President and Congress any longer than absolutely necessary."

"Next, what about the millions of you who have one of those Dominus for President rings now imbedded beneath your ring finger? Miss Pam Betts has developed a painless way for them to be extracted. Please see visit your local Magical

Healing Clinic as soon as possible to have it removed."

"Yes, my fellow Americans, today, Liberation Day, thanks to the incredible efforts of the Rodents, the long running tyranny has been ended! Mop up operations will undoubtedly be ongoing for quite some time, unless those guilty parties come to their senses and surrender. Personally, I would not want to experience Eliminator Cross's spell. However, much remains to be done. This I would like to address next, if I may."

"Over these many years, Dominus Malefic and his Death Stalkers have committed a vast quantity of crimes, from murder to abduction, mutilation, and even rape. There are hundreds of victims of his crimes out there in the world, not just our own country. Hundreds more have lost husbands and wives. This is to say nothing of the millions turned into automatons."

"As many of you are aware, the Western States have formed the new department which I now head with the greatest of honor, the States Justice Department. Part of our goal has been to seek real *justice* for the victims of crimes. After pursuing this approach for many months now, the results are quite impressive. Victims are now getting some compensation from those that victimized them, at least momentarily anyway."

"As Acting President, I am making this new program National in scope as well as worldwide, for the victims of Dominus and his gang. Yes, all the victims of his tyranny anywhere in the world will be compensated monetarily, in proportion to the offense. Again, our country is deeply in debt to the untiring efforts of Miss Pam Betts in maintaining a database of the crimes committed over the years by Dominus and his men. We know that this compilation is far from complete. Some crimes may have even gone unreported for one reason or another. If you have been the victim of a crime committed by Dominus Malefic or one of his Death Stalkers, please contact your nearest Department of Justice and report it. They will check to see if your situation is already known and in our database. If it is not, after verification, yours will be added."

"As soon as possible, the Justice Department will begin making a monetary restitution or compensation from the money that we have confiscated from Dominus and his men. Please bear with us; this will take us some time to tally up. Everyone who was a victim or their heirs will receive a proportional amount. We all know that money cannot undo a crime, nor bring back the loved ones who were slain, but it is our small effort to assist those victims in creating a better life afterwards. It is the very least that we can do."

"Now you may be wondering just how much money we are discussing. Yes, divide a sum by the sheer number of victims over all these years and you would not expect to see much. However, I would like to share some astounding news about this with you today. As the expression goes, hold on to your seats." He paused to allow his audience to respond.

"Due to the incredible Sleuth Pam Betts, we now know that Dominus Malefic is an assumed name, yes, an alias. She has uncovered his real name: Simon Mac Fluide. Yes, Dominus really is that billionaire financial recluse who no one ever sees. Now you know why no one ever sees Simon!" Again, he paused, knowing many were gasping from that revelation.

"I am pleased to announce that Miss Betts has identified all known holdings of the far flung Mac Fluide Enterprises. The very moment that Dominus was captured, the head of the States Security Department, Misty Wells, ordered her entire department immediately to take over these many companies and secure them, preventing any theft of assets by company personnel. All of those companies are now securely in the hands of Security Department personnel."

"Fred Angel, head of the States Law and Justice Department and his subordinates, under the leadership of the federal attorney Mary Hampton, are, as we speak, beginning the lengthy liquidation process. When they have finished, they will have one, dare I say, monstrous pile of money with which to divide among the many crime victims and their heirs. Please give them time to do their work, and then Dominus will be assisting you to attain closure and a better life as a result."

"Sorry, Hugo, I am not yet done." Amos grinned at the tele-prompter. "There remains one huge, monumental problem. We have millions of people in five entire states that are now hooked on the heroin-laced Health Care pills. Somehow, these millions must be helped. This is a massive health care problem to say the very least."

"During our long struggle against the tyranny of Dominus or Simon, we have gained the support of many others from overseas. One of these unexpected sources is the giant Folquet Enterprises, located in France. In secret these past months, that corporation has voluntarily been searching for a cure for those addicted to these pills. Only two days ago, we received word that they have found a possible cure and are ready for trials. We hope that soon we can begin the detoxification of those that are now automatons, returning them to their right minds and off their addiction. Even if the cure works, it will be many months before everyone in the effected states can be cured. Yes, my fellow Americans, there is great hope for the future."

"One final note, if you please. Once the millions have been cured of their addition and horrific side effects of these pills, Folquet Enterprises promises to conduct further research on these pills to see if they can be made safe for use in healing, as was promised by ex-President Snow. As I understand their recent report, this may well be possible. I quote from the CEO of the Folquet Enterprises, 'If we can find a safe reformulation that truly heals without any ill side-effects, we will begin a program to produce these pills in quantity and make them available at no cost to any who may need them.' Now that is *truly* humanitarian."

"If I may, another word," Amos decided he still didn't want to relinquish the spotlight. "Our country and even the entire world owes these seventeen brave wizards and witches of the Rodents a debt of gratitude that can never be repaid. I find it ironical that the vast majority of the Rodents are women. They accomplished the seemingly impossible in less than *one hour* this morning. Utterly incredible, utterly unbelievable, the Rodents may well be the most powerful wizards and witches in the world!"

"As you know, the many magical departments at the federal level were eliminated and many of those personnel moved over to the new States Justice Department. As of this minute, I have issued an Executive Order that places the States Justice Department at the federal level. All personnel and organization remains the same, only now they once more serve our whole country, not just those western states. We will be implementing the highly successful Justice programs nationwide very soon. Thus, all states will see a real reduction in crime rates, without the horrible side-effects of making their populations automatons."

"One of the other projects that we have been working on is a total, complete revision of all the laws of the United States. In due time, we will replace the nightmare book of laws with this new set. Right now, it takes teams of lawyers to figure out nearly anything. The common man has no chance of knowing what is or is not legal. When we are done, a high school graduate will be able to read the laws and understand them. Yes, they will be that clearly written. I admit that it will likely take some years to get this project done, but I promise you that it will be done."

"Okay, I'm told that I am not allowed to take questions. Ah, the heck with that. I'll take your questions, but please, one at a time."

"Bill Jones, NBC. President Slaughter, you've

mentioned a few names of the members of the Rodents. Can you give us all their names? Can you arrange a meeting with them? We, and the whole country, would like to see them and give them our thanks."

"At this time, I am not at liberty to divulge all their names. I suspect that they still have much work to do in apprehending the many treasonous criminals who are still at large. In time, I believe that they will agree to a meeting. I will say this; all but three are still merely students at the prestigious Arthur Bradbury's School of Magic. As such, they are still considered minors, if only for a few more weeks."

"Pete Jenks, ABC. President Slaughter, in the limited time that we have had since the events of this morning, our sources tell us that Miss Barron has no hands and that Miss Stokes-Compton has no arms at all and that she went to the Chicago School of Magic, where she was about to be expelled for fighting her professors. Is this the same young woman who has appeared in several Teen Fashion magazine photo shoots? Is there any truth to these rumors?"

Lindsey moaned and Ashley giggled. Lindsey said, "They sure know how to dig up dirt on us don't they?"

"Wouldn't be news otherwise," Ashley joked.

"Think twice about being interviewed," Wilma cautioned. "We always let Sam do all the talking."

"Miss Barron had the misfortune to be the victim of illegal corporate dumping of toxic chemicals. She was the victim of Thalidomide poisoning and was born without hands, but they were regrown during her first year at Bradbury's.

Today, she is just fine. Miss Stokes-Compton is also the victim of Dominus. He arranged for a car accident that killed both her parents when she was little more than a baby. It now appears that her father was about to expose to the world that Dominus was in fact Simon Mac Fluide. Imagine how different things might have been if he had been able to do just that so many years ago. Anyway, in that accident, she lost her arms, but survived. She attended several schools of magic before starting her third year at Bradbury's. There, she too has had her arms regrown and is in perfect health. Both of these young women deserve our highest respect."

"Okay, Hugo is giving me the high five. I'll end this first press conference. I will let you know when I have further announcements. Thank you for your time and patience."

Hugo's face reappeared. "There you have it, perhaps the most incredible news ever. He covered so much ground that we will have to spend hours making this all clear. Let's review the key points of our new President's first speech to the nation."

Professor Cho Lin turned the TV off. "Now then, will *one* of you Rodents please illuminate just what *did* happen this morning? And no, there will be *no* interviews until after you graduate and are gone from here!" They all giggled, though they knew she was serious.

Lindsey began, "Well, first, you must know that Deiter, Pam, Ashley, Amanda, and I have developed a secret Eliminator technique, which must remain a secret, at least until we have captured every one of them. You, Wilma, you are right. We should have one spokesperson. Pam, you are the best qualified. Will you take on that role, please?" Pam grinned. She knew that Deiter would brag too much, that Jim was too carefree, that Emilio was not quick on the take to grasp new situations, that Ahana was only interested in making music, that Andy was too into old bones to care too much about these matters, and that Tom was too quiet and shy.

"Okay, I prepared a list of defensive spells that we all cast upon ourselves before we left." Pam began a detailed description of the hour's events. She used Emilio's theory of their location, somehow coming down from the roof, as a reasonable explanation of their secret use of the Beyond. While none of the Professors believed this, they accepted it for now.

When they had finished answering all their questions, Professor Cho Lin allowed them to return to their dorm. Classes were still cancelled for the rest of today, but would resume tomorrow. As Lindsey, the last to leave, was near the door, Professor Cho Lin whispered, "You know, one day last summer, I would have sworn that I saw your head hanging down from the sky, your beautiful long hair dangling downward. Emilio's description reminded me of that. Any truth in that?"

Lindsey smiled, "You saw what you saw, but I best not say anymore at this time." She scooted out the door as quickly as she could, leaving Cho Lin deep in thought.

When the teens entered Yellow Hall commons, where

the entirety of their fellow Yellow Hall students were crammed in still watching the TV, spontaneous clapping broke out, followed by yelling and cheering. Then, everyone wanted to know all about it. Emilio and Pam began their lengthy explanations, while the others decided to disappear into their rooms. Deiter and Peaches received a similar response when they entered the Black Hall commons. Both were very happy to relate the events to hundreds of eager ears.

Chapter 19—One Shot, One Kill

Aneta continued to scour London for signs of this Simon fellow and her mutilated sister, but grew more and more disheartened with each passing day. She took to following the news on the tele, in hopes that something, no matter how remote, might appear, even a death notice, anything.

On April 7, she, like many in the entire world, were glued to their sets. All coverage was about the developing crisis in the States. On the MAG news, a picture of Dominus was shown. Aneta nearly jumped out of her chair. “That’s him! That’s the man who took Milankova! Called himself Simon something. Darn it! He’s in the US, not London.” She packed her bags, intending to head there, though she had no idea where to begin looking. The United States was a huge place, compared to her country.

Just as she was about to check out, Amos Slaughter began his lengthy speech. When the revelation that Dominus Malefic was really Simon Mac Fluide, Aneta shrieked. “Now I have him!” She felt sure that she could find where this man lived now that she knew his real last name. Hence, she delayed her trip to the States and began hunting for homes owned by this man. Unfortunately, she was again frustrated. While he owned several companies, none of these had ever seen him with any woman, let alone how she described the condition of her sister.

Rebuffed, she again began watching the tele, wondering what she could possibly do now. All hopes of ever finding Milankova vanished from her mind. Slowly, revenge took its place. “That man must pay for what he did to my little sister! I swear I will kill him myself!” She continued to watch the news from the States.

Then on April 15, a short notice caught her attention. “Simon Mac Fluide, alias Dominus Malefic, will be transported from Denver Maximum Security Prison to the Federal Court in downtown Denver tomorrow to be arraigned on well over a hundred charges ranging from murder to rape to mutilations to high treason against the United States. He is due in court at ten a.m.” Aneta immediately checked out of her cheap London motel and cast her Teleport spell, arriving outside the Denver courthouse. Her keen eyes surveyed the whole surrounding area. She spied what she desired and cast first an Invisible spell followed by another Teleport spell.

Perched high above the granite steps leading into the large, stately building, she watched all that day. Frequently prisoners in handcuffs were led up the steps into the courthouse, later returning the same way. Even those being Teleported here arrived at the bottom of the steps and then climbed them to enter. Satisfied with her observations, she moved to her choice of locations. Now she would wait. Aneta was patient, highly trained for such operations. She Summoned her baby and set it up, tested it, placed one fifty caliber explosive shell in its chamber and locked it. She slept in her perch through the night.

Dawn came. People began appearing on the streets as Denver came to life once more. Around nine, police brought a man in handcuffs and leg cuffs into the courthouse. She looked through her sights and made a slight adjustment. She checked on the winds, but they were calm this morning. She waited patiently. It all happened in a blink of an eye.

Promptly at two minutes before ten, three men materialized at the base of the granite steps. Two Security men held Dominus between them; he was heavily handcuffed and leg cuffed. They took one step up the stairs leading into the court house. She gently pulled the trigger. The silencer did its job. Only a faint psst sound emitted, drowned in the nose of all the approaching TV cameras. A large hole appeared between Simon's eyes; the back of his head exploded, leaving a six inch area devoid of bone and brain matter at the back of his head. The lifeless body of Simon Mac Fluide slumped to the ground, though the Security men attempted to support him for a couple of seconds before they realized that their prisoner had been assassinated while in their custody. All this had been caught live by the six television crews working this assignment.

Aneta waved her wand and Teleported some distance away. Still invisible, she stowed her baby, cast Shrink on it, and placed the tiny case in her pocket. Satisfied, she hailed a cab and asked to be taken to an inexpensive motel.

At Bradbury's Lindsey and friends were working a problem that Professor Herbert had assigned. A Message appeared before Herbert's eyes. Pam looked up and wondered what that was all about. She had not long to wonder. "Class, excuse me. I've just received word from Professor Cho Lin, and I'm supposed to relay it to all of you. It seems that Dominus was assassinated while entering the federal courthouse in Denver this morning, just around ten. He's very dead." The class applauded, but he quickly got them back on their problem solving work.

Over lunch, everyone dashed to the commons to watch the news. Indeed, they all got to see the video replay of the assassination. Actually, there was little to see. Cameras began focusing in on Dominus, held between two Security men. Some thought that they heard a faint noise, but a small hole suddenly appeared in the forehead of Dominus, right between his eyes. His body slumped, held up only by the two men, who slowly lowered him to the ground. Their wands flashed in all directions, but nothing further happened. Discretely, the messy backside was not shown on TV, although the six different crews digitally recorded it. The sixty-second clip was repeated several times. Then they rushed off to eat lunch.

While they were eating, everyone in the school was talking about the assassination. Emilio commented, "Well that was a professional hit, if ever there was one. Did you see that perfect placement of the shot? Dead center. Must have been a real marksman who did it."

Speculation ran wild about who was responsible. Pam commented, "Well someone must have really hated him for what he has done, so much so, that they hired a professional hit man."

Just then, Pam received a Message.

Need your help. Will send all videos along shortly. Study them this evening. Must find assassin. F.

"Well, that's more like it," Pam said, and then explained what her dad wanted her to do. Pam counted the minutes until Spell Casting class was over. Sure enough, she had a top security package waiting her. She explained what she needed, and Professor Cho Lin allowed her the use of a DVD player and TV in the Admin Hall. Naturally, all the other Rodents wanted to see too. Since her dad had not said that she was to keep this secret, they all gathered for a viewing of the six disks provided by the six camera crews.

"Good god! He's got no back of his head!" Emilio exclaimed, stating the gruesomely obvious. Quickly, all the girls left Pam to her work, even the guys grew disinterested. The recordings were only sixty seconds long. All pretty much showed the same thing. Pam, however, saw things differently. Her father needed a clue, and by golly, she was going to find it for him. First thing, copy these to her computer. Ten minutes later, she pulled them up on her laptop and began observing them all once more.

An hour passed as well as countless viewing of the assassination. Just when she was about to give up and request an on sight viewing, she spied something in the upper left corner of one tape. She replayed that tiny section in very slow motion and saw a tiny flash of light. There was the dark outline of a person there, invisible at first, but who became visible as the light flashed. She saw a wand motion and recognized a Teleport spell! She was on to something.

Pam made a copy of these few seconds of video and then uploaded them to her triple secure server in her dad's office. Next, she loaded up the Department of Magical Misuse's image enhancing software, a program far too large to fit on her laptop, though she had once tried to install it there. For another hour, she tried various enhancement technologies until she finally got an improved frame. Bingo. There was a strange looking rifle, a person dressed all in black except for the blue eyes. She smiled, "Gotcha!" She sent an email to her father with the image attached, and then printed one off for herself. A few minutes later, she showed Professor Cho Lin the photo of the assassin and thanked her for the use of the school's video equipment.

A couple minutes later, Pam showed her fellow Rodents the enhanced image. "How on earth did you ever spot this? I didn't see this in any of the tapes," Emilio exclaimed, awed at her skill.

Pam was about to reply, "Well, you ought to have looked." She thought better of this and said, "I stared at them for over an hour before I spotted it. It was very faint. This image is the result of an image enhancement program my dad has." Emilio felt better about it now.

"Told you it had to be a professional hit man," he commented. "One shot, one kill. That's their motto."

"No, that is the motto of the snipers in the Special Forces," Pam corrected him. Speculation now turned to a disgruntled member of the US Special Forces. Then, it was back to studies. Pam didn't get to bed until nearly one that night, valiantly writing three compositions, instead of her choice of one of the three. She didn't even open her poem book.

Chapter 20—Attempting Normalcy

Casper and Fred both insisted that the Rodents refrain from going after the many remaining wizards and other criminals in the employ of Dominus until after they graduated. Besides, they wanted to give these men time to come to their senses and surrender. During the last weeks of April and May, a good many actually did, hoping that their action would make their penalties lesser. Additionally, once the Department of Law and Justice personnel took over the confiscated properties and companies being held by the Security Defense personnel, they were then free to go after the lesser wizards and normals who had participated in the tyranny of Dominus. These Security men apprehended a large number of these as well. In fact, by June 1, only fifty wizards remained at large for the Rodents to round up.

The next morning classes went well, except for Pam, who completely flunked another poem quiz, having merely randomly guessed answers. During the breaks between classes, most all their classmates did ask for their autographs, however. Deiter was eager to sign; Pam, most reluctant.

No, it was in Spell Casting class that they discovered the viewpoints of their classmates towards them had altered utterly. Uniformly, their mates shied away from them. Soon they saw that they were being considered gods or super powerful wizards and witches, not just the usual sixth year students. Kathy found this change in attitude most disconcerting.

Pam ignored them. She was far too interested in their tasks in class. Professor Arthur explained, “For the remaining few weeks, you have two choices before you. One, you can go back and try once more to learn various spells that you failed to master. Two, you can begin to invent new Specialty spells of your choice. All I ask is please, let’s not have anyone ‘doing a Deiter’ on us.” The class giggled and chuckled. He’d become famous for his spell casting blunders, which in the end proved highly valuable. Mass Disarm was highly useful indeed.

The next day, in Spell Casting class, Lindsey announced, “Well, today I’m going to see if I can master Deiter’s Mass Disarm spell. We all have the Mass Message spell down, and this one of his was invaluable. Anyone else game?”

“Sure, I have to admit that Deiter’s spell really helped us apprehend all those Death Stalkers,” Pam went along with Lindsey. Soon, her whole group decided to try it. She and her fellow Rodents had opted to try to invent new spells. Most of the rest of the class wanted to try to pick up some of those they had failed to learn before. Deiter was the teacher, naturally; it was his spell.

“You see, you just have to be utterly convinced it is going to work, only you just forget to specify who is to be disarmed. Have in mind that everyone will be disarmed when your wand activates,” he explained.

They began to practice it for the next few hours. Pam

was the first to "do a Deiter" as everyone now referred to it. All their wands went flying about the room. "Look, Pam's done a Deiter!" Peaches exclaimed, visibly excited that someone else could now do this.

Ashley picked it up next, then Lindsey, and then Amanda. The others continued to work on it until at last Peaches managed to do a Deiter and cheered loudly over her success. Emilio and Kathy finally gave up in disgust; they were not even close to doing a Deiter.

Near the end of the three-hour class, Professor Arthur brought in Peggy West of Red Hall. Professor Jerry, who had been overseeing Lindsey's group, halted them and nodded to Arthur. "Class," Professor Arthur said with tremendous pride, "I would like to announce to all of you the Miss Peggy West has just mastered the Full Wish spell, becoming the first Bradbury's student to do so in fifty years!" She beamed with pride. Lindsey and her friends clapped loudly and cheered her.

"Thanks, this is *so* cool! Now I'm a *real* power witch!" Peggy proclaimed. Indeed, Peggy was the talk of Bradbury's for the rest of the week. Some even teased her, "From now on, Red Hall will always be winning the school track and soccer trophy!" Those that overheard this one laughed heartily. Of course, Peggy had no such wishes in mind. Red Hall students were very passionate about things, but running miles was definitely not one of them, although a few were excited about soccer.

Around the first of May, two key events occurred. First,

Lindsey suddenly realized that she really didn't know all that much about cooking complete meals. True, they had helped around their homes, and Lena even helped them learn to plan meals, but cooking a really fine meal all by herself, this Lindsey had never done. If she were going to get married, Lindsey realized that she would be responsible for their cooking. She didn't relish spending hours in the kitchen, so she proposed that they invent a Cook Complete Meal spell.

Every girl in the class thought this was the best idea ever and wanted to join her. The fellows groaned and decided to think of something else. When she explained it to Professor Jerry, he too laughed and said, "Oops, this one is way out of my line of casting. Let me bring in someone more appropriate, okay." Lindsey agreed but wondered who that would be—perhaps one of the staff who handled the cooking in the secret kitchen below the dining hall.

To everyone's complete and utter surprise, Professor Janice Smith walked in to their classroom, wand held firmly in her right hand. "I understand that you all wish to invent a Cook Complete Meal spell. Is this correct?"

"Yes, you know—a wave of the wand and the meal all gets done. Honestly, we don't want to spend hours in the kitchen everyday preparing meals and all that. We don't mind doing it occasionally, but not every day. That's drudgery," Lindsey explained. Professor Janice smiled, her brilliant red lips contrasting with her pure white teeth.

"Well, then, follow me to the kitchen. The cooks have given us the run of the place for two hours each day. Mind you,

I will require proper wand activation." Lindsey stifled a giggle.

Once in the kitchen, Professor Janice explained, "You see, every spell *mimics* some activity. In this case, we want a spell to mimic what must be done to prepare a complete meal, say a dinner. Thus, first you must know in *total* detail every step that must be done. Only then can you work on creating a spell to carry that out. Today, ladies, put your wands aside. I want you to prepare your meal, omitting no steps. Pay keen attention to each step, each action that you are taking. You will need to mimic these when you cast the spell."

"That's an interesting clue," Pam whispered to Lindsey, "spells *mimic* actions." The teens set to work cooking their complete meals. Two weeks later, all the girls had mastered their newly invented spell, which was labeled Cook Complete Meal.

The second event that occurred on the first of May was far stranger. In the late afternoon, a young woman arrived at the gates of Bradbury's. She pressed the button and Professor Cho Lin responded. She opened the gates. "Hello. I am Professor Cho Lin Sung and acting Governor of Bradbury's. How can I help you?" said politely. Her eyes noticed no new cars in their lot, so presumably the woman was a witch. She was around thirty, Cho Lin guessed, as the woman tossed back her shoulder length brunette hair. Her blue eyes met those of Cho Lin.

"My name is Aneta Deniska, a witch from Prague, Czechoslovakia. I have heard on the news that you have a Miss

Pam Betts here and that she is a Sleuth. I would like to speak with her about my sister. I believe it is a matter of life and death for my sister, though already we may be too late."

When the buzzer announced that someone was at the gates, Cho Lin had cast See True on herself. Thus, she concluded that this woman was who she claimed. Further, her eyes indicated no lies. "Miss Betts is still a student here. Yet this is Saturday, and she is not in class. I will insist that I am present when you talk with her. Is that acceptable?"

"Yes, yes, thank you so much." The woman seemed sincere and followed Cho Lin across the campus, now green with spring. "You have such a pretty campus here, not like Prague." Cho Lin graciously accepted the compliment.

"Say, as you probably also know, many of the Rodents go to school here. Perhaps you may wish other Rodents to hear what you have to say to Miss Betts," Cho Lin probed.

"It is very, how you say, humiliating, embarrassing. Only girls please. Very nasty business."

"Okay, I'll ask Miss Barron, the Dispeller, and Miss Stokes-Compton, the Class 4 Diviner, to accompany Miss Betts. Perhaps they will also be able to assist."

"Yes, yes, perhaps. Is she really Class 4? There are none of those anymore," she asked.

"Very much so. Ah, here is my office in the Administration Hall. I've Messaged them, and they will be waiting for us." Cho Lin held the door open for her.

A minute before this, Cho Lin sent a Mass Message to Pam, Lindsey, and Ashley, asking them to come to her office in the Admin Hall at once. A young witch was requesting to meet with Pam. "I wonder what this is all about?" Pam said, as the three got to the office ahead of Cho Lin.

"Dunno, but must be important," Ashley replied, glad of an excuse to get out of doing her poem homework. Pam still had not even opened the book this entire term.

The door opened and Professor Cho Lin ushered in a poorly dressed young woman, clearly of foreign descent, but well groomed. She had very pretty blue eyes, Ashley noted, though there was a cloud of gloom over her.

Cho Lin introduced the teens to Aneta Deniska. "She is from Prague and has asked to meet with Sleuth Pam, here, but I thought it prudent to have our Dispeller and Diviner on hand as well. Aneta, can I get you anything to eat or drink?"

"No, thank you. It is more than enough to be allowed to talk with Miss Betts."

"Pam, please, just Pam," she suggested. Aneta smiled slightly. She liked those who dispensed with formalities better.

"Let me begin at the beginning, now back around January. I have a sister, Milankova, who is nine years younger than me. She's twenty-one. Our parents have passed on, and I have been looking after my sister for many years now. I worked nights as a security guard at a factory, after I got out of the army. Milankova is not like me; she is very beautiful and has begun a modeling career, very pretty. But she also is a bit wild; she likes to dance and party, probably a bunch too much. She defies me and goes to nightclubs while I am at work. I can do nothing to stop her."

"Then I come home and she not there. I wait up until morning, but no Milankova. I file missing person report. I search hospitals, even morgues, but not find her. Days go by. I quit my job and search all of Prague for her. Then policeman calls me to the station to tell me news from London. They found her arms in the Thames River by London!"

"I go to London at once, search all of Thames. I expect to find the rest of her body, but no, I didn't find a thing, not even her clothes. Then, I think that she may still be alive. I was in army, so I know how to watch unseen. I know that she only likes to go to the finest nightclubs and party. I stake out all the best ones, watching with my night vision goggles from a distance. After a couple weeks, I finally see a Rolls Royce, expensive car, pull up to Denny's. A man got out and then helped a woman out. She looked so much like my sister! But I could not be sure. Man takes car, how you say, wallet, no, valet. I watch people get cars back. I go Invisible and hide where I can see them when they come out. I wait. I am very patient."

"At last, the man comes out with the woman. I see her very good. She is Milankova! But he has mutilated her. She has only short arms, down to elbows. I see her eyes, they are wrong color, but then I realize they are glass eyes; she has been blinded. It is worse. He has done something awful to her lovely breasts. They are now as big as her head, I think. He made her wear very strange boots that I've never seen before. She is like made to walk on her toes I think, very high heel."

"I wanted to rescue her right there, but I admit I was so

shocked to see what he had done to my poor Milankova that I froze, but he heard me, I think, because he looked around and then got into the car. I was going to try to Fly and follow him, but as the car drove away, it vanished. Teleport I believe. Must be powerful wizard to take car with him."

"I ask valet man who this was. He tells me Simon but gets last name wrong. I spent a week searching all of London for home of man with wrong name. Then I search for all Simon's but that is no good at all. I keep watching clubs, but I see them not again."

"Then you had your big battle thing. Tele showed pictures of captured evil man, here called Dominus, but I recognized him. He was the man who took my sister and mutilated her body! In London, he is called Simon. Tele shows your Amos man identifying him as Simon Mac Fluide. So now, I research London for a home owned by him. I found a few businesses, but they never saw him with any woman. I felt defeated again."

"Then I want revenge. He did this to my sister. I cannot find her. She probably now dead. He must pay. I see he is going to court. I take him out. We say: one shot, one kill. Only put one shell in my baby. Milankova has revenge now. I still try to find Milankova, but still cannot. I hear Pam is big Sleuth. I decide I come to ask Pam to help me find my sister. I can pay a little money, but I promise to work hard and get all money Pam wants, if you can help me find her. Please, you help Aneta find sister, please."

Pam grinned—the irony of it all. Dominus was killed by

a woman seeking revenge for what he had done to her sister. Dominus went to his death never realizing how powerful women can be, that was the biggest error he made. "Summon Image." Pam cast her spell, and the image she had made appeared in her hand. "Now things make more sense, Aneta. Is this you?" She showed her the enhanced image.

Aneta smiled. "You good Sleuth. That's me. Czechoslovakian Special Forces. No see me. One shot, one kill. Clean kill. He pays for crime against Milankova."

"Cool. Well, Aneta, we have been rescuing women who were mutilated just as your sister has been." She proceeded to describe several of those times. "He considered them his toys, his play things. Often we find around four women mutilated similar to the way the Milankova was. He also has another woman who is in charge of helping them, only he cuts off her legs so she cannot escape or get away and has to stay there and help the women. Always he has a Death Stalker around to look after them. So Dominus has made another toy house in London. The question is: has that wizard who is looking after them still there or has he abandoned them, leaving them to starve to death?"

"It is bad. I know. Milankova is probably dead, my fault. I should have kept her from going to nightclubs. If can find her, I take her body home to Prague, bury her beside our parents. I got revenge for many other women too, I see."

"Okay first things first. Summon Laptop." Pam's wand activated, and her laptop appeared in her lap. A minute later, she was scrolling the many listing of the extended Mac Fluide enterprises. "Yes, you are right. Simon owned three businesses in London proper, but no homes. Yet, this has to be a home, if he stuck to the pattern he has always followed. Now since we have found and raided all of his other toy houses, he probably took extra care to keep this one hidden from us. With his ego, he probably kept the name Simon, but bought the house under a fake last name. However, the funds must have come from somewhere. Another possibility would be to search all sales of homes in London say from last June through December, possibly January this year."

"How can you do that?" Aneta asked.

"Well, I will need to get permission and an access code from the London authorities. Let's see, I know." She sent a detailed Message to her father.

"While I am waiting on that, let me search bank records. Probably he paid one lump sum for the house. I'm sure that he never wanted to bother with making monthly loan payments. What is a good guess on how much he might have spent on a house in London?"

Lindsey chuckled, "Search me. I have no idea of house prices."

"Oh!" Ashley spoke up. "Try a million dollars. It just sort of came to me that this time he wanted a quality house so he could put up better protections against us raiding it."

Pam grinned, "We've spooked him. Okay, I will search for all single transactions across his entire enterprise looking for one that is between say nine hundred thousand and fifteen hundred. There. It is off and searching."

"What? You have all his business records on your computer there? How possible?" Aneta asked.

"From Mary Hampton. We've confiscated everything he had. She's gotten all his financial dealings into a large database. It is not on this computer. I am running against the Department of Magical Misuse's large mainframe computer. Otherwise, this search could take quite a while."

"Ah, here come the search results now, filling up a table on my computer, so I can search in more detail. Now let's remove all those not going to London. Well, bingo! Got him! Better cancel my request to see the London database." She sent her dad another Message.

"Look, on November 15 last year, he wired 1.2 million dollars from his TV station in Florida to a bank in London. One minute and I'll have the details of that purchase." Indeed, a minute later, she had the bill of sale displayed on her screen. "He bought a new home on the small side. Here's the address."

"Oh thank you, thank you. I shall go now and try to rescue Milankova or take her body back to Prague," Aneta gushed her tremendous relief at finally knowing where her sister might be located.

"Oh no you don't, Aneta. There is highly likely to be one or more Death Stalkers hiding out there. I can't let you go up against them all by yourself! Besides, what if there are a half dozen women being kept there, all like your sister? How are you going to be able to care for so many women in dire trouble?"

"But I have no one to ask for help," Aneta replied,

pitifully. She knew her limitations well. Perhaps with all of Milankova's savings, maybe she could get her eyes back or maybe her arms. She'd have to have a long discussion with her about that, assuming she was not already dead.

Cho Lin spoke up, "You are here, and the Rodents are here. Allow us, please. Now Ashley, can you possibly get us more information? I will let the other Rodents know. I believe you have a short mission ahead of you." She grinned.

"Have you got a picture of your sister? That will help a lot," Ashley asked. She stared at the picture and then at the MagGoogle map that showed in good detail the location of the home. She closed her eyes and relaxed. At first, Ashley was a bit startled. Everything was utterly black! Then she remembered that Milankova was now blind. Words began appearing, and she concentrated more, picking up a distant conversation plus a growing fear.

When she opened her eyes, all the Rodents were present, patiently waiting for her. "Hi all. We must act soon. I found them. Cho Lin, you are right. Several Death Stalkers are hiding out there. Right now three of them are arguing about disposing of the women, claiming Dominus is gone and that they are just dead weight. One wants to keep them as his play toys. I can't tell how many are there—at least three. Milankova is still alive, but she is becoming very scared. I heard what she was hearing, that is, the men talking downstairs about disposing of the women. We had better do something quickly."

"Okay, Rodents, you have my permission to take this house, capture the Death Stalkers, and put them into the

Maximum Security Prison as before. However, if the women are there as we suspect, you are to Teleport them here to Bradbury's immediately. Understood?"

"Yes, Professor," Lindsey gave her a playful salute. "I'll cover their healing costs," she added.

Cho Lin retorted, "You'll do nothing of the kind! Just bring them here fast."

"Okay, spells time," Pam announced. She handed the list to Aneta. "Can you cast these on yourself now?" Aneta nodded and began casting Skin of Stone. A few minutes later everyone had their protections up and were ready to go.

"What's the plan?" Deiter asked. "Our secret weapon?"

"Yes, Pam, Ashley, you are with Deiter. We'll Magic Door into the front room. I'll keep their nastiest spells defused, work on Dispelling any protections they have, and then go for their capture. All set? Okay, let's study the map to make sure we don't get lost and off we go."

Three minutes later, one by one the eighteen alighted on the street before the nearly new home on a residential street. At first, no one saw the house for which they were seeking. Lindsey took a closer look and removed the Mislocation spell, which caused them all to fail to see the home itself. Next, she removed the Repulsion spell that prevented them from moving in closer to the front door. She noticed that the door was also enchanted and removed the magical energies from it.

"Stay alert. Probably more traps and guards inside. Okay, Magic Door time," Lindsey ordered. The Invisible group cast their spell nearly simultaneously, stepping out inside the front room. At once, a spell activated, "Intruders! Intruders!" Lindsey silenced that spell, dispersing its magical energies rapidly. Five Death Stalkers, wands at the ready rushed into the room, looking wildly around them. At once, Lindsey went to work on them.

They had very few protection spells on their persons. However, they quickly dispelled the many Invisible spells and began to shoot Disintegrate spells at the invading women. These Lindsey easily dispersed long before they could form enough to discharge. Webs flew thick into the living room, covering everything in a giant mess. Large gloved hands began to pound or grip the men, who at last discovered Lindsey, just standing there looking at them with her wand at her side. She did not need it at all, for what she was doing.

Fear now swept over the men, even more so as one of them mysteriously vanished from sight; then another one was gone. Dispelling a number of the webs, two tried to retreat, but Fern caught one with her Gripping Fist from behind and held him securely. He wrestled and tried to get his wand in position to cast a Dispel Magic on it, but couldn't. Audrey cast a Bind spell on the other retreating man. The carpeting swelled up and tripped him. As he hit the floor, the carpeting wrapped around him holding him tightly. The last man merely dropped his wand and raised his hands. The next instant, he too vanished from sight.

Fern called out, "Audrey and I will hold these two until Deiter takes them away."

"Okay, everyone fan out and search this floor. See if it has a basement. Peaches, guard the stairs leading to the second floor. Yell if anyone else comes down it. We don't know if there are any more Death Stalkers in here. Don't take any chances," Lindsey ordered and began following Jim as he headed back the way the man had come. Various voices called out "Clear" until at last Lindsey was satisfied that the first floor and basement were clear of others.

Pam, Ashley, and Deiter arrived. "I'll collect the evidence," Pam stated flatly. "Have you found the women yet?"

"No, they are probably kept upstairs, because that way the steps become a barrier and they cannot escape the house," Lindsey theorized, based on all their previous encounters. "Okay, guys, you remain down here and on guard; give Pam a hand if she needs something. If the women are up there, it is better for them if you are not present, not until we can cover them or something."

Lindsey led the way up the steps, looking for traps or other signs of magical protections or counters. "Gosh, I hope this is the last time we ever have to do this," she said to Amanda, who was right behind her. Wilma, now Levitated, hovered above the girls, ready to blast any surprise attacker, before he could get to the teens.

At the top of the stairs, the decor changed to the velvet red wallpaper that Dominus always used in his toy houses. The layout of the rooms became obvious. A long hall began just before the master bedroom. A secure gate blocked the stairs so that the blind women could not accidentally fall down the stairs. Without hands, they could not open it. Down the hall was a large master bath. At the far end was a closed door, probably where the women were kept. As they passed each room, one or more of the Rodents checked it out, pronouncing it clear.

At last, Lindsey reached the closed door. She heard women's voices inside. Aneta came up close to her and whispered, "Do you hear them? Alive?"

Lindsey nodded. "Remember, they are all likely to be under the Idiot Mind spell. Here we go." She opened the door, startling a woman who sat on a pillow on the floor whose her legs were missing below her knees. Soft padded cushions were attached; presumable she walked much as the Venezuelan woman had. She had a matronly air about her caused in part from the Idiot Mind spell.

Five beds lined the walls and a large couch was in the middle of the room. Four more women sat rigidly upright on the couch. The scene was all too familiar to these teens. Wearing nothing but a very tight corset and hose and those crippling ballet boots, each was missing their lower arms, had their busts grown to mammoth sizes, and had glass eyeballs, making then permanently blinded. All five were under the effects of the Idiot Mind spell. The four did move their heads more or less in the direction of the door, totally confused about what was happening.

Aneta rushed to her sister, taking her arms in her hands. "It is me, Aneta. I've come to rescue you, Milankova. What has he done to you? Are you okay?"

"Aneta? Is that you, really?" Her overly tight corset caused her to gasp for breath every few words. "Oh, I am perfectly fine. Simon is taking good care of me. He's taken me to the finest nightclub in London. I have a pretty new dress around here somewhere, only I can't see it. I am doing fine. Can you tell him I want to go dancing again real soon? I do like to go out. I just wish I could see better. He tells me what I would be seeing. So I really am not missing anything, now am I? Can you find my pretty green party dress?"

Meanwhile, the matronly woman barked harshly, "You should not be here. Simon is very strict about visitors. If you don't leave at once, I have to report you to Simon. He will be very angry. Might hurt you. You must leave. Don't you hear me? Don't touch that woman! I am respon. . ." she couldn't quite remember that big word and added, "I care for these women. You know. I brush their hair and put on their makeup. Now you all must leave. We are all perfectly fine. We don't need your help. Please leave. You are not welcome."

Wilma moved in front of the matronly woman and said, "Excuse me. What is your name? Where are you from originally? I am called Wilma."

"Oh, Millicent, Millicent Bindleweather. I've been a Londoner all my life. Pleased to meet you Wilma. Bloody American are we?"

With Millicent calmed down, Lindsey moved to one of the other women, the one with pixie blonde hair. Taking her arms in her hands, she said, "Hello. I am Lindsey Barron. Who are you? Where did you live before coming here?"

"Alice Small. Here, London, if we are still in London. I am lost. I can't see anything anymore. Simon says I have beautiful new eyes. Are they beautiful? I hope so. I can't walk well. Milankova, she can. She walks so good. Simon took her to a nightclub. My feet hurt too bad. I want to go to the nightclub too. Can you take us to the nightclub? I won't be able to dance though. Milankova says she can dance. I can stand though and walk to the bathroom."

Amanda followed Lindsey's lead, taking a hold of the next woman's hand. All these were probably twenty-one at the most, except the matronly woman, who was more like thirty or forty. "Hello, I am Amanda Whitewater. What is your name? Where did you live before here?"

In a thick Scottish accent she replied, "Zoe Smith. Edinburgh, that's in Scotland, you know. What is going on? Men downstairs are bad men. Want to dispose of us. We don't want to be disposed, whatever that is. Where's Simon? He looks after us. He promised to take us to a nightclub. I can't walk good enough. Milankova can. Bought her fine new dress. Simon is good man. Brings us chocolates. Don't let bad men dispose me, please."

"No one is going to hurt you, I promise," Amanda replied.

At the same time, Ashley took a hold of the fourth woman's short arms. She noted that Dominus had done more than just slice off their arms at their elbows. This time he also changed the shape of their upper arms, turning them into a conical shape, barely an inch across at their elbows. "Hi my name is Ashley. What's yours?"

"Oh, hi. I am Jamie Lyn Homestead. You sound like Simon. American?" Ashley replied that she was from Colorado. "Great. I'm from Atlanta. That's Georgia. I am a dancer, but only Milankova is good now. She can walk. I can't much. Don't know why I can't. Hard to keep from falling down. Feet hurt. Still Simon is kind. Brings me chocolates. Milankova is his favorite. She walks good. Simon gave her a new dress. Simon took her to dance club. I want to go too. Can't walk good yet. I promise to try. Bad men down stairs. What does dispose mean? They want to dispose of us. Milankova says that means something bad. She's not sure what."

Lindsey wanted to tell them right now that Simon was the bad man and that he was dead. However, she refrained, knowing that with their current intelligence level and point of view, that would only create more difficulties. She spied Aneta looking for traps on her sister. Cho Lin had warned her that Dominus often booby-trapped the shoes and corsets so that they cannot be removed.

Wisely, Wilma spoke up, "Okay, listen up you lovely women. It is time that you all get a chance to go to a nightclub. So we are going to take you there right now. Once we get there, I am sure that you all would like something nice to drink, right? So we'll have drinks waiting there for us."

"Millicent will come along with us. While she cannot dance, she can watch and help you all with your makeup and stuff. She will have a good time too, while watching over you." Millicent looked pleased with this. After all, she had been cooped up here for months as well, and she did envy Milankova, who had been to the nightclub with Simon.

Lindsey sent a detailed Message to Doctor Caterwall. Then it was time to move the women. Milankova was insistent on wearing her new dress. Aneta relented, found it, and with the help of several girls, finally got it on her sister. Meanwhile, no other dresses could be found, as Lindsey expected. However, sheets were wrapped around the other four women, with Wilma casting a spell on to Millicent, which made her believe she was looking at fine dresses not sheets.

"Now ladies, you are all dressed up. We will be arriving shortly at the nightclub. However, we must all walk a short ways inside. I know that Milankova can walk well, but if you can't we will carry you inside. Okay?"

All four expressed great relief. "I can walk, Aneta," Milankova said quite insistently. Aneta still kept her arm tightly around her sister. Lindsey gave the signal and the five cast their Teleport spells.

"Here we all are, just outside the nightclub. Of course, it was just an illusion, compliments of Cho Lin. They cast their Magical Doors once they stepped a few feet past the gates and arrived in the emergency room of the Infirmary. Again, for Millicent's benefit, it looked to be a fine nightclub indeed.

"Oh goodie. Tell me all about it, Aneta," Milankova begged. Aneta didn't quite know what to say. It was just a very simple, static illusion.

Lindsey came to the rescue. "Okay, here come our drinks. Aneta, will you help your sister with her fancy drink, please?" This defused everything. Lindsey also knew that the potion tasted awful so she added, "Boy, isn't this the finest tasting drink that you have ever had? I bet it costs a fortune." Cho Lin grinned at her. The power of suggestion on an Idiot Mind worked wonders. All five drank theirs without a complaint. Almost at once, the potion began its work.

A minute later, all five were sound asleep. Yes, tomorrow they would have headaches, a side effect of the removal of the Idiot Mind spell. However, now the doctor could go about his work. "Kids, time to check for traps. Don't remove anything from their bodies until we have triple checked for traps. Pam, you are the tally person. Now let's get cracking."

An hour later, the only traps they found were the glass eyeballs. He'd used the same poison capsule technique with these that he had used on Lindsey and Ashley. Doctor Caterwall explained the Deiter-Kathy removal techniques and set the group to work. Kathy showed Aneta how to alter the Wall of Force to slide it behind the glass eye, being careful not to remove it. Once the wall was completely around it, then it could be removed. Each time this was done, a small explosion occurred within the contained wall, splattering shards and poison, which was totally contained within the now spherical force walls.

Next, they quickly removed their corsets, nylons, and boots. He examined them very carefully but found nothing else amiss. At last, he had them move the five to their beds where they would have to remain for the next week. Finally, he began administering the heavy regrow potions to the five women.

"How is she?" asked Aneta, after he had finished setting up the IV for Milankova.

"In a week, she will be as good as new. Not to worry, Aneta; she's safe. However, for the next couple of days, none of these women will be allowed to move from their beds. So someone will have to be with them at all times. Plus, during the next week, they will need to consume as much of my special fortified milk as you can get them to drink. It's needed to rebuild their bones, you see."

"I promise I will be with her all times. Others too."

"Of course you will. We have lots of students here who will be coming in shifts to help look after all these women."

Indeed, Peaches had already begun a schedule sheet, circulating it among the halls. Soon the lists were overflowing with volunteers.

At suppertime, Aneta was replaced by several teens, and Pam invited her to come dine with them. She learned that Aneta was Brown Hall when she was in magic school years ago. "After we eat, my dad wants to chat with you, is that all right with you?"

"Is he going to arrest me for killing the bad Simon?" she asked a little concerned.

"I don't think so. Besides if he does, I will argue in your defense." That seemed to satisfy her.

Around seven, Fred met with Aneta and Pam privately. Fred had Aneta relate her whole story once more. Then he spoke, "Well thank you for being so honest with us, Aneta. I have discussed this with President Amos Slaughter, and he says that no charges of any kind will be filed against you in the matter of the assassination." Aneta looked very relieved.

"Now then about your future. As I understand it, you like to work security?"

"Yes, but it doesn't pay well in Prague."

"Well, how would you like to come work for the US Security Defense Department? We pay very well."

"What? You are offering me a job, here, in America?" she asked quite shocked.

"Yes indeed. We are shorthanded just now and in need of good security men and women, especially the one shot, one kill type. Are you interested? Your sister can be here with you. There are lots of modeling jobs to be had. She will prosper, I do believe."

"Yes, oh yes. Thank you, thank you, thank you all for everything. Now I will earn money to pay back school for healing my sister."

"About that, Aneta. I have entered her case as well as the other four women into our database of victims. When we get the money finally sorted out, she will receive a substantial amount of funds to help compensate her for the mutilations and crimes that Simon committed against her. She will be more than able to pay the school for her care. Don't give it another thought. Do you know much about America, like in what part of the country that you would like to live?" Aneta had no idea, which then gave the teens another task on which to work.

That night, while Lindsey was watching over the patients, she gathered up the five corsets, nylons, and boots, throwing them in a sack in her room. She'd discard them later on, if they were not needed as evidence. As she watched the sleeping women and the ghostly images of new arms and eyeballs appearing, Lindsey wondered how many more women like these were out there somewhere, as yet undiscovered.

Pam too was very worried about this. Somehow, she had missed this transaction, and Aneta had accidentally saved her from the error. How many more mistakes or clues had she missed?

Over breakfast, Pam confided in Lindsey. "I don't know who else I can really say this to but you, Lindsey. I made a tragic mistake in that I missed that house of Simon's, and it very nearly cost these five women their lives. Lindsey, how many more things have I missed? What if there are more out there that I have overlooked?"

"I know Pam. I was thinking on that last night too, you know, while watching the sleeping women. How many more of them are out there that we don't know about? How many will die because we just don't know about their plight? It scares me, Pam; it scares me."

Pam made a decision. She went to see Professor Herbert, her math professor and Elementary Education teacher. Pam explained her mistake, though he told her that it was not a mistake. "Sir, time is critical. I have an idea." He listened and agreed. Pam then headed to the school's computer.

The next morning in their math class, Professor Herbert explained the problem and solution. "This week, you are going to put your math skills to work. The recent women that were rescued were staying in a home that Simon bought using a fake name. The funds, of course, came from one of his many businesses. Hence, no one knew about this home, and the women very nearly were killed by the Death Stalkers. Thanks to the Department of Law and Justice, we now have the complete banking and finance records of all those companies. Our task is to go through all these entries, looking for additional hidden purchases of homes or properties that may have fallen through the crack." He outlined the procedure to use, illustrating just how they were to apply the math that they learned to this complex problem. Then, he turned them lose on the problem. He and Pam supervised and answered questions as they arose.

On the next to last week of May, they finished their exhausting study. Only one more home showed up. Emilio had found it. Dominus had purchased a home in Singapore using the name Simon Bolivar, of all choices! This time, acting Governor Cho Lin insisted that Pina Pong, Governor General of the Southeast Asian schools, accompany the Rodents. This was her country.

Around ten, she met them near the address of the dwelling. "So good to see you all again. Welcome to Singapore. I suppose we should get down to business. I have had this home watched since I got Cho Lin's Message. No one has gone in or out, but that doesn't rule out by magical means. I will let you deal with this Lindsey. I am your back up. I have fifty men waiting, Invisible, of course. Just say the word, and I'll send them in, okay?"

Lindsey grinned. "Sure. Okay, execute Pam's list everyone." Pina Pong watched as the seventeen began casting their protection spells. She noted that they left out none that would be useful in such a circumstance out. Then Pam, Ashley, and Deiter Teleported away. "Our secret Eliminator weapon," Lindsey teased Pina, who grinned. Obviously, these teens knew what they were doing! She had studied the reports sent to her by Amos. One hour and Dominus, Death Stalkers, the President, and all her cabinet were captured, not one killed, and no Rodent harmed. These teens had to be incredibly powerful, and she was thankful that she knew them. However, she was still curious, but could not locate the three.

Lindsey gave the order, and the Rodents went Invisible. Magical Doors opened, and they entered the building. She didn't see Lindsey disarming a dozen guards, wards, and alert spells that covered the front of the building. Several minutes later, Lindsey Messaged her. It was clear, but no one was inside. Lindsey wanted her to enter, which Pina did at once.

"Well, this was definitely a secret hideout," Pam pointed out. "We found many of his things and discovered a secret room beneath the basement. Have a look." Inside the large extra-dimensional room, Pina saw a large stockpile of canned food and water. A bed, desk, and clothes wardrobe was all that occupied the space. "You'll want this," Pam continued. "It appears to be a list of people that he had influence over, along with what appears to be plans to take over your country."

"We never knew! Terrific find. I assure you that those who were plotting to overthrow our country will be apprehended. This is invaluable information." Pina began reading the documents.

Audrey muttered, "Something is not right."

Ashley noticed Audrey's hint. She closed her eyes and began to concentrate, using her special skills. A bit later, she exclaimed, "Someone is here somewhere. There must be another secret room around here somewhere!"

Lindsey took charge. "Rodents, cast Open Doors over this whole place. Probably it is down here somewhere." Seventeen spells detonated covering nearly every inch of the walls in this forty-foot square room. Suddenly, the sound of stone sliding on stone broke the silence. A door opened near the large shelves holding the food and water. The room was entirely black. Light! Lindsey silently cast, and the room illuminated. It was about twenty foot square, containing a kitchen counter and sink, a bed, toilet facilities, and a woman lying on the floor, barely conscious.

She, like all the other victims of Simon, had been mutilated in a similar fashion. She was definitely from Singapore. She had very long black hair, the same type of blue glass eyes, forced to wear a tight corset, greatly enlarged breasts, very tall heels which were locked in place so that they could not be taken off, and of course she was missing her lower arms. Blood covered the floor beside her head. Pina took charge at once, Teleporting her to their Infirmary. She returned a little later.

"Well, her name is So Won. She's been a prisoner here for many years; we are not sure exactly how many. She is the one who uses that food and water, though she has a very hard time with it. Simon has not been here for some time, and she had an accident. She stumbled and fell onto the closing mechanism, which shut the door, and she was never able to get to her feet after that. She is very dehydrated and has not had anything to eat in days. Even if she could have managed to get up, she does not know how to open the door. She expected to die in there, unless Simon returned. Once more, another owes you her life. I thank you on her behalf. She is still pretty much delirious."

"Thanks, I will add her name to the database so she will receive monetary compensation along with all the others," Pam explained.

A while later back at school, Pam breathed a huge sigh of relief. She now had more confidence that nothing had been overlooked, that there were not others out there in dire peril. Finally, Pam could relax.

Also during May, Yellow Hall had their final sports events, which became nestled among all their other activities. The first Saturday in May was the track meet between Brown Hall and Yellow Hall. Lindsey allowed all the alternates to race. Yellow Hall won the meet as Amanda left their last runner two hundred feet behind her when she crossed the finish line of the twenty-mile relay race.'

The next Saturday was their final soccer match against Blue Hall. Lindsey decided to allow all the younger players to start the game. Later on, if Yellow Hall was in real danger of losing, she'd put herself and the other sixth years into the match. Fern, playing acting captain in Lindsey's absence, coached them to an easy victory. Yellow Hall had once more captured the school track and soccer trophy. Fern felt like a million! She and the players who would be returning next year stood a good chance of winning. At least, they would be competitive after losing so many sixth years. Black Hall still had not recovered from similar losses of their top players the previous years.

Chapter 21—End of Term

"Well, they are gone now," Lindsey said on Sunday morning, as she and Pam lounged around the dining room. Sunday mornings were serve yourself times. They remained here long after most others had grabbed a bite and left. The rescued women had fully recovered, both physically and mentally. Lindsey, herself, had cast the spells that erased their emotional trauma of their mutilations and captivity.

"Aneta and Milankova will be staying in Denver so we can visit them when we go dancing. I'm glad that she took a Security Defense position in Colorado," Pam replied, toying with her hair. "At least, I can rest better now, knowing that we've done everything possible to find other women. Do you realize we only have one more week left until we graduate? A few finals, the Formal Dance, and then graduation—hardly seems possible. Of course, then we will be free to go after the remaining Death Stalkers that have not given themselves up or been captured. Once we get that done, then Tom and I are getting married. I wonder what exactly I will do after that? I suppose I shall set up a Sleuthing operation somewhere."

"I hear you. I think Amanda's idea that we hold one big ceremony is a good one. I am really, really going to miss Bradbury's, Pam. My whole life has really begun here. Before that it was just misery, when I was little going to that one room school in Plano. I can't imagine life without Bradbury's, but then I guess I will have to, won't I?"

"Know what you mean. At least Kathy and Emilio have big plans. So do Amanda and Ahana. I know Tom's planning to start his own computer programming company. I'll help him all I can," Pam added. "Well, I guess I will go work on the log of just who we must apprehend yet. Ashley needs the list for her divination work. She and Jim want to get married as soon as we get them all rounded up and is in a big hurry to do so." Lindsey smiled. They all were and for the same reason.

"I wonder how I will like being married and all that?" Lindsey mused.

"Oh, let's not start in on that now or I will never get Ashley her list. Cya," Pam got up and headed for the study hall.

Lindsey got up and resolved to finish her last paper and prepare for the last poem test. She'd finished her math and was ready to cram for that last exam as well. The day passed slowly for her.

On Monday, they had their last set of exams in their traditional studies, namely math and English. Pam didn't answer a single poem question, however, but turned in all three essays, as she had been doing all this term. Now they had to wait for their grades to be posted. Lindsey felt hollow. There would be no exciting schedule of classes for next year appearing after their grades were posted! She realized just how comforting that small detail had been, something to look forward to all summer.

Deiter caught up with her. "Say, are you ready for our last Formal Dance?"

"Yes, but I feel so sad about it, our last one, very last one, Deiter."

"Yes, but we can go to all the Formal Dance nights at B & B's," he countered. She brightened up.

"Can we go every Friday night?"

"Lindsey, you dress up, and I'll go every night of the week!" She flushed, but knew what he meant. She loved the way he looked in his fancy suit.

"Promise."

"Promise. What are you going to wear to our last dance? It ought to be super special, you know, being our last one and all that," Deiter asked.

"I know. I'm going to wear my Inaugural Ball gown, in honor of Governor Alister, who bought it for me. My small tribute to him," Lindsey decided, remembering when he had given it to her. His incredible generosity struck home to her once more.

"Cool. I like that. I've a little tribute to him of my own. I found it in a small shop in Iowa, of all places. Wait til you see it," Deiter teased her and refused to tell her what it was.

"Excuse me, Deiter, here comes our track and soccer team. I got to officially do my last duty as captain." The team, led by Fern, came up to Lindsey, right on time she noted.

"Okay, it is my duty as your team captain to nominate next year's captain. If you don't like my choice, you are free to elect whoever you choose. My choice is Fern Whitewater." Fern grinned and was pleased to have this honor, one that only her older brother, Tom, had held.

"I promise to do my best for Yellow Hall," Fern pledged.

"I've another bit of news for you," Lindsey continued. "Next year, the Nationals are back on and will be held the third Saturday in May in Des Moines as usual. I think they just didn't want us running the last two years, probably afraid that we would win three years in a row." Her team giggled, but knew she was joking. "All of you practice up this summer, and I think you have a shot at going to the Nationals. The key is the total time for the twenty-mile relay race. Get it down to an average six-minute mile for the duration, and you will have a good chance of going. I hope you all make it!"

Everyone cheered. This was good news indeed. Lindsey wondered if the hot twins from New York would be moving back there. If so, Fern would be hard pressed, as she would lose her best two twenty-mile racers. Those were always the hardest to find.

The other teens liked Lindsey's idea to wear their Inaugural Ball gowns that Governor Alister had bought for them. "We will be a visible tribute to him," Ashley stated what they were all feeling. Again, they took all afternoon to get ready for the dance. All the while, Lindsey kept wondering what Deiter's surprise would be.

When they finally went down to the dining hall to meet their dates and eat supper before the dance, Lindsey spotted Deiter at once, and her face spontaneously broke into a broad smile. He was wearing a formal black suit with a top hat. The outfit was perfect if you were living some four hundred years ago. It was similar to the one that Governor Alister always wore when he opened the first formal dinner here. Deiter, too, was paying homage to Alister. Lindsey rushed to him and gave him an exuberant hug and kiss. "Perfect!" she whispered into his ear.

"Of course," he whispered back. "You look fabulous as always, my love." She blushed.

Professor Cho Lin officiated. "Tonight, Formal Dance night, marks the end of another year at Bradbury's. This year, more than any other, has been fraught with change, some good, and some bad. Our country has been in utter turmoil, but is now on its way to recovery and will be stronger than ever before. I'm so very proud of the way that every one of you students handled the various life situations that we all faced this year. In spite of everything going on in the world around us, you continued to study hard, and no one's grades have suffered. That would have made Governor Alister Broadwell most proud of you all."

"I have followed your wishes. When you return in the fall, a bronze statue of Governor Alister will be standing tall among the green field behind your dorms." Spontaneous clapping broke out, interrupting her, but she smiled and was pleased that the students appreciated this gesture.

"Tonight, our meal is Governor Alister's favorite. I should know; I have fixed it for him often enough." Several Red Hall girls giggled. "I hope you enjoy your chicken and pea pods as much as he always did. So let's let the festivities begin." She waved her wand, and the whole room changed into a romantic, dimly lit, elegant dining room, complete with thousands of candles. Oh's and ah's echoed around the room.

Lindsey felt cheated. This year, the dance lasted only a couple minutes; she was sure of it. "That's the shortest dance ever, Deiter! How come it is over already?"

"Love, we have been dancing for over three hours! It really is midnight, dear, look at the clock," he teased.

"Oh! Well, I think it ought to go on later or we should start earlier or something," she pleaded, knowing it was pointless.

"I know. I love every minute with you. Time just flies." He gave her a warm good night kiss and headed back to Black Hall, while she silently cast her Magical Door and stepped from the dining room into her bedroom, where her four dear friends were chatting as they undressed and got ready for bed.

The next morning, the teens were sleeping in, all except Amanda, who rarely did so. "Hey everyone, wake up. The grades are posted. Come on. Let's see how we did." Moans and groans circled around the room, but everyone stirred and dressed quickly to go down to the dining room to see how they had done, all except Pam, that is.

Covering her head with her pillow, she wailed, "I don't want to see mine. I can't face it. I flunked Poems. I want to just stay here and pretend I don't exist." The other four ignored her and dashed down to the wall on which the thousand student's grades were posted. Of course, one could only see their own grades; the wall was magically enchanted to prevent seeing other's grades.

"Wow! A in Potion Making III," Kathy exclaimed. "Way

cool, but I never ever thought that I'd get an A in math! For the first time in my entire life, I got all A's!"

"Duh, I don't know how I did it, but I got all A's too," Emilio replied.

In fact, all of Lindsey's friends had straight A's this year, an amazing feat, but not too surprising because of the heavy emphasis on magic this sixth year.

"Come on Pam; everyone got all A's!" Lindsey tried to coax Pam out of bed a half hour later. "You have to go see your grades."

"No, I will be the only one who has an F!" Pam wailed. Finally, all four teens cast a Levitate spell on Pam, lifting her out of her bed. While suspended in the air, they dressed her over her protests. Lindsey then open a Magical Door to the wall below their rooms, and all four brought the floating Pam through the door. They positioned her body before her name and said look. She kept her eyes tightly shut.

"Okay Pam, if you don't look, I will have to cast a spell on you to make you look," Lindsey stated in an annoyed fashion. It was fake; she was just teasing her friend.

"All right. All right, but put me down first," Pam gave in at last. "Now you can make fun of me, when I am the only one to flunk," she declared. Finally, she looked over her grades. "Oh my goodness. There must be a mistake! Cho Lin gave me a 90 in English, not the F."

"Well, are they all A's too?" Amanda asked annoyed with Pam.

"Well, yes they are," Pam replied, but thought better of

saying, like they have always been. Lindsey breathed a huge sigh of relief. She knew that Pam would have been utterly crushed if she had blown her straight A's throughout these past six years.

Just then, all the Rodents received a Message to report to the Admin Hall at once. Professor Cho Lin wanted to see them, and it sounded urgent. "I wonder what has happened this time," Pam said as they all raced there. "I should have looked at the news this morning. I'm slipping again, too much partying with Tom last night." Lindsey wanted to box her ears, but couldn't because she was jogging too fast.

When they entered the room, Wilma, Monane, and Jim were already there. Standing beside Professor Cho Lin was Mary Hampton! Lindsey wondered why Mary was here. Was something wrong back home?

Wilma spoke first, just as soon as everyone was in the room. "I have been acting as liaison for the Rodents. You see, when the Rat Pack went after Dominus years ago, Sam Barron was our official liaison to the government. I took that upon myself, since none of you are of age, except Jim. The Rat Pack was remunerated for its efforts in capturing Dominus and the Death Stalkers. Since the Rodents were about to do the same thing, I discussed our financial remuneration with Amos. Mary Hampton is acting as the US Federal Representative to the Rodents. Mary?" she nodded to the young attorney.

"On behalf of the entire country, let me extend our undying gratitude and thanks for what you have done already and for what little remains to be accomplished. I am extremely pleased have been chosen to make this presentation to you. It is the very least that we can do for you for what you have selfishly done for our country and all its citizens, wizards, witches, and normals. When I call your name, please come forward to receive your check. Miss Lindsey Barron."

Lindsey was a bit confused, though Wilma was smiling from ear to ear. She walked up to the smartly, professionally dressed woman, who was holding a check in her hand. Lindsey took the check and shook Mary's hand firmly. Then she looked at the check. Five million dollars!

"There must be some mistake! This check is for five million dollars! Am I supposed to divide it among the Rodents?" Lindsey asked. At the same time, the others gasped at such a huge sum.

"No, dear, that is all yours for a job very well done. Each of you will receive a similar check. Miss Ashley Stokes-Compton." Ashley squealed and held her hand over her mouth as she walked up. Five million dollars? Unbelievable, beyond words. All the teens were overwhelmed. Not Wilma or Monane, for what the Rodents had done, the government was getting off dirt cheap, in their minds.

"We are rich!" exclaimed Fern.

"No richer than rich," Deiter amended her statement.

"Now I can open Kathy's Potions right away," squealed Kathy, awestruck by her good fortune.

Lindsey now realized how her father, Sam, had acquired the small fortune that he had left her in his Secure Vault in Denver.

Once all seventeen had their check, Mary added, “Of course the government would like to call upon your services from time to time.”

“Absolutely!” Lindsey gushed.

“One more thing. We cannot keep you from the press any longer. Already, Lena has driven two pesky reporters off your ranch with her shotgun.” That’s my mom, Lindsey thought, giggling.

“So I have arranged a big interview session with the press on June 5 at the KMAG studios in downtown Denver. Fred Angel, head of the States Law and Justice department, will accompany you there.”

“Boy, do we ever need a spokesperson now,” Lindsey exclaimed.

“Don’t worry. Pam knows how to deal with the press,” she said frankly. “But what about you two, Wilma, Monane?”

“Kids, we’ve decided that now is as good a time as ever to come out of hiding. I’ll explain to the reporters about Bill and Able. That will give them something to write about. All these years, they thought the main members of the Rat Pack were men. Ha. Only Sam. That ought to raise the ante a bit, don’t you think?”

Lindsey laughed. Pam pointed out, “That was Simon’s downfall. Eleven of the Rodents are female. Three out of four Rats were female. Powerful magic users are not just men. Only a fool believes that.”

Everyone laughed loudly, even Professor Cho Lin. Then, Mary had to return and the meeting ended. However, the teens could only talk about their incredible good fortune for the rest of the day.

The next day was graduation day. First, the teens packed their belongings. As usual, Lindsey and her roommates had to purchase more duffle bags. How did their possessions keep growing so, Lindsey wondered. As the day grew on, they all became more nervous. Soon they would be handed their two diplomas, and after that in the morning, they would be leaving Bradbury's forever. Some were eagerly awaiting this, especially Emilio and Kathy, who had big plans in the works, as well as Amanda and Ahana, who were going on a three-month rock band tour. Lindsey and Pam felt just the opposite, Lindsey more so, since Bradbury's was the center of her life.

At last the supper hour came, Lindsey sighed as she headed down for what she believed would be her last dinner at Bradbury's. She was a little surprised to see Wilma, Monane, and Jim waiting for them, even more so when she also saw her mother and father with them. Her mouth dropped open when she recognized that all the Rodents' parents were gathered together in the back of the room. Why? This had never happened at a graduation before. She looked at the front. There were the large stacks of diplomas as usual and the large Bradbury's Cup for the winning track and soccer team, which would be Yellow Hall's once more.

Then, she saw that there were a number of other people, some rather old, sitting with Professor Cho Lin. Who were these people she wondered. Her friends, like her, were as surprised as she was, waving to their parents in the back.

There were three others sitting there by Professor Cho Lin's side. All wore long robes, colorful but regal. Then, she recognized one of them. It was acting President Amos Slaughter, the head of the States Justice Department. But who were the two much older looking men?

"Pam," she whispered, "what's going on? There is Amos, but who are the other two old guys?"

"Have you forgotten your first year History of Magic already?" Pam asked incredulously. "The one on the right of Amos is Arthur Doms. The one to his left is William Sturm. They were instrumental in building relations with the normals when the wizarding world went public. They are incredibly famous men. What are they doing here? Why are our parents here?"

"What gives?" asked Deiter, who had just arrived, taking a seat beside Lindsey instead of at the Black Hall table. All throughout the room, the thousand students were whispering similar thoughts to each other. Nothing like this had ever happened at graduation before!

At last, acting Governor Cho Lin rose. Lindsey held her breath, what was going on? "Extremely distinguished guests, parents, faculty, and students, I am pleased to welcome you all to the Arthur Bradbury's School of Magic Graduation 2183. Tonight our school has the highest honor possible. It is with great pride and humbleness that I am being allowed to introduce these three men to you. This is Acting President Amos Slaughter, Head of the States Justice Department, Order of Merlin, Knights of Truth. To his right, Arthur Doms, retired,

Order of Merlin, Knights of Truth, and to his left, William Sturm, retired, Order of Merlin, Knights of Truth. Never in the history of Bradbury's have we had such important guests at our school. At this time, I will turn the proceedings over to Amos." She sat down, Lindsey still had no idea what was going on. What was the new President doing here?

Amos rose and looked out over the many students and the rows of parents at the rear. "Tonight is a very special night for the whole world, not just the wizarding portion of that world." Lindsey notice that all three men wore identical golden medallions around their necks and prominently displayed on their chests. She resolved to get a good look at them afterwards. Why was tonight special?

"Since the dawn of time, the wizarding world has sought out the best of the best to honor them for their achievements. These very few wizards and witches have demonstrated power, power beyond the normal. Yet, with that all that immense power, they have shown wisdom, intelligence, compassion, and understanding for their fellow man, wielding that great power for the good, the betterment of mankind. Down through the ages, there have lived thousands upon thousands of wizards and witches. Yet, among them, but a handful can reach this highest standard of excellence, this pinnacle of power, used to better all mankind—oh, so dreadfully few, I'm afraid to say."

"In my own lifetime, until tonight, I have never had the opportunity to honor such a person, though my esteemed colleagues here beside me have done so three times. It is said that these are the best of the best, for these cherish truth above lies, wisdom above stupidity, generosity above avarice, bravery above cowardice, and a dedication to mankind above self. It is the highest possible honor for Arthur, William, and me to be here with you tonight to bestow this award, this title upon those who have displayed what is greatest among us all. And for William, who is now ninety years young, this night holds an even greater honor, for it was here that he first bestowed this highest of honors upon one of your own, the revered Governor Alister Broadwell."

The room broke out into spontaneous applause at the mere mention of his name. Still Lindsey had no idea what they were doing. Perhaps this was a posthumous award for him. He certainly deserved it.

"Normally, if we are incredibly fortunate, we may make one such award in our lifetime. Not so tonight. Yes, we three are here to present the Order of Merlin, Knights of Truth award to seventeen of the world's greatest wizards, the members of the Rodents." Lindsey nearly fainted. Pam felt very dizzy. Emilio choked. He was hungry and had sneaked a piece of roll from the table.

The room sat in a stunned silence. "When I call your name, please come forth to receive your robe and medallion. Wilma Weltsi, alias Bill West." As she walked to the front, the room finally grasped the magnitude of the award, the highest ever bestowed on any wizard or witch! Students and adults exploded in applause and cheering, whistling and yelling. Wilma shook his hand and received her certificate, moved on to shake Arthur's hand and received her robe, and moved on down to shake William's hand, as he handed her a golden medallion identical to his. She then stood off to one side, awaiting the others to join them.

"Monane Tumble, alias Able Monument." Amanda and Fern shouted louder than before. This was their aunt! "Jim Whitewater." Again, the two tried to out-yell everyone else; he was their brother.

"Lindsey Barron, leader of the Rodents." Lindsey was so nervous that she thought her legs would not support her. Somehow, amid the thunderous noise, she found herself shaking the hand of Amos, and he put her certificate into her hand. He whispered to her, "Thank you." Mechanically, as if in some kind of dream, she moved on down the line, shaking hands with two of the most famous wizards of all time. How she managed to get in the line next to Jim, she had no idea.

"I hope I don't faint," she whispered to Jim. He cast a silent Calm spell on her, she looked at him, "I didn't know you could do that. Thanks."

He grinned and whispered, "Lindsey, you aren't the only one who can cast spells this way."

"Ashley Stokes-Compton." On and on came the names. Pamela Betts, Deiter Cross, Amanda Whitewater, Tom Ryker, Emilio Lopez, Kathy Townsend, Audrey Lemon, Peaches Colt, Ahana Orondarka, Andy Rains, Orenda Orondarka, Fern Whitewater." After Fern had finally joined the other sixteen, Amos added, "My, that is a lot of Whitewaters." Giggles and chuckles echoed around the room.

Amos, Arthur, and William then turned to face the seventeen and began slowly to clap to them. At once, the room joined them in the loudest applause of the evening. Finally, Cho Lin rose, "We would love to have you three join us for dinner, but I know that the President has urgent business to attend. Thank you all for giving Bradbury's the high honor of hosting this unprecedented ceremony." The three walked towards the door. Now Lindsey spied the many Secret Service personnel surrounding the three, escorting them away. They had been very discrete, she thought.

"I know that the many proud parents would love to personally congratulate their children, so let's allow them to do so while we feast on roast duck with almonds." She waved her wand, and the food began appearing. The seventeen hurried to the rear to their parents, where hugs and kisses predominated for a few minutes, followed by an examination of the robes and medallions. At last, they dined together there at the rear of the hall.

An hour later, the remains of the meal had vanished into the basement dishwashing area, and the usual graduation time ceremonies began. "First, I am proud to present the winners of the Bradbury Track and Soccer Cup. Again, this year it goes to Yellow Hall. Will their captain, Lindsey Barron, please bring your team up to receive your ribbons and the cup?"

Yellow Hall burst into loud applause and cheering, as their team marched up, received their ribbons, and all held up the large trophy. Lindsey hoped that Fern would get this honor next year, but she had her doubts.

Finally, the actual graduation began. One by one, over a hundred names were called. In a daze, Lindsey walked up and received her High School Diploma and her Magic School Diploma. For her, this had been a dizzying day—a day beyond all imaginations. At last, the ceremony was over. While the other students filed out to finish their packing, ready to head home for the summer, Lindsey and the others chatted with their parents and the other parents as well.

Mr. Cross took Lindsey by surprise, when he began to chat with her. "Lindsey, I want to personally thank you for what you've done for my son. I know that you have been instrumental in helping him achieve this highest of awards. Thank you. No other Cross has ever had it. Thank you."

Lindsey didn't quite know how to respond to this, but merely said, "Deiter is the greatest." This brought a big smile to his face. An hour later, the parents left, and the seventeen sat around staring at each other; this had been a wild evening indeed.

"I can't believe it!" Pam said flatly. "Order of Merlin? Wow! Do you know that there are only fifty-one living wizards and witches who have this title? Well, I guess we just added another seventeen to that total. Alister had it, you know."

Lindsey's eyes teared at the mention of his name. "I wish he could have been here today. It would have been his finest hour."

"I know, Lindsey. He would have been so proud of us all," Deiter consoled her.

"Well, it is getting late. I suppose we had all better get packing," Ashley suggested. They all said goodnight and headed to their rooms.

About ten minutes after that, Pam and Lindsey received a Message from Cho Lin.

Please come to Governor Alister's old office at once. It is not an emergency. C. L.

As the two headed out across the lawn, enjoying the cool evening air and smell of grass, Lindsey commented, "I wonder what she wants? Probably to personally congratulate us or something."

"Suppose so. She did say it was not an emergency," Pam replied, though she was still curious. Once inside the old office, both were surprised to find Professor Herbert there as well.

"Good evening Order of Merlin holders," Professor Cho Lin said with a grin. "Surprised you didn't we?"

"I almost fainted, truly I did. Jim cast a Calm on me or my legs would have given out," Lindsey replied honestly. Both professors smiled.

"Now then to business. As you probably know, Herbert and Elaine are retiring as of now. Both stayed on until you were through, as Alister wished. It has always been the policy here at Bradbury's for any professor who is leaving to make their suggestion for who will be their replacement professor. Of course, the final decision always rests with the Governor, or Acting Governor in this case. Herbert," she turned to him.

He cleared his throat, "Well yes. I have already given Cho Lin my request for the person to replace me, and she has agreed. Now it is up to you, Pam. I have nominated you to be my replacement here at Bradbury's, teaching all the levels of math to our students. I do not know of any finer mind in math than yours. It will also be very prestigious for the school actually to have an Order of Merlin on their faculty. Please consider my request."

Shocked, Pam's legs gave out. Lindsey reacted swiftly to keep her up and steady. "Me?" her voice cracked and squeaked. "Me? Teach here? Are you sure? I mean I nearly flunked poems this term."

Cho Lin laughed. "Don't worry, Pam. You will never be called upon to teach poetry."

Pam regained her composure—her mind raced with conclusions. "So that's why you had me taking Elementary Education this year!" Herbert flushed and nodded affirmative.

"I would love to be a teacher here! That would be simply the greatest thing ever! Are you sure that I am old enough and qualified to do it? I mean I don't know how to use the machinery and all that."

"More than qualified, Pam," Cho Lin said graciously. "Then you accept your new position Professor Pam Betts?"

"Yes," she squeaked, cleared her throat, and added, "Oh yes, yes indeed, but I suppose that I will have a lot to learn and do before the fall term. When do I get started?"

"Go home, relax, and finish your Rodents duties. If you will come back on July 1, we will have plenty of time to get you all situated for the fall term. Will that be satisfactory, Professor Betts?" Cho Lin grinned, knowing that Pam was reacting to her new title.

"Absolutely. Great. Incredible. Wow. I have to tell my folks and Tom, though my dad will be disappointed that I'm not joining the Magical Misuse Department," Pam began to wonder what her father would think.

"Don't worry. He already knows about this. We talked it over with him before the ceremonies tonight. Pledged him to secrecy, of course. Thanks Pam." Pam and Herbert left, chatting about the teaching of math.

"Now then Lindsey, there is another matter before us. However, we must wait a few more minutes. Tea?" The two shared a pot of Darjeeling.

A half hour later, Governor General Lacy Brooms entered the office. "Sorry, got a bit delayed by our new President. Hi, Miss Barron, congratulations, Order of Merlin, well deserved." Lindsey shook her hand and thanked her.

"Now then, we can get down to business," Cho Lin stated. "Governor Alister left us both a letter. I've read mine and have followed his instructions exactly. I was instructed to give you this letter after you have graduated. Here, take your time and read it carefully, please." She handed her a sealed envelope.

Lindsey opened it as if it was the most precious item in the world. To her, it was. Alister's last words to her were more precious than gold. She read, fighting to hold back her tears.

Dear Miss Barron,

If you are reading this, then my body has passed on. If it did not die from natural causes, then it was by the hand of Dominus, and I can safely say that was the biggest mistake he ever made, for it undoubtedly convinced you and the others to go after him as soon as possible, though I hope that in doing so you have not forsaken your studies.

I can safely say that you will be successful in ending his tyranny. Why can I make this bold statement from the grave? (That was a tease, by the way.) Because only recently have I come to realize fully the singular flaw that he has, a fatal flaw, the flaw that pervaded him during his entire lifetime. To him, women were nothing but mere toys, mere object with which to play. He did not consider any woman to be anything more. Yet, unless I am horribly mistaken, it will be women who finally bring him down.

Here, Lindsey paused to wipe her eyes. She thought, "Yes, eleven out of seventeen of us are women; you are right."

Now that I am gone, it is still my responsibility to nominate my replacement. After considerable thought, I am nominating you, Lindsey, to be the next Governor of Arthur Bradbury's School of Magic. You have all the prerequisites. Above all them, you have shown nothing but compassion for all students, regardless of Hall affiliation. You are generous to all in need. You have, I feel, the uncanny ability to sense the good in others and to bring that to fore. Plus, you have shown time and time again that you have the patience to allow others to work out something for themselves without just outright telling them how to do it. These, to me, are the most important requisites for a good Governor.

If you accept this position, Cho Lin will give you another, far lengthier letter from me. In it, I will share my philosophy and how I ran the school.

It has been my great pleasure to watch you grow and mature from that little girl with no hands who bravely entered the world of magic six years ago. I count you as one of my greatest finds, while Dominus has been my greatest failure.

No matter the direction that your life may take, remember this from your old Governor. Always dwell on your successes, never on your failures. I know that it is hard to follow that sometimes. With Dominus, I was not always able to follow my own advice.

No matter what you chose to do with your life, I wish you the very best of luck.

Your Admiring and Loving Governor Alister Broadwell

Lindsey forgot to keep from crying. Tears streamed down her cheeks. Both older women were silent, allowing her to time to grieve. Finally, Lindsey wiped her eyes and looked up.

Cho Lin spoke first, "Lindsey, he told me roughly what the main content of your letter would be, that he is nominating you to be the next Governor here. Your letter may remain your private letter."

"Thank you." Lindsey appreciated this. It was as if Alister himself were here speaking to her.

"Now then down to business. Lacy?" Cho Lin said.

"Yes, Lindsey. I have received a letter from Alister, in which he made his nomination of you quite clear. As required, I have discussed your prerequisites with Cho Lin and several key professors here. They confirm that you do have them. However, I am required by law to verify them from you yourself. After all, students are sometimes known to fool their teachers. Now then, Lindsey. Can you cast the Make Permanent spell effectively?"

"Yes, many times."

"Good. Can you cast all the various protection spells as covered in the various Grade 0 through 7 spell books?"

"Yes, we use them all the time in the Rodents pack."

"Can you cast Move Object sans words, sans wand?"

Lindsey laughed, "You better believe that one! Golly, that one gets a real work out as Yellow Hall Floor Monitor." Lacy smiled; she got the point.

"Can you cast See True?"

"Yes."

"Can you cast the In Case Of spell?"

"Yes."

"Can you cast Disintegrate?"

"Yes."

"Can you cast Enchant Magic into an Item?"

"Yes."

"Can you cast Teleport?"

"Yes."

Can you cast at least twenty spells sans words, sans wand?"

"Yes, nearly all them now, through Grade 7." Lacy's eyebrows rose. No one had ever achieved that. Now she began to understand how this eighteen year old could have brought down Dominus!

"Finally, have you taken at least one Administration Management course?"

"Yes."

"Do you feel that you can use the data and principles in that course?"

"Sure."

"Excellent. You have the prerequisites, Lindsey. As Governor General, I hereby accept Governor Alister's choice for the next Governor of Bradbury's. Now then, Lindsey, do you want this job and the responsibilities that come with it?"

"Do you really mean it? Me? I'm only eighteen." Lindsey asked, quite unsure that this was for real.

"Yes, indeed. I can think of no better replacement," Lacy replied sincerely.

"I—it—I—it would be my fondest dream come true! Bradbury's is my life! I mean back in Plano with no hands, that was just survival. Bradbury's is all I know. I was dreading leaving tomorrow. I promise to do my very best, but aren't I taking it away from others—like Cho Lin or Delius? I would feel horrible if I somehow stole their promotions."

Cho Lin chuckled, "No my dear Lindsey. I'm a teacher, not an administrator, though I do a fair job with it. That's why Alister made me his backup. Same with Delius; his heart is in teaching, but he does covet my backup position, though Alister refused to give it to him because he is so biased towards Black Hall students. No one here wants the job because we are all doing what we love to do, teaching."

Much relieved, Lindsey said, “Okay. I accept it. Golly, this is the best thing that has ever happened to me! Incredible!”

“Well, let me be the very first to congratulate you, Governor Lindsey Barron,” Lacy shook her hand. She added, “Strange that you didn’t ask about the salary. Usually they do, though Alister, come to think of it never did either.”

“Oh I don’t need money. My dad left me a fortune, and then miraculously I just got five million from the government for taking out Dominus. I don’t need money.”

“I heard about that. Well, just so you know, you’ll get one hundred fifty thousand per year as a starting salary. Now I must rush off; my husband has been complaining that he is being neglected. It’s after eleven already. Cho Lin will fill you in on the details. We’ll have a summer meeting sometime in July. Until then, good luck.” Lindsey shook her hand and she left.

“Now then, there is one action that I must have you do before you leave. Professor Elaine Mac Elroy is obviously also retiring. Like Herbert, she has made her wishes for a replacement known to me. If you disapprove of her choice, we need to post a job opening and handle some interviews in late June.”

“Okay, that makes sense. Who does she want to replace her?” Lindsey asked.

“She wants Sandy Rains-Whitewater to replace her. She’s had her eye on her for several years now. Sandy has just graduated from Denver University and is fully qualified, though she doesn't have any teaching experience."

"Way cool!" Lindsey replied at once, but then wondered if Cho Lin also thought Sandy would be a good choice. "What is your opinion, Cho Lin? I mean if you had to okay it, would you accept her as our new English professor?"

Cho Lin smiled. Lindsey was not letting her feelings for Sandy interfere with her actual responsibilities, she thought. "Yes, I believe Sandy would work out just fine. I was able to watch her several years when she was a Yellow Hall Floor Monitor and saw how she interacted with all students. I think she would be an excellent choice, Lindsey."

"Great, then let's do it. What do I need to do?" Lindsey signed several forms, and Cho Lin promised to handle the official notifications and other details.

"That's that. Now then, Lindsey, I will give you the same orders as Pam. Go home and relax. Then go capture the remaining Death Stalkers. Come back on July 1, and we will begin going over everything. Yes, there will be enough time before the fall term starts. It is very quiet around here in the summer. Oh, I almost forgot. You will need to live here on campus so that you can protect the students at all times. I'm your backup when you need to be elsewhere, that is, if you still want me to be your backup."

"Absolutely, Cho Lin. I'd be lost without you."

"I know that you and Deiter are planning to get married this summer. I am sure that you will find the accommodations that Alister had here to be more than satisfactory. Until July then?"

"July!" Lindsey shook her hand and Teleported back to her room. She just had to tell everyone what had just happened. However, their room was empty. She placed Alister's precious letter on her desk and noticed a big sign.

We are all down in the dining room celebrating Professor Pam. Come join us. We didn't want to interrupt you. Amanda.

Lindsey cast her Magical Door and raced through it. There were all of her dear friends chatting with Pam and drinking sodas.

"Hi Lindsey!" Deiter called out. "Would you believe Professor Pam? Incredible." Pam was happier than Lindsey could ever remember seeing her.

"What did Cho Lin want of you, Lindsey?" Amanda asked, not wanting to be in the dark any longer.

"From now on, everyone, you will address me as Governor Lindsey Barron of Bradbury's! Alister chose me to replace him! Lacy Broom came and made it official!"

Pam jumped up from her chair and flew into Lindsey's arms, hugging her tightly. Then everyone cheered and talked like mad. It was well past one before they headed off to bed.

At breakfast the next morning, news had spread to nearly everyone on campus. Student reaction in the dining hall ranged from an utter awed silence to cheering. One by one, as the professors arrived, they congratulated both Pam and Lindsey. All said that they would chat more around July 1. Evidently, the professors all took off on a vacation about now.

After eating, Lindsey began her usual litany of Move Object spells, helping get all the students and their piles of bags onto the bus. Many commented that she shouldn't be doing this, since she was now their Governor. She laughed and said she was still Floor Monitor until she got home.

Of course, when she arrived home, she and Pam had another huge round of congratulations from their parents and friends. Nadia was ecstatic about her new appointment. The day passed rapidly, and the chatting, furious.

Chapter 22—Cleaning Up Loose Ends

On June 2, Pam compiled the latest list of Dominus henchmen who had not surrendered and had to be rounded up by the Rodents. The Security department could handle many others. These remaining fifty-three were considered difficult men to apprehend, a bit too risky for the Security forces. Pam printed out the list along with all pertinent information about each, as well as a photograph where available. She gave Ashley a copy as well as Lindsey.

"Okay now what?" Pam asked. "We have some really bad wizards on this list."

"Probably with this many to get, there is likely to be one who is in an ideal position for us to capture at any given moment," Ashley speculated aloud. "Give me a few hours to see what I can divine."

Three hours later, Ashley and Pam began to draw up what Pam called their "capture" list. It gave the name of the wizard, the ideal time and location for them to strike. Audrey wandered in and told them that the day felt right, adding more confidence to their list. Lindsey then sent the Mass Message, and a half hour later, the Rodents were going over the capture list while sipping sodas in Lindsey's front room. "Seventeen to one, overkill, perhaps?" Kathy jested.

"One Dispeller, though," Lindsey batted back. "Okay, let's get to it." They cast their many protection spells and set off for the first address.

Jackson was hiding out in his private hideaway. He'd cast various spells on it so that no one could ever see his house, and at first their eyes passed over it. No one could approach the front door, each finding their feet moving away from it. Ever since Dominus fell, he'd added more and more spells and was now hiding in his basement, afraid to come out, but hoping everything would blow over in time. Yes, he needed time, time for everyone to forget about him.

Lindsey and fellow Rodents began systematically dispelling the magic guarding Jackson's home. Finally, they were able to enter, only to find numerous more traps and spells. Indeed, he's set up over a hundred traps and thus felt safe in his basement. "How many traps has this guy set?" Deiter complained after disarming ten himself, not counting all that the others were dispelling. He missed a Ball of Fire, which detonated, causing no harm to the Rodents, but setting the house on fire. Deiter quickly worked on extinguishing it.

"Upstairs is clear," Jim called out.

"Must be hiding in the basement like a scared rat," Wilma decided. After ten more trap removals, the group began heading down the steps. Jackson began firing off Disintegrate spells as rapidly as he could cast them. Lindsey simply focused and caused each to fizzle. Frustration and fear swelled in Jackson's mind. Pam, Ashley, and Deiter now took their positions in the Beyond, and he reached down pulling Jackson to the Beyond. Simultaneously, Pam and Ashley cast their Idiot Mind spells. Jackson became a rigid statue. A minute later, Deiter deposited Jackson into the prison complex, and the three rejoined the others.

Lindsey was already giving orders for the next hit, as she began calling them. Slowly they worked their way down the list. Towards the end of the day, they had one more to grab, a man named Torson. Following their proven methods, the group began dispelling the protections he had on his secret hiding place, an extra-dimensional space in a train station. They had just gotten the last barrier dispelled, when Torson acted. He cast his power spell, and time slowed down to a crawl for the Rodents. He rushed out past them and attempted to stab Lindsey in her heart. His knife blade snapped as it struck her Skin of Stone, which saved her life. Seeing her thus heavily protected and his spell about to end, he Teleported away.

"Where'd he go?" Jim called out. "He was just there a moment ago."

"Teleported," Amanda and Monane called out nearly simultaneously. Both had seen the distinctive trail left by the spell.

Deiter called out from the Beyond, poking his head down into the room. "Got him. Trapped him during his Teleport. Pretty cool. Just cut his streaking energy line and here he is. Pam took care of him. He's now in prison. Time for supper?"

"Sure glad you had Skin of Stone on you," Fern

commented, as they packed up to leave. "He would have killed you. What spell was that anyway?" Lindsey explained about this top-level spell, telling her she'd get her chance at it next year.

Back at Lindsey's ranch, Pam crossed six off her list. "We've got three hours before Ashley thinks we should go after Paul. I'm famished."

So it went the next day. However, on June 5, they had to stop to deal with the KMAG interview. Thus far, they had put fifteen more behind bars. As they dressed up for the interview, Ashley commented to Pam, "Say, if you get to the point where you want to end the interview and can't, here's what you say." She whispered it. Pam grinned mischievously.

"Say, what should we wear to this interview?" Amanda asked.

"Clothes," Deiter commented playfully. "No, make that no clothes." Amanda threw a pillow at Deiter, who ducked but not in time.

Wilma had some advice. "Look, we will be photographed as a group and on camera for the first time. Millions will be watching, and the pictures will be everywhere, especially all over the Internet for years to come. We should dress accordingly."

"We should look very feminine," Audrey commented. "I don't know why, it just feels right."

"Feminine it is," Lindsey ordered. "I think Inaugural Ball gowns are a bit much though."

Wilma chuckled, "Right, a bit much."

"I can help with this," Mary Hampton offered, she'd just come in on the tail of their conversations. "I have all your checks deposited. Your receipts are on the kitchen table. You should look like professional women, such as me."

"But we don't have any outfits like yours," Lindsey admitted. "I mean we have formal gowns and fetish outfits, but nothing like yours."

"Then, let's do a bit of quick shopping. I know just the place." While the few men dressed in their suits, the women Teleported into Denver. When they returned, each wore a white silk blouse, a woolen skirt, with matching jacket. Each, however, was a different color. Three-inch matching colored pumps completed their outfits.

"Golly, it looks like we are going with eleven attorneys or bankers," Deiter jested.

"Glad you noticed," Lindsey teased him back.

"We'd better get going. Pam is the spokesperson, right?" Wilma asked, making sure that they had everything straight. Pam nodded. A minute later, they arrived outside the KMAG studios in downtown Denver. Wilma led them inside; the couples holding hands where possible.

An assistant met them just inside the door. "What an honor meeting all of you. Please follow me to the waiting room. The photographer is about ready for the group photographs. We'll be doing the photos first and then the live interview."

The photo session went well, and they were given their pick of which digital image would be used. Pam cleverly hit a few keys on the photographer's laptop and emailed herself a copy. Later, she gave a copy to all the others. Lindsey had a color prints made and had one framed for her new office and one for her parents.

The live studio was brilliantly lighted, but the heavy air conditioning kept them comfortable. Normally, Hugo was used to interviewing one on one, not one on seventeen. Further, due to the importance of this group, KMAG had little choice but to allow reporters from the other seven major networks to join him, making it eight to seventeen. Eight sets of cameras faced the group, times three. That is, each had three cameras, front, left, and to the right. Another eight cameras were positioned slightly to their rear so that they could focus on the reporter asking the current question. Many boom microphones hung above their heads. It was more than a little intimating to the seventeen. Even Wilma and Monane were a bit uneasy about this.

Pam sat in the middle with Lindsey on her right and Wilma on her left. Both would be her support. Ashley was beside Lindsey, while Monane sat next to Wilma. The others finished out the long line on either side. Immediately behind Pam sat Fred Angel, head of the States Law and Justice department. He was there to ensure that they were treated fairly and properly.

Finally, Hugo and the other seven reporters joined them, and Hugo explained how the interview would be conducted. "First, let me thank you all for coming. This is truly an historic occasion. Because of this, KMAG is allowing the other seven major networks to join us. We've agreed that each station is allowed to film and show their own video. However, we all cannot be talking at once. We've agreed that there will be only one reporter asking questions at one time. Thus, you will be taking questions from only one of us at a time. Naturally, I will go first. As we understand it, Miss Pam Betts is your spokesperson?"

"That's correct, Mr. Whitefield," Pam replied flatly. "Though Lindsey may also wish to speak. She is the Rodents' leader."

"Right. Okay then we will go live in one minute. All set everyone?" he called out.

His producer gave him the thumbs up sign. A man called out, "And five, four, three, two, one, live."

"Welcome one and all to this historic event being held live in the studios of KMAG in downtown Denver. This is your favorite announcer Hugo Whitefield. Because of the importance of this event, KMAG is graciously sharing our studios with the other major stations." He quickly introduced the reporters and their stations.

"As I began, this is an historic event unfolding here. We have with us the entire Rodents, as they call themselves, a name perhaps invented by the late Governor Alister Broadwell, who ran the Arthur Bradbury's School of Magic and where most of these have just graduated a few days ago. Graduated yes, but more importantly each has been awarded the Order of Merlin, Knights of Truth award. Yes, all seventeen! This alone is historic. In the past, ordinarily only one such medal is awarded at one time, but in this case, well you certainly know why! Ladies and gentlemen, I give you the Rodents who single-handedly captured Dominus Malefic and most of his Death Stalkers, along with the treasonous President Snow and her whole cabinet."

An applause machine made it sound like there was a crowd looking on and applauding them. Lindsey thought this was a bit much, however. Hugo went on, "Let us begin by introducing to the world each member of this esteemed group of wizards and witches, or rather I should say witches and wizards. It seems the women greatly outnumber the men." He grinned broadly, and they all knew that he was trying to add a little of his brand of humor to his reporting.

"In doing so, you are about to hear a great revelation, yes, you heard me, a *major* revelation. Many years ago, the famous Rat Pack captured Dominus. All these many years, we have known those members as Sam Barron, Bill West, Able Monument, and Mabel Pruit. Alas, Dominus' thugs killed Sam and Mabel many years ago, but Bill and Able, as you have heard many times these past six years, are still around and still in business. However, what none of us knew is that Bill West is really Wilma Weltsi, and Able Monument is really Monane Tumble!"

"Yes, they have probably set the world's record for the best use of the Morph Self spell ever! Later, we will ask them about this, but on to the introductions that I know you are wanting. The leader of the Rodents is Miss Lindsey Barron, daughter of Sam Barron. She is their Dispeller, who by all reports has skills far beyond that of her father. Yes, she has just become the Governor of Arthur Bradbury's School of Magic!"

"Their spokesperson is Miss Pam Betts, a Sleuth, and now Professor of Math at Bradbury's, who has been responsible for uncovering much about the activities and crimes of Dominus and his gang. Next, we have Miss Ashley Stokes-Compton, the adopted sister of Lindsey and a Class 4 Diviner. Yes, you heard me correctly, Class 4! The world once more has a Class 4 Diviner. Mabel Pruit was the last one. Ashley is also a fashion model for Teen Fashion magazine."

"Wilma is one of their two Eliminators, and Monane is one of their two Trackers. Continuing, next we have Miss Amanda Whitewater, their other Tracker. Note, there seem to be many Whitewaters in this group. Let's keep them straight. Amanda is their Tracker. Yes, the Whitewaters are Apaches, as is Monane, which may account for their unusual skills."

"Their other Eliminator is Mr. Deiter Cross, who has been training under Bill West or rather Wilma." Hugo pretended to have made a goof. Grinning and flashing is brilliant white teeth, he added, "I, too, keep thinking of them as Bill and Able. Continuing, next is Mr. Jim Whitewater, who works for the Security Defense department. Mr. Tom Ryker, son of Bill Ryker, head of the Arizona States Law and Justice department. Mr. Emilio Lopez. Miss Kathy Townsend. Miss Audrey Lemon. Mr. Ahana Orondarka, Iroquois, and better known as the leader and founder of the rock band Eli's Rockers. Mr. Andy Rains, an Arapaho. Miss Peaches Colt. Both

Mr. Rains and Miss Colt are now registered casters of the Restricted Wish spell! Miss Orenda Orondarka, the younger sister of Ahana. And finally, Miss Fern Whitewater, the youngest sister. Like I said, many Whitewaters here."

"Ladies and gentlemen, I give you the Rodents and the seventeen newest members of Order of Merlin, Knights of Truth!" Again, the applause machine worked overtime.

Hugo, white teeth shining behind his large smile, then said, "Now the whole world would like to hear just how your band managed to capture the most powerful wizard of this century and his band of Death Stalkers. How is it that the Rodents have managed to do what the rest of the wizarding world has been unable to do? And are the rumors true that you have invented some new, ultra-powerful spell, which was used to capture him?"

Pam had rehearsed how she would answer the request to tell how they had captured Simon. "When Dominus killed our Governor Alister, we all resolved to capture him ourselves, since none of you adults were obviously going to do it. Audrey told us that one day, the time would be right. Ashley then used her divination skills to determine the precise day and hour, down to the minute when we should strike. He was planning to send a group of over fifty Death Stalkers to attack Erin Sacs in the Battle for Virginia. He was giving them their orders in the same warehouse in Montrose, Colorado, in which his men created those Dominus for President rings, only now the warehouse was totally empty. Ashley told us that we had just a few minutes to get him and his men, while he was there issuing their marching orders."

"Yes, they outnumbered us almost three to one. However, I insisted that each of us have all possible spell protections on our persons when we entered. Dominus knew that Lindsey was our Dispeller. To protect her better, the rest of us Morphed Self into Lindsey, so when we attacked they saw seventeen Lindseys, giving her time to work her magic."

"Lindsey's first job was to dispel or remove all the protection spells that Dominus had on his person. Then, Deiter, Pam, and I exercised our secret weapon and captured him, giving him to my dad and Casper, who were at the prison in Denver. During the time that Lindsey was doing this, which of course was the most dangerous period for the rest of the Rodents where we were outnumbered three to one, Deiter did one of his famous tricks to help. We call it the Mass Disarm spell. All the Death Stalkers including Dominus had their wands thrown about the warehouse. That gave us all the time we needed, you see."

"With Dominus gone, Lindsey dispersed all spells that the Death Stalker cast, while the rest of us dispelled their protection spells and began to subdue the lot. One by one, Deiter, Ashley, and I used our secret weapon to apprehend them and take them to prison. It took less than a half hour. Then, we did the same thing with President Snow and her cabinet, who were all in one room, sitting like zombies watching the news coverage of the battle going on in Virginia. Simple, really. Took about an hour all told. And no, we have not invented a new all-powerful spell, unless you call Deiter's accidental modification of the Disarm spell a new invention."

"Would you care to elaborate about this secret weapon of yours?" another reporter asked a follow up question.

"Of course not. We still have a lot of Death Stalkers out there to apprehend yet," Pam said very flatly, getting across the idea "like what a stupid idea that was."

Another reporter asked, "Dominus has attacked and mutilated Lindsey several times, along with Ashley and even you Pam. Just when did you decide that you were going to get him? How did it feel finally to get your revenge on Dominus for what he did to you? Why didn't you just kill him? Wouldn't he be likely to escape from prison again?"

Lindsey was growing slightly annoyed with the questions, but Pam fielded this one nicely. "It appears that your education is lacking. Revenge is a poison. No one gets real lasting satisfaction from mere revenge. How silly. No, we went after the obtaining of Justice, not only for ourselves, but for all of those others, particularly women, whom Dominus had harmed, as well as for the attempted destruction of our whole country. We've been working all along towards this goal, from our first year at Bradbury's. However, I will say this. The murder of our Governor sealed his fate. We swore to bring him to Justice as soon as the time was right. Having Dominus dead gets no one real Justice. As you know, I discovered every company, every asset Simon owned. Those were confiscated at the very instant we put Dominus in prison. As you probably know, those assets will be divided up and monetary compensation given to all those he has harmed over these past many years. I know that money cannot bring back a lost loved one, but it can help survivors build a better future for themselves and others and help bring them some closure."

"Darn, she's good," Deiter whispered to Lindsey, who smiled.

A reporter for the People Tell All station asked, "Ashley, you grew up totally armless. How is it that you could even get into magic school and let alone cast a spell? Rumors say that you were expelled from the Chicago School of Magic for fighting with your professors. Any truth to that?"

Lindsey fumed. Silently she cast Darkness. Suddenly, the whole set went completely dark. Pandemonium broke out, with engineers and producers shouting orders. Lindsey dispelled it after only a couple seconds. Lindsey calmly said, "Next question." Hugo stared at her.

Producers and engineers finally restored calm and Hugo resumed, "We apologize for that technical failure here at our studio. We are interviewing the famous Rodents. I believe Rosamund wishes to ask our guest the next question."

A woman with bright red lipstick, probably a Red Hall graduate perhaps, asked, "We know that you and your classmates have located and rescued a large number of women who Dominus mutilated and kept as his, well I will be blunt, his sex slaves. We also know that on several occasions he did pretty much the same thing to you Lindsey and Ashley. Some are saying that Dominus was about to capture you and treat you the same once you had your eighteenth birthday. Any truth to that? Can you tell our viewers out there what it felt like to be so mutilated? Did you not want revenge? It is only human."

Lindsey fumed. She thought of those women who may well be watching this interview, who were struggling desperately to recover their lives. She cast her Darkness spell once more. After a few seconds, she dispelled it. Pam tried hard to keep from laughing. Kathy failed utterly and began giggling. Hardly any Rodent could keep a straight face, not even Wilma.

When the lights came back, Lindsey asked, "Yes, Dominus had plans for us, but we were never in any danger of that coming to pass. We both have learned to disrupt a Restricted Wish spell cast against us. As for how it feels, if you like, I can remove your arms, blind you, enlarge your breasts to the size of your head, slap a tight corset around your waist, and lock on some extremely high heels on your feet, and then you can accurately relate to all of your viewers firsthand how it feels. I will only take me a second to do that. Are you ready Rosamund?" Lindsey kept a sober face, though her friends were stifling giggles.

The reporter, suddenly in a panic, shrieked, "No! Please, I'm sorry."

Hugo, watching Lindsey very carefully now, smiled and said, "Next question." He was glad that he had not asked that one.

"Is it true that Ashley passed on key information that she divined to Erin Sacs so that he and his band could take the actions that he did?"

Ashley answered this one herself. “Sorry, but at no time did I directly communicate anything to Mr. Sacs. I have met him a couple of times, though. Sorry.” The reporter just couldn’t believe her reply, but it was the truth, she had not. Others had done it for her.

Hugo then asked the next question. “This European Connection, as we are calling it. Rumors are going around that members of the Rodents were somehow responsible for bringing the huge French conglomerate Folquet Enterprises onboard. Is this true and how are they going to assist us and why?”

Pam answered, “Yes, some of us held discussions with them. As you know, we now face the biggest drug rehab situation ever, with five whole states under the influence of heroin-laced pills. Their labs have come up with a cure in pill form. As I understand it, the first shipments are due to arrive soon. It will take time, but within a reasonable period, I believe all can be cured. It is my fondest hope that, after that is done, these Frenchmen will be able to reformulate the pills so that they can safely be used to keep us all healthy. That would be a tremendous boon to all mankind. So perhaps something of great value has come from all this treason and tyranny.” Pam did not mention any reason why they would do this, however.

Just then, Audrey worriedly said, “Something bad is coming.”

Ashley sensed it too, “Lindsey a bomb I think.” Sixteen wands were drawn, but too slowly. Lindsey spied a man running into the back of the studio.

He screamed, "Dominus's revenge to you all!" He opened his jacket to reveal a huge bomb strapped to his chest. With a grandiose gesture, he pressed a button in his hand. The reporters and their crew and producers just stared at him shocked, surprised, and stunned. A massive explosion followed.

However, Lindsey reacted at once, casting her Force Wall around the man, forming it into a large sphere. The explosion was muffled and totally contained with her wall. Calmly, she said, "Would someone roll that messy ball outside before my spell expires? I don't want to get my new dress dirtied the first time I've worn it."

"What just happened?" screamed a producer, and then all those in the station reacted at once. Pandemonium broke out among the reporters, crew, and producers. However, the cameras were still rolling, so to speak. The Rodents remained seated and calm, though Wilma said, "Thanks, Lindsey. That was a close one. I was about to Disintegrate him, but would have been a trifle late."

"I got it all! I got it all!" screamed one cameraman on Lindsey's far right. His camera had been in position an accidentally filmed the whole episode. Hastily, the producers replayed the scene for all the eight stations.

Shortly, the producer gave Hugo a sign. Far whiter than normal, Hugo resumed. "Ladies and gentlemen, yes, a mad bomber has just attempted to detonate a bomb right here in our studios! You are seeing this live from the KMAG studios."

"Sorry, Hugo," Lindsey pointed out, "he *did* detonate the bomb. I put a Force Sphere around him to contain the blast. Can we get on with the interview?"

"But how? We saw," he stopped, remembering just what he had seen. "You didn't have your wand out, did you?"

"Of course not. Don't need it for that spell," Lindsey replied calmly.

Hugo was speechless for a few seconds, and then enthusiastically reported, "Incredible. We, I have just witnessed perhaps the most incredible display of Dispelling Magic I have ever seen! You have just seen the world's best Dispeller in action, right here, live on KMAG! Miss Barron sans anything just prevented the insane bomber from killing everyone here in our studios! What a display of Dispeller skill!"

Lindsey began to laugh nearly hysterically. When asked what was so funny, she replied, "If you replay it, you will *see* me sitting right here just as I have been sitting this whole interview. There really wasn't anything actually to *see*, not like running the twenty-mile relay race. That's what's so funny. They didn't actually *see* anything, just the result. Sorry, I couldn't help myself. That is so funny!"

Now Wilma began roaring with laughter as well, and then the rest of the Rodents joined in too. Finally containing her mirth, Wilma added, "You never *do* see anything from a good Dispeller."

Finally, the interview got back on track. The next reporter asked, "Thank you for saving our lives. Now then,

President Snow is in jail. What do you think her punishment should be? Should she be charged with High Treason for her part in all of this?"

Pam replied, "During her run for President, she was hospitalized. During her stay in the hospital, one of the Death Stalkers put a Dominus for President ring on her finger, while she was unconscious. After he melted the rings onto their fingers, she was thereafter under the control of Dominus. She was an unwilling victim of Dominus as well. I hope that they take that into consideration. She probably had little that she could do about it, except cut her finger off, which would have been the smart thing to have done at the time, but then, that is hindsight, isn't it?"

"Is it true that you have invented a new special spell which was used to capture Dominus?"

"No, sorry. We did invent a Cook Complete Meal spell. We're somewhat lazy you see, we didn't *invent* a new spell to capture Dominus," Pam replied honestly. No, they had sort of "misused" an existing spell. "By the way, just for the record, that mad bomber who just killed himself was Jason Tacks. He was on our list of Death Stalkers to apprehend. Gang, we have one less to capture."

"And now we are out of time. I hope you have enjoyed this historic interview, complete with an actual Dispeller action right before our cameras. I thank all of you Rodents for taking time out from your important work to address the entire nation today. This is your favorite reporter, Hugo Whitefield saying so long for now." The hot lights went dark and a scurry of action accompanied the many crews as they began dismantling their equipment.

Hugo leaned towards Lindsey and whispered, “So it was you who cast the Darkness spells, not some freak equipment failure?”

Lindsey flashed her eyebrows. “Never can tell can you? We don’t answer such questions.” He grinned; he liked this powerful teen.

“I say, let’s have another session some time, without all these other reporters around, shall we?” he asked.

“Maybe,” Lindsey was un-committal.

A short while later, back in Lindsey’s front room, Ashley went through the list of Death Stalkers once more. She altered a few times and one date. Then, the Rodents went to work once more. On June 10, the last of the most wanted men were in custody. Lindsey pronounced their current assignment finished. Everyone cheered, for now they could make their plans for the future.

Chapter 23—A Giant Wedding

On June 11, Lindsey and her friends sat sipping sodas in her living room. The topic was weddings, naturally. "Look, Amanda has to get married soon. She and Ahana have a three-month band road trip scheduled to begin on July 1," Lindsey pointed out.

"Besides, I want to attend all your weddings too," Amanda pleaded. "I don't want to miss them."

"Don't forget honeymoons," Pam said wryly. Kathy grinned.

"Well, we certainly cannot wait until next summer," Lindsey added the obvious.

Lena volunteered a suggestion, "Why don't you set the dates for all of your weddings to be say June 20? Have one big wedding and use the B & B Dance Hall as you had suggested earlier. That gives you time for a honeymoon and everything. You know that we all support whatever you want."

That settled it. June 20 would be their day. Now they began making all sorts of plans. Each of the families had to invite their relations and friends; the list of attendees grew and grew. Nadia and Jolina volunteered to handle the decorations and the catering of the giant reception to be held immediately afterwards. All told, seven couples would marry at the same time, and thus well over a thousand guests and friends would be attending. Fred Betts insisted upon a large number of

Security forces be present, though they would remain discretely in the background.

Choosing dresses and bridesmaids proved to be their toughest decisions, particularly so for Lindsey, because nearly all of her close friends were also being brides. Fern and Orenda were going to be bridesmaids for Amanda, naturally. Monique offered to be Pam's bridesmaid, which Pam wholeheartedly accepted. Audrey and Peaches chose their bridesmaids from their friends in Brown Hall and Black Hall respectively. Kathy's younger norm sister would be hers. This left only Ashley and Lindsey without any. As an orphan now adopted by Lloyd and Lena, Ashley had no other friends than these, ditto with Lindsey.

Nadia and Jolina came to their rescue. "Look you have to have a bridesmaid, who better to be her than me?" Nadia begged. Thus, Nadia would be Lindsey's, while Jolina would be Ashley's. Then dresses nearly became an unsolvable problem for the teens.

"They are supposed to be a very special dress for our very special day," Kathy explained.

"Yes, but why do we get such a dress that we are only going to wear one time? That seems silly to me," Pam stated flatly, annoyed with the idea of never wearing it again.

"But you are only going to get married once, well hopefully anyway. You want it to be more special than special," Kathy argued. After much discussion, Pam finally came around, and the teens agreed to get a special dress. What kind became the next problem. Quite wisely, the fellows made themselves scarce at these times when they were going over their plans.

Next, the idea that they all wear identical gowns, perhaps with different colors was suggested. This met with failure when Kathy pointed out that brides always wore white to denote their purity. Pam pleaded her choice, “I always feel very special when I wear that billowing Inaugural Ball gown, so I want mine to be something like that. I want to feel special for Tom.”

Nadia and Jolina suggested that they wear a fetish wedding gown, compete with outer corset, long and slinky. For a time, Lindsey considered this option. Kathy wanted to her dress to be strapless, “It’s all the rage you know, shows off a lot of skin too.” Lindsey didn’t like that idea at all. Just when they all thought it was hopeless, they decided to each have their own look.

On their special day, the bridesmaids cast dozens of Calm spells. Over a thousand parents, relatives, and friends watched them marry and celebrated with them at the reception. Nadia and Jolina transformed the dance hall magnificently, with seven different arches mounded with flowers, beneath which each couple stood for the ceremony.

Thus, on June 20, they became Mrs. Lindsey Barron-Cross, Mrs. Pam Betts-Ryker, Mrs. Amanda Whitewater-Orondarka, Mrs. Ashley Stokes-Compton-Whitewater, Mrs. Audrey Lemon-Williams, Mrs. Peaches Colt-Rains, and Mrs. Kathy Townsend-Lopez. Yes, waltzes predominated throughout the reception. That evening, the seven couples

Teleported to Tahiti for their honeymoon. All loved the islands.

On their return, they went their separate ways. Ahana and Amanda packed up and headed off on the Eli's Rocker's First World Tour. Kathy and Emilio headed to Pueblo to start up their business, Kathy's Potions. Jim and Ashley took off on a grand tour of the world. To Lindsey's surprise, Audrey and Bill moved into a vacated home on her ranch, joining with Lena to form Lena's Organic Produce company. Andy and Peaches headed off to Denver University, where he continued his archaeology studies, and she studied to become a PE teacher and swimming coach.

Deiter and Lindsey along with Tom and Pam packed their things and headed to Bradbury's. Tom planned to start up his computer programming business, while Deiter was still exploring his options as an Eliminator with the States Department of Law and Justice.

Chapter 24—Governor Lindsey Barron-Cross

On July 1, Lindsey sat in the chair that Alister had used, behind his enormous desk, which was now hers. Alone, she began reading the second, lengthier letter that Alister had left for her. Cho Lin had brought her a pot of tea, the letter, and then left, wisely allowing her some private time to read it. Lindsey had to stop and wipe her eyes several times.

After reading it through several times, she went back to one section.

Cho Lin will shortly be telling you that your first action must be to accept or reject the school seekers' suggestions for all the new first year students. This must be done soon so that the seekers have time to visit all the new students and notify them of their selection.

I would like to share a few words of advice on this, Lindsey. The seekers only cover our state. However, during the year, I always keep my eyes open across the whole country, looking for worthy students there as well. Look at grade school reports, local papers, and so on. Don't forget to examine other magic schools; that is how I came across Ashley.

Always look for worthy students. Look at not only their potentials but also their personalities and how they interact with others. Bradbury's has a reputation for accepting only the best. Maintain that long-standing tradition and you will never go wrong. Sometimes, I admit, the facts as presented by the seekers are not conclusive. In those cases, I always went with my gut feeling, which was never wrong, except with Dominus.

Also, try to balance out students between the five Halls, though that is not always possible. What Hall a new student will join is not known until the seeker actually visits the student and their parents. I try not to play favorites to the different Halls, though I must admit that sometimes my Yellow Hall background comes out.

Lindsey sent for Cho Lin, who brought in the seeker's combined database of possible candidates for this fall's new first years. "How did Alister handle these?" Lindsey asked. "I mean did he accept them all usually or did he reject a lot of them?"

"Oh he pretty much goes with their choices. However, he always reads over each one. I do believe that he frequently finds one or perhaps two per seeker that he challenges. In those cases, he had the seeker meet with him and discuss the case firsthand. Sometimes, he went to view the person himself. You know, go invisible, and watch the student. Now last year was a big mess, what with hundreds of transfer requests. This year, we have retained ninety percent of those that transferred here during the last two years. I don't blame their parents for not wanting to rush back into the affected areas, not until the automaton mess is worked out," Cho Lin replied quietly.

"Okay, then I'll start in on them now. Can I call you and

have you double check me this first time?" she asked.

"Of course. Message me when you are ready."

It took Lindsey over an hour to go through the details of the one hundred potential new first year students. Then, she called in Cho Lin once more. "I've only found two that I think we ought to reject. Both seem to be bulling the other students, bragging a lot, and were supporting the fact that wizards are better than normals."

"Ah, you spotted those two as well. I would agree with you on those. Actually, you and I think alike on these. Those were the only two that I would have rejected. As Acting Governor, I took the liberty to go over the lists in early June. Excellent."

"This Jan Feldspar case—on the surface, I agree with the seeker's report that she ought to be accepted. Perhaps this one I should see for myself. However, it seems that the seeker has a question mark under financial. What does that mean?"

"Ah, that's the potential special needs case. Lillian and I talked about her. Lillian says that Jan is completely blind, born without eyeballs, birth defect by all accounts. Her parents are norms and could not possibly afford our tuition. Seeker Lillian is not sure if her parents actually know if there is any magical means to correct her eyes or not. Even if there is, she doubts that they could afford it. Jan is the sixth and youngest child; her father works as a janitor. If we accept her, she will likely need a full scholarship."

"Okay, then I will visit her myself this afternoon. Do I just leave this as is for now?"

"No, you mark this one as Under Study. Later, you update her entry. Now just enter your disapproval of the two and say why in the appropriate columns, save the database, and then hit the post button. Our five seekers will be notified immediately and will begin contacting the students personally."

"Now in about two weeks' time, the seekers will have gotten the data we need to sort them into their Halls. Alister always looked that over too. I know that for the last six years, he always had a hand in who was rooming with you and Pam, and then later Ashley. It's not by chance that he roomed you, Amanda, Pam, and Kathy together that first year. He knew that Pam was good with computers and very bright in grade school, that Amanda had a very kind and generous heart and loved to run as you did, and that Kathy was always looking out for others in grade school, helping with anything she could."

Lindsey chuckled, "Well, he certainly did a superb job with us. Now I'm also supposed to look all over the country and also at other magic school for possibilities."

"He would do a bit of that every day, while reading the newspapers and such. It really is too late this year for you to do that. If you like, I can set up subscriptions for all the papers he used to get."

"Please. Thanks."

"When you get back, I'll take you to meet the staff, which maintains the school and grounds," Cho Lin promised. "See you in a while."

Lindsey studied the directions. The girl, Jan Feldspar,

lived in Pueblo. She MagGoogled for a map of Pueblo and printed out the map showing the girl's home. She cast Invisibility on herself, went out the main gates, and Teleported to Pueblo. Quickly, she found the house in question and set about watching for the girl. She was in luck. The front door opened and many kids came scrambling out. The older boys raced off ahead of the four girls. "See you at the park," a younger girl said. She and an older sister ran off after the boys. The oldest girl, probably seventeen, led the youngest girl, holding her hand and talking with her.

"Okay, here comes that nasty hole in the sidewalk," she said, slowing down while Jan moved her feet more carefully than before. "Okay, smooth sailing to the park." Lindsey watched as Jan now undid a collapsible striped stick and began tapping her way along. Her older sister let go of her hand. Independent, Lindsey thought.

At the open park, the older sister asked, "Are you going to be okay now? Remember where the swings are at Jan?"

"Of course I do. You go play while I go swing," Jan said, tapping her way across the sandy, grassless ground to the swings. She folded up her stick and began to swing. Was that a Push spell she just cast? Lindsey was startled to see magical energy activating from Jan's hands! Lindsey became keenly interested, watching Jan very closely. After about a half hour, several older boys came up to the swings.

"Hey, how about letting us swing, blind kid? You shouldn't be on a swing. You can't see what you are doing anyway," one boy said snidely.

"Go find your own swing," Jan replied testily.

As the same boy came up to her to pull her off the swing, Lindsey saw magical energy forming around Jan's hands as she held onto the swing chains. The next instant, it discharged, giving the boy an electrical jolt! He jumped back quite surprised. "Hey, just for that, I'm going to tell Alice on you. Now you are in big trouble, blindy." The boy stumped off to tell her older sister about what had happened. He got no satisfaction, as the older teen told him that four other swings were vacant and to leave Jan alone. The boys grumbled and headed elsewhere. Lindsey had seen enough; she Teleported back to Bradbury's.

Cho Lin, we absolutely *must* have Jan here as a first year! Lillian's report is an understatement! While I watched, she cast something close to a Push spell and then gave a bully an electrical shock. How do I tell Lillian that we must have her period?" Cho Lin chuckled and explained that she could add all the comments that she desired in the Comments column. Lindsey did so, adding if Lillian ran into difficulties recruiting Jan to let her know, and she would help convince them to allow Jan to come here. She also marked Jan as the top priority for Lillian.

Next, Lindsey met personally with the staff at Bradbury's. A few she had seen when she was a student, the workers who helped handle the blown up bleachers when the Mad Bomber was on the loose and some kitchen staff. Sixty staff were divided into ten cooks, six dishwashers, twenty maids who did the cleaning and handled the many dirty clothes, seven grounds keepers, and seven janitors/jack of all trades, who swore they could fix anything, and ten who ran the book store/mail services. One of the cooks, she knew—Juanita from Venezuela, who had looked after Ashley and her when Dominus had imprisoned them in the abandoned mine. She spent over an hour chatting with the staff, who took an immediate liking to their new boss.

She also learned that most of them were about to go on vacation themselves, only a skeleton crew would be around for the next six weeks. Juanita said, “When you are ready to eat, let me know. I will have your tray waiting. It is so strange to see the tray just vanish though,” she grinned. Lindsey gave her a big hug.

Around five, she headed into her new living quarters. In the back of Alister’s office, a door led into a magically altered space. Actually, it was a closet enlarged to that of a large house! There were ten rooms total, including two studies, two bathrooms, and a master bedroom. Deiter came along shortly, and the two headed into their dining room. “Never knew this even existed,” Deiter commented as they sat down, and Lindsey cast Move Object, bringing Juanita’s tray to her table.

“Figured out anything today, Deiter?” she asked.

“Nope, still looking and checking. I never knew that figuring out what I wanted to do was going to be this hard! I want to be with you, but beyond that, dunno. The Security Department is hounding me to join them. The Law and Justice folks have been begging me to join them. I’m ignoring the ten police departments across the country that have offered me a job by mail. Jeesh."

"Well, we have all the money we could possibly want. You ought to do what you really want to do," Lindsey replied.

Deiter winked at her, "Tonight, dear. Got to wait until tonight for that." She blushed.

"Besides that," she teased him.

The next evening, Deiter arrived home extremely pleased and happy. "Lindsey, I have the job I am going to like! Fred Betts just hired me. I am the western state's department of Magical Misuse's Strike Patrol Captain. I will lead a group of ten, and we get to go round up violators of magic and the like anywhere in the western states. Awesome. I report directly to him, but the other state's heads can request my Strike Patrol's aid at any time! Way cool!" Lindsey was pleased, though a little worried that he didn't have a Dispeller along with him.

"Before you start dashing around the country, we ought to go get all my dad's things out of my vault, now that I have a place for them," Lindsey suggested. Deiter promised they would do that on Saturday.

The following morning, after Deiter left and she sipped her tea and looked at the mountain of newspapers sitting on her desk, Lindsey spied a letter that had just come. The letter was from France, the return address caused her heart to race slightly. It was from Simone Folquet.

Dear Mrs. Lindsey Barron-Cross,

We heard of your marriage, and I want to congratulate you. That was an interesting interview that you had with KMAG. We saw it over here too. Congratulations on the Order of Merlin!

Michelle now has her GED. Sharp sister. Michelle talked about Bradbury's for weeks after her visit. When she was a little girl, I continually promised her that when she was twelve she would go to school there. I have no idea if anyone can learn magic when they are thirty-three years old, instead of twelve. Plus, she now fully realizes how difficult it is for her to get around in those awful boots that she is forced to wear.

I owe it to her at least to try to see if she can learn magic. Could we possible come for a visit and discuss this?

Okay, I would like to see the old campus myself. Let me know. A Message is fine.

Sincerely,

Simone Folquet

Lindsey immediately sent Simone a Message to come to the parking lot around ten this morning, if this was convenient. Since all the professors were now on vacation, excepting Pam who was frantically preparing for her fall classes, Lindsey felt it was safe for him to come at this time.

At ten, Lindsey stood waiting for them in the parking lot. She blinked, and they arrived, Simone and Michelle. "Thank you for seeing us," Simone said, shaking her hand. He wore a suit and his thick beard hid his facial features well.

Michelle wore a silk blouse and tall jeans that nearly touched the ground, helping to hide the fact that she was walking on her toes in these boots. Her blouse was not tucked in, which helped hide the fact that she had a twelve-inch waistline. She was slower getting to Lindsey and excitedly shook her hand. Lindsey gave her a hug as well. Michelle now wore makeup, just enough to highlight her beauty, rather like Isabella, Lindsey thought. “Congratulations on getting your high school degree, Michelle. You do look so much better than the last time you were here.”

“Thanks, I really am doing so much better now. I try to get out some, but with these boots, well you know with what I have to deal. This place is so beautiful. I cheered for joy when Simone and I heard on the news that you were the new Governor of the school! Congratulations to you, Lindsey!”

“Okay, let’s go to my office first. I’ll make us a Magical Door, as soon as we are inside the gates. Less to walk that way.” Michelle grinned and walked slowly inside. A bit later, the three sat in her big office.

“Simone, this discussion should be just between Michelle and me. I know that you would dearly love to wander about the campus, but only Pam knows your story. There is the risk that someone might recognize you in spite of the beard. If you don’t mind, Pam will go with you and fend off any queries. Your cover story is that you are checking out the campus to see if it is suitable for your first year student, which is not too far from the truth. Okay?”

“Thank you!” Simone said with enthusiasm. Pam knocked and greeted them both. Then she and Simone headed off to tour the campus. Actually, Pam went wherever Simone wanted to go.

When they had their privacy, Lindsey asked, “Michelle have you ever cast any kind of a spell or perhaps had strange things occur around you?"

Michelle's face fell, "No, neither. I always dreamed of being able to so the things Simone does, though."

"Well that's okay that you haven't. I have to ask these questions to see if there is any chance. Now how about this? Ever felt any kind of tingling sensation in your hands—oops, pardon me, I forgot you only had your upper arms for so long. Make that tingling sensations say at your elbows? I know you could not see, but any sensations?"

"Oh, well yes, kind of like electricity. I stuck my fingers in a light socket when I was ten. I got shocked, but was all right. I always have had that funny sensation at my elbows. Is that important?" she asked curious about it. She was blind at that time, and of course, could not see what it was, if there even was anything visible to see.

"Yes, that is very important. Michelle, I need to take you to our bookstore to see if we can get you a wand that will work for you. You will need to answer a bunch of questions, which are used to match the wand to the new witch. This is one of the first things that a new first year does—visit the bookstore and get their first wand. True, they don't know how to use it yet. I'll use my Magical Door so you don't have to walk too much, okay."

"Fantastic! A real magical wand! Wow!" she displayed a childish enthusiasm.

A few slow minutes later, Lindsey and Michelle walked up to the counter, behind which rows and rows of wands lay stacked on shelves. Michelle was so excited that she forgot to pay close attention to her walking and nearly stumbled. Lindsey cleverly caught her, preventing a spill. "Sorry, I got too excited there. I have to pay very close attention to my walking."

"I know, been there," Lindsey was reminded of Deiter supporting her as she slowly walked to classes two November's ago. "Excuse me. I would like to see if we can find a wand that is right for Michelle here."

"Oh hi Lindsey. Michelle, is it? Lost yours?" Ben Aker asked politely.

"No, we think she may possibly be able to learn to cast spells at her age. So assume that she is a new first year, and let's see if there is a wand which will activate for her," Lindsey explained.

"Sure thing. I must say, Michelle, you are the prettiest first year I've ever seen. Now if you will just go down this list of questions and answer them honestly, we'll see what we come up with, okay. Just mark them with this special pencil." He handed her the pencil. Lindsey had not realized before now that the pencil that she had used six years ago when she timidly came up for her first wand was magically enchanted. Now it made sense that it was, since it tabulated her answers, giving Ben the wand of choice immediately.

Lindsey wondered if Michelle would have trouble standing for so long on her toes, but this Michelle was used to doing. After some fifteen minutes, she finished. Ben took the paper and looked at the results. "Ah, power house one—oak with a platinum core. Nice." He produced a golden box and opened the lid, revealing a splendid wand. “Pick it up and wave it around a little,” Ben suggested. Michelle did so.

As she waved it around in the air, the magical energies began to flow and flow rapidly. “Woo hoo! Wow, it tingles as my elbows always did. Cool!” Lindsey carefully dispersed the energy that was flying wildly around the room.

“Careful, Michelle, your wand is definitely attuned to you and is activating. From now on, you need to be very careful with this. Think of it as a loaded gun.”

“Oh, I’m sorry. Wow, it feels great though.”

“Thanks, Ben, put it on my account, please. Michelle, it’s back to my office now.” Ben watched this curious woman taking such small steps. Suddenly, he got a flash of her boots though and became very curious about this very pretty woman with the long, curly black hair and bright eyes.

A bit later, with Michelle sitting comfortably in one of the stuffed sofa-like chairs in Lindsey’s office and examining her very own wand, Lindsey Messaged Cho Lin, who came at once. “Professor Cho Lin, this is Michelle Folquet. Michelle, this is one of our professors here at Bradbury’s. I need to chat with her for a bit. Will you be okay if we talk in private a bit? Then, Professor Cho Lin may want to chat with you.”

“Sure, very pleased to meet you,” Michelle said. Lindsey took Cho Lin into the next room and cast a Silence spell on the door. She did not want the woman to overhear them. “Okay as you know, this is Simone Folquet’s sister, Michelle, who should have attended Bradbury’s when she was twelve. I have just verified that she has all the potentials of any first year, perhaps more. Her wand is acutely attuned to her. I would like very much to see if somehow she could learn magic from us. She already has her high school degree, so it is only the magic classes that she needs. Plus, because of her age, she might progress more rapidly than our kids. What do you think?"

"Well, we ought to try. After all that Simone has done for the US and asking nothing in return, we should, but we've never had any students remotely her age here. Of course, no school has, for that matter. With her boots, will she even be able to get around the campus? She will feel terribly out of place if she is sitting in classes with twelve year olds."

"I know. What about having the professors work with her after hours? I know it is asking a lot of you professors, so I will have to increase your pay of course. Would that be possible?"

Thinking aloud, Cho Lin said, "Well, there are three theory classes for the first years, but only one hour of actual casting. We simulcast the theory classes so she could watch them from another room. Only one professor would need to spend an hour with her each evening, much like an elective. I think it is doable, except for one thing. As you well know, she will need a twin, a partner with which to practice the spells. You would also need to get Professor Janice's agreement. She still handles the first years and their spell casting."

"Makes sense. I have asked her to drop by later this morning anyway. I got the notice from Lillian that Jan Feldspar will be starting this fall, so I need to make sure that she is willing to handle the special needs student. I can kill two birds with one stone."

"Say, I saw Pam walking a strange bearded man around the campus. Who is he?" Cho Lin asked.

"Simone Folquet. He brought his sister here this morning from Marseille, France. Pam is giving him a tour."

"*The* Simone Folquet? Wow. I sure would like to meet that man. What he is doing to help our country is beyond magnanimous!" Cho Lin said enthusiastically.

"Okay, done deal. How about at lunch?"

"Perfect, I will wear a fancy dress—need to impress our foreign visitors. I will go chat a bit with Michelle on my way out."

A half hour later, Professor Janice entered Lindsey's office. She wore slacks and a blouse. She was on vacation, but had answered her Governor's call. She was a bit nervous about the surprise call, however. Lindsey had just finished giving Michelle instructions on filling out the very lengthy form, which would suggest which Hall was right for Michelle. "Thank you so much for coming on such short notice, Professor Janice." She led her into her side office, closed the door, and cast Silence on it. Janice grew even more nervous, suspecting that Lindsey might be about to fire her.

Janice said, "Is this about replacing me? I know that I was overly harsh on you during your first year here at Bradbury's, but I wanted you to either succeed or fail rapidly so that you were not strung along on false hopes, you know, casting with no hands to even hold a wand."

"Oh no, no, nothing like that!" Lindsey suddenly saw

what Janice was thinking, that the first thing she would do is fire her for having so badly mistreating her. “No, you proved yourself more than worthy of teaching here when we were all attacked by the fifty Death Stalkers. You never gave up an inch of ground, though you took a horrible burning.” Janice visibly relaxed.

“No, it is two very different matters I need to discuss with you. First, Bradbury’s is accepting a special needs student this fall, a Jan Feldspar. She is blind. Birth defect. She has no eyes—well she has some ugly glass eyes. I watched her out playing yesterday. Honestly, she is highly attuned to magical energies. I saw her cast a Push spell to get herself going on the swing, and she darn near electrocuted a bully who taunted her and was trying to take the swing away from her. With that much control of raw magical energies, we must see that she is trained to use it properly. She will be Red Hall, by the way.”

“Well, that is nice. Red Hall?” Janice over saw all the Red Hall girls. “I see. Well it would be very dangerous to have her grow up and really pack a punch like that. I agree. I assume her parents are poor?”

“Yes, so full scholarship.”

“I’ve never tried to teach a blind person before.”

“She reads braille so I will have her textbooks converted to braille. She’s going to have twin problems, isn’t she? I mean in your Spell Casting class.”

“Absolutely, it will be very difficult for her. How will she be able to see the proper wand motions to make? She can read the braille commands and such, but the wand? I don’t see how? I mean with thirty students—I cannot spend all my time holding her hand so she can feel the proper motions to make."

"I know that. I believe I have an answer for that too. You remember Michelle Folquet, the thirty-three year old sister of Simone Folquet? She visited here last Christmas along with Simone's wife, Isabella?"

"Yes, poor thing, having to wear those horrid boots. And such a tiny waist. Just awful. Why?"

"Well, I want to accept her as a first year student too. She was supposed to come here when she was twelve. I looked up her records, and she had been accepted back then. I've tested her today and honestly, the wand took to her better than most—oak with platinum, a power combination. She already has her high school degree so she only needs to sit through all the magic classes. Cho Lin believes that she could take the three theory courses by watching them in another room on simulcast, that way she won't be embarrassed by having to sit in a class of twelve year olds. However, again, I must ask you if you would be willing to deal with her after suppers for an hour, handling her Spell Casting class, rather like an elective course, with corresponding pay of course."

"Here is what I was thinking. Twin Michelle up with Jan. Michelle has had a tremendous amount of reality on what it is to be blind. She was blind from age twelve through thirty-two or so. They would have a tremendous amount in common. Further, neither will be able to move around swiftly, though for vastly different reasons. You can have Jan merely study about the spells in her Casting class and then after supper,

Michelle can help her perfect the wand motions, leaving you to just supervise and not have to 'hold her hand' all the way through the class. What do you think of this plan?"

"Governor Lindsey, you have impressed me! Yes, that is positively brilliant. After all, Simone Folquet is giving our whole country massive assistance, well his companies are. If we can do this for his sister, that is the least we can do by way of thanks. Your plan should work out well, especially for me, lightening my load with the special needs student. By the way, what Hall will Michelle be in and will she room with Jan?"

"Let's find out shall we? I have my suspicions, but let's see what the test shows, shall we?"

They rejoined Michelle who had just finished the lengthy questions. Lindsey took the sheet, and it automatically produced the results. Lindsey was not surprised, though Janice was. At the top of the form beside her name and in large letters was Red Hall. Janice looked very pleased indeed.

"Her brother is here having a tour of the campus. Simone will be dining with us in a half hour. Professor Janice, if you have the time, you are welcome to join us and Professor Cho Lin for lunch."

"Oh, I am a mess! I was on vacation, but how can I pass up this opportunity! I'll be back in a half hour. I do hope that everything is all set with these two students, Governor Lindsey."

"They will be by the time you are back," Lindsey smiled, and Janice left.

"Michelle, I have good news for you. We all believe that

you will be able to learn magic here at Bradbury's starting this fall. You will be in Red Hall. I know that it is going to be very awkward being with all these twelve year old first years. I have a plan to greatly minimize that, if you are willing to help another student who really will need your patience and aid. She is a special needs student of Red Hall. She is blind. Birth defect, no eyes at all. Here's the plan." Lindsey outlined in detail how school would go for the two.

"You see, both of you will be slow, careful walkers. By working together, living in the same room, you can both help each other. She will not care that you are so much older, since she can't see you, only that you will be there for her."

"Fantastic! I would love to help her. Honestly, I could walk her to all her classes if she needs it. Perhaps if everyone saw that my job was to help her around, they would not think too much of it. I can say that I am being paid by sitting in on these courses. Then, you all don't have to bother with this cast-thing, whatever that is."

"Okay, that is even better! I want you to let me know if this arrangement does not work out. Will you?"

"Yes, I promise. I can't believe it! I am coming to magic school! I never believed that I would, but it's happening! Can we tell Simone? He will be so happy!"

"Yes, we are going down to the dining room for lunch now. I'll tell him all about it. Professors Cho Lin, Pam, and your Spell Casting professor, Janice, will be joining us. Welcome to Bradbury's, first year Michelle Folquet!" Michelle rose and hugged Lindsey tightly.

As expected, Professor Janice arrived precisely on time, hair and makeup perfectly done, professional dress, with hose and her usual tall heels. “Oh, I am so delighted to finally meet you, Mr. Folquet!” she gushed a bit too thickly. Cho Lin merely grinned.

An hour later, Simone and Michelle left for Marseille. He was the happiest man in the world. His long-standing promise and vow to this sister had been fulfilled. She was going to Bradbury’s!

“Lindsey, he looked awfully familiar—like I should know him,” Cho Lin commented after they had left.

“I agree. Those eyes! I’ve seen those eyes somewhere before. Awfully familiar. Are you sure we have not met him before?” Professor Janice asked.

Lindsey sighed. She would have to share Simone’s secret, now that Michelle would be here. “Cho Lin, when will be the first time that all the professors are back here and I could hold a meeting with all them?”

“They are all due back on August 15 to begin preparing their fall lessons. Why?”

“Okay then, I will send everyone a Message. At the meeting on August 15, I will have a very long story to tell you about Simone Folquet.” Cho Lin and Janice grinned, evilly, a tease of course. Pam suppressed a giggle. This fall term promised to be a very interesting term indeed!

With all the massive confusion surrounding the capturing of Dominus, no one noticed the error that was made, concerning the disposal of his remains. Instead of cremation, the body of Dominus Malefic was embalmed and inadvertently buried in a local cemetery. That error went unnoticed for nearly ten years.

The End.

A Favor to Other Readers

How about helping other readers? Many readers rely on reviews to make the decision whether to buy a book. You can help them make their decision by leaving your opinions and viewpoint in a short review of the positive things of this book. Writing the review and expressing your opinion only takes a few minutes, and other readers will appreciate your efforts.

Click this link: Volume 6 States Justice
scroll down to Customer Reviews; click on Write a Review, and enter your review. Thank you.

Author Information

Visit My Amazon.com Author Page

Vic Broquard Author Page

Follow My Blog

Vic Broquard's Blog

Follow Me on Social Media

Facebook

Google+

LinkedIn

YouTube

Other Books by Vic Broquard

Without Warning (fantasy)

The Trident Series: (fantasy)

Volume 1 The Trident and the Book

Volume 2 The Trident and the Scepter

Volume 3 The Trident and the Resurrection

The Adventures of Elizabeth Stanton Series: (science fiction)

Volume 1 The Evolution of the Path

Volume 2 The Great Messiah

Volume 3 Of Kings and Queens and Troubadours

Volume 4 Chaos in the Aftermath

Volume 5 Power Plays

Volume 6 Age of Exploration

Volume 7 Abducted

Volume 8 The Emperor and Empress

Volume 9 A Job Worth Doing

Volume 10 Degradation

Volume 11 The Second Crusade

Volume 12 When Worlds Collide

Volume 13 Dark Ages

The Lindsey Barron Series: (fantasy)

Volume 1 The Rod of the Apocalypse

Volume 2 The Board of Governors

Volume 3 The Crown of Moses

Zoran Chronicles Series: (fantasy)

Planet of the Orange-red Sun Series: (science fiction)

www.ingramcontent.com/pod-product-compliance
Lightning Source LLC
Chambersburg PA
CBHW070859260626
47162CB00007B/2502

* 9 7 8 1 9 4 1 4 1 5 5 1 1 *